THE WEDDING, ETC.

RECKLESS SERIES BOOK 3

CC GIBBS

PUBLISHED BY SUSAN JOHNSON

Copyright © 2020 by Susan Johnson

All rights reserved.

No part of this book may be reproduced in any form or by any electronic or mechanical means, including information storage and retrieval systems, without written permission from the author, except for the use of brief quotations in a book review.

In Memoriam:
Fletcher 1987-2018
Forever in my Heart

CHARACTERS

Bride and Groom
　　Nicole Parrish
　　Rafe Contini

Groom's family
　　Camelia, Rafe's mother
　　Anton (Gore), Rafe's step-father
　　Titus, Rafe's young step-brother

Bride's family
　　Melanie, mother
　　Matt, father
　　Isabelle, sister; Bax, her boyfriend
　　Keir, brother
　　Dante, brother
　　Rafe (Buzz), brother
　　Ellie, sister
　　Dominic Knight, Nicole's maternal uncle
　　Kate, Dominic's wife
　　Rosie, Kate and Dominic's daughter

James (Jimmy), Kate and Dominic's son

Rafe and Nicole's friends
    Fiona, Nicole's friend from childhood
    Henny, Rafe's friend from childhood
    Mireille, Henny's wife
    Basil, Rafe's friend from childhood
    Prince Giacomino Santori (Jack), Rafe's cousin
    Ganz, Madeline, Ray, Crissy: hackers extraordinaire
    Gina and Webster: undercover operatives
    Zoe, Webster's young daughter
    Carlos Sanz, Rafe's personal bodyguard
    Simon, Rafe's bodyguard/driver
    Davey, Rafe's bodyguard/pilot
    Alexei Rovira, Rafe's personal physician

Secondary Characters
    Natalie, Rafe's housekeeper in Paris
    Josephine, Rafe's housekeeper in Monte Carlo
    Mrs. B, Nicole's family's housekeeper
    Vincent Weiser, Rafe's mentor/company attorney
    Isabelle Tansy, Contini Foundation director
    Costa, wedding/ event planner
    Chomak, Rafe's major domo in Geneva

1

In Paris, on October eleventh, the night before the wedding...

Rafe sat up in bed and stared at Nicole. "You could have told me what you were going to do," he said, trying to keep the fury from his voice.

Nicole came up on one elbow and stared right back. "You might have said no."

"Damn right I would have." He jerked the sheet up over her nakedness; his life was being blown to shit. He didn't need the distraction.

"Then see. I was right."

His nostrils flared. "As in?"

"*As in* I wouldn't be pregnant if I'd told you I was going off my birth control."

He was trying hard to hold it together, but he felt the world shifting under his feet. "Jesus, are we ready for this?"

"I am." Nicole's voice was smooth and easy, like her

smile. "And you don't have to do anything. Your job is done."

He lifted one brow. "You gonna eat me now like some of those insects do?"

"I could eat you if you like," she said with a flirtatious little grin.

His hooded gaze darkened. "Don't fuck with me. I'm not in the mood."

"I'm sorry," she said, unintimidated. "But you never would have said yes. You've lived a different life. Children weren't something you'd miss. They'd never been part of your world. You know I'm right."

He was watching her, cool and unblinking. "Out of curiosity. Why didn't you wait until after the wedding?"

"You mean once I'd snared you?"

"Yeah, that's what I meant."

Her eyebrows pulled together just a touch. "Let me ask you this? Do you love me less now that you know?"

He took his time before he answered; you could practically see the struggle going on. "No."

"Then there's something else I have to tell you."

His head came up as if he scented danger. "Are you okay? I mean other than"—he jabbed a finger toward her stomach.

"I'm fine, but"—she took a small breath, then sat up.

He didn't even notice the sheet falling away; his pulse was spiking, his heart suddenly drumming in his chest. Something *was* wrong. What if he lost her? He couldn't bear it. His life would be over. Scooping her up in his arms, he dropped her on his lap and held her close. "Whatever it is, we'll deal with it," he said, soft and low. "I won't let anything happen to you. Just tell—"

She put a finger over his mouth to silence him. "It's not me; this is about you and my fears. Ever since the night of

Maddy's birthday, I've lived in terror that you could be taken from me. You think you're indestructible, that you can handle any crisis that comes your way, but I wasn't so sure." The words were tumbling out in a rush, as if she'd been holding them back a long time. "I was selfish. I wanted your child, so even if, God forbid, something happened to you, I'd still have part of you. Don't tell me I shouldn't feel this way because I do. It's not something you can talk yourself out of. So there"—she sucked in a breath—"that's my reason for not telling you before." She stared at him, her blue gaze straight on. "And if you don't want to marry me, I understand."

"There's not a chance in hell you're getting out of this marriage," Rafe said, brusquely. "You can forget about that." He shut his eyes for a second, took a hard in-breath through his nose, sorted through the tumult in his brain, finally got a grip on the I-can't-believe-this-is-happening. She was and always would be the only person he loved with every fiber of his being. He moved his hand down to her stomach and gently spread his fingers over the beginnings of a new life. "So, we made a baby," he said, a touch of wonder slowly rising in his voice. "How about that?"

She watched him, her eyes wary. "You sure you don't mind?"

He shook his head. "I've loved you from the first time I saw you. I'll always love you."

"Me *and* the baby—both of us, right?" She was less uncertain now, a dawning happiness in her eyes; he'd said he'd always love her.

"Yes, both of you," he said, his voice deep and sure, his large hand warm on her stomach. "How much time before—"

"You're a daddy?" Her smile was sunshine bright. "Eight

months. So you have plenty of time to get used to the idea."

"You'll have to help me out," he said, with a wry twitch of his mouth. "I've had zero role models."

"You're so good with your half-brother, Titus. It's the same thing, only you have to be a little more careful when the baby's tiny." She threw her arms around his neck and kissed him hard. "I'm so excited! Tell me you'd excited too! You are, aren't you?"

He adored her full steam ahead persona, the one that assumed the world shared her enthusiasm. "I'm getting more excited by the minute," he said, only half teasing. The thought of Nicole having his baby was like staring out the window and suddenly seeing a new world: the sun warmer, the grass greener, the sky bluer. His child would be loved unconditionally; he'd make sure of it. "I'll try to be a good dad," he said, quietly.

Immune to his reservations, she spoke with jubilation. "You're going to be just perfect!" Then she laughed a little breathless sound. "May I announce the baby at the wedding reception? Say you don't mind," she added without waiting for his answer. "I'm just over the moon happy and I want everyone to share in our joy."

He smiled. "I don't mind. Say the word and we'll have fireworks to celebrate."

"Really?" Her eyes were huge. "Can you do that in the city?"

She took such pleasure in life; she'd even taken charge of her fear and had his baby. She loved him and for that he'd give her the world. Fireworks were nothing. Short notice if he needed permits for tomorrow, but make a few calls—the mayor of Paris, the president of France if necessary. "If you want fireworks, pussycat," he said, calmly, "piece of cake. I'll arrange it."

2

Rafe Contini, billionaire CEO and playboy of note, came awake at the brisk knock, shot a glance at the hint of dawn outside his bedroom windows, another at the digital display on the bedside clock and silently swore. *What the fuck?*

"Breakfast! Braaaak...fest!" a female voice trilled.

"Oh Christ," Nicole groaned.

Pushing himself up into a sitting position, a tick of annoyance fluttering over one high cheekbone, Rafe gazed at his bride-to-be. "You know who that is?"

Her eyes still shut, Nicole sighed. "It's my mom."

For a man who'd controlled every facet of his life since adolescence, it took Rafe a moment to tamp down his temper and school his voice to a necessary civility. "Tell her we'll be down later. At a more reasonable hour."

"She gets up at dawn. This is reasonable for her. Maybe she'll go away."

Another flurry of knocks failed to open his fiancee's eyes and when the rapping intensified, Rafe softly exhaled. "She's not going away. Want me to take care of it?"

Suddenly, he was looking into a joyful, brilliant blue gaze.

"Would you? I'm such a coward when it comes to confronting my mom." Nicole pushed a lock of hair from her forehead in a placidly sensual way that brought a ghost of a smile to Rafe's lips.

Her eyebrows shot up. "What?"

"I already said I'd do it. Although," he added, his voice mellow, "I find your sex kitten persona endlessly fascinating."

"While *I'm* grateful," she murmured, with an oblique, teasing glance from under her lashes, "that you're a fearless, smooth-talking bad ass who can send my mother away without pissing her off."

No argument there; he'd perfected the threat/charm methodology to a nicety. "And you need your sleep." Leaning down, his dark silky hair brushed her face as he kissed her lightly. "You were up way too late fucking my brains out."

"My pregnancy hormones are going crazy." A twitch of a smile. "Hope you don't mind."

Sitting back, he gave her a lazy grin. "Not likely." Nicole had been hotter than hot from the first day they'd met, their sexual compatibility one of the many reasons he loved her. And if pregnancy made her even hornier…hell, life was good.

The sound of the sitting room door opening and closing disrupted the spiritually attuned moment.

Rafe scowled. *Seriously? Walk right in?*

Nicole jerked the covers over her head.

Approaching footsteps brought Rafe vaulting out of bed. "Be right with you!" he shouted, sprinting for the bathroom. Grabbing a robe from the back of the door, he shrugged it on, snatched an elastic binder from the dresser as he sped past, and entering the sitting room seconds later, drew the bedroom door shut behind him. Fastening his hair back with a deft flick of his wrist, he smiled at Nicole's mother standing in the middle of his Anatolian carpet, in his goddamn *private* apartment at fucking *five forty-three* in the morning. "I'm afraid Nicole's still sleeping," he said with incredible restraint.

"Oh dear, and with so much still to do," Nicole's mother murmured, a perfectly calculated sinking sound to her voice. "We'd better wake her." Strikingly petite, looking fresh as a daisy in blue slacks and a yellow sweater, every blonde hair smoothly in place, Melanie Parrish bore no resemblance to her tall, dark-haired daughter.

"We were up late going over some last minute wedding details," Rafe said in lieu of the truth. "I think it best if we *don't* wake her. If you'll excuse us, Mrs. Parrish, we'll be down for breakfast later."

A non-plussed look flitted over his future mother-in-law's face. "Are you sure? I don't think Nicole would mind getting up considering our busy schedule."

Then Melanie Parrish calmly waited to be accommodated.

Nicole's family had arrived in Paris two days ago, and in that brief period of time, Rafe had recognized that together with the Parrish housekeeper, Mrs. B, Nicole's mother, in a looks-can-be-deceiving way, ran a well-disciplined household.

But when it came to management skills and command, Rafe's authority had been honed in an atmosphere so fraught with danger that any opposition short of actual gunfire was easily managed. Not that he was about to make an enemy of his future mother-in-law. Giving her his best, boyish smile long used to potent effect, he said, "I'm afraid if Nicole begins the day fatigued, she won't be able to enjoy all the wedding festivities. So let's allow her a little more sleep. She'll thank us, I know."

Recognizing the tall, powerful man guarding the bedroom door wasn't about to move either physically or figuratively, Melanie softly sighed. "I suppose you're right."

"If the wedding celebration isn't likely to continue well into the night, I wouldn't quibble. But the fireworks don't even begin until eleven." Rafe dipped his head, his smile rueful. "And knowing my friends, they'll party until morning."

"Fireworks?" Melanie and Mrs. B had practically memorized the extensive program.

"Last night Nicole mentioned she'd like fireworks, so"— Rafe lifted one white terrycloth clad shoulder in a small deprecatory shrug—"I have people working on it. But the minute Nicole wakes up, I assure you, we'll come down for breakfast."

"Mrs. B made Nicole's favorite cinnamon, caramel coffee cake."

Rafe was beginning to understand from whom Nicole had inherited her stubbornness. "Definitely incentive," he said, blandly. "I'll tell Nicole." Walking across the sitting room to the outer door, he opened it and stood aside. "Would you do me a favor when you go back downstairs? Ask my housekeeper to check that the caterers set up the chocolate fountain in the children's area. There was some question as to where it went." A flash of perfect white teeth. "Actually, it was a small argument I'm sure Natalie won. Tell her Dominic's little girl, Rosie, asked."

Melanie understood she was being dismissed with the same suave ruthlessness her brother, Dominic, exhibited. As she moved toward the door, she said, with a twinkle in her eyes, "I can see why you and Dominic were initially at odds."

"Just a slight disagreement quickly rectified." Rafe smiled as she walked past. "Nicole's happiness took precedence."

Turning back in the hallway, Melanie looked at him for a moment, her chin up, her gaze assessing. "At first I worried that Nicole was dazzled by you and your lifestyle, caught up in the wildness and notoriety. But there's no doubt she's happy. *You've* made her happy. I've never seen her over the moon before."

Rafe wanted to say, *You have my word Nicole will always be happy,* or less tactfully point out, *Your brother wasn't always a saint either,* but discussing his thoughts with a semi-stranger would have required a different childhood than his. "We're both very happy," he said, instead.

Melanie recognized the same reticence that characterized Dominic, understood she wasn't going to be further enlightened and politely smiled. "When Nicole wakes, tell her the hairdresser is scheduled for ten thirty."

"I will," Rafe replied, rather than explain that Paris's most celebrated hairstylist had moved his salon lock, stock and barrel to the premises. Nicole's appointment was at her convenience.

After Nicole's mother disappeared down the hallway, he shut and locked the door. Returning to the bedroom, he stopped at the foot of the bed, and thought, as he had so often since the day they'd first met on his yacht in Monte Carlo, how lucky he was. "Hey," he said, gently. "All clear. You can come out from under the covers. Although," he added, with a lift of his brows as Nicole's head emerged, "you realize you weren't actually hidden."

Nicole tossed the covers aside and raised her arms. "Come hold me," she murmured, sultry and low.

He smiled. "Are we changing the subject?"

"Yes. I need sex. Thank you by the way for saving me. Now hurry."

Her lush body, all soft, voluptuous curves and warm, pink flesh, wasn't likely to elicit a no from any man with a heartbeat. Although he tried. "You should sleep," he said, even as his erection surged upward with impressive speed.

"Ha! You don't mean it!" Nicole pointed at the raised fabric of his robe with a gleeful smile. "You're always so good to me." She wiggled her fingers in fidgety impatience. "I'll go to sleep immediately after, I promise."

Reminding himself that she was more fragile in her pregnancy and the day ahead enervating, Rafe deliberately curbed his lust. "Sleep first. It's going to be a late night."

Her pout was paired with a clear blue-eyed gaze. "Please, please, pretty please with cherries or kumquats or whatever you like best on top. Please…I'm begging."

He had no idea how to say no, his life one of habitual acquisition when it came to women, assuaging desire as natural as breathing. "I'm trying to be sensible." An infinitesimal pause; sexual restraint was virgin territory for a billionaire playboy. "Come on, you need your sleep," he cajoled, calling on a rarely exercised sense of virtue. "It's going to be a helluva long day and an even longer evening."

"Don't want to sleep," Nicole muttered, a stubborn jut to her jaw. "I'm not tired. I'm horny."

"Jesus, you're not making this easy. I'm trying to be"—he blew out a breath—"fuck, I don't know…understanding, benevolent…different from my usual self."

"If you were benevolent, you'd screw me." Her voice was

fretful. "And I don't want you to be different. I want you to want me just as badly as ever."

He had no defense with his heart involved, no practice in any event, refusing a naked woman begging for sex. "Keep this up, pussycat," he murmured, her unremitting, highly gratifying sexual demands last night not likely to encourage resistance, "and I'm going to have to take a leave of absence from work."

She grinned. "Okay."

A strange notion to even contemplate when he'd never *not* worked, when uncompromising academic achievement, followed by a steadfast commitment to Contini Pharmaceuticals were all he'd ever known. "You have to *promise* me you'll go to sleep afterward."

Her smile lit up the room, the universe. "Yes, yes, whatever you say."

Rare license from his willful fiancée. "Can I get that in writing?" he asked, softly sardonic.

"Depends how quickly you accommodate me."

Before her cheeky purr had completely died away, his robe was on the carpet and he was resting between her thighs, the weight of his body lightly brushing hers, his face inches away. "Now listen," he said, gently. "We need some new ground rules so we don't mess things up. I'm more than willing to give you as many orgasms as you want, for as long as you want. I have no problem accommodating your rising tide of horniness either. *Up* to a point."

She went still; there was a slight cant to his brows, gravity in his amber gaze.

"That means no craziness until we talk to someone who knows more about pregnancy than we do. Relax," he added, at her worried look. "You still get what you want. Just no rough stuff."

She relaxed.

"And I promise no one will bother us again, so take your time, make a list, check it off twice, whatever." His smile was serene, unencumbered, a man in charge of his world once more. "And when your every little desire is satisfied, I'm going to have someone bring up a piece of Mrs. B's caramel coffee cake for you."

She smiled. "You're absolutely perfect. *Tout ensemble*. See I'm learning French."

He laughed. "That's sweet, but delusional." Reckless playboy and hard-ass businessman were closer to the mark. "Now I have one last order, suggestion, proposal, whatever word best eliminates argument." His golden gaze fixed on her was warm with affection. "Immediately after you've eaten, you have to go to sleep. You need your rest now more than ever."

In a moment of total clarity, she understood, heart-pounding, that she could lose herself completely in loving him. Or maybe she'd known from the moment she'd walked into his stateroom in Monte Carlo and he'd smiled at her. "Hey," she said, her voice tremulous like her smile.

"Hey," he whispered, understanding. "The stars were aligned that day."

"And here we are," she said, feeling a moment of improbable bliss.

"On our wedding day no less."

"You're smiling. Didn't think it would happen, right?"

"Never in a million years."

She grinned. "I bewitched you."

"You did," he said, quietly. "With your brilliant blue eyes and stunning beauty and that frisson of shimmering desire you brought in with you." His voice softened. "Like now."

"Oh, jeez, that reminds me. My mother might walk in a"—

"I'll take care of it."

The familiar phrase made her smile. "You're going to spoil me."

"I am. Now how many kisses do you want?" Her startled look made him chuckle. "Looks like we're moving on"—a quick lift of his brows—"to your favorite part."

She could see the smile in his eyes, so she was pretty sure of her answer before she said, "Tell me you don't mind if I'm"--

"Demanding, insatiable"—he grinned—"always in a hurry? No, I don't mind." His breath was warm on her mouth. "Not now, not ever." Although perhaps a modicum of prudence wouldn't be out of the question after a long night of screwing.

But a few moments later, no matter her libido wasn't entirely averse to gentle kisses if the ready-for-sex tingles vibrating through her senses were any indication, she pulled back and met his gaze. "Are you trying to tell me I should be less greedy?"

"Not necessarily. Let's just catch our breath."

"I knew it." She grimaced. "I *have* been too demanding. I should have better control or *some* control, oh hell, I have no excuse. Sorry."

He smiled. "No need. I just think a little moderation might be in order. You didn't sleep much last night."

"Oh, that," she said, brightening. "I already said I'll go to sleep right after. There." She wiggled her hips. "Problem solved."

He cocked one brow. "You've been in a mood lately."

She smiled. "My nympho mood?"

"Not a word I'd use," he said, neutrally, having known

women of that partiality. "Let's just say you've been on a roll."

"Come on, it's not as though you aren't amped up too." His rock-hard erection was pulsing against her stomach. "And look, we've had time to catch our breath, see"—she inhaled, exhaled, flashed him a radiant smile—"calm, steady respiration, not to mention you totally know how to work that moderation part, so how about if we—oh *MY!*"

She gasped at his sudden, plunging downstroke.

He grunted at the jolt of raw pleasure.

They both went still, stunned by the intense, X-rated impact, sheer, blinding bliss lighting up their brains.

More familiar with X-rated sensation, Rafe quickly recovered and dipping his head, kissed her cheek. "Ready for a replay?"

Still awash in a rosy euphoria, Nicole didn't/couldn't/chose not to reply.

"Hey." Whisper soft and teasing.

She took a small breath, eyes shut. "I heard you."

Her answer was super faint; not good, worrisome in fact. "Time for a break."

"No."

Jesus, he could barely hear her. "It might be a good idea."

Her eyes snapped open. "No!"

He smiled. "You're alive."

She gazed up at him, her eyes half-lidded. "I was in a feel-too-awesome-to-move zone. You're damn good but you know that, and don't grin. I'm trying to ignore why you're so good."

"*We're* good, pussycat," he said, soft and low. "Us, together, okay?"

"So diplomatic, Contini, but now that I'm lucid again..."

He laughed. "Ready to rock?"

She moved her hips in a leisurely back and forth motion. "I'd say we both are."

"Then right after you go to sleep. Agreed?"

"Jeez, don't look so serious. My sleeping's not the end of the world."

"I worry. So, agreed?"

"I love when you use that cool, dispassionate, master-of-the-universe tone. It makes me all hot and"—

"Answer me."

That look. It sent a little shiver down her spine. "Yes, yes, I'll sleep."

"Thank you." A charming smile. "Now what's on the menu? Fast, slow or something in between? I'm only asking because you've been pushing me all night."

"Says the man with the perpetual hard on."

"Just being accommodating, pussycat."

A tiny lift of her brows. "In that case..."

"Looks like I'm back on the clock," he said, lightly teasing.

But clearly, he was going to have to be the adult in the room when it came to sexual boundaries. Withdrawing marginally, he forced his dick deeper by slow degrees, particularly conscious of finite distances, softly yielding flesh, sentient gradations of pressure—on alert for a specific response. Ah...like that. He smiled faintly as Nicole shut her eyes, made a small helpless sound that ended in a low throaty purr and began gently rocking to sustain the pleasure; that familiar purr a not-to-be-missed cue to zero in on all her favorite sweet spots.

Moving inside her with deftness and delicacy, he concentrated on every impressionable, feverish, nerve-rich surface. There. And there. And her absolute certifiable, hard core, personal preference—right the fuck *there*.

On her precious little G-spot.

Exhaling a low, rapturous groan, Nicole arched up into Rafe's flamboyant cock, slid her hands down the heavy muscles bordering his spine, touched the smooth dip in the small of his back, and held on tight, reveling in the wild, soul-stirring ecstasy, the feel of him deep inside her seething hot and beautiful, sensory overload battering her senses. "Do--not--move," she ordered, half-breathless, shaky, his massive dick jammed against every humming, strumming, jacked up nerve in her pussy, a delicious, edgy ache pulsing between her legs.

He waited a ten count before moving because he was on his best behavior. "Don't panic," he said, withdrawing slightly, ignoring her protesting squeal.

Grabbing his hair, she jerked his face close. "I said don't move!"

"Hey, look, I'm back," he soothed, slipping inside her again with lithe grace and finesse, smiling as her fingers loosened, her hands fell away and a soft sigh replaced her little princess bitchiness. He could have added *I know what I'm doing* but instead settled into a leisurely, sure-to-please driving motion of his lower body, his powerful muscles functioning in a supple flex and flow, his downstroke smooth and silken, his upstroke lingering, the added bonus of a velvety drag on her G-spot and clit coming and going, offering new meaning to the term stroke of genius.

She squirmed against the impressionable, unerring pressure, impatient, frenzied, wanton desire at fever pitch.

"You like that?" he murmured, biting her earlobe lightly. "Want a little more?" Her soft sigh was part shaky, part honey soft, irresistibly compliant, and forcing his cock a stellar distance deeper, they both felt the tenuous yielding, the quixotic abrasive drift, the sudden hot-blooded rush as he stopped, completely submerged.

He drew in a sharp breath.

She uttered a low, barely-there moan.

The sound of license, he decided, permission certainly, and gripping her hips, he pulled her closer.

Her gasp ended in a tiny shriek.

Every muscle in his body went rigid.

"More," she whispered, her voice shaking.

Fuck no.

Sinking her fingernails into his back, she hissed, "More, *now*!"

Christ, her nails stung. Jaw clenched, the temptation to give her what she wanted was intense. Instead, he reined in his temper along with his dick that wasn't as easily curbed, and said, tightly, "I'm trying not to hurt you."

Those taut, bit off words required a quick reset. Offering a conciliatory smile, she lowered her voice. "Nothing hurts, I swear." Shifting her hips in a slick, slippery undulation, she held his gaze. "See?"

"You're sure?"

"Pretty much--yes, yes, absolutely sure," she quickly added, as he frowned.

"Okay, but I'm shutting you down after this. We're not taking any chances. Got it?"

"Yes, and thanks." A dazzling smile. "Really."

He grimaced. "You'll say anything right now, won't you?"

She hesitated, not wishing to offend him when the feel of his massive dick inside her was so incredibly, unbelievably good the thought of writing poetry commemorating the occasion wasn't entirely out of the question. "Maybe if you told me what you want me to"--

"Jesus, *really*?"

"Pardon me all to hell," she said, just as pissy. "After the last couple months, it's not a news flash that I like your dick. Oh, shit, are you going to cut me off now?"

Her artless candor was one of her many charms, not to mention her hot little cunt wrapped around his dick offered zero incentive to cut her off. He softly sighed. "No."

Throwing her arms around his neck, her smile was big and wide. "You're always *so* good to me. I adore you every which way to Sunday."

He smiled faintly. "I appreciate your total adoration, hey —don't punch so hard or I might change my mind." Grabbing her fist, he held it for a moment, his gaze suddenly turning serious. "We're taking it easy from now on," he murmured, releasing her hand. "Understand?"

"Yes, yes, whatever you--oh, ohhh, God..." Her voice trailed away at the gluttonous shock as he gently maxed out in her pussy and every over-sensitive, bone-melting, nerve in her body absorbed the blissful delirium.

Assuming the small silence and the flood of dewy moisture drenching his dick was gratitude, he took advantage of the brief hush to add, "Even if you're racing for the finish line, we're keeping it under control, okay?" Christ, she was drifting away, her hands clamped hard on his back, as if holding on tightly to the shimmering splendor. "Nod, if you heard me."

No nod, that little mewing sound pure, overwrought horniness.

Breaking her grip, he withdrew enough to gain her attention and waited for her eyes to open.

"I heard you," she muttered. "It just wasn't convenient to answer."

"You have no bloody restraint, so listen up. For your

safety—don't scowl like that—and my peace of mind, a reminder of"—

"*Your* rules." A soft petulance.

"Call it what you like."

The rare sharpness in his voice gave her pause. "I don't want to fight, okay?"

He sighed. "Let's just not be reckless."

"Okay, you're in charge. Better now?"

"You know it's not about who's in charge. It's about"—

She stopped him with a finger to his mouth. "You're right."

He grinned. "You must really want it."

Her quick, sardonic up glance made him laugh.

He was still chuckling when he dropped a kiss on her nose. "We're doing this one my way. You can complain later."

"Wouldn't dream of it."

"So docile, pussycat. That freight train barreling down the tracks?"

"Big time. Now stop talking."

For a man who had until recently only known women who accommodated him, his bride-to-be was a startling change. But also, heaven-on-earth, so screw it. Literally.

Making the no-brainer adjustment apropos who accommodated whom—a constant since he'd met Nicole--he put his splendid body, legendary dick, and superb sexual talents at the service of the woman he loved.

Despite years of excess in the perfidious world of vice, he had a natural propensity for simple pleasures and improvisation. And he seduced with understated delicacy and sweet nuance, with a connoisseur's eye for every quiver and tremble, with as much patience as Nicole would allow.

Which wasn't much.

In her usual go-for-broke fashion, she was soon past the point of no return, trembling, her breathing ragged; pre-orgasmic ripples were fluttering up his dick.

Slipping his hands under her bottom, he spread his fingers for better purchase, pushed deeper into her sleek, glossy heat, flexed his stiff dick minutely upward to target her clit and G-spot and lodged hard against both nubs of engorged flesh, hit all his marks with virtuoso precision.

She whimpered.

He paused for a moment while she gently panted, then moved forward a fraction more until his erection came to rest, full stretch, in her tighter-than-tight pussy.

Crammed with cock, nirvana glowing on her retinas, she began to shudder.

He recognized that little shudder, the rhythm of her heartbeat pulsing wildly around his dick in a not-to-be-ignored sexual prompt. Going utterly still, he held his erection against the very limits of her soft flesh, then gently pushed a precise, delicate, impeccable distance more, and began to silently count. *One, one thousand, two, one thou--*

Nicole's scream catapulted up into the low-ceilinged room, ricocheted off the medieval rafters, bounced off the plaster walls, her climax detonating a nanosecond later in wild, spiking rapture. The fierce, frenzied shock waves flared through her sex, raced up her spine, burned through her nervous system at warp speed and dazzled her brain in dizzying splendor.

Intent on catching her orgasmic wave, Rafe arched his back, flexed his quads, and mid-point in a powerful forward thrust alarm bells blasted through his brain. With a decade of unconstrained vice in his past, it took a couple hard breaths to tamp down his raging libido and a nanosecond more to curb his freedom-loving dick. That done, he gave his head a shake, came up for air, and jumped on Nicole's lightning fast climax with a tense and nervy, critically tempered caution that curiously amplified sensation. For the first time in memory, his orgasm took on an out-of-body dimension, at once real and unreal, annihilating in its urgency, epically intense, and he came and came and came, flooding Nicole's warm, welcoming body in a raw, high-velocity, damn-near monumental deluge.

Jesus C Christ! His chest heaving, dragging air into his lungs, he blinked to clear his vision, eased his fingers open and softly exhaled. Fuck, he was glad he was marrying her. He couldn't imagine life without that pulse-quickening, nuclear-level, orgasmic freak out.

His heart still pumping hard, he smiled at Nicole who lay eyes-shut and softly panting beneath him. "You okay?"

Slowly returning from her color-me-happy journey to orgasmic fulfillment, she opened her eyes and smiled back. "I'm grand. All tingly and floaty, still glowing from within thanks to your awesome skills. Meanwhile," she added with a flicker of a smile, "you're your usual calm self."

"Au contraire. I'm still trying to catch my breath. Thank you by the way. That was incredible. You're incredible."

Her mouth twitched into a tiny smile. "Incredible. Really?"

"Swear to God. And irresistible, and every possible kind of wonderful and brilliant and beautiful...but"—he held her gaze, his plans back on track—"now, you have to rest."

Rolling off her, he grabbed a towel from the bedside table, slid it between her legs, then pulled a pillow under his head, lay back and took her hand in his. "Shut your eyes, go to sleep."

"You have white sheets everywhere...here, Monte Carlo,

Geneva, San Francisco." She slid her hand over the crisp fabric.

He did a double take at the abrupt change of subject. "I guess," he said, neutrally. "Go to sleep."

"Why do you have white sheets everywhere?"

He turned his head, smiled. "No special reason. Come on, you have to sleep." His sadistic father's preference for red sheets was one of many depraved memories he chose not to exhume.

"Is it okay, then, if we have colored sheets on occasion?"

An infinitesimal hesitation. "Sure."

"I heard that."

"I said sure."

"You didn't mean it."

"I do, okay? Have any color sheets you like."

"Because you love me."

He laughed and pulled her close. "No shit. Now *fucking* go to sleep. It's going to be a helluva long night"

"Don't want to. I'm too psyched."

He glanced down and scowled. "Jesus, babe." Suppressing the caustic comments racing through his mind, he pulled away, his gaze cool. "What the fuck you doin'?"

He never called her babe; that was what he called all the women before her. "I know I said I'd go to sleep," she said, sitting up, meeting his scowl straight on, hoping he'd understand if she explained her feelings properly. "I'm really sorry, truly I am." She pushed a fall of hair behind her ear in a quick, nervous gesture. "But I told you I feel lit up from within after that mind-blowing orgasm. And I'm pretty sure if I tried to shut my eyes, they'd snap right open again. Don't be mad. I can't help it."

He softly sighed; damned if she wasn't adorable--and

apologizing. Mark that one on the calendar. "You sure now? Seriously? You can't sleep?"

She shook her head, gave him a little smile.

"Just cause I love you, you're not always going to get your own way," he warned, rolling up to a seated position in a ripple of hard abs. Then his voice softened, and leaning over, he kissed her. Climbing out of bed a moment later, he turned, gently pushed her down, pulled the covers over her and gazing down at her a moment later, smiled a smile that could have warmed from space. "Enough with the suspicious look, Tiger. You don't have to sleep. I'm just going to get your cake." He raised one brow. "Coffee?"

"Milk."

It took a moment to register, then he flashed a grin. "For baby." Bending low, he brushed her mouth with a kiss, straightened and walked to his dressing room. After slipping on boxers and a pair of grey flannel slacks, he passed through the bedroom with a wave. "This won't take long."

A moment later, he dropped onto the sofa in the sitting room, picked up the house phone and dialed the gypsy housekeeper/notorious autocrat and meddler who ran his Paris home.

Natalie picked up on the first ring. "Sorry, the Madame woke you," she said in her rough Romany-French. "I tried to stop her."

"Not a problem." Rafe's Parisian French was flawless. "I took care of it. Now, I need someone to bring up a tray with a piece of Mrs. B's coffee cake, a glass of milk and a pot of coffee. They can leave it in the hall. And be nice to our guests, Natalie. A couple more days and they're gone."

"I know how to be diplomatic."

Rafe laughed. "I've noticed. A pleasant surprise."

"The staff has been warned as well to be on their best

behavior. I won't have your reputation besmirched by some wayward employee."

"Jesus, that's why I'm getting skittish looks. You scared the shit out of everyone, didn't you?"

"I merely mentioned that you pay premium wages and others do not."

"Come on, Natalie, lighten up with the staff. We're not hosting royalty. And if you need additional help, get some."

"Humpf, we already have all those outsiders you hired underfoot."

"We needed them, Natalie. Flowers, chairs, lighting, music, help for the chef. Want me to delegate?"

"No."

"I didn't think so. Hopefully, Nicole's going back to sleep after she eats. I have a number of calls to make. And if it looks as though we need a guard at our door, have Carlos send someone up."

"I will. Nicole needs her rest with a baby on the way."

Her comment didn't surprise him. His belief in magic might be tenuous, but Natalie's second sight was undeniable. "You knew before me, I suppose."

"Of course."

"Yet you didn't see fit to tell me?"

"Not my place."

Rafe snorted. "You just wanted to make sure I married Nicole."

"I knew that from the moment I met her. I chose not to alarm you."

"Since I'd only known Nicole two days," he drawled.

"Two days longer than you'd been with any other woman," she reminded him. "It's not all magic. Deductive reasoning plays a part. But the signs were clear. Your marriage was fated."

Arguing mystical portents with Natalie was useless. "Tell me then, has Fate indicated whether we're having a boy or girl?"

"Don't ask. If you really want to know, you can find out yourself, however..." Her voice trailed off.

"You wouldn't recommend it."

"Bad luck," she muttered, darkly.

"Nicole might not agree with you."

"Naturally, I wouldn't presume to interfere."

"Of course you would," he said. "So listen. You're not to frighten Nicole with any of your gypsy superstitions. I don't want her unnecessarily agitated. This pregnancy is to be as trouble-free as I can make it. My child is to be safeguarded and protected." His voice had taken on an edge. "Neither is to suffer a moment of distress. Not *one* single moment." His tone was sharp now. "Is that clear? I need your promise."

"You have my word, Rafail. Nicole's pregnancy will be faultless, the child strong and healthy. I would have given you warning if the signs were malevolent."

He hadn't realized his pulse was racing until Natalie's firm avowal tempered his vehemence. "Sorry." He let out a small sigh. "The bloody demons are never completely exorcised, are they?"

"He hasn't been dead long enough."

Neither put a name to the man who'd wreaked havoc on Rafe's life, as if their silence lessened the brutality.

With practiced skill, Rafe dismissed his oppressive past. "If you'll get that tray up soon, I'd appreciate it," he said with smooth urbanity. "I'd like Nicole to go to sleep."

"Five minutes," Natalie replied, understanding the abrupt shift in tone. "I'll add something for you to eat as well. I'd suggest you sleep too, but Carlos said you woke him in the middle of the night with several tasks, so I won't waste my breath."

"I'll sleep after the wedding. Fireworks have yet to be arranged, not to mention news of the baby disrupted some plans."

"The honeymoon in Bali for one."

"Yes. A location without insects is required."

"Nicole won't care where you go. She doesn't want the things you can give her like all the other women."

"One of her many charms," Rafe said, a smile in his voice. "Now, the food post haste, Natalie. I can't get any work done until Nicole goes to sleep."

"Rafe!" Nicole called out. "I *need* you!"

He smiled. "Gotta go."

Setting down the receiver, he came to his feet, crossed the sitting room and pushed open the bedroom door. Bracing his hands high on the doorframe, he smiled at the beautiful, flushed, sexy-as-hell woman lounging nude in his bed. Ignoring the jolt of lust spiking through his senses, he shut down his reckless impulses and spoke with a forced calm. "Natalie's sending up some food. Are you hungry?"

"Starved." Nicole grinned. "Sex and food are my priorities, first and second, or second and first, I can't decide. Really, darling, you look insanely hot hanging there in the doorway, bare-chested, hard-bodied and seriously fuckable. Come fuck me. The food can wait."

"No it can't. I'm starved too."

"Come a little closer," she whispered, stretching her arms above her head, slowly drawing her legs up, offering him a titillating centerfold view of dewy pink flesh, "and tell me you want to wait."

Fuck no. "Look, I'm trying to be—careful, prudent...whatever."

Sitting up, she linked her fingers in her lap, looked up at him from under her lashes and smiled sweetly. "Come on-- be nice to me. It's our wedding day."

He laughed. "Cute as a cupcake, but so not you, Tiger. And I'm on my best behavior because I don't want you falling asleep in your soup at the reception dinner. You need to rest."

She frowned. "Maybe I won't marry you."

"Sure you will." A faint arrogance in his gaze.

She wrinkled her nose, sighed. "I know."

"We both know," he said, very softly. "Now be a good girl. Behave."

"Yes, sir," she whispered, rolling over, coming up on her knees and looking at him over her shoulder. "Spank me and make me behave."

He was saved from an intractable dilemma by a soft rapping on the sitting room door. "Food first, pussycat, then we'll talk about sex."

"If you think you can talk me out of it, you can't."

He was aware. Dropping his hands from the doorframe, he held up a finger. "If you promise to rest after"—he smiled —"you get sex for dessert."

"I want *that* in writing."

"Not a problem. Eat fast."

But he was grateful Natalie had recognized his appetite, his favorite breakfast food scenting the air as he carried in the tray and set it on the bed. Taking a seat beside Nicole, he lifted the silver covers one by one and tossed them to the foot of the bed.

"Oh my God!" Nicole exclaimed, sitting up straight, her eyes alight. "Forgive me for drooling, but that is one amazing display of food."

Lining up the plates before them, Rafe ticked off the

items. "Waffles with strawberries and Chantilly creme, Spanish omelet, spinach frittata, bacon and sausage, croissants, blueberry/banana smoothie, porridge—do you eat oatmeal?" At her nod, he pointed at the last plate. "And Mrs. B's famous caramel coffee cake."

"The streusel topping with caramel drizzles is fabulous," Nicole said.

"I see that."

"Would you like some?" She was already scooping up caramel with her finger.

He understood no wasn't the right answer. "I'd love some."

In the aftermath of a night and early morning of Zen-perfect sex, breakfast was leisurely, affectionate and in Rafe's case, super polite, as he consumed, with Nicole's coaxing, more of Mrs. B's coffee cake than he would have liked. On the other hand, Nicole agreed to eat some of the omelet and bacon in addition to the waffles and coffee cake she preferred; they were both on their best behavior.

With breakfast over, Rafe carried the dishes into the sitting room and on his return, stopped in the doorway. "You can change your mind."

"You promised."

He smiled at her little pout. "I was just checking."

"I keep feeling I should apologize." She grinned. "Every once and a while, sorta, maybe...or not."

"Hey, forget it. I'm one happy guy."

"Oh, good. I worry just a teeny, tiny bit that my constant demands might offend you."

"Not gonna happen," he said, his grin infectious.

But with his morning agenda up against hard time constraints, he concentrated on offering Nicole the orgasms she wanted. It wasn't an imposition for a man who'd spent a good deal of time perfecting his skills, nor was he averse to the concept of mutual pleasure. And had not the bedside clock slid into his line of vision occasionally, reality might have been more easily dismissed. His darling, however, was burning hot and impatient which nicely balanced the time/pleasure equation and before long, Nicole was satisfied, fully content and drowsy.

"If my mother comes up, save me," she murmured. "I'm going to sleep."

"Don't worry about your mother. We get along." Resting on one elbow, he winked at Nicole's raised brows. "Correction, I know how to say yes when I have to. Look, Tiger, I'm more than willing to smooth all the bumps in life for you because I love you and want to take care of you, keep you safe, make you happy."

"Me and the baby."

"Yes, of course." His hesitation was minute, then he quietly said, "Promise me one thing."

"Anything." The feel-good post orgasmic endorphins were still swirling through her body and brain.

"Don't ever keep something from me like you did this pregnancy. If you want or need something, tell me, ask me, demand it for Christ's sake. I don't like the word, trust. It has too many psycho-pop connotations, but something in that general vicinity would be nice. This is important to me. Otherwise I wouldn't ask."

While she didn't know many details, she understood his family life had been difficult. "I understand. You have my word. You're happy about the baby, though, aren't you?"

Maybe. "Yes."

"See—I was right," she noted with a light-hearted smile.

He didn't know if she was or not. He'd always had and would continue to have enemies; a baby created a new level of security problems. He smiled. "Let's just say I'm getting used to the idea."

"Well, I'm happy enough for both of us, so take your time getting used to the idea."

Her self-confidence charmed him; it always had. "You have the advantage of prior knowledge," he murmured, sliding his fingers lightly over her tummy.

Her smile was dazzling. "And you have months to come to terms with the notion of fatherhood." At the sudden arctic chill in his eyes her smile vanished. "I've made you angry."

The word, fatherhood, had unleashed a flood of revolting images of his father normally locked away in the nether regions of his brain. By will and practice, he slammed the door shut on the lurid memories. "I'm not angry with you. But if you could avoid using the word, father," he said, his voice carefully neutral, "I'd appreciate it."

She quickly mimed locking her lips. "Done. And if you don't want to talk about the baby, I won't."

Rolling onto his back, he shut his eyes, ran his palms over his face, turned one hand slack wrist over his eyes and lay motionless.

She tried to recall what she might have said to elicit such stark withdrawal, how their casual conversation has so suddenly altered. Clearing her throat, she quietly said, "I apologize for not telling you about the baby before."

"It's okay." His voice was low, unhurried, as if he were somewhere else. "Don't worry about it."

A silence fell.

Eyes closed, he was still as the grave.

Tell me what you're thinking, she wished to say, but knew

better; he was a man of inexhaustible restraint. And effortless strength, she reflected, surveying his long, muscled form occupying a good share of the bed—tempting her. Quickly looking away, she chided herself for such shameful considerations when she should be comforting him. Or apologizing again. *Or, oh God!* Struck by sudden fear, she blurted out, "Are you thinking about backing out of our marriage?"

His eyes shot open. "Are you fucking crazy?"

Affronted by his snarl, her fear vanished. "Are *you*?" she snapped.

Goddamn right," he growled and a second later she was looking up into amber eyes, very close, flame hot and laser-focused. "Crazy for you, pussycat," he whispered. "Wanna fuck?"

She smiled. "Welcome back from wherever you were."

"You don't want to know. So whadda you say?"

"This your default mode?"

A flicker of one brow. "Are you interested or not?" He had no intention of explaining his default mode.

His arrogant smile meant he knew damned well she was interested. "I suppose," she said, as if a point for her side mattered.

He laughed. "We keeping score?"

"Only if you let me win."

"I always let you win." His voice went soft. "It gives me pleasure."

Suddenly conscious of the power and authority that allowed him to speak with such assurance, reminded as well of the dangers of the world in which he lived, she felt a small spark of terror. "Tell me you'll always be with me." Tears welled in her eyes. "Promise!"

He traced the curve of her upper lip with the pad of his

finger, then dropped his head and brushed her lips with his. "I'll love you forever, pussycat."

"You'll never leave me? You have to say it!"

"I'll never leave you."

He spoke with such certainty she almost believed him capable of overcoming every danger, defeating every enemy, assuring them a blameless future.

"You worry needlessly, sweetheart," he said, wanting to erase the furrow in her brow. "I'm here. I'm not going anywhere. You have my word."

"Oh God, I'm going to turn into a whiny, overbearing, emotional wreck dominated by hormones. And it's all your fault."

He chuckled. "So what's new?"

Her eyes flew open then narrowed dangerously.

"Hey, I was joking. Seriously, you've always been the soul of discretion."

"Liar."

He shrugged. "I love you, pussycat, whether you're sweet, angry, or anything in between. It's called unconditional love."

"Thanks," she whispered. "You're always steady as a rock."

That's what came from being raised in the eye of an emotional hurricane. "One learns," he said.

3

It was nearly eight by the time Rafe entered his office downstairs. "Sorry to keep you waiting," he said to the man coming awake on his sofa. "But Nicole was restless last night."

"It must be love." Jacque Morin tossed aside the beige mohair throw and sat up. "You wouldn't have used such a tactful expression in the past." The men had known each other since childhood; attended the same boarding schools, shared friends, entertainments--occasionally lovers.

Rafe smiled. "Tact wasn't necessary in the past. It was a game. Everyone knew the rules. Love is different. Deeply satisfying. Magical. Don't look at me like that. When it happens you'll know."

"Hopefully not for a decade or more." Jacque ran his fingers through his untidy, sun-streaked hair. "I'm too bloody young to get serious."

"That's what I said. Then I got lucky." Rafe grinned. "I'll try not to be insufferable about my good fortune. Show me what you brought."

Jacque's father was the financial director of a multinational, centuries-old Parisian jeweler. Following in his father's footsteps, albeit in a more dilettante way, Jacque had grown up in the business and knew it well.

"Over there." Jacque indicated a small leather satchel on a nearby table. "You said, blue gems, right?" Slipping his feet into black leather moccasins, he stood up and moved toward the table. "At two in the morning, I'm not fully alert."

"Nicole has blue eyes."

"Ah, yes...I remember you saying that."

"Speaking of blue eyes, are you bringing Charlotte to the wedding?"

"I was or I probably will--if she gets over her latest tantrum."

Rafe laughed. "She's not going to give up on her engagement ring. You know that, right?"

"So?" Unlocking the clasp on the satchel, Jacque opened it, pulled out a black velvet cloth and flipped it open on the table.

"So nothing. She's your problem, not mine. At the moment I don't have any problems." Rafe thought of the fireworks still in flux. "Well, nothing of any consequence. Umm, I like those earrings. And that." He pointed at the glittering pieces Jacque had set out. "A unicorn?"

Jacque looked up and smiled. "One of our most profitable themes. Love, desire, and fantasy are ageless. You've seen the medieval tapestry of the Lady and the Unicorn at the Musee de Cluny, right?"

"Long ago. A school tour as I recall. I'll take both of those."

"Do you want prices?" Jacque was emptying the satchel and spreading the items out in a colorful display.

Rafe shook his head. "Send the invoice to my Geneva bank."

The array of jewelry was stunning, the major gems largely in shades of blue, the design elements augmented with other precious stones. Whether earrings, bracelets, brooches, necklaces, jeweled boxes, all were one-of-a-kind bijous by master artisans.

"The boxes could be used to hold the jewelry," Jacque pointed out.

"Perfect. I'll take it all. Nice touch on the satchel monogram, too. Thanks." Reaching down, Rafe picked up a heavy gold link bracelet, centered with an enamel medallion depicting a black and white Escher architectural pastiche. Clipping it on his wrist, he flipped up the lid and studied the photo inside. "Thanks for this," he said, softly, gazing at a small headshot of Nicole captured by one of the security cameras on his yacht the day he and Nicole had met. Her hair was wet from her swim in the Mediterranean, her eyes brilliant blue, her fresh-faced beauty breathtaking. Shaking away the ripple of fear that always struck him when he thought how close he'd come to never meeting her, he flicked the medallion lid shut, took a small, calming breath and said, "I appreciate your help with those last minute items I needed."

"Not a problem." Jacque gave Rafe a considering look. "No one would have bet a cent on you becoming a daddy."

"No argument there. I wouldn't have either."

"A surprise you said. I assume that's not for public consumption."

"No, nor would I have mentioned it if I wasn't ordering baby rattle charms in the middle of the night." Lifting a delicate gold link bracelet from the table, Rafe surveyed the personalized charms he'd had made for Nicole commemorating their whirlwind romance: an enameled facsimile of his yacht, another of his carriage house in Monte Carlo, a lovers knot, a crenellated tower like that on his island in the Adriatic, a flowered blue bikini, and the two he'd ordered last night—a blue and pink baby rattle. Sliding the charm bracelet into his pants' pocket, he nodded at the glittering jewelry. "Leave it there. Natalie will take care of it." He put out his hand. "Thanks for your help. Call me at two in the morning whenever you want. I owe you."

"I might." Jacque shook Rafe's hand. "Or better yet, I might have you apologize to Charlotte for me. No one can soothe an angry woman better than you."

"Jesus, just do her a favor. Give her an engagement ring. You've been off and on for what—three years now? It's an engagement...a promise that's all. Hell, she might change her mind before you do."

"I'll think about it."

Rafe smiled. "Consider--the make-up sex might be worth it. Let me know if you want me to call her." He moved toward the door. "I still have a couple things I have to do before Nicole wakes up. Thanks again. I'll see you tonight."

Taking a back corridor to Natalie's office, Rafe knocked once, walked in without waiting and saw his housekeeper pouring cognac into a coffee mug. "Pour one for me. Light on the coffee."

She shot him a disgruntled look over her shoulder. "I expect a bonus once our guests have left." Pulling over another mug, she tipped in a good portion of cognac, set down the bottle and picked up the coffee carafe.

"Name your price. Hey, enough coffee, add a little more cognac. It's been awhile since I've had to be polite to so many people this long."

"Try never," his housekeeper muttered, turning to him with mugs in both hands. "At least here in Paris. You always slept alone, ate alone, drank alone--like a monk."

"Yeah, well, not any more. I'm not complaining. Nicole makes this houseful of people all worthwhile."

"But we're both counting the days." She handed him his coffee.

"Forty-six hours to be exact. Now, what's it going to cost me to keep you happy?"

"My cousin needs a new car. He blew his engine last week."

"Just make sure the title's in Drago's name. His smuggling business is an accident waiting to happen."

"And you never take chances," she murmured, sardonically.

Rafe grinned. "Touche. I'm sure Drago will continue in good health for many years."

Natalie's full-throated chuckle acknowledged Rafe's glossy hope. "Thank you. Now I won't have to put a hex on you future mother-in-law." She drank her coffee in one long draught as if punctuating her statement.

"Come on, Mrs. Parrish is nice."

"You want me to step aside?" she asked, dropping her mug on a pile of perilously stacked papers. "Let her and that Mrs. B give orders?"

"God no, I need you to run this place properly? Just suck it up for a couple more days. Buy your cousin two cars if it helps. Buy him a whole fucking fleet." Draining his mug, he handed it to Natalie rather than take a chance of initiating a paper avalanche. "Are we fine now, cause I have to see Carlos."

"He's in his apartment, on the phone with the mayor. He woke her up."

Rafe turned back at the door. "Carlos knows how to apologize. By the way, have someone wrap that satchel in my office, would you? It's for Nicole. And if you need me, give me a call. I'll be back upstairs once I talk to Carlos."

Natalie dropped his mug with a thud. "You should have eloped."

"Nicole wanted her friends and family at her wedding. That's why we didn't." His eyes narrowed. "Any other advice?"

"Hmpf." A shake of her hennaed head set the diamonds in her ears ablaze.

"Here's a polite head's up, Natalie. I'm the luckiest man on the face of the earth, so whatever Nicole wants she can have. And you and I and everyone on our team are going to see that she gets it. That's a *fucking* order," he added, gruffly.

"Yes, sir."

Natalie's tone was chill, her black eyes spitting fire, her small, plump figure ramrod straight. *Shit. He could visualize nuclear chaos in his household.* "Look," he said, not in the mood to apologize, but recognizing he could have spoken less confrontationally, "this necessary degree of hospitality isn't easy for either one of us. You're used to running this place unimpeded. I'm not comfortable with a crowd of people I barely know invading my privacy. But bottom line, I want Nicole to be happy, now more than ever. This wedding celebration is about her friends and family because it matters to her. We could have been married by some clerk in some city hall in the middle of nowhere for all I care. Okay?"

"I understand." Natalie took a small breath. "I apologize."

Rafe was tempted to ask whether hell had frozen over. Instead, with the wedding fully entrain and Natalie's management skills required at every turn, he said, "Me too. And thank you. You're the heart and soul of this establishment" He smiled faintly. "Also, on a separate topic, I'm going to need your continued assurances that Nicole's pregnancy is going swimmingly."

"Doctors don't know everything," she said, smoothing her colorful gypsy skirt over her substantial hips in a firm gesture of certainty.

"My feelings exactly." Rafe glanced at the clock on the wall. "Twenty-four hours, tops, and the wedding festivities are in the rear view mirror."

"You should sleep a few hours."

"I'll try. I still have things to do though. Starting with Carlos." Pressing the ornate door handle, he opened the door. "Wish us luck with the mayor."

"Money works better than luck. Carlos knows that."

"In that case," Rafe drawled, "I'm sure the permits will be awarded promptly."

"Did you ever doubt it?"

"Not since I was very young." Walking out, he shut the door behind him.

4

When Rafe had purchased the cloister house, Carlos had chosen an apartment overlooking the courtyard. "Safe," he'd said the first time he'd surveyed his surroundings, then testing the oak door with a series of knocks, had declared, "Solid. Good."

Rafe opened that solid, medieval door quietly, entered the room and shut the door equally softly.

Carlos held up a finger without turning, then continued to listen to the person on the phone with an occasional "Yes, of course," or "No, certainly not," while Rafe settled into a leather club chair and half-dozed. At Carlos's final expression of gratitude and a promise to have a check immediately dispatched to the mayor's favorite charity, Rafe opened his eyes.

Placing the receiver in its cradle, Carlos swung around in his desk chair. "The mayor had her assistant finalize the details. We have the permits."

Rafe smiled. "Thank you. How much to expedite it?"

"Five hundred thousand. I didn't want a lengthy conversation at this late date."

"What charity?"

"A refugee neighborhood association. Not far from your community center."

"Excellent. I wouldn't have cared, although I wince at charities affiliated with religious orthodoxy."

"I may have mentioned that."

"I don't know why I'm even asking. Thank you for taking care of it. It's done. That's all that matters."

"My thoughts exactly. Fuck doctrinaire differences. Just get the permits." Carlos leaned back in his chair. "I have to welcome some new security people I brought in, give them a heads up. Any comments or advice?"

"Warn them this marriage is a once in a lifetime occasion so everything has to go off without a hiccup." Rafe grinned. "No pressure."

"They already know. The tabloids have trumpeted the rarity of your marriage with scandalous headlines and X-rated photos from your past." Carlos smiled faintly. "The gossip rags are going to miss you."

"The voyeurs will find someone else to feed their lurid curiosity," Rafe said with a dismissive shrug. "I'm out of that loop."

"They're hoping you're not. As are some of your female wedding guests I suspect."

Rafe grimaced. "My mother invited those women, not me. I was surprised she knew them. The world's way the hell too small."

"You'll have to stay out of their way."

"No shit. At least avoiding them shouldn't be difficult with the huge, fucking crowd. Neither of our mothers understood the concept of small and intimate wedding."

"Apparently not. Your guest list is huge *and* a damn rich target. That's why I brought in added security. By the way, congratulations on the baby. I don't want to say, I told you so, but I did." He met Rafe's look of surprise. "Natalie told me. You okay with the news?"

"More or less. You know me. I can be a go-it-alone, selfish prick so it took a little adjustment." Rafe smiled. "But Nicole's worth a helluva lot of adjustments." A small frown canted his brows. "My only hurdle is making sure Maso's depravities are locked away so fucking deep they'll never surface. I won't have the taint of my father impacting my child."

"You'll manage. You always have. Even when you were young."

"The forgetting is easier now with Nicole. The memories less frequent."

"Love is the ultimate distraction."

Rafe nodded. "A definite improvement over perpetual work and no name sex."

"No name sex with an endless succession of dazzling women." Carlos pointed out the obvious, not entirely sure Rafe was the best candidate for marriage.

"Available women," Rafe corrected.

"Beautiful, available—whatever; you fucked them all. Are you sure you can pivot on a dime? That life style is one of long-standing."

"Too long. So yes, it won't be a problem."

Carlos recognized that firm, determined tone. He'd first heard it fourteen years ago when Rafe's mother had introduced him to her son. Maso Contini had been gone for a month, his enemies were ever present and Camelia had been worried enough about her son's security to have taken the initiative in a marriage where she seldom did. She'd hired Carlos.

"I can take care of myself," Rafe had said, already tall at

twelve, looking Carlos in the eye with a confidence rare in someone so young.

"Then I won't have much to do, will I?" Carlos had replied, calmly.

Rafe had turned to his mother, and his voice had softened. "Are you sure, Mama? He's not going to like this. It's going to make him crazier than he already is."

"Carlos has promised to deal with Maso for us."

Camelia had looked so relieved, Carlos had seen Rafe's defiance instantly alter.

"You'll protect my mother?" the young boy had asked, his amber gaze uncompromising.

Carlos had nodded. "I will."

"Very well."

The boy's decision was quick and sure, his mother's welfare paramount. And in those early days it was moot who knew more about survival in Maso Contini's household. Perhaps they'd learned from each other how to deal with the vile man who callously and without conscience defiled all he touched. In those years of conflict, the boy and young bodyguard had forged a deep bond of friendship.

Heaving himself out of the chair, Rafe slowly stretched, then dropped his hands and shook himself awake.

"You should sleep," Carlos said, coming to his feet.

"Maybe later. I have to change the honeymoon venue. And if you'd do me a favor and bolster Natalie's non-existent manners with praise or offers of money, I'd appreciate it. I need her. No one runs this place as smoothly as she. I already promised her the usual family tribute, in this case, a car or cars," Rafe said with a shrug. "But she has a short fuse, so do what you can. I have to go back upstairs. I don't want Nicole waking up alone."

Carlos smiled. "Go. She needs you."

"It's a good feeling." Rafe smiled faintly. "Who knew love and contentment were one and the same?"

"It's about time you found out."

Rafe's gaze narrowed. "You have something to tell me?"

"Nope."

"Fuck if you don't."

"Get the hell out of here. We both have things to do."

Rafe jabbed his finger at Carlos. "Later, then. Love and contentment? You're not getting out of this."

Carlos watched the door close, his thoughts traveling back in time. Young love. You have such hope...and ignorance. Thinking it could never end. He sucked in a breath. This wasn't the time to get maudlin; he had a thousand things to do.

5

"Ith *too* eight!" the toddler shouted, pushing past his sister, running into their parent's bedroom and making a beeline for the bed.

"It's okay, Rosie." Dominic Knight offered his five-year-old daughter an indulgent smile. "Mommy and I are up." Quickly setting down his cell phone, he smoothly caught his son in mid-leap and set him on his lap. Waiting for Kate to wake, he'd been answering his emails, an unending task for a CEO of a privately-held global enterprise.

"Daddy, Daddy!" Jimmy shouted. "Me know eight! Small hand on froggie!" At two and a half, he was learning to tell time from a clock featuring animal babies.

Dominic smiled. "Good work."

"Me smart!" the little boy declared with high-decibel, toddler excitement and the unimpeachable assurance of a much loved child.

"You are," Dominic agreed, giving him a hug. "I'm proud of you."

"Jimmy woke up really, really early," Rosie explained in her responsible, older sister tone. "I told him Mommy wanted us to sleep late after Auntie Nicole's rehearsal dinner lasted so long, but he wouldn't listen, so I set up his favorite race car game on his computer." She spoke with her father's quiet reserve.

"Thanks sweetheart." Dominic set the squirming toddler on the bed between himself and Kate and lifted Rosie onto his lap. "I appreciate you keeping Jimmy occupied. Mommy *just* woke up a minute ago." He shot a grin at his wife. "She was a sleepy head this morning." Champagne made Katherine amorous, for which he was always appreciative. "If you like," he murmured, gazing at his rosy-cheeked wife with affection, "the children and I could have breakfast while you sleep a little longer."

From her snug nest under the honey-colored duvet, Kate gave him a lazy smile. "No, I'm awake...and hungry. Champagne gives me an appetite," she added with a hint of amusement in her eyes. "I hope Emilie's arrived." She looked at her daughter. "Has she?" They chose not to have live-in help so their cook's arrival time depended on the extent of gossip at the local markets.

Rosie nodded. "She fed us hot chocolate and croissants. But Jimmy ate superfast so he could wake you."

"Me go wedding today!" the toddler whooped. "Me wear Spidey suit! Me show you!" Scrambling over his mother, he grabbed her cell phone from a bedside table--unlike his father's, her phone wasn't off limits. Punching the photo app with unflappable two-year-old confidence, he quickly found his photo and held the phone out to his audience. "See!"

Jimmy's style sense was irrepressibly individual, and largely super hero related. His suit had been a compromise with an applique of Spiderman prominently displayed on the jacket.

"I love it," Kate said, ruffling his hair. "You look very grown up."

"Me almost dis!" The little boy held up three fingers. "Daddy let me drive his race car when me dis!" Three fingers punched higher.

"I said you can drive *with* my help," Dominic reminded him.

A small silence fell; Jimmy's willfulness patent. But he was a sweet, bubbly child as well and a moment later his pout turned into a smile. "K, Daddy. Me let you."

Kate caught Dominic's eye and they both smiled.

"After you've had breakfast, Daddy," Rosie said, interrupting her parents' silent exchange, "come help me decide on shoes to go with my new dress." Rosie understood her father was the arbiter of fashion in the family.

Dominic raised an eyebrow at Kate. "Want a vote?"

She grinned. "Wow, you asking me? You must be in a good mood."

He winked. "I am. You can select your own earrings for the wedding."

"I better help Mommy." Rosie spoke with a gravity that belied her years. "No offense, Mommy."

Kate smiled. "I'd appreciate your help, darling. Daddy says the color of my dress is"—she gave Dominic a searching glance.

"Plum," Rosie volunteered. "Those tear-drop pearl earrings Daddy bought you would look nice with it."

"Me'n Tor yike pums!" Jimmy cried, jabbing his thumb at the Thor image on his pajama top.

"I do too." Kate smiled at her young son. "Let's go get some."

"Me tell Emee!" Leaping up, the toddler wobbled across

the large bed, jumped to the floor and raced toward the door. "Me get there first!"

"If you'll give Emilie a head's up, sweetheart," Dominic said, setting Rosie on her feet by the bed. "She's not going to know Jimmy's asking for plums. Mommy and I will be there in a minute."

"Want me to make two espressos? Emilie let me practice this morning."

Kate smiled at her daughter who, despite her unusual maturity, was still young enough to favor bunny print pajamas. "I'd love an espresso and I know Daddy would too."

"Sugar for you, Mommy?"

"Just a little."

As the door closed on their daughter, Dominic pulled Kate into his arms, lowered his head and kissed her gently. "Thanks to you we have the most darling children in the world."

"You're welcome." Kate grinned. "We did good, didn't we?"

Rosie had her mother's looks: red hair, green eyes and a fresh, pure beauty.

Jimmy was a toddler version of Dominic: dark, ruffled hair, blue eyes and boyish features that would someday mirror his father's stark handsomeness.

"They're perfect," he whispered. "Like their mother."

"You get credit too, Mr. Knight," she purred. "We're a team."

A toddler shriek echoed from the kitchen.

Dominic chuckled. "Jimmy has no patience." His smile widened. "He takes after you. By the way," he said, softly, "thanks for last night. You were adorable."

"Insatiable...impatient."

A flash of a smile. "That's what I meant."

"I should be thanking you," she whispered, stretching upward, and kissing his smiling mouth as he lowered his head. "You never say no."

"I never will. You've given me a life, Katherine—a family, love." His eyelids drifted a fraction lower. "I'm forever in your debt, and," he added with a wicked grin, uncomfortable expressing emotion, "it's not as though I'm averse to sexual marathons. In fact..."

She felt his erection surge against her hip. "Don't you dare."

"Not a phrase likely to stop me," he drawled.

"The children might come back."

He groaned.

"Also, Emilie's here, Rosie is making us espressos, Jimmy is already screaming"—

"Okay, okay, duty calls."

Reaching up, she lightly traced the curve of his bottom lip with the pad of her finger. "How about a rain check?"

An instant smile. "You got it. We don't have to be at Rafe's house until four."

"Nicole said three-thirty and I *doubt* either child will take a nap. They're both excited about the wedding."

"What about that new Disney movie? They could watch that."

"Jeez, are you a fifteen-year-old with a hard on?"

He grinned. "You wouldn't like a fifteen-year-old with a hard on. Relax, I'll make it work."

She grinned back. "I know you will. But right now, I really *am* hungry. I must have burned off a thousand calories last night, so..." Sitting up, she pulled a white cashmere robe off the bedpost, slipped her arms into the sleeves and slid off the bed.

"Come on, *I* did all the work," Dominic playfully noted.

Leaning over, he picked his grey sweats off the floor in a supple flow of honed muscle, reversing direction with an effortless strength, shoving his legs into his sweats and coming to his feet.

"And did it extremely well," Kate murmured, watching her husband pull the sweats over his lean hips, enamored as always at the splendid sight of him: tall, broad-shouldered, sleek and toned, a powerful, disciplined body.

He looked up from knotting the tie at his waist. "What?"

"I'm just admiring the view."

"While you, and all that...spectacular sumptuousness"—a sweeping downward motion of his hands marked her voluptuous form under the soft white cashmere—"are for my eyes only." His voice was a low growl at the last, his narrowed gaze restive. "You're so goddamned fuckable, Katherine. You don't know how tempted I am to keep you locked away from prying eyes."

"If only we didn't have two young children I might let you. However...we do *and* they're waiting." She held out her hand and smiled. "Come."

Her simple, welcoming gesture touched him with joy. Even now, years after Katherine had entered his life, he never forgot that feeling of joy--once unknown to him--had arrived in all its amazing wonder with her.

Reaching out, he took her hand, leaned down and kissed her cheek. "You make me happy."

"The feeling's mutual," she murmured, recognizing the dozens of things left unsaid in the soft hoarseness of his voice.

That they'd met was perhaps a fortuitous act of fate, but after that first meeting, random chance played no part. Dominic had managed, controlled, occasionally coaxed, but always determinedly shaped the direction of their lives. Selfishly at first—he'd had no practice with altruism—but ultimately with consideration for Katherine's feelings as well.

Still, love had taken him by surprise.

To say he was skeptical would have been charitable; in fact, he'd rejected love out of hand. But the sensation, quite separate from lust and desire, persisted, consumed him, tormented him, artlessly seduced his formidable cynicism and slowly, the mangled mess of his life, crammed deep with secrets, crumbled.

Dominic took a small breath, as he often did, when he thought about the million improbable coincidences that brought him to this moment. "If I ever do something to make you unhappy," he said, quietly, "you must let me know."

"Of course I will. And if I do anything to make you unhappy," Kate said with a grin, wanting to ease the worry line between his brows, "tell me very diplomatically."

He laughed. "Or not at all."

"Better yet." There. He was smiling again. "Speaking of happiness, I hear a sibling disagreement escalating." A toddler scream, countered by Rosie's mild reprimand, was quickly followed by the cook's rapid flow of admonishing French.

Grabbing a shirt from a nearby chair, Dominic pulled Kate toward the door. "Jimmy sounds frustrated." He gave her a grin. "Like you at times."

"While Rosie's like you. Reticent. Controlled."

"Fuck, don't say that," he muttered as they walked down the hallway.

"It's fine. She's not a martinet. In fact, she's very kind and thoughtful."

"Unlike me." Releasing Kate's hand, he slipped the T-shirt over his head, shoved in his arms, let it slip downward.

"I didn't say that." Smoothing the fabric over the long, fluid line of his back, she recaptured his hand. "You're unsparing in your love for all of us, and our children know it. They'll be fine, whatever they decide to do."

Dominic rolled his eyes. "Jimmy wants to be a race car driver."

"He'll get over it."

"I'm not so sure about that."

Kate leaned into Dominic's arm and smiled up at him as they moved through the sun-drenched living room. "Then you'll have to see that he's not hurt in that dangerous occupation."

"Shit, no problem," he said, dryly. "Anything else?"

"You might think about giving Rosie a few tasks at Knight Enterprises. She wants to replace you as CEO someday."

"You're fucking kidding."

"Not in the least. She's quite serious."

He gave her a sideways glance. "How do you know all this?"

"Motherly intuition."

"You're freaking me out just a little," he said, softly.

She grinned. "It's a gift. Ask my Nana. Now smile, here we go into the lion's den," she said, brightly, pushing the kitchen door open. Walking into the large, sunny kitchen, she surveyed her two, scowling children. "Tell mommy and daddy what the problem is and your daddy will fix it"—she winked at Dominic—"won't you Daddy?"

This he knew. It was his strength. The capacity to manage the unmanageable had made him a billionaire at a very young age. "Let's talk it over," Dominic said. "Jimmy you first, then Rosie, and we'll figure this out so everyone's happy. And in case you were wondering if I remembered your movie list, I did. I brought home those two new Disney movies."

"Which movies, Daddy?" Rosie asked, politely, although excitement lit her gaze.

"Movie!" Jimmy screamed, dropped his second croissant of the morning and jumped off his chair.

"The one about the horse," Dominic replied first because that was Rosie's choice. "The other one is that super hero movie you wanted, Jimmy. They're in the bag on the entry hall table. Take it easy, now," he cautioned, as both children raced away. "And don't knock over the vase of flowers on the table!" he called out as they disappeared from sight.

"Excellent work, Mr. Knight," Kate murmured.

He winked. "It's a gift. Morning, Emilie, Katherine tells me she's starved. What's on the menu?"

6

hit. The sound of voices coming from his apartment was audible as Rafe reached the top of the stairs. He had a good idea to whom the voices belonged and when he walked into the sitting room, his expectations proved correct. Nicole's mother, Mrs. B, Nicole's sister, Isabelle, and her youngest sister, Ellie, greeted him with smiles.

"Morning ladies." A smile, a dip of his head, his gaze shifting to Nicole, seated between her mother and Mrs. B on the sofa, her discomfort plain. "You're up," he said, softly, his straight on look saying *I got this*.

At his unspoken message, Nicole set aside the hairstyle magazine in her lap. "We were trying to decide on hairdos for the wedding."

"I see. If I might steal you away for a minute," he said, walking toward her. "I have a question about the honeymoon arrangements." He gave their visitors a swift, all-encompassing smile. "A weather front is disrupting our flight plan. We have to decide if we want to re-schedule or add a layover."

Nicole was on her feet before Rafe had finished his explanation. "Excuse me," she murmured, easing past Mrs. B and the magazine covered coffee table, deliverance, escape, *freedom* within reach.

As she approached, Rafe took her hand, and drew her toward the bedroom. "You looked like you needed rescuing," he whispered.

A nod, her voice pitched low. "Thanks."

He winked. "Anytime, anywhere, pussycat."

A moment later, he ushered Nicole into the bedroom, shut the door behind them, and watched with mild concern as she collapsed in a sprawl on the nearest chair. "That bad?"

"I was trying not to scream." She shot him a grateful look. "You arrived in the nick of time."

"I'm sorry I didn't get back sooner." With Nicole's peace of mind more important than their visitors' sense of affront, he turned the ancient key in the lock without regard for the scape of metal on metal. Turning back, he contemplated Nicole's obvious weariness, her hastily donned robe with the buttons out of sync, and said, flatly, "They shouldn't have wakened you."

Nicole sighed. "In their defense, everyone's super excited. Apparently, our wedding has become a major social event." A teasing glimmer lit her gaze. "That's on you, cause I'm just a California girl without an entourage or trust fund. And keep in mind," she said with a small shrug, "ordinarily I wouldn't have been sleeping late, but"—

"I kept you up."

"That wasn't your fault."

True, but only up to a point. "I could have shown more restraint. That *was* my fault." His reputation for vice wasn't in question; he knew the difference between enough and too much.

"You don't have to apologize," she said with a flick of her fingers. "It's not only lack of sleep making me twitchy. I'm dealing with other strange, baffling emotions, most of them antisocial, all of them unsettling. So I don't feel like chatting about stupid hair styles, or being polite, or"—

"You don't have to." Rafe's amber gaze held a boundless tenderness. "I'll deal with the commotion, your family, problems that arise. Stay in here until the wedding—relax, sleep if you can. I'll wake you when it's time to dress and help you button, zip, snap, whatever. Francois will do your hair, or not," Rafe quickly added at her grimace. "It's entirely up to you."

She took a small breath to suppress a disconcerting urge to weep, pushed herself upright in the chair as if good posture would strengthen her resolve, and forcibly tamped down the incipient shakiness in her voice. "That's sweet of you, but I can do my hair myself and my dress isn't fussy, it just slides on and...oh God, sorry"—she swallowed hard to stem her tears. "How embarrassing..."

Any show of bewilderment was so foreign to his strong-willed Tiger that Rafe immediately crossed the few feet separating them, swept her up in his arms and kissed her gently on the cheek. "Tell me how to help--short of calling off the wedding," he added in an attempt to cheer her, "and I'll do it."

"I wish I knew." Her smile trembled briefly. "But I don't. I'm weepy when I never am, my emotions are in shambles, and at the risk of scaring you, I'm this close"—she raised her hand, her thumb and forefinger a hair's-breadth apart—"to major histrionics."

Hell, high-strung and nervy was business as usual for his

pussycat, but he knew better than to say so. "You're newly pregnant. Everything's bound to be strange and different," he murmured, carrying her to the bed, sitting down, settling her on his lap. "Explain these novel feelings to me. I'm a good listener and"--he smiled--"the best fixer-upper on the planet. You need something taken care of—your dress ironed, a light bulb changed, some personal therapy--I'm your man." Her little giggle was encouraging. "You think I can't? Watch and learn, Tiger. I can do anything."

"I know," she whispered.

"I'll take care of you," he said, softly. "Hand to God." At the flicker of her brow, he smiled. "Any god you want. Seriously though"—his voice was low, soothing--"we should sign up for Pregnancy 101 soon so we don't make too many blunders."

She blushed, gave him a ghost of a smile. "I've done a little reading already."

He bit back his first ten replies because getting pissed again about having been blind-sided by her pregnancy wasn't useful. "Then I have some catching up to do," he said, smoothly.

"I'm trying to understand how to manage the first trimester, particularly my crazy, rollercoaster emotions."

Which comment required further suppression of impolitic replies. In his ignorance, he'd written off her heightened sensibilities as wedding nerves.

More fool, he.

Quelling his flash of temper, he reminded himself that he loved her no matter what *and* he of all people was long past moral outrage. "So tell me what you've learned," he said with a well-mannered smile.

"Right now the nesting instinct is really appealing to me. Apparently, it's more prevalent toward the end of pregnancy, but I can't help how I feel. The thought of a cozy, secluded home somewhere with just you and me, and no one else until the baby is born is my current dream-come-true."

Not to mention a staff to cook and clean and do the wash. Although, considering her dodgy mood swings, he chose not to mention the practicalities. "Then that's what we'll do." He brushed a wisp of curls off her forehead with a special gentleness. "So this nesting instinct...is it common?"

"Meaning what?"

Her snappish glance was so close to normal he decided his Tiger was getting back in form. "Nothing," he said, promptly. "It was a neophyte question. I don't have any problem shutting out the world until the baby arrives. All you have to do is tell me where you want to be when we lock the gates."

"The carriage house in Monte Carlo."

An infinitesimal hesitation with Contini Pharmaceuticals headquartered in Geneva. "Fine," he said. "Monte Carlo it is."

Taking note of his minute equivocation, Nicole sighed. "That was selfish of me. You have to work, don't you?"

Considering he owned a global corporation employing twenty thousand employees, his answer was predictable. "I do, but don't worry. I'll manage the logistics."

"I just want to be with you." Her attempt at a smile ended in a quivering bottom lip. "Sorry"—she rubbed away the tears welling in her eyes, but one spilled over, then another. "Oh God, I don't even know why I'm crying."

"It's okay," he whispered, wiping the wetness from her cheeks with his shirt sleeve. "Having a baby is a big deal. If I knew how to cry, I would too."

His startling comment snapped her out of her weepy

mood. "You don't know how to cry?" She stared at him. "Seriously?"

"Seriously." He smiled. "Feel free to cry for both of us, pussycat."

His reply was casual, easy. But then he'd been very young when he'd learned two important lessons. Never cry. Never show fear.

She squinted at his glibness. "That answer's ready for prime time."

A smile. "Always."

Another sideslip, *nothing to see here,* all the mysteries hidden deep.

An aberrant thought suddenly spiked through her senses, followed by a burst of elation; perhaps foolish her more rational instincts warned. *Don't overestimate your powers.* As if, her bitchy alter-ego instantly rebuked; of course her love would triumph over Rafe's hidden past, overcome his resistance to any conversation touching on the personal, bring him happiness. She just knew she could and had--at least partially; she understood her limits. But there was a smug assurance in her smile and a teasing note in her voice when she said, "You might regret giving me leave to cry. Wanna take it back?"

He liked that she was smiling again. "Nah, I'm good." Her naivety was charming; as if a few tears mattered to him after the life he'd lived. "And whenever you're restless or unhappy, or if you want or need anything, just tell me." He touched her cheek. "There's nothing I can't give you."

An eyebrow lift, a hint of a grin. "Such arrogance."

"Uh-uh, practice." And a level of authority granted few men.

"I can make you happy too, you know."

"You already have." Flicking open the Escher medallion,

he held up his wrist. "Look. That's you the day you changed my life."

Staring at her likeness, she felt a lump rising in her throat. "I'll never forget seeing you...that first time." She let out a little sigh, remembering his stark beauty, half-undressed, then quickly dressed and smiling at her. "Do you ever wonder what would have happened to us if I hadn't walked into your stateroom?"

"I try not to." A faint frown slid across his brow. "It was the biggest roll of the dice *ever*." He sucked in a breath at the improbable circumstances that had brought them together. "Having won against those odds," he said, gruffly, "don't plan on straying far from my side." His arms tightened around her, and he struggled to shut down his worst instincts. "Sorry." He took a breath. "I shouldn't give orders like that, or at least not in that tone of voice." A slow exhale, his voice when he spoke, softer. "The thing is,...my kind of love isn't virtuous or gentle. It's unprincipled, possessive, bone-deep jealous, and damn near"--he went still, knowing he was getting it wrong, not sure he knew how to get it right, the underlying threat in his words deplorable. "Look," he said, "it's a bitch wanting to own someone in this day and age. I know better; I know that kind of love is fucked up." He shrugged, a tense twitch of one shoulder. "I have no excuse, other than my twisted childhood, but"—his amber eyes were inches away, unblinking, taking some personal inventory—"so help me God, if you ever so much as look at another"—he abruptly held up a finger, dragged in a breath. "Give me a second." He could feel himself moving into major certifiable territory, his lawless feelings so huge and powerful the air burned. Christ, don't be a dickhead. Pissing off Nicole hours before their wedding was insanity.

The transformation was instant. His smile was angelic,

his tone apologetic, his expression so totally sincere it colored the world flat-out beautiful. "I'm such a controlling jerk." A slow, sweeping smile. "Please, ignore what I said."

But a muscle was still twitching over his cheekbone and Nicole understood only sheer will had curbed his temper. Turning marginally on his lap, she took his handsome face between her palms, a hint of edginess still evident in his golden gaze. "If it makes you feel any better," she offered, "my love is equally uncompromising. Just for the record, I don't share."

He laughed. "That's my line." Of recent origin; sharing common in his past.

"Then we both understand the rules."

"Whoa." A lazy grin. "Back up a little. I don't remember signing on for any rules."

A spark of surprise on her face. "Don't tease."

"Who said I'm teasing." Suddenly he was looking into huge, blue eyes, beginning to fill with tears. "Don't cry," he whispered. "I was joking. Show me where to sign. Seriously, I'll sign anything." An outrageous statement for a man who'd always given that far-off stare whenever the word, commitment, had entered the conversation.

"Oh, Lord...see...what's happening...to me?" Her stammering lament ended in hiccupy sniffles. "I cry over everything and nothing. It's mortifying, but I just...love...you so... much, and I've never loved anyone before, so...it's not fair unless...you love me as madly as...I love you," she finished with an enchanting pout he would have liked to photograph. And if her mood hadn't been so dicey he might have.

Touching the corner of her mouth with a light, brushing fingertip, he said, gravely. "Loving you madly isn't a problem. Keeping my madness to manageable levels is the tough part. So don't ever worry about how much I love you." He gazed at her for a moment, sensitive to all the monumental and subtle changes she'd made in his life, the untrammeled happiness she brought him. "You're in my heart"—he smiled—"and keep in mind I didn't know I had one before we met. Thanks to you I know I do, thanks to you my world is cloudless, my life complete. But," he said, very, very, softly, "you must *never* leave me."

"Oh Lord," she moaned. "We're both obsessed."

"It's okay. That's why we get along. We're both crazy in love. It doesn't get any better than that. And I should know."

She frowned. "Don't say that."

"But it makes all the difference in the world, pussycat. The absolute certainty, the one-in-a-million, ten million, endless millions gamble that's paid off for us. We have that kind of love, you and I, and," he murmured, kissing her lightly, "I'm going to make sure it stays that way." He ran his fingertips down her arm. "Tell me you forgive me for being an ass."

"If you give me a free pass for being a crybaby the next eight months."

He put out his hand. "Deal."

Her grip was strong but there was a wobble in her voice when she said, "I'm never going to be a saint. I hope you don't mind."

"Jesus, Tiger, as if that's what I want," he murmured, pulling her closer, resting his chin on her head. "You're the smart ass princess that makes my life worth living. Promise you won't change."

She nodded, sniffed, rubbed her wet cheek against his shirt.

Recognizing the next wave of tears was imminent, he slid the charm bracelet from his pants' pocket. "I brought you a present. Give me your wrist, and I'll put it on." Filing away the memo apropos gifts arresting tears, he twined the gold links around her wrist and locked the clasp. "See if you recognize the charms. There are a couple blue ones if you need *something blue* for your wedding day."

"You *are* romantic," she said, softly, fingering the jeweled mementos of their whirlwind affair. "They're beautiful." Seeing the two rattles, she looked up and smiled. "Fast work, Contini."

He grinned. "I woke a friend in the middle of the night."

"That's a really good friend."

"He is. You'll meet Jacque at the wedding. Speaking of friends, why don't you text Isabelle and warn her you're going to rest. I would, but I don't want your family to think I'm controlling."

"It's not a problem." She smiled. "Isabelle knows our relationship is egalitarian."

"Good," he said, politely, rather than mar their content. "I'm glad Isabelle understands. Where's your phone?"

A few moments later Isabelle texted back. *I thought you looked tired. I'll explain to Mother you're going to rest until the wedding.* And shortly after, they heard the apartment door shut.

"Now you're going back to sleep." Flipping over the covers, Rafe lifted her off his lap, and smoothly deposited her on the bed. "No arguments," he said, curtailing her protest. "Think of the baby. He or she needs to rest even if you don't."

"You're guilting me," she grumbled.

"Damn right I am." Straightening the indigo blue coverlet under her chin, he tucked her in. "Do you need a drink or snack?"

"I need you."

"I'll be right over there." He pointed at his desk. "I'll take care of some emails." He'd given his employees the day off in honor of his wedding, but some areas of his company never closed. And to those outside business contacts who required his personal attention, his wedding day was irrelevant.

But once Nicole fell asleep, he retired to the sitting room, leaving the bedroom door ajar so he'd hear her when she woke. There were several tasks yet to finalize for the wedding.

7

He called Carlos and Natalie and let them know he was in his apartment until the wedding. After running through the activities still to be completed with each of them, he said, "Nicole's sleeping, so text me if you have any questions."

Next, he cancelled the honeymoon in Bali, informing his steward at his beach house there that the staff could stand down, apologizing as well for the last minute change in plans. "Something unavoidable came up." Rafe didn't give a further explanation. It wasn't as though Jan didn't understand his employer's erratic lifestyle; on more than one occasion Rafe had walked in unannounced with a rowdy group of friends.

"The staff and I would like to offer you and your bride our best wishes, sir," his majordomo said with the cultivated manners of a bygone era. "We look forward to seeing you at some later date."

"Thank you, Jan. Give my thanks to the staff as well." Jan van Maas was the quintessential retainer; sophisticated, cosmopolitan, a seventh generation Balinese educated in

Paris. Rafe had asked him to stay on, along with the staff when he'd purchased the property almost a decade ago. "Once our schedule allows, we'll be out for a visit." Since Nicole's pregnancy was semi-private until the wedding, he didn't elaborate; time enough for that later.

"Very good, sir, we'll put the vintage champagne back in the cellar."

"No need, there's plenty. You and the staff use it to celebrate our wedding. And I'll be sure to give Nicole your best wishes. *Au revoir*."

Setting down the receiver, Rafe considered canceling the pre-wedding group photo. The photographer was set-up in the refectory, but should Nicole sleep late, the families would be kept waiting. And bottom line, he couldn't imagine shepherding twenty-some people into place for photos could be quickly done. Pulling out his cell, he found the photographer's number and tapped it.

"Change of plans," Rafe said. "We'll do pictures after the ceremony. Sorry for the last minute notice. I'll have Carlos warn everyone."

When Carlos answered, Rafe asked him to give the family a head's up. "Just say we're postponing them until after the wedding."

"Gotcha."

"No wiseass remarks?"

"Hell no, it's your wedding. Although, one small word of advice. Don't keep Matt Parrish waiting. He's protective of his daughter. I'm sure you understand the feeling."

"Yup, in every way imaginable. So don't worry, we'll be there on time."

Having disposed of all the last minute details, Rafe poured himself two fingers of Macallan 32 and began answering emails. Mindful of the four o'clock deadline, however, he kept an eye on the clock.

They had to be downstairs by three forty-five at the latest. Since Nicole had spurned outside help, he was guessing she'd need more time than usual to bathe, do her hair, and dress. Although showering and suiting up was a fifteen minute exercise for him, he'd best do what he had to do before waking her. She was going to need help with her gown.

At two o'clock, he shut down his laptop, quietly moved through the bedroom to the bathroom, and leaving the bathroom door open, quickly showered.

"You left me!" Nicole called out, Rafe's shadowy form visible in the steamed bathroom mirror. "Hurry back before I go into decline!"

"Be there in a minute!" Pulling on a pair of boxers, Rafe rubbed a towel over his hair, smoothed it back with his hands and walked into the bedroom. "I thought only Victorian ladies went into decline," he said, smiling at his sleepy-eyed fiancée.

"I'm being pampered like a lady of leisure so I'm allowed."

"Continually fucked you mean," he drawled.

"Speaking of that you look scrumptious," she murmured, the lift of her brows appreciative. "All sleek grace, brute strength, testosterone to spare, so"—Rafe was watching her with a hint of a smile. "Is there time? Say yes."

"Yes."

"Because you're super talented."

He grinned. "And you have a hair-trigger."

"Only with you. I never felt"—

"Don't." A small shake of his head.

Reminded of his jealousy that night at his Monte Carlo club, she smiled sweetly. "Have I told how much I'm looking forward to being Mrs. Contini and teaching you not to scowl?"

His frown melted away. "Sorry. And thank you. I'm looking forward to having a wife"—he grinned—"and a baby. I like surprises."

She caught his eye. "No you don't, but you love me."

"Yes, that." Love was new enough for him that at times like this he was still feeling his way; a distinct anomaly for a man of action. Opportunely, however, Nicole was looking for a fuck and that happened to be his default position with women. So back on familiar ground, he set aside the ambiguities of love, slipped off his boxers and gently said, "There's not much time."

"How much time."

"Ten, fifteen minutes." Sitting beside her on the bed, he stretched out his legs, winked. "Think you can do it?"

"Better question," she said with a cheeky grin, her gaze flicking to his dick. "Can you?"

"Seriously?" The smirk in his voice went with the disarming smile that had captivated endless women in situations like this. Gripping his cock, he pumped his fist up and down three, four times, then quickly released his hold, fingers spread like a mic drop. "This do?"

"Show off." His towering erection was world class and seriously fuckable. A thought wildly seconded by an off-the-charts desire streaking up her spine.

"He's good under pressure."

"I don't want to hear it."

"What I meant to say is the hottest chick in the world wants some action, and he got the message. Okay?"

She smiled. "That works for me."

"Excellent." He grinned. "Now, come here." He patted his lap and held out his arms.

She scrambled up, he swung her over his lap and as she straddled his legs and settled on her knees, her smile was a flash of sweetness. "A thousand thanks. My crazy hormones don't have an off switch anymore."

"I'm thinking it's pretty much Paradise found for me," he said dropping a quick kiss on her nose. "But, unfortunately"—a flicker of his brows—"more earthly issues are intruding. I hear organ music starting up."

"Oh, shit. Really?"

"Chapel doors open at two thirty." He held her gaze. "So--a couple enough?"

"I'll settle for one."

"That's my sweetheart." He raised her enough to guide his erection into her creamy warmth then watched her slowly slide down his dick, the image so totally hot and sexy, such a goddamn thing of beauty, it made him think there might be a heaven after all. And he moved just a little to refine the sensory impact.

Her eyes widened for a second before she uttered a soft, weightless sigh. "Has anyone ever told you your dick has mad skills?" she whispered, bottoming out on his thighs, filled, gorged, glutted with cock, the fit, super tight, the pressure so sublime she held her breath for a moment to let the tiny, glittering explosions tap dance down her nerve endings.

Whether her question was real or rhetorical, he played it safe and lied. "No, never. Your sweet little pussy getting in the zone?" he asked, changing the subject, his large palms exerting the faintest pressure on her hips to turn up the heat.

"Ohmygod"—her breath caught—"that feels *so-o-o* good..."

His muscles shifted, and with a casual push he forced his erection upward so the all-consuming goodness touched every skittish, trembling surface of her sex, spread ripples of raw, molten lust through her body, excited every lurid give-it-to-me nerve. "Ready to max this out?" A whisper, a promise, a certainty from a man with an enviable sexual repertoire.

Her lashes lifted faintly, her blue gaze, flame hot. "Go for it."

A comment he would have acted on yesterday without a qualm; now he was facing countless constraints. On the other hand, after years of flagrant lechery, he had an encyclopedic grasp of sensual nuance, granted, more often excessive, uninhibited and some might say, problematic, but for his sweetheart, he could do soft and gentle. Sliding his large, wide hands under her bottom, he slowly raised her up his rigid length with an effortless lift, then down again in a languid, lazy rhythm, shifting her weight lightly in his palms, adjusting the ideal angle for maximum sensation, carefully testing the limits of penetration, paying attention to her breathing, her hot, pulsing tissue, moving in her with all the subtle mastery at his command.

She squirmed at the extremity of each hilt deep invasion, her wetter than wet sex slipping on his thighs, her adrenalin pumping, her body purring and pulsing, little warm, wanton fuzzies flooding her senses. "Make this... spectacular bliss last—forever..."

If only; the organ music was freaking him out. "I'll see what I can do," he said, lying his ass off with the clock ticking in his head.

"Oh God, oh God, oh God, what are you doing, don't

stop, no, no, don't," she panted, a frantic, fuck me tremor flashing through her body. "Oh, Lord—thank you...that's heavenly..." she purred as he eased her back down his erection.

"I know what you like," he whispered, zeroing in on all her favorite erogenous zones with perfect understanding and precision even while mentally watching the chapel fill up in the multi-tasking portion of his brain.

"Do that again," she gasped, every brain cell on fire, a pink glow of pleasure drugging her senses. "I'm dying..." Lavishly filled with cock, she was rocking gently, eyes shut, pleasure washing over her in waves, her body stoked, ravenous, orgasmic momentum rising at dizzying speed. Suddenly grabbing handfuls of Rafe's sleek, black hair, she pulled his face close and kissed him hard, hard, hard—a nanosecond before that first kick-ass, glorious spasm spiked through her pussy with high-pressure, killer intensity.

Score, he thought with a glance at the clock. Splaying his fingers wider on Nicole's hips, he held her impaled on his dick with the artful pressure of fairy tale fame--not too soft, not too hard, just perfect; a lesson mastered at fifteen in the least bookish, non-fairytale venue in Southeast Asia.

A second later, he inhaled her wild, take-no-prisoners scream as the full force of the orgasmic wave crashed through her body, quickly shifting his shoulder a second later to cushion her head as she collapsed on his chest, over-whelmed by the fierce, jarring convulsions.

Holding her gently in his arms while the stunning rapture cooled and her tremors waned, he half-smiled, conscious of a vast content. His beautiful, rosy-cheeked, high-octane darling gave and took pleasure with spendthrift abandon. She was an absolute treasure; awesome, adorable, and totally his.

The last phrase not for public consumption.

Nicole believed in equality.

"One more for the road?" he whispered.

It took effort for her to open her eyes, and another moment before she smiled. "Sorry, you didn't get a turn."

"I'm fine. I'm asking you." A politesse only; her libido was still racing on a one-way-street.

"Then, yes, please."

He smiled. "Give me a kiss, pussycat. and we'll see about fine-tuning the magic."

Her mouth lifted to his, his dipped to hers, and as they kissed, he ran his fingertip over her clit that was jammed against his dick, exerted a subtle pressure, felt liquid desire drench his finger and swallowed her soft, breathy gasp. "Too tight?"

She shook her head, a little whimper escaping as he softly pressed her showy clit.

A warning to move his inked dick a modicum higher into her sleek, throbbing sex with care. "Everything good?" he said, low and hushed, giving her an out.

A blissful, melting sigh.

Lifting her hands to his shoulders, he said, softly, "Hold on," flexed his thighs and pushed deeper. "You want me to stop, tell me."

She panted, her eyes slits.

He read that as a yes and spreading his hands wide over her ass, he raised and lowered her, slowly at first, setting a cautious pace, until with a little shiver, she leaned in close and whispered, "I'm not one bit fragile."

He smiled; carte blanche in a whisper. She was also wet and covetous, trembling with need, and moments later, completely submerged, he gave her what she wanted in a brilliant, breathless, race-to-the-finish orgasm.

As if on cue, the clock in the sitting room chimed the quarter hour.

A visible flinch, a quick breath through his nose, then he kissed her cheek, and lifted her free of his erection. Laying her on her back, he covered her with the quilt and came to his feet. "I'll be back in five minutes."

"Make—it…ten…a day or two would be better…"

He stood for a moment, debating their narrowing options, correction, lack of options; the wedding, the guests; Nicole's father couldn't be kept waiting. Swinging around, he walked into the bathroom.

Turning up the heat, he opened the taps on the ornate, malachite tub and quickly washed up again while the tub was filling. Then he picked up Nicole from bed, carried her into the bathroom, gently eased her into the water and took a seat on the broad tub edge.

"The world is still hazy," she murmured, sliding lower in the water. "I need a second."

That worked for him; he needed a second to get his dick under control. Her voluptuous breasts were just cresting the surface of the water in ripe, rosy mounds, while her sleepy-eyed, post-orgasmic half-smile was so fucking give-it-to-me alluring, it took every shred of restraint he possessed to keep from climbing in with her. He reminded himself he wasn't some undisciplined, horny sixteen-year-old, nor was he particularly impulsive by nature. And if she hadn't shifted slightly so her full breasts jiggled in the water, sending a wired jolt to his dick, he might more easily have heeded his advice. Swearing softly under his breath, he slid back another foot. "I don't trust myself," he said, gruffly, "so I'll rinse your hair for you but otherwise I'm keeping my distance."

She stared at his colorful, tattooed dick, solid as stone,

Hokusai's Great Wave brilliantly portrayed in stunning detail. "And I know better than to comment on him"—she pointed—"or argue when you're looking at me with that grim expression." His transformation to politely bland was instant. She sighed. "I don't have your chameleon skills, nor, apparently does your cock. It's *huge,* damn you. Go. Do us both a favor. Get some clothes on." She pointed at the spray hose coiled above the faucet. "I'll rinse my hair myself."

Relief flooded his senses. Sexual abstinence was foreign to him. "I'm right next door if you need me." He glanced up as the eighteenth century mechanical clock above the tub began to chime, the scantily dressed ballet dancer pirouetting at each strike.

After three chimes, silence.

"I heard, I heard," Nicole said to Rafe's telling look. "I'll be done before you."

Recalling the first time she'd said that when they'd showered and dressed in Monte Carlo, Rafe smiled. "Not a chance, pussycat. Besides, you need me to zip you up."

She winkled her nose, then slid under the water.

Striding into his dressing room next door, he took out a clean pair of boxers from a semainier, put them on, walked to the closet wall, opened all the doors, and slid his new suit pants off the hanger. Stepping into the fine navy wool, he pulled the pants up over his hips, swiftly zipped and buttoned and moved to a number of shelves stacked with shirts. Selecting a white shirt from Borrelli, his Neapolitan shirt maker, he tossed it on the rosewood table in the center of the room. A navy foulard tie, socks, belt and a pair of navy tie shoes joined the shirt on the table. Once he helped Nicole with her gown, he'd finish dressing.

It was too hot in the bathroom for a suit.

The Wedding, Etc.

Suit pants, however, were a safeguard against reckless urges.

He was waiting with a warmed towel when she rose from the water. Wrapping the white towel around her shoulders, he lifted her from the tub and set her on her feet.

She smiled. "A personal valet. I like it."

"That makes two of us," he drolly replied, flipping a corner of the towel over her wet hair. "And if we weren't on a tight schedule I'd personalize it even more. But we are, so don't move, don't say a word while I dry you."

"Wow, so many orders and we're not even married."

"I've been trying like hell to *get* us married." He slid the towel over her shoulders and arms, down her body with a studied detachment. "We have to be ready in twenty minutes." He kneeled. "Lift your foot."

"Ummm, nice...I felt your breath right on my--hey!" she squealed as he grabbed her around her waist, stood and swung her onto the marble countertop.

"We don't have time for you to feel *anything*," he muttered, drying her foot. "Now sit still. And that *is* a fucking order."

"I love when you talk rough and growly like that."

He groaned. "Be good."

"Sorry." A rueful twist of her mouth. "I didn't mean to"--

"It's okay." He didn't sound annoyed, just firm as he finished drying her other foot and dropped the towel. "We have to get this show on the road though. People are waiting." But Nicole was naked, inches away, smelling of some sweet fragrance, and when she said, "Kiss me," he had to take a deep breath before he said, "No."

"Then I'll kiss you." Sitting up straighter, her opulent breasts swaying gently at her movement, she gave him an impudent smile. "One kiss, that's all."

His predatory instincts read that little swing of her tits as a gold-framed, personal invitation and a restless energy suddenly lit his gaze. Raising his hand, he gently trailed his fingertips over the swell of one breast, then the other with a connoisseur's appreciation. "They're bigger," he said, softly. Pressing lightly, he sank the pad of his finger into her pale, cushiony breast. "So soon, pussycat. I'm impressed."

There was something in his self-assured tone, a pronounced, almost professional assessment that commanded her attention, spiked through her senses, coiled hot and aching deep inside her and left her trembling.

"Are you cold?"

It took her a moment to respond and when she looked up, wanton desire flared in her eyes.

"I didn't think so." His smile was shameless and very close. "Now about that kiss," he murmured, running the backs of his hands up her inner thighs, gently spreading her legs, moving between them.

The fine wool of his trousers was soft against her skin, strangely seductive, her nakedness heightened by that infinitesimal abrasion. She felt the small pulsing between her legs intensify, felt her body open in welcome and restive and needy, uttered a low, fretful groan.

"You sound impatient," he whispered, watching her nipples swell and stiffen. "Would you like me to kiss you here?" He touched one taut, rosy peak. "Or here," he asked, sliding the pad of his finger over her top lip, cupping her bottom with his other hand, drawing her close, and holding her firmly against his rigid erection so they both felt the wild rush of unguarded lust.

"Anywhere..." she whispered, hot and breathless.

"No time. Only choice one or two."

A quicksilver lift of her chin, challenge in her gaze. "Make time."

"You're throwing off sparks, Tiger." His smile was easy, like his tone. "I wish I could help you out, but I'm trying to get us to the altar and we're running late." Grabbing a fistful of her wet hair, he tugged, tilted her face up and went nose to nose with her. "So chill."

She shifted her hips, rubbed against his rock hard dick, gave him a small smile. "I wish I could help you out," she softly mimicked. "But I can't. So hurry."

"No."

She met the dangerous glitter in his eyes with a calm stare. "Be nice." Her lashes drifted lower, and her tone took on a cajoling resonance. "Come on, how long can it take?"

"Too long."

"No it won't. Faster than the speed of light, I promise."

There was nothing more beautiful than Nicole looking at him with those luminous, laughing eyes. "Jesus, Tiger, you're making it hard to say no." And, bottom line, getting bogged down in pointless argument with the minutes ticking away was counterproductive. "Okay," he said, but a razor-fine edge swirled through the single word. "You asked for it." A quick breath to remind himself not to step over the line, then dropping his head, he kissed her fast and hard, with a wildness that dazzled, blurred the borderlines of sensation, demonstrated a blunt I'm-calling-the-shots authority that he knew switched on and geared up every carnal nerve in her body.

Her soft moan was warm on his lips, the little twitch of her hips adding inches to his dick, her scent of arousal invading his nostrils.

"How do you do it?" she whispered, a molten heat burning through her body, spiraling downward with feverish impact, drenching her sex in opalescent horniness.

"Instinct, pussycat." He licked the ripeness of her lower lip, slid his thumb along her jaw in fluid, unhurried possession. "And I can smell you," he whispered. "Ready to rock and roll?"

Adrift in a hyper-lurid delirium, her senses fully engaged in fevered pleasure, the low resonance of his voice was distant, remote from the intoxicating sensuality drumming through her body.

Raising his head, he looked at her for a silent moment, let out a sigh. Was he ever, even remotely, that untroubled. Squinting against the unpleasant aggregate of memories, he spoke more sharply than he intended. "Answer me. Do you want to come or not?" Tapping her nose to gain her attention, he added in his playboy drawl, "Look at me, babe."

The notorious word, babe, cleared a blazing path to her brain, and blinking to banish the sexual fog, Nicole stared at him. "Did you say, babe?"

Christ, she was a gorgeous, testy bundle of fuck me now. Although her audacity had amazed him from the first, sent his adrenalin spiking, forever changed his perspective on women as entertainment. He smiled, his ill humor forgotten. "I was just wondering if you wanted to come yourself, or if you'd like some help."

Something in his casual, take it or leave it drawl peeled away the last layer of lust, wiped her mind clean of all the soft warm fuzzies, brought her jealousy center stage. "So you don't care one way or the other?" she said, a hint of bad weather in her voice.

He smiled. "Of course I do, more than you know...and if we had time I'd show you how much. Since we don't..." Giving her shoulders a soft shove, he watched her catch herself, lean back on her hands, begin to open her mouth in protest. He held up a finger. "You want to come or discuss the complexities of life?" His gaze was astute and not unkind.

She let out a sigh.

"Smart girl. Now relax."

"You never raise your voice."

"Sometimes I do. I try not to."

"I should do that," she said. "Try harder."

He gave her a long, uncritical look, thinking back to those handful of seconds when she'd walked into his stateroom and his life of sustained dalliance had ended. "I'm looking forward to a ridiculously successful marriage." He smiled. "Don't fuck it up by changing."

The sweetness of his smile made her heart flutter. "I'm being selfish when we're pressed for time. I can wait."

He shook his head. "The organist can keep our guests entertained for a few minutes more."

"Really?"

An artless warmth lit her eyes; it was impossible to describe the pleasure he felt. "Really," he said, brought his mouth to hers and kissed her until her eyes drifted shut.

She was swaying gently, homed in on the raw heat rising inside her when he slid his hand down her belly, and slipped two fingers palm deep into her succulent cleft. She was slick, softly throbbing and when he touched her wildly beating sweet spot, and rested his thumb on her clit with the precise weight most likely to please, she sucked in a dreamy breath that trailed away in a little sigh.

"Feel good?" he whispered, delicately running the pad of his thumb up and down her engorged clit. That she didn't reply was expected; he was gradually adding a third finger to her sex.

Demonstrably overwrought, panting open-mouthed, she trembled slightly at each additional measure of penetration, her body expanding by slow degrees to allow him access, the rising pleasure intense.

"That," he murmured, once his third finger was fully submerged, "is a real...tight fit." He looked up. "You okay?"

No matter her silence, the flush rising up her throat and face, the ragged tempo of her breathing was unqualified sanction. She was peaking fast, as usual. Good. Not entirely blind to the astonishing number of people waiting for them in the chapel downstairs, he concentrated on getting her off.

Moving his fingers inside her in small measured, carefully calibrated degrees he brought his fingertips to rest with incredible lightness, right *there*...on the Holy Grail of sensation...and gently pressed.

She gasped.

He smiled and added a miniscule more pressure on her swollen clit. Not too hard, just hard enough.

Just. Like. That.

Her frenzied moan reverberated on cue, testimony to his affection and the years he'd spent practicing the finer points of fornication. And a split second later the fierce ecstasy assaulted every shuddering nerve in her body, deep inside, on the hot surface of her skin, in her fingertips and toes, up and down the fluttering tissue of her exquisitely stretched pussy.

Feeling every ripple around his fingers, he skillfully massaged her wet, throbbing flesh, caressed her pulsing G-spot, and swollen clit with an expertise that hit all the right notes--a sideways twist here, a little grazing stroke there, a trailing sweep of his fingertips over that little G-spot bundle of nerve endings that lit up emergency flares in her brain. Then with a finely tuned attention, he waited for that breathless, spring-loaded moment that would take her over the edge.

Oblivious to Rafe's vigilant gaze, lost in a wonderland of heated bliss, Nicole gave herself up to the heavenly rapture tumbling through her senses: gentle as mist, solid as an imprint on her soul, rash, fiery, poised for moments in utter stillness. Eyes shut tight, she wantonly embraced every delight, captive to the sumptuous, dizzying pleasure slip-sliding hot and lawless into every susceptible crevice and fold, enchantment hovering irresistibly on the horizon. "I love you, I love you, I love you," she breathed, over and over again in a hushed, dissolving litany of adoration.

Her words were soft as gauze and beautiful, when in the past, he'd always dreaded words of love. Now the simple phrase held a mystical significance, a richness and bounty beyond price. In fact--

"Oh God, oh, oh, oh *God!!!*"

Jerked from his musings, he understood the import of Nicole's sharp wail. But then fucking had been his currency, the nearest thing to religion he had, an aptitude, a skill, a habit. Smoothly readjusting his fingers, he murmured, "Come on, pussycat, let's take you home..." Focusing on every sensitive, feel good nerve and pleasure zone, he masterfully stroked and teased her pussy, her clit and G-spot with a soft, silken, exquisitely targeted finesse until she was uncontrollably whimpering and her molten tissue was vibrating wildly against his fingers.

When she suddenly went tense, he knew the next dance steps. No jarring moves; wait for her to draw in a breath...

He felt her sweet spot flutter against his fingers a second before her orgasmic scream rang out, whirling sharp and silvery, bouncing off the tiled ceiling and walls, ricocheting round the small bathroom while he deftly prolonged her climax for long, blissful, rapturous moments. Until, at last, shaken to the core, she collapsed, breathless and replete.

He caught her sudden weight, held her close for a moment, briefly debating whether he had time to take care of his aching cock. *Yes, yes and yes.* Adjusting her in the crook of his arm, he'd just pulled out his erection when the clock chimed the half-hour. He froze. *Shit.* A smooth, fast arc of time versus lust versus pissing off Nicole's family— yeah that--raced through his brain. With a disgusted grunt, he shoved his dick back into his pants, jerked up the zipper and said, gruffly, "We have to go."

"Not yet." Her voice was barely a wisp of sound.

"Sorry. No more excuses."

She slowly opened her eyes. "Not even a little excuse?" Taking in the firm line of his mouth, and his steely gaze, she sighed. "Apparently not."

"Everyone's waiting." His libido reined in, he spoke in a meticulous kind of way that echoed his restraint. "Hundreds, actually." He ran his hand down her arm, gave her a rueful smile. "You going to be okay?"

She exhaled, sat up, straightened her shoulders. "Maybe...okay, okay, yes," she corrected, his straight on look negating insurrection. "It's not my fault though. You're just so *incredibly* hot."

"Literally," he muttered, interested in changing the subject. "It must be fucking ninety in here. We'll go next door. It's cooler and your dress is in the closet."

Not waiting for an answer, he lifted her into his arms, carried her with a neutered politesse into his dressing room, seated her next to his clothes on the table and handed her a comb. "I'll get a hair-dryer from the bathroom."

During his brief absence he took the opportunity to give himself a lecture on courtesy to family and friends, to a small fraction of their guests as well. He also reminded himself that once the wedding was over, they had all the time in the world for unlimited sex. So don't be stupid.

Nicole's smile was unabashedly sunny when he returned; she, too, had moved out of the fast lane. "I thought this was going to be a small family gathering," she noted, opting for a less fraught topic. "It turned into a red-carpet extravaganza? What happened?"

Rafe shrugged. "Ask our mothers."

"Let's never do this again—not the wedding," she quickly added at the sudden chill in his gaze. "The crowd."

He grinned. "Quick save, pussycat. But yeah, count me in."

"That's the reason we get along. We're both selfish hermits."

His grin widened. "One of the reasons. There's a couple more, although they're probably selfish too, but"—he held up the hair dryer, then plugged it into an outlet under the table.

She wrinkled her nose. "How much time do I have?"

He handed her the hairdryer. "Ten minutes."

She laughed, recalling the evening in Monte Carlo. "So I don't have time to check my email."

"Not tonight, Tiger. We're fucking getting married in ten minutes."

Fortunately, their compatibility included speed dressing, and by the time Nicole had dried her hair and arranged it in a loose knot at her nape, Rafe was dressed, save for his tie and suit coat.

Holding out a pair of white, lace panties, he gave her an impudent grin. "For virgin brides."

"Lucky you found one," she said, smart-assed and sassy as he slipped the panties over her feet and up her legs.

"Damn right I'm lucky." Lifting her off the table, he set her on her feet, slid the panties up her hips, then dipping his head, kissed her smile. Taking her by the shoulders, he turned her to face the mirror, slid her gown from a hanger, moved in front of her and bending low, held out the dress so she could step into it. "Hang onto me."

Steadying herself on his shoulder, she placed one foot then the other into the circle of white silk charmeuse falling from Rafe's hands in graceful folds, and stood motionless while Rafe slid the delicate fabric up her body. Slipping her arms under the wide silk straps, she adjusted them on her shoulders and flipped the sheer white cape into place.

Arranging the slip-style bodice over her breasts, she twisted left and right, checking to see that her boobs were covered since the dress was open to the waist in back. She glanced at Rafe. "Nothing shows?"

"Nope. Tres sexy though, pussycat."

She touched the gauzy cape draped over her shoulders and arms. "This is a cover-up."

Rafe rolled his eyes. "It's see-through. Hey, no problem, I like it. Turn so I can zip you up."

Sliding his hands under the sheer floor-length cape, he smoothed the wide silk straps crisscrossing her back, zipped the short zipper, fluffed up the elaborate white silk bow resting at the base of her spine, then ran his palms over her luscious ass. "Jesus, Tiger," he whispered, his breath warming her ear, his gaze holding hers in the mirrored doors, "you're one beautiful bride."

She winked. "You're just saying that because you helped pick out this dress."

He laughed and stepped back. "You threatened to cut off my balls if I didn't agree."

"I was also persuasive," she murmured, turning to face him.

"Fucking A. The dress shop owner couldn't stop blushing when we walked out of the dressing room."

Nicole gave him a lift of her brows. "That's because she was wishing you were fucking *her*."

No way he could respond honestly to that comment when the woman had written her personal phone number on the dress receipt. Fortunately, his cell rang, saving him from a lie. "That's probably Carlos wondering where the hell we are." Pulling his cell from his pants pocket, he tapped the answer icon. "We'll be down in a couple minutes," he said, sliding the phone back into his pocket.

He lifted his chin a notch. "Jewelry?"

"My pearl earrings. On your dresser."

"Shoes?"

She smiled. "Those new red ones, if you don't mind."

He grinned. "Seriously? You're asking *me*?"

She pursed her lips. "Maybe. They *are* red."

"I like red."

Her smile was impossibly lovely. "Good."

"No problem." He could have said more; he could have said *I'm not likely to say no to you about anything unless it might hurt you.* But a novice at laying his heart at a woman's feet, it kept it simple and lifting her up on the table again, went to fetch the red shoes and earrings.

A few moments later, he buckled on the shoes, while Nicole slipped the studs in her ears. "You just need your tie now," she said. "I'll do it for you."

He hesitated. He'd learned how to tie a tie as a youngster from an old tailor who'd lived in Geneva forty years and still spoke with a strong Neapolitan accent. Tying a tie was an art, Ando had insisted, a personal statement. You want the right knot, not too tight, not too loose, an expression of your mood he liked to say. "You know how?" Rafe asked, his tone faintly challenging.

"I have three younger brothers. So yes, I do."

He was surprised it mattered who tied his tie. But then he'd always been an island unto himself, not in the habit of relinquishing control of anything in his life. For a moment more, he contemplated his bride-to-be, seated on the table, a beautiful, ethereal figure in shimmering white, save for her bright red shoes, her smile open and warm. "Okay," he said.

She smiled. "You were wondering how to say no."

He shook his head. "Just rifling through the debris of my youth. Wholly irrelevant now." Taking a step forward, he flipped up his shirt collar, picked up the tie from the table, slid it around his neck, let the ends slip down his chest and raised one brow. "Show me what you got."

She gave him a cheeky grin. "Lucky I can work under stress."

Her movements were swift and sure, a fluid twist of her wrist brought the wide end of the tie over narrow end. Slipping the wide end up between the collar and the tie, she brought it back down, spooled it underneath, then up again through the loop and down once more. A last smooth fold over, a slide up, underneath, over and she was tightening the knot, easing it up to his collar button. Flipping his shirt collar back down, she made a slight adjustment to the triangular knot and gave it a pat. "There."

He looked at her narrow-eyed. "Where did you learn that?"

"A traditional Windsor? U-tube. I can tie any knot you want."

His mindless jealousy assuaged by her U-tube reply, he

took a step to the side, looked in the mirror, then leaned over and kissed her. "My compliments, Tiger. It's perfect."

Setting her on her feet in an effortless show of strength, he took her hand. "This is it," he said, very, very softly. "You ready?"

Her smile was a burst of pure happiness. "From the first moment I saw you."

"Yeah. It was like something out of a movie seeing you walk through that door. I'll never forget it." He gazed at her, his smile a tangle of sweet recklessness and quiet gravity before it turned brilliant with his more familiar arrogance. "Come on, Tiger, let's make this legal."

8

Fiona, Isabelle and Nicole's father were waiting in a small anteroom next to the chapel entrance.

"Forgive us," Rafe said, as they entered the room, taking note of Matt Parrish's frown. "I lost track of the time."

Nicole touched her father's arm. "It was my fault, Daddy. Rafe let me sleep. I was tired after the frantic pace of the last few days."

"Explain that to your mother." Matt Parrish smiled faintly. "She's the one who worries."

"I will, Daddy, right after the wedding."

Suddenly, the door flew open, the event planner rushed in and after a quick, scanning glance, exclaimed, "Thank God, you're here!" With disaster averted, his voice dropped in volume. "Everyone's seated, the organist is"—he paused briefly, searching for a word other than hysterical—"anxious. She wasn't sure whether she should repeat the prelude or play something else. I told her to repeat the musical prelude as many times as necessary." He'd also told her in no uncertain terms that for the money she was being paid she could play the prelude until her fingers turned blue. He forced a smile. "I'll cue her whenever you're ready for the processional and Wedding March."

"Just a few more minutes, Costa," Rafe said, understanding if not relating to his planner's agitation. "Tell her she can move on to the processional once I'm at the altar with my groomsmen. She has the musical arrangements—in order, right?"

"Indeed she does." Having coordinated scores of parties for Rafe, Costa Michelopolus knew his client had an eye for detail. "I'll relay your instructions to her." The slim, immaculately dressed man with perfectly gelled hair turned to Nicole's bridesmaids, Isabelle and Fiona. "You ladies will enter the chapel next. Any questions?"

Costa had been directing the wedding festivities the last few days in such an exacting, punctilious, albeit capable way, Isabelle couldn't resist teasing him. "Is there an open bar?" At his startled expression, she grinned. "Just kidding."

"Ah…I see. I'm sure you'll find the bar well supplied," the planner said, smoothly. His celebrity events had extravagant budgets, Rafe Contini a particularly generous host.

Viewing the exchange with amusement, Rafe turned to Costa and gave him an understanding smile. "It'll soon be over, and you can relax."

"Yes, of course." Although he wouldn't relax until Rafe and his bride left on their honeymoon.

Rafe squeezed Nicole's hand. "I gotta go." He dipped his head to meet her gaze. "See you at the altar?"

She took a small breath. "Wow."

Rafe kissed her cheek. "No backing out now, Missy. I'll sue you for breach of promise."

She giggled. "In that case I have no choice."

"There you go. My kind of bride."

"Coerced?"

"Nah, just a little rebellious." A flash of a grin. "I like that."

"Stop," she whispered, her cheeks flushing. "My dad's here."

"In that case," he noted, his voice instantly urbane, "I'll see you in five." He turned to the other occupants in the room and nodded. "We'll meet again in the chapel."

Recognizing Rafe's sideways glance, Costa plucked a boutonniere from a table near the door and quickly followed him out into the hall.

"I'll text you when we're actually ready," Rafe said, standing still so Costa could slip the small blue iris into his lapel buttonhole. "God knows if Henny's sober."

"Sober enough. I just saw him." Making a small adjustment in the angle of the flower, Costa stepped away.

"Good. After you receive my text, have the organist begin the processional, escort the bridesmaids to the chapel, then come back for Nicole and make sure that she isn't shaky. She's been tired lately." He blew out a breath. "Fuck, this is serious, isn't it?" His eyes narrowed and his mouth twitched. "I suppose the odds are shit. Have you heard?"

Speechless, Costa realized his worst fears had come to pass. Rafe Contini, the least likely man to marry, was thinking about bailing. He wasn't surprised; the British bookies were betting he'd back out.

"Jesus, Costa, you're white as a ghost. Relax. You think I'm going to let anyone else have her?"

Now that was the Rafe Contini he knew: imperious, headstrong, predatory. Costa's heart started beating again. "No, sir, I never thought you would."

Rafe squinted at him. "Did you bet against me? You did."

"No." Costa took a small breath, and wondered if he was

kissing away a spectacularly wealthy client when he said, "I admit, I thought about it. I've known you a long time and this is unprecedented behavior for you. But you smile a lot now when you rarely did in the past, so I bet a quid you'd go through with it."

Rafe laughed. "Christ, only a quid? Have you no faith?"

"I never bet more than a quid." Nice and neat, like there were rules.

A wide, charming smile. "Amazing restraint. Well, let's see that you make a few quid on this wedding, shall we?" Giving Costa a pat on the shoulder, Rafe walked away.

His gaze thoughtful, Costa watched the young man whose parties had almost single-handedly paid for his villa at Cannes disappear down the medieval corridor. Having catered to the billionaire class for so long, he'd become a cynic when it came to romance, but in this rare instance, he was prepared to change his mind.

Rafe Contini was in love.

This was one time he should have bet more than a quid.

9

When Rafe saw the tall, reed-thin, elderly man waiting outside the door to the sacristy, he knew why he was there. Vincent Weiser had been his grandfather's lawyer, had survived Maso's erratic ownership tenure, and continued his loyal service to Contini Pharmaceutical under Rafe's leadership.

On reaching him, Rafe stopped and smiled faintly. "Come on, Vincent," he said, kindly, "you heard me the first hundred times I said no to a pre-nup. I appreciate your concern, but don't worry. Everything's good."

"I'm here on another matter, Rafail."

His extra sensitive, tiptoeing around tone was out of character for a man who could bring a hostile witness to tears without breaking a sweat. Under any other circumstances, Rafe wouldn't have been immune to the peril. However, preoccupied as he was with his imminent marriage, he thought, *Couldn't this wait? I'm getting married in five minutes.*

At Rafe's hesitation Vincent said, "I won't take much of your time."

Suppressing his sudden surge of annoyance, reminding himself Vincent was the least likely man to inconvenience him on a whim, Rafe scrubbed the impatience from his voice. "Okay, I'm listening."

"If the issue wasn't time-sensitive, I wouldn't have bothered you. But I was concerned you might leave on your honeymoon before I could speak to you and, well...this isn't something I can personally resolve."

Rafe's brows shot up. "Sounds serious."

"I'm afraid so."

A new alertness marked Rafe's gaze; he almost said, *Who died?* "Look," he said instead, "my life's always been high-maintenance. Just tell me, Vincent. Whatever it is, on this day of all days, I'm more or less impervious to bad news."

"Your uncle has laid claim to Contini Pharmaceuticals."

Hell, this wasn't life or death. This was about money. "Cesare's got balls, I'll give him that. Grandfather bought him out years ago. How much more does he want?"

"He wants it all." The aged lawyer's voice was strained, a wariness skidding across his face.

Rafe gave him a quizzical look. "What the hell's going on?"

Weiser's grey-eyed gaze was guarded.

"Vincent," Rafe said in his gentlest voice, "I don't have time to fuck around."

The Contini consigliere sighed. "The lawsuit alleges you're not Maso's son."

"Alleges?" Soft as silk.

This time the sigh was deeper. "They have evidence, they say. Your aunt refused to be involved, so Cesare contends he's sole heir to Contini Pharma."

Rafe's breath caught and for a moment the entire world went silent. "He can't be serious."

"Serious enough to file a lawsuit."

In that second, a grand, surging tide of improbable scale and depth and full awareness swept through Rafe's dark, tangled past and a vast, uncluttered truth lay before him. His heartbeat quickened, and it surprised him how easy it was to let it all go. "Jesus, if that's true, and Maso's just a random asshole,"--a slow shake of his head, relief curving his mouth, a puff of easy laughter punctuating his smile—"think about it…I could have saved myself a lifetime of rage and loathing."

"It's no laughing matter, Rafail. Your uncle could seize the company."

"Like hell," Rafe said, grimly, the smile wiped from his face. "There wouldn't be a company if not for me. Maso was a total fuck-up. I was fourteen the first time I countermanded one of his crazy, bat-shit orders. You remember. Everyone was scared shitless." He smiled. "Everyone except you. You said, 'I'll help you,' and you did and have countless times since." Rafe dragged in air through his teeth, exhaled in a quick rush of breath, said, fast and low, "Who else knows about this?"

"Just Cesare's people. I haven't told anyone."

"Good." Something solid and decisive in Rafe's voice. "It's Friday, nothing can happen until Monday. We'll take care of it then."

"You're not going on your honeymoon?"

"No, not because of this." A smile rippled across Rafe's face. "It's something else. One last question. Do you know if Cesare's allegation is true?"

"I don't. I haven't had time to do any checking. The papers were just couriered to me. Your mother might be a better person to ask."

Rafe shook his head. "I prefer not having that conversation. Look, our families leave Sunday. Why don't we meet in my office Monday morning at six," he suggested, wanting to make sure Nicole was still sleeping when he went downstairs.

"I'll be there, with more information if possible. And I apologize again for marring this momentous occasion."

"Nonsense. Nothing's marred. Nicole's making me the happiest of men today. My uncle is of no consequence. Life's thrown worse things than this at me and"--Rafe smiled, held his arms open wide—"see, completely untouched. Now, if you'll excuse me, the minister is waiting. Tell Katya I'm looking forward to seeing her newest pictures of your grandchildren at the reception."

Stiff-arming the sacristy door open, Rafe strode in, took note of the clergyman's overwhelming relief and after a glance at Henny, understood why. Henny was pouring Jagermeister down his throat, and from the tilt of the bottle, he'd already drunk a good share.

"Perfect timing," Basil said, pushing away from the wall where he'd been patiently waiting. "Henny's still sober."

Swallowing, Henny turned and jabbed the bottle at Rafe. "I figured you changed your mind."

"That's because you're not thinking clearly," Rafe drawled, crossing to the desk the minister was using as a barricade to the tumult. Leaning across the desktop, Rafe shook the man's hand, apologized for his lateness, and Henny's lack of restraint. "I think we're finally ready." Moving back a step, he drew the bottle from Henny's grasp and set it on the desk. "I'll return this in fifteen minutes. The ceremony is short."

Henny grinned. "Is that a subtle message not to drink from my flask in the chapel?"

"It's not even remotely subtle. Behave. This is important to me."

Henny's expression instantly sobered and brushing his palms over his close-cropped ginger hair, he dropped his arms and stood ramrod straight in his best military school posture. "You have my word," he said, and touched his fist to his chest. "From the heart *mon ami*. I wish you all the happiness in the world."

Rafe smiled, placed his clenched fingers on his heart. "We all made it, didn't we? Who knew?"

"Basil too." Henny lifted his chin toward his friend. "Tell him."

"Claudine and her children are with me. She filed divorce papers this morning."

"Hey, wow...congratulations," Rafe said, softly. "Only good times from now on...for all of us." His uncle was forgotten, the lawsuit as inconsequential as the man. "Come on, let's get me married, then you're next Basil."

A few minutes later, the three men, who'd been friends from childhood, who'd survived the nightmare of numerous boarding schools, whose deep and abiding friendship was the only real family each had ever had, were waiting at the altar with the minister.

Rafe stood tall, dark, and spectacularly handsome in an elegant, navy bespoke suit, the small blue iris in his lapel an incongruous note in the sheer physicality of his hard, lean form.

Inured to gossip after years in the scandal sheets, he ignored the speculative glances and the low undercurrent of conversation buzzing in counterpoint to the organ music. With so many guests aware of his former lifestyle, his sudden marriage had generated curiosity. He expected Nicole's announcement at the reception would offer to some at least, a conventional answer. As to his former friends-in-vice, who discharged their responsibilities to a pregnant partner with a check, let them wonder.

He didn't owe anyone an explanation. He never had. Nor was he likely to satisfy anyone's curiosity today.

By sheer dumb luck, love had hit him like a stun gun, he'd been smart enough not to fuck it up and here he was.

As if in confirmation of that full-throttle, freight train of events, the sonorous tones of the processional marked the start of the ceremony. A piquant murmur of anticipation hummed through the air, the majority of the guests swiveled to watch the bridesmaids walk down the flower-bedecked aisle while a cynical minority kept their eyes fixed on the groom.

Might he bolt?

Calm, relaxed, Rafe exhibited zero misgivings. He exchanged quiet comments with his groomsmen, smiling occasionally, laughing once at something Henny said, politely greeting each bridesmaid as she took her place at the altar, seemingly unaware of the world-wide interest in a billionaire playboy's unexpected nuptials.

The private chapel was heady with the fragrance of spring flowers flown in from around the world because Nicole had once casually mentioned she loved spring flowers; Rafe had seen that she had them. Huge baskets and bouquets of blooms were artfully positioned throughout the interior, garlands of colorful blossoms looped gracefully arch to arch down the nave, twined round the supporting piers, floral wreaths decorated the chandeliers, the tulips, iris, peonies, and anemones all in perfect harmony with the brilliant stained glass windows. Tall, heavily chased silver torchiers marched down the outer aisles, framed the flower-adorned altar, the flickering candlelight illuminating the chapel in a golden glow.

Rafe felt his pulse quicken. In a few minutes Nicole would step inside the chapel, walk toward him and perhaps lamentably, because he was not and never would be a humble man, he'd say to himself, *She's mine.* Or, he reflected, smiling faintly, Nicole, equally confident, might say the same. She was unapologetically possessive, a thought that would have been anathema to him in the past.

No longer, he thought with content, the ways of the human heart unfathomable.

As the opening bars of the Wedding March announced his bride, he lifted his gaze to the entrance doors and smiled. Nicole was framed in the Gothic arch, her gown a shimmer of white in the flickering candle glow, her fair skin fairer in the half-light, her dark, gleaming hair in casual disarray, the small bouquet in her hand a bright spot of color in the faint shadows. She was a beautiful enchantress who'd brought him warmth in a cold world, love he'd never known, and in her clear-eyed, unstoppable way…a child… and with that miracle, a sense of wonderment and hope.

Linking arms with her father, Nicole glanced up, said something that made him laugh, the moment so intimate, Rafe experienced a tidal wave of jealousy. A rational man, he instantly quashed his disorderly emotions. Of course she loved her father.

Unwanted, a parallel and unpalatable thought slipped past his defenses, the memory of the man who may or may not have been his father so foul, for a split second he felt a toxic brew of memories wash over him. Catching himself with casehardened practice, he closed down those noxious memories and drew a line straight back to self-preservation. Click.

The Wedding, Etc.

His smile was in place as Nicole and her father approached.

She was always struck by his smooth, polished façade. She found it wildly attractive: the raw strength beneath the elegant tailoring and well-mannered grace, the apparent modesty of the best-looking man in any room, the relaxed authority of the truly powerful. A little flutter of arousal warmed her senses, merciless and indiscrete; the reason without mystery.

And when she smiled at him, he knew.

Matt Parrish interrupted the impressionable moment, kissing his daughter on the cheek before giving Nicole's hand to Rafe. "Be good to one another," he said, softly. "You can be a headstrong, Nickie, so I'm talking to you. I don't know you well, Rafe, but be kind to my girl."

Nicole smiled. "We will be, Daddy."

"You have my word, sir." The term of respect was deliberate, a mark of Rafe's sincerity. It was also unprecedented for a man with a deeply honed sense of command.

Nicole's father had no more than turned away to take his seat than Rafe reverted to form. Plucking the bouquet from Nicole's grasp, he leaned past her, handed it to Isabelle, and with a one armed hug, pulled Nicole into the warmth of his body. "There now," he murmured, smiling down at her. "That's more like it."

She grinned. "If we're entertaining our guests, I might as well give you a kiss." Twisting slightly, she rose on tip toe, pulled Rafe's head down and kissed him.

Cupping her hands, Rafe lifted them away and turned to the minister who was staring at them, aghast. "Nicole likes to tease," Rafe said, smiling pleasantly, taking her under his arm and drawing her close. "Let's dispense with all but the essential legalities today."

"Wunderbar," Henny said a shade too loudly, put his hand over his mouth and glancing at Rafe, said through his fingers, "Sorry. Take your time."

"I'll see what I can do," the minister replied coolly, thin-lipped and reproachful.

The minister's remit, apparently, offered little room for abridgment and the ceremony advanced at a measured pace.

Never inclined to overt drama, Rafe ignored the minister's snail's pace. If he could sit through hours-long R&D presentations, he certainly could wait for the clergyman to finish what he considered necessary.

Nicole was less calm or knowing his Tiger, Rafe decided, less appeasing. He did what he could to assuage her restlessness, murmuring soothing phrases that while well-meaning sounded pitifully trite. Promptly casting aside useless platitudes, he offered her lavish rewards instead if she'd be patient.

Her smile was instant. "You don't have to," she whispered, "but thanks."

Pleased she was smiling, he upped the ante.

Leaning into him, she spoke in an undertone. "You're a darling, but you-know-what is making me jumpy and that's not exactly fixable." She took care not to use the words, baby or pregnancy, in the largely silent chapel.

The bride and groom's capricious behavior had precipitated the extraordinary silence, the guests exchanging curious and/or mildly shocked glances at the couple's casual disregard for protocol. On more than one occasion a nudge from a bridesmaid or groomsman was required before they responded to the minister. The guests decided that Nicole was as unconventional as her uncle Dominic Knight, while no one was completely surprised by Rafe's behavior. He'd always lived without limits.

As the clergyman continued to drone on, Rafe wondered where the hell Costa had found such a martinet. Increasingly on edge, Nicole wondered how much longer she could control her jitters.

As they exchanged simple wedding bands, Rafe frowned faintly. "You gonna make it?"

Nicole nodded, but her bottom lip was quivering.

In a blur Rafe slapped his large hand over the open book of divine service held by the minister, ignored the man's flash of fear and said, tersely, "Bring this to an end *now* and your parish gets five million. Make it ten."

A nanosecond passed while theological principle, fear of being punched, the dream of a new activity center were prioritized at warp speed; the truism, money trumps principle, winning in the end. "I now pronounce you man and wife!"

"Thank you for your understanding," Rafe murmured, more aware than most of the power of money. Turning to Nicole, he lowered his head and whispered, "Ready to go?"

"Tell me you're mine." She tried to smile and didn't quite manage. "I don't know why but I need a true blue, forever yes."

Taking her hands in his, he leaned in close. "Yes, a thousand yeses. A million. Yeses to infinity."

Her smile was real this time. "Now I need a kiss."

He grinned. "You must be feeling better."

"Tip top, thanks to you." She giggled a little. "Kiss me."

"Yes, ma'am," he whispered, his words warm on her mouth. "Any special place?"

He inhaled her laugh and wondered if everyone felt as impossibly happy as he did on their wedding day.

"I absolutely adore you," she whispered in her open, generous way.

"Thank you for marrying me," he said simply.

Their kiss was lengthy and depending on your point of view, either excessive or extremely affectionate. Those who knew the couple best, thought them a perfect match. Those who knew them less well, viewed the extended kiss with arched brows.

Eventually, the minister cleared his throat loudly, and muttered, "I dare say."

Stifling a flippant reply, Rafe lifted his head and winked at Nicole. "That's our cue, Tiger. Allow me to show you off." Taking her by the shoulders, he turned her slowly. Towering behind her, his hands resting lightly on her shoulders, he spoke in clear, deep tones. "I'd like to present my wife, Nicole." She leaned into him a little and his voice softened. "She's made me the happiest of men today. Please wish us well."

The hip hoorays began with Henny, quickly rose in volume until they filled the nave with raucous cheer and after a nod from Rafe to Costa to the organist, triumphant recessional music flooded the chapel.

Hand in hand, cushioned in happiness, their hearts full, Rafe and Nicole exited the private chapel on a fortissimo wave of buoyant jubilation.

10

The photographer was waiting in the refectory, the enormous room bustling with activity. The wait staff was setting the tables for dinner with white damask tablecloths, antique blue and white Limoges china, silver flatware said to have been saved from plunder during the French revolution, and rows of sparkling Baccarat crystal once owned by a prince of the blood, all testament to Natalie's love of auction catalogues and Rafe's indifference to cost.

Spring flowers were arranged in an undulating river of color down the length of the tables, with hundreds of candles tucked amidst the blooms. A twenty man crew was at the ready to light the candles just prior to dinner.

Waving everyone in through the broad entrance, Costa directed the group to the north wall where stained glass windows rose from floor to ceiling.

Per orders, the photographer, with Costa's help and a few significant looks from Rafe, completed the picture-taking at record speed. Costa orchestrated the various poses with parade ground precision, moving each group into place with brisk efficiency.

The sequence of photos followed a conventional pattern: the bride and groom, the bride and groom with their attendants, with Nicole's family, with Rafe's family, then several group photos with the entire gathering of relatives, attendants and their significant others.

As the last group disbanded, Rafe offered a smile to the photographer, to Costa, and last, to the group at large. "Thank you all for your patience. May I suggest drinks in the Chapter House? Costa will show you the way."

"Nicole looks tired," Kate murmured, a moment later.

"She looks *adoring*," Dominic said under his breath, as they moved down the corridor with the stream of family and relatives. "Talk about a dissonant note. That's not Nicole's style."

"She's in love."

"I understand, but why the personality change? You didn't change."

"Are you implying that I'm not adoring?"

He grinned at her.

"Well, I could be."

"No you couldn't."

"I figured you already had years of female adoration," she said, sweetly. "I thought I'd switch it up."

He laughed. "So you're doing it for me."

"I hope you're not complaining."

Pulling her out of the teeming crowd, Dominic held his wife in a loose but confining embrace until the multitude had passed, acknowledging a comment or two with a smile, a lift of his chin, a promise to share a drink later.

As the last guest passed by, Kate hissed, "You better not make a scene."

Pushing her up against the wall, Dominic planted his hands on either side of her head and leaned in so his body pressed lightly into hers. "Or what? Don't answer that," he added, at the small heat in her eyes. "I just wanted to take the opportunity"—at her arched brows, his voice softened-"to tell you I'm not interested in adoration. I have zero complaints."

"And you and I will never agree on Nicole."

He laughed. "That too."

"Okay, I accept your apology."

He rolled his eyes, dropped a kiss on her nose, and stepped back. "Let's go see how the kids are doing before we have a drink."

"There're two nannies for every child in the playroom. They're fine."

"Indulge me."

She smiled. "Once a control freak…"

"As I recall"—his voice drifted lower—"sometimes you like it."

She put her hand over his mouth. "Dominic, for heaven's sake, there are hundreds of people about."

Taking her hand from his mouth, he twined his fingers through hers and began walking. "We'll just take a peak in the play room. Five minutes and you'll have a drink in your hand."

"You're lucky I'm easy going."

Rather than point out the discrepancy in her statement, Dominic gave her a smile. "I am, sweetheart. Thank you."

RAFE AND NICOLE were seated in a corner of the refectory, Nicole on a facsimile of a throne some Mother Superior apparently had viewed as suitable to her station, Rafe opposite her on a dining table chair, her feet in his lap.

"I suppose we have to go and be polite to everyone."

"Eventually." He was gently stroking her ankles with his thumbs. "Let them drink for a while."

"I'm not drinking."

"I know. The staff will serve you non-alcoholic bubbly."

"Discretely."

"You *could* tell everyone up front, make your announcement before dinner."

She smiled. "Don't want to."

"Drama queen," he drawled.

"I want to see the shock on everyone's faces."

"I could put you up on a chair in the Chapter House."

"If I wanted you to, you could."

He laughed. "Remind me to spank you tonight for your willfulness," he murmured.

"Ummm...sounds delicious." Her smile was teasing, her tone without restraint. "Will you spank me hard?"

Taking note of the sudden attention from nearby waiters, Rafe placed a finger to his mouth. "Mind your manners, pussycat. You're going to turn on all the wait staff, they're going to forget what they're doing and Natalie will cause an uproar."

She smiled. "You're always so disarmingly calm. How do you do it?"

He thought for a second. "Difficult to explain." Like the last survivor on a lifeboat prefers not talking about how he survived. "When you're rested though, I could use a drink."

She was beginning to recognize those quiet moments of suppression and with tactful dishonesty, said, "I'm ready now. The sooner we go, the sooner you can have them announce dinner."

He grinned. "And the sooner you can tell everyone about our baby."

She blew him a kiss. "Exactly."

"Sounds like I have my marching orders."

With a flutter of her lashes, she spoke in her best Southern belle purr. "Ah'd nahva presume to usurp y'all authority, kind sir."

He laughed so hard, she eventually felt justified in retaliating. "Don't blame me if Natalie notices you—oh, oh, here she comes."

Still chuckling, Rafe turned to look.

"Gotcha. And it wasn't *that* funny."

"Fucking A it was." He held up his index finger. "Before you go off on me, I love your take-no-prisoners persona. I'm not looking for someone to walk all over, okay? That said, it's about time we go smile, make small talk with our guests and as soon as courtesy allows, I'll herd them into dinner." He grinned. "Then, I'll wait with bated breath for your surprise announcement."

"I hope you're not saying you mind."

"I wouldn't dare," he said, serenely.

Her brows rose slightly at his tone. "I don't have to ask for permission."

"I'm already aware of that." His gaze flicked downward to her stomach, than back up again. "Obviously."

"Oh, God," she said, feeling herself blush. "Now you're mad and we haven't been married an hour."

He shook his head. "Not true." His eyes met hers. "You're the love of my life. Although," he added with a lazy smile, "if I want you to ask me for my permission I know a couple ways to make you do that. See, you remember."

"That's not fair," she muttered, lust spiking through her senses in a flame-hot rush. "You took advantage of"—

"Your fondness for orgasms?" He watched her quick survey of the room. "Not going to happen, pussycat, unless you like an audience. Your call, of course."

"Because an audience has never been a deterrent for you." Her indignation was sabotaged by a sudden breathlessness.

"I confess, Natalie's a slight obstacle, but manageable." He smiled faintly. "Are you asking?"

"No, damn you." Her voice was hushed, heated. Shaky.

Quickly lifting her feet, he set them on the floor and half-rising, reached out, picked her up and placed her on his lap. "I'm sorry," he whispered. "I've made you angry when I only meant to tease. If you want me to make love to you just say the word, I'll clear the room."

"Would you really?"

"Of course. I'd do anything for you."

She took a calming breath, cautioned herself to tamp down her unruly desire and temper, and slowly exhaled. "Now *I'm* sorry. I don't know what to say, other than I'll probably be apologizing a lot in the next eight months. I'd like to think I can improve, not be so temperamental but"—another sigh—"I'll try at least."

He was tempted to say, *Don't bother, I can take care of myself,* but she looked so forlorn, he didn't want to seemingly dismiss her sincerity. "We'll both try to improve, okay?" A more difficult task for him than her, he suspected, considering his authoritarian tendencies.

"I don't suppose we could leave yet." She wrinkled her nose. "Wishful thinking, right?""

He smiled. "Neither of our mothers would approve."

She sat up straighter. "So we just suck it up."

"Pretty much." He glanced at his watch.

She put her finger on his mouth. "Don't tell me unless you're going to say everyone will be gone in fifteen minutes."

"Okay, what I will say is it's too bad you can't drink because I intend to drink my way through this evening."

"What if I said if I can't drink you can't either."

He went still.

"Too bitchy?"

"Maybe." He wasn't looking for a fight.

"So I could extract say, a pound of flesh, for your drinking tonight."

He grinned. "At least."

"Ummm...I like when you owe me." She slid off his lap and held out her hand. "Let's go. And while you're imbibing to your heart's content because I'm awesomely kind and considerate, I'll think of something I want from you."

"Anything in the world." Coming to his feet, he took her hand and gave her a broad smile. "Just name it."

When they entered the Chapter House a few minutes later, Rafe played the host with aplomb, guiding them from group to group with ease, his skill set perfected after years of socializing at business functions. He and Nicole graciously accepted everyone's good wishes; some more sincere than others, some obviously specious, most warm-hearted.

As previously arranged, a fresh whisky appeared whenever Rafe's glass was empty. His staff was familiar with the drill, mingling at receptions one of his least favorite activities. Not that any of the guests were aware of his feelings. He was the perfect host.

Having been raised in a large family, Nicole was less of a recluse. Although she was more than willing to play the passive role and smile, accept congratulations, bask in the glow of her husband's affection. Rafe was blatantly solicitous, including her in every conversation, holding her hand throughout, kissing her on the cheek from time to time. Most guests were left slack-jawed; Rafe as doting lover was startling.

"You're aware of the astonishment left in our wake," Nicole whispered as they moved to the next group of people. "Are we on show?"

"Not necessarily. It's no secret I love you." He smiled. "Don't tell me I'm embarrassing you. As I recall, you once said you couldn't be embarrassed."

"I'm not. Just checking. I thought you might be playing to some exes."

One-night stands were, by definition, not exes. That would imply a modicum of permanence. "Nope," he said. "Haven't seen any. And if you have any exes here, don't tell me. Best to avoid bloodshed."

She smiled. "Neanderthal."

He pulled her to a stop, dipped his head to meet her gaze. "FYI, with you I am." He'd spoken more gruffly than intended and as her eyes widened, he smiled in apology. "Sorry, that was out of line."

She'd regained her composure. "Okay."

His new wife was staring at him, her 'okay' provisional at best. "I really am sorry. I don't handle crowds like this very well," he lied, not about to explain his unreasonable thoughts on conjugal possession. "I think we've been dutiful hosts long enough. Why don't I have dinner announced?"

He signaled Natalie with a glance, she in turn signaled a dignified butler Costa had hired who looked as though he'd come straight from central casting. The tall, stately man moved to the center of the doorway leading from the room and proclaimed in portentous tones, "Dinner is served in the refectory!"

11

Dinner was sumptuous, Rafe's chef taking the opportunity to display the full range of his culinary expertise. Marshalling sous chefs, pastry chefs, two specialists in ice sculptures, together with a prima donna sommelier Costa had hired at extravagant and unnecessary cost, the chef thought, when Rafe was no less knowledgeable himself, the dinner was literally a work of art: classical yet unaffected, elegant and at times, earthy, splendid to the eye, and served with a royal flare.

Standing at the back of the dais occupied by the wedding party, Costa directed the glittering production, immodestly aware that the household of the Sun King himself could not have improved upon the occasion.

The menu was princely, the first course offered three soups: tomato shrimp bisque, creamed leek and potato soup with julienned vegetables, pumpkin-lentil consomme. Salads followed: spinach with strawberry vinaigrette, roasted red peppers with walnuts and raisins, clementine, olive and endive salad, melon carpaccio. The entrees were: Beef tenderloin in puff pastry with Perigueux sauce, lobster

Thermidor, duck a l'orange, trout with almonds, veal scallops with apples and Calvados. The vegetable choices consisted of: baby artichokes and shallots, asparagus Pompadour, potatoes Anna, creamed morels with black truffles, petit peas. There were twenty-four options for dessert: pastries, puddings, cakes, sorbets, cheeses.

Rafe ate with his usual hearty appetite; soup, salad, three entrees, several vegetables, declining dessert in favor of a century-old port. Nicole tasted several dishes, favoring the melon salad, lobster, asparagus, morels, finishing her meal by selecting five pastries, lining them up in front of her, and contemplating them with a satisfied smile.

"I should take a picture," Rafe murmured.

Nicole looked up. "I hope that's not sarcasm."

"Au contraire. You look happy. I like when you're happy. Should we bring one of the pastry chefs with us to Monte Carlo?"

Her smile broke. "Yes! Oh hell"--she made a face--"better not. I'll gain fifty pounds." A second later her expression brightened. "Then again butter is supposed to be healthy for the brain and we want our baby to be healthy and smart, right?"

"Absolutely."

She giggled. "Are you going to agree with everything I say for the next eight months?"

He smiled. "Of course."

Having heard Nicole's giggle, Isabelle leaned over and looked past her sister to Rafe. "Of course, what?"

"Of course he's going to love me forever," Nicole answered.

Rafe smiled. "Every day til the end of time..."

"That's so sweet." Isabelle sighed. "It makes me all misty-eyed."

"Then we better change the subject," Nicole remarked with sisterly understanding, "because you've been misty-eyed a lot lately. Here, try this chocolate pyramid confection topped with coconut meringue." Nicole pushed the plate toward her sister.

Isabelle's tears were averted by the universal female panacea of chocolate and a second later Fiona stood up to make a toast, further diverting Isabelle's tearful mood. Next, Henny toasted the newlyweds with a rambling discourse on friendship that only came to an end when his wife, Mireille, rapped his arm and pointed at his chair. Immediately sitting, he lifted her on his lap and ignoring their audience, kissed her ardently. Although Henning Graf von und zu Steindorff-Lehn had a reputation for doing what he pleased, when and where he pleased. It came from his mother's side of the family those who knew him understood; the von Tresckow's had never believed in rules. Not that the sophisticated gathering was long distracted from their dining and gossip, the din of conversation quickly resuming, rising into the high, arched ceiling, the volume only subsiding when another toast was proposed.

As the last course of coffee, port and dessert wines was being consumed, Nicole pushed her chair back, rose to her feet and picked up one of the microphones on the table. After a quick smile for Rafe, she turned to face their wedding guests, put the mic to her mouth and said, "I have an announcement to make." The sound system was first rate, the exhilaration in Nicole's voice unmistakable, her emphasis on the word, announcement, tantalizing.

Surprise gave way a split second later to a tomblike silence, no mean feat in a room the size of a small stadium.

With admirable calm Nicole allowed the dramatic hush to intensify.

She's as shamelessly impudent as her husband, many thought, glancing at Rafe to assess his reaction, only to find his expression blank.

Once everyone's attention was laser focused, Nicole opened her arms wide in a buoyant gesture, swept the mic back to her mouth, smiled broadly and exclaimed, "I want to share the most amazing, wonderful, *joyous* news! We're having a *baby!* I'm absolutely thrilled...*we're* thrilled!" She glanced at Rafe. "We *are*, aren't we?"

She had no filter, no instinct for privacy. Understanding what was expected of him, Rafe quickly came to his feet, took the microphone from her hand, and turned to their astonished guests. "We're enormously pleased and happy... and yes," he added, "definitely *thrilled.*" Dropping the mic, he wrapped his arms around Nicole, pulled her close and kissed her.

Amazing indeed, many decided, that a playboy conspicuous for his selfishness and debauch should decide to start a family.

Clever girl, others thought who knew Rafe's dislike of scheming women.

How did she do it? the young women in the audience wondered, wishing they had been as cunning.

On one fact alone everyone agreed; it explained the hasty marriage.

As their guests reacted with varying degrees of disbelief, Rafe smiled at Nicole. "You wanted shock, pussycat, you got it."

She giggled. "Thanks for not minding a little drama."

"No problem." His entire life had been steeped in drama; this was no more than innocent amusement.

Suddenly, clapping erupted, the cadence slow and rhythmic at first, gradually intensifying in volume until it reached a seething, clamorous tattoo, augmented by wild cries of speech, speech, speech!

Nicole nudged Rafe. "Say something."

He grinned. "Suddenly you're out of words?"

"I am." Her smile was dazzling. "My work is done."

His brows rose. "Hardly, but I get your point." He gave her a wink. "Let me show you how to clear a room in record time." Turning to face their guests, he held up his hands to quell the noise and once a modicum of quiet was restored, spoke in a carrying voice. "Thank you for your enthusiastic response. We're pleased and delighted to be having a child. I've promised Nicole I'll be helpful in every way. Thank you, Henny," he added, putting his hand over his groomsman's mouth to arrest his comment. "I'm sure we all know what you were about to say. I'd like to point out that the band is beginning to warm up next door, they're taking requests and the bar is open for business. We'll join you there in a few minutes."

The scraping back of chairs was immediate.

Rafe turned to Nicole and lifted one brow. "See?"

"Smart ass."

"Damn right. I married you, didn't I?" Bending low, he put his mouth to Nicole's ear. "Isabelle looks like she's about to burst. Why don't you girls go and escape the curious. I'll meet you in the hallway outside the powder room in ten minutes. I have a feeling Henny and Basil might have a few questions as well."

"Sweet *and* understanding." She smiled up at him. "How do you do it?"

"For you it's easy." He looked past her and smiled at Isabelle. "She's all yours," he said, then lowered his voice. "I see our parents heading this way. Go. Ten minutes, talk fast, then we'll face our families."

Rafe had had Natalie set aside a small suite near the refectory for Nicole to freshen up between festivities. Nicole, Isabelle, and Fiona quickly disappeared and a few moments later were ensconced in the small sitting room next door where the subject immediately turned to Nicole's announcement.

"Sorry, I couldn't tell you before," Nicole said, smiling at her bridesmaids seated across from her on a matching club chairs upholstered in antique needlepoint. "But it's only the first month so you didn't have to wait long to hear the news."

"I still can't believe that you and Rafe decided to have a baby so soon?" her sister said. "I wouldn't have bet a nickel on it. Didn't you always say as the oldest child you'd babysat enough for ten lifetimes?"

"I changed my mind. We both felt really, really, lucky that we'd met, and"—Nicole smiled—"one thing led to another." No way was she baring her soul, nor was Rafe's initial reaction for public consumption.

"Awww, that's sweet," Fiona murmured. "Although you could practically see the sparks fly that day on Rafe's yacht. You met, POW, end of story."

"Speaking of that day," Nicole said, preferring to change the subject, rather than offer up half truths about her pregnancy, "I saw you and Jack in the Chapter House. How are things going?"

Fiona smiled. "We stay in contact. I've seen him twice since summer. He came to Stanford once and I flew to Rome a couple weeks ago. We're both busy, so"—Fiona wrinkled her nose—"in terms of a future, who knows. In the meantime, he's a super glorious date, sheer perfection in every way."

"And a prince," Isabelle chimed in. "Don't forget that."

"He doesn't really use his title, or at least not much. Did I mention I met his mother when I was in Rome? She came over to Jack's for lunch."

"No," Isabelle said, giving Fiona a pointed look. "I wouldn't have forgotten that. Meeting mother isn't exactly casual dating."

"Jack's easy going. Don't make too much of it. I'm not."

Nicole grinned. "Do you want me to ask Rafe to ask Jack how much he likes you?"

"No!" Fiona frowned at Nicole. "He hears that, I'll never see him again."

"And you'd like to."

"Of course. He's gorgeous and nice and don't either of you say, rich, because I don't care about that any more than you do. And he's super good in bed, so don't even ask."

Nicole held up her hand. "I promise. No comments to Rafe."

"And if he asks, you tell him you know zero about it, us, mostly my feelings on the subject, okay?"

Nicole nodded. "My lips are sealed."

"Come on, get real," Isabelle said. "Men don't talk about that stuff and if Rafe actually did ask, Jack would make some non-comital remark about good times."

Nicole made a face. "True, so...next question. Did you like Jack's mother? She's Rafe's aunt."

"She was nice, easy to talk to, not at all pretentious. She and Jack seem to have a good relationship...warm and friendly."

Isabelle smiled. "It's always a good sign when a guy gets along with his mother. Bax and his mom are buds. She's an artist, a really good one. He bought a gallery for her in San Francisco."

"You never mentioned that before." Nicole's brows rose

marginally. "How does a massage therapist afford a gallery in one of the country's highest priced real estate markets?"

"Don't ask me, ask him. He should be here soon. I got all weepy last night talking to Bax on the phone, missing him like crazy, so he said he'd come to Paris and kiss away my tears."

"No shit. Does Mom know?"

"About what?"

"About Bax for starters. I'm guessing you haven't exactly confided in her about your world class stud. That's what you call him, right?"

"As if I'd tell Mom anything even remotely sexual."

"Especially when you're supposed to limit your physical activity for six months after your life-threatening car accident."

"I'm just introducing him as a friend who happens to be in Paris." Isabelle's gaze narrowed. "That means you don't know him, Rafe doesn't either."

Nicole mimed locking her lips. "Got it. I'll warn Rafe." They'd met Baxter in San Franciso once or twice, but didn't actually know him, so no lie there.

"Now that's what I call a personal fly-in service," Fiona teased. "Maybe Bax can help you out with more than kisses."

Isabelle grinned. "I'm way ahead of you."

"Black or red?"

"Not with this floaty blue bridesmaid's dress. And he likes blue."

"Lace?"

"Of course, with ribbons and bows."

The three women were all smiling, their conversation familiar, the dress-for-success a long-standing concept when it came to sexual allure.

"I can't wear a bra with this gown," Nicole said. "However, my panties are white so I'm marginally adhering to the theme of virtuous brides."

"Are there any left?" Fiona quipped.

Isabelle grinned. "Where's the fun in that?"

"Hey, to each to their own," Nicole said. "If virtue's your thing, go for it."

Isabelle did a little bunny twitch of her nose. "What if you find out too late that your husband's a dud in bed?"

Nicole smiled. "Wouldn't know about that."

Fiona punched the air. "To independent women!"

"Amen, and to dear sisters and friends." Nicole gave them a blanket smile. "It wouldn't be the same without you guys here."

"We wouldn't have missed this wedding for the world." Fiona gaze was teasing. "Especially since you always said love was an illusion, a brilliant lie, a unicorn. Now I get to smugly say, *I told you so.*"

"I have to admit, it's pretty damn nice," Nicole murmured. "Consider me radically transformed."

"Speaking of radical changes, your announcement was equally out of left field," Isabelle said with a twinkle in her eye. "What do you think Mom's going to say?"

As if on cue, Rafe opened the door, stepped inside, shut the door and quietly gave notice. "Our families are about to descend on us, your mom in the lead."

Nicole groaned. "Is it too late to hide?"

Rafe dipped his head, and held her gaze. "Want me to play interference?"

"If only." Sitting up straighter, she squared her shoulders. "I can do this."

"We'll do it together." His voice was easy, his expression indulgent. "We're not obliged to explain ourselves to anyone." His smile was for her alone. "It doesn't matter what other folks say, okay?"

"Easy for you to say. She's not your mom."

His grin flashed. "What's that line about you can't please everyone? Come on, take it easy."

"Do you mind? I'm freaking out and you're being reasonable."

"You don't have to freak out. I'm here. I'll take care of you. Now, give me a smile and I'll let them in."

A sucked in breath, a tiny smile.

After opening the door, Rafe crossed the room, and stood beside Nicole's chair. "Chin up, Tiger," he said, softly. "It's gonna be fine."

What he didn't say was if it wasn't fine, he'd kick them all out.

12

"Oh, dear, are you feeling unwell?" Nicole's mother exclaimed, coming through the door so swiftly the skirt of her Dresden blue taffeta gown flared out behind her. "You're looking pale."

"I feel fine. Really, Mom, I'm great."

Melanie came to a stop before Nicole. "Are you're sure?" Leaning over, she put her palm to Nicole's forehead. "You're a little warm, dear. Should we call a doctor?"

"Come on, Mom. I'm not sick, I'm just pregnant."

A raking glance, a scintilla of a frown. "I'm sure you know best," Melanie Parrish said in a carefully rationed tone of nominal acceptance. "Although, I must say, your announcement was a *bit* theatrical *and* unexpected." Glancing up at her husband who'd come to a stop beside her, she turned back to Nicole. "Just the other day Daddy said he thought you were thinking of graduate school next term."

"I still might." Nicole looked up at Rafe. "Our plans are up in the air at the moment."

"We only recently found out about the baby," Rafe said, pleasantly. "We're still slightly dazed."

"That's only natural." Melanie suddenly smiled at Nicole. "My heavens, where have all the years gone? It seems only yesterday you were a little girl and now you're all grown up."

"And really happy, Mom." Nicole glanced up at Rafe. "We both are."

"Very happy," he said, softly, gazing at Nicole as if the room had emptied in the last few seconds.

Speaking briskly to gain their attention, Melanie said, "Do you happen to know the due date?"

A second of silence, then Rafe turned his head.

"The due date," Melanie repeated. "So we can plan."

Rafe looked at her blank faced, a corner of his mind unsettled by what his reclusive nature considered a personal question. Deciding to defer to Nicole's judgment—it was her mother after all—he touched her cheek, leaned down and whispered in her ear.

Once Rafe's comments fully registered, Nicole looked up at her mother, her face glowing. "Mid-June."

"Your birthday month," Nicole's father said, grinning. "Good timing."

"Thanks, Dad."

"Congratulations to you both." He took his wife's hand. "And if you need any help, your mom and I know how to babysit"—he winked at his wife—"right Mel?"

"Yes, of course," Melanie said. "We'd love to. Anytime at all."

"You can count on our help too," Rafe's mother, Camelia, said. "Isn't that so, dear?" She smiled at her husband, standing beside her.

"Absolutely." Gora had never taken care of a baby in his

life other than to oversee Titus' nursery staff, but if that's what Camelia wanted, he'd learn. With a lift of his chin, and a conspiratorial smile, he added, "You two kids sure know how to silence a room. My compliments."

"Hush." Shooting her husband a quelling glance, Camelia turned back. "We're delighted to hear your news." She smiled at Nicole. "Did you say June? Rafe's birthday is in June."

Nicole looked up at Rafe. "When?"

"The seventeenth."

Nicole stared, wide-eyed. "No way! That's my birthday!"

If anyone in the room needed further confirmation of the headlong pace of Rafe and Nicole's courtship and marriage, that small exchange was solid proof of their adrenaline-fueled love.

Lifting one brow in query, Rafe held his wife's gaze.

"Could be," she quietly said.

Bending low, he kissed her cheek and whispered, "If that's the case, Baby opens presents first." Standing up, he smiled at the small group watching them. "We're pleased you're all were here to share our joy. The next few months should be interesting, busy and certainly eventful. Nicole tells me she wants to go to our place in Monte Carlo. You're all welcome to visit," he said out of courtesy, although the ultimate decision on visitors would be up to Nicole.

"Monte Carlo?" Melanie blurted out. "I thought you'd want to be in San Francisco for the birth."

"We haven't planned that far ahead," Rafe said, smoothly. "Nicole was thinking the weather would be pleasant in Monte Carlo this time of year. We just thought we'd head south once everyone leaves."

"We don't have any long range plans, Mom," Nicole said. "There's plenty of time to decide on logistics."

"But you *have* seen a doctor." A grave look, a faint frown when Melanie didn't immediately get an answer. "Really, dear, that's not something you should put off."

"I'll do it soon, Mom. Rafe has a doctor on staff."

Matt squeezed his wife's hand in warning. "Your dad thinks I'm interfering." Melanie smiled. "He's probably right. But make sure you see a doctor before too long."

Aware of her mother's polite restraint, Nicole smiled in return. "I'll be bothering you for a whole lot of advice in the coming months, but it's still early days, okay?"

"Of course, dear. I understand. It's just exciting for us, too, right Matt?"

"You better believe it." Matt Parrish grinned; a big, easy going personality, he was a perfect match to his wife's more exacting view of the world. "No pressure, Nikki, but don't forget this is our first grandchild."

Nicole laughed. "I'll see what I can do, although I'm not guaranteeing perfection."

"I'll make sure Nicole stays healthy," Rafe said. "That I guarantee."

Despite his soft tone, no one misjudged the power of his pledge.

As a small silence fell, Camelia decided that commenting on her son's protective qualities and sense of purpose might sound defensive and remained silent. As for Gora, he knew better than to speak his mind when he'd wondered from the moment Nicole made the announcement if she'd planned the pregnancy without Rafe's knowledge. Not that it mattered. Clearly, Rafe loved her.

"If you feel up to it, Nikki," Matt Parrish said, tactfully breaking the silence, "I'm waiting for the first dance."

"Since you're one of the best dancers I know, I'd love to."

Rising from the chair, she held out her hand to Rafe. "The second dance is yours."

Taking her hand, Rafe pulled her close. "And the next thousand," he whispered. Looking up, he smiled at Melanie. "We'll have to show them how it's done, Mrs. Parrish."

"Mom's a really good dancer. How about you?"

Rafe shrugged. "I manage."

There it was again, everyone noted—manifest and inescapable. The newlyweds were largely unacquainted with each other, a source of both wonder and alarm.

Indifferent to the raised eyebrows, more interested in clearing the room, Rafe drew Nicole to the door, opened it wide, stepped aside and said to their guests, "Please, after you. I believe the bandleader has Nicole's request for that first dance, right sweetheart?"

"Yes, it's one of your favorites, Daddy," she said, adding for Rafe's ears only, "Such finesse. I'm in awe."

"I'll show you another kind of finesse later," he whispered.

Leaning into his body, she gazed up at him from under her lashes. "What if I can't wait?"

"You have to."

The raspy undertone, the blunt authority, the infinite possibilities in that simple statement triggered a rush of heart-tripping lust that left her breathless.

"Two seconds and they're gone," he murmured, watching their guests approach, realizing a pulse-beat later Nicole was trembling. Holding her close, he shifted slightly to shield her and as their parents, Fiona and Isabelle walked by, he offered them his well-honed, social smile. "It's been a busy day and Nicole tires more easily in her condition. Give us a minute and we'll see you at the dance."

Before anyone could answer, he shut the door.

"My goodness!" Even though she wasn't easily shocked with a brother like Dominic, Melanie was shocked.

"I should apologize for Rafe," Camelia said. "He can be impulsive."

Gora also spoke up in his son's defense. "Rafe's in love and perhaps more devoted than courteous. Please excuse his behavior."

"Of course we will," Matt said. "Rafe and Nicole have been surrounded by people for days. It's bound to get on their nerves."

On the contrary, Gora reflected, Maso's cruelty had given rise to a nerveless resiliency in Rafe. In deference to the joyful occasion, Gora quickly dismissed noxious memory and said, "While we're waiting for the bride and groom we could toast them with the Napoleonic brandy I brought." Signaling one of his bodyguards, he quietly gave instructions, then turned back with a smile. "Some brandy from Napoleon's coronation was discovered in a cellar in Brittany. We'll have to see if it's still drinkable."

A few moments later, as the small party walked into the Chapter House, Kate waved them over to the table she and Dominic were sharing with Dominic's ADC, Max, and his wife, Olivia. Rafe and Nicole's parents joined the two couples, while Isabelle and Fiona went off to find their boyfriends.

During the pre-wedding entertainments, old friends had renewed friendships, and strangers had met so everyone knew everyone. No more than a few moments after greetings had been exchanged, the muscular bodyguard in a bespoke suit tailored to conceal his shoulder holster, set down several dusty bottles, gave Gora a respectful nod and joined his companions near the door.

After a waiter brought glasses, Gora did the honors,

opening the first bottle with care, sniffing the cork, pouring a small portion, tasting it and looking up, smiled in satisfaction. "It aged well."

In short order, a toast to the bride and groom was drunk, followed by a discussion of the discovery of the brandy and the vagaries of Napoleon's ill-fated reign. Very soon, however, the topic of the evening took center stage and various toasts to the health of the expected baby made the rounds of the table.

"Speaking of babies," Olivia said, glancing at her watch, "I should check on Cressy. She can be fussy."

"I'll go with you." Max came to his feet. "Andy might need a lecture on manners. He was an only child so long he doesn't always play well with others."

"Maybe it's just boys," Kate remarked. "Jimmy has a mind of his own too. I expect the nannies are tearing out their hair by now."

Camelia smiled. "Titus doesn't normally interact with so many children. I'll come along and see how he's doing."

"Since our youngest, Ellie, is familiar with crowds," Melanie noted, "and the other children can take care of themselves, I'm going to dance with my husband." She gave Matt a grin. "They're playing our song. Did you request it?"

He smiled. "I did and two more you like since you're wearing your dancing shoes. If you'll excuse us"—he waved to the table at large, rose from his chair, picked up Melanie and swung her up into his arms.

She was giggling as Matt strode away.

"Still a love match, I see," Max said, turning to Dominic.

"She was nineteen and Matt twenty-two when they married and I doubt they've ever had a fight." Dominic arched one dark brow. "Fucking soul mates."

"Like us," Kate teased, rising from her chair and bending to kiss Dominic on the cheek.

Dominic glanced up and grinned. "A little wilder than that, thank God."

"Hey, I can be soulful."

"Really?" His gaze was amused. "Give me a clue when that happens."

She punched him on the shoulder. "Let's just say I know what you like and it's not soulful, it's"—she leaned over and whatever she whispered in Dominic's ear made him reach up, cup the back of her head and pull her mouth down to his.

"Hey, you two get a room," Max drawled.

Lightening his grip, Dominic gave Kate a roguish glance. "There's an idea. Want me to come with you?"

"Yes, no, maybe later," she said under her breath before standing upright and speaking in a normal tone. "I'll let you know if Rosie needs a good-night kiss when I get back."

"I'll be right here, drinking Gora's illustrious brandy."

After the collection of parents departed, the two men, once bitter enemies, now tenuously related by marriage, were alone at the table.

Leaning back in his chair, relaxed, Gora raised his glass. "A brandy this good demands a special occasion."

"And what better occasion than your"—Dominic's pause was infinitesimal—"step-son's wedding?"

Gora's expression was the unreadable one honed in situations more perilous than this. "Indeed. Speaking of occasions," he added with a barely there smile, "I have another case to celebrate the birth of the child. Were you as surprised as I?"

"Genuinely. I didn't think Nicole was interested in

having children." Dominic shrugged. "Apparently she changed her mind."

"Will she make a good mother?"

Dominic's eyes narrowed, his glass arrested mid-tilt. "Meaning?"

"It's a simple question. You know her, I don't."

"Okay, simple answer, yes." A stiff nod. "What about Rafe? Is he father material?" Dominic tossed back the brandy and set the glass down with enough force to turn heads at the adjacent tables.

Indifferent to the awakened interest of their neighbors, the two powerful men stared at each other, silent and watchful, their jaws clamped shut, family loyalties cutting both ways.

Gora sighed, shifting the dynamic, their prickly history drifting away like smoke. "Father material?" A little cock of his eyebrow. "Fuck if I know. It's not as though Rafe ever *had* a father."

"Tell me about it," Dominic muttered.

"Same, although at least you knew what yours looked like. Mine left my mother with six kids under seven when I was a baby. Beat her up, took what little money she had and walked out."

An up glance, Dominic's expression bland. "I'll bet you saw what he looked like at least once."

Gora's face went still. "No comment."

"While we're on the subject, was Maso your work?"

Gora shook his head. "Although I was on his trail. He'd started siphoning large sums of money from the company, gambling recklessly in Macau and losing. It couldn't go on." Gora ran his finger around the rim of his brandy glass. "I was in Bangkok when he died."

"Not a coincidence."

"No, an informant notified me and just as I landed I received an update. Maso was having a party in a hotel penthouse with the dredges of society; the hotel manager was concerned. I'm guessing the manager didn't want to be thrown into jail on some random murder charge. When I arrived, I cleared everyone out of the suite, but Maso was already beyond help."

Dominic's lip curled. "Lucky break."

"The police investigated. It's all in their report."

"I could ask how much that cost, but I won't."

Gora gave him a sideways look. "You know the price. You had a playhouse in Bangkok once."

"A lifetime ago."

Gora smiled thinly. "I just didn't want you to get too righteous."

"Don't worry, I have a good memory. I suppose your first wife's death in Istanbul—what--a week or two after Maso's was another coincidence."

"I asked you once about killing your mother and you said, 'This isn't about my mother.' Similarly, this isn't about my first wife." A gentle smile. "Is there a reason your mother isn't here?"

Dominic spread his hands. "Fair enough."

"Look, we both have pasts, although if I need an excuse, yours was considerably more privileged than mine."

"True. But people still can fuck you up, short circuit anything resembling normal emotions. Fortunately, emotion is a detriment in business. Knight Enterprises saved my sanity and better yet, I found Katherine in the bargain. Convincing her to stay was the hard part." Dominic grinned. "She wasn't willing to settle for an emotionally distant man."

"Unlike the legions of other women."

Dominic shrugged. "Money brings you all the fucking variety you can handle. Katherine was different. You understand that. You waited a long time for Camelia."

"I wanted more for her than the life I lived. Every day was a gamble."

"So you branched out."

"Enforcing is a young man's job."

Dominic smiled. "The twenty million you took from my factory in Bucharest must have helped."

"It didn't hurt but I already was financially secure. And you got your money back. In fact, if not for me, you wouldn't have met Katherine. You're welcome."

Dominic frowned. "Bianca was the bitch from hell so I paid that debt in spades, motherfucker. *You're* welcome."

Gora smiled. "Let's call it a draw. And Bianca gave me Titus, so"—he shrugged—"her family's iniquitous bargain was worth it. I could have said no when they pimped her, but I'm glad I didn't. Holding Titus for the first time,"—his voice softened—"changed my life."

"It catches you off guard, doesn't it?" Dominic made a slight gesture with his hands, smiled in memory. "Rosie's first look was wide-eyed, like she was interviewing me, and suddenly it was over. She owned every inch of me."

Gora thought for a moment before he spoke. "I'd never deferred to anyone in my life, always laid down the ground rules myself, expected to be obeyed." His eyes closed for a second. "Then Titus was born. The nurses complained he never slept, so I hired more nurses; they complained he didn't eat, so I brought in a team of nutritionists. Nothing helped, so I engaged a battalion of child psychiatrists, terrified they might find some mental affliction impossible to remedy." He raised an eyebrow. "Not to be discounted considering his parents, but," he said with a nod, "a king's ransom later, Titus was pronounced free of all defects. The psychiatrists all departed, but the screaming continued until finally out of desperation I moved a cot into his room next to his crib, lay down beside him and overnight he turned into an angel. The nursery staff was ecstatic." Gora blinked, took a breath. "I couldn't bear screwing up again. Rafe had gone through hell because of me. I'll take that guilt to my grave," he added, softly. "God knows how he came out whole, strong and unafraid but he did. And Titus did as well." Gora raised his glass. "To survival."

"Amen." With a nod, Dominic lifted his glass. "To happiness."

"To motherfucking luck," Gora said, softly.

Both men drained their glasses, recognizing that beyond personal courage and ruthless determination lay random fate, the long shot, the indiscriminate accident and if you were lucky enough: love, family, and a life worth living.

13

"Would you like another drink before we go?" Basil asked.

Claudine smiled. "You're welcome to come with us to see the children's playroom."

"Thanks, maybe later." Gina Wojcik pointed at her half full glass. "I'll just nurse this one." She smiled. "Pace myself."

Ever considerate, Basil held Gina's gaze. "You're sure?" Everyone else at the table, Henny, Ganz, Ray Morgan, and their significant others, had gone off to dance.

"Absolutely. I just flew in from Rio. I could use some quiet time." After a high-intensity month investigating a money laundering operation, followed by a delayed flight, a race against the clock to reach the wedding on time, hours of drinks, dinner, endless toasts and idle chit chat, she was ready to relax.

The wedding had been beyond splendid, the newlyweds so deep in love even the most cynical observer couldn't help but be disarmed. She was pleased not to have missed the happy occasion. And in the course of the evening, thanks to the attentive wait staff dispensing liquor at every turn, all the obscure nerves and instinctive flashing signals that normally kept her alive, had retired for the night.

Her sensory receptors, however, were still fully operational and the sweet ambergris/cedar cologne drifting into her nostrils elicited fond memory long before its wearer came to a stop behind her. Turning slightly, she looked up and smiled. "I heard you were here." She'd also heard Webster's cheating wife and her boyfriend had died when the Maserati they'd been in had missed a curve at one hundred forty miles an hour.

"Zoe was having so much fun playing with the other kids, she didn't want to leave." Taking a seat beside her, Webster Eames settled his sleeping three-year-old daughter in his lap, unbuttoned his slate grey suit coat, and stretched out his long legs. "She likes me to stay close."

Gina knew that too. After the accident, the police had found his daughter traumatized and alone in her crib. When the authorities reached Webster in Dubai, he'd chartered a plane, and on reaching home had immediately withdrawn from the world to care for Zoe. "I hear it's a virtual amusement park in there," Gina said. "Not that I'm surprised. Rafe's parties are always grand affairs."

"Yeah, it's a mini-Disneyland. Zoe's shy though so she didn't let go of my hand until one of the nannies sweet-talked her into going on a ride. After that, I was lucky to get a wave."

"Apparently, the chocolate fountain was a hit too." Gina nodded at the stains on Zoe's pink party frock.

Webster grinned. "Yeah, this pink number is toast." He lifted his chin. "Looks like you could use another martini. Chopin? Extra olives?"

"Good memory."

"Always an asset in our business." Webster turned, caught a waiter's eye, ordered two and swiveled back. "Nice dress."

Gina wore a deep violet silk boucle version of the little black dress.

"I like the color." He winked. "And the fucking pricey jewelry."

Gina earrings were large violet, tear-drop diamonds suspended from even larger cabochon emeralds.

She smiled. "They were a gift. One of my clients liked my work."

"Ah." Softly put.

"Don't be a dick. I did my job, he was grateful." *We're not all like your wife.* Realizing she'd been both snappish and judgmental, she quickly moderated her tone. "I was called in after a big heist in Antwerp and was lucky enough to locate the diamonds before they were recut. The earrings were my bonus."

"Sorry. One gets cynical."

"Hey, it goes with the territory doing what we do. I'm the last person in the world to believe in happy endings. You know that."

"The story's legend." He smiled faintly. "Remind me never to piss you off."

"No worries. You're one of the good guys." Despite his lethal skills, Webster looked like the wholesome rugby bloke he'd once been: handsome, clean-cut, fit and muscular.

He blew out a breath, opened his mouth, shut it again.

She watched him trying to decide what or how much to say about the scandal surrounding his wife's death. She wanted to tell him it didn't matter, that as far as she was concerned, the difference between good and bad was relative *and* personal.

He finally grimaced and said, "How long did it take you after that...episode in Trieste to get your head on straight?"

She didn't know if she should be sympathetic or honest. In truth, she'd never had a moment of regret when it had been kill or be killed that day. As for being deceived by the man she'd loved, she'd only felt rage at her stupidity. "It took a while," she lied, because clearly Webster was hurting and complete candor would be unkind. She understood the five stages of grief included anger at some point, and while she'd bypassed the other four stages, it didn't mean Webster could. "I don't remember exactly how long. It happened quite a few years ago." *Three years, six months, twenty-two days, to be exact.* "If it's any consolation, the pain eventually fades."

Webster shook his head, half-smiled. "You lie worse than I do."

She laughed. "You're not some scumbag trying to off me. I do better under pressure."

The waiter didn't bat an eyelash at her comment. He smoothly set down their drinks and as smoothly withdrew.

Webster gave him a nod as he walked away. "Well trained."

"I've seen him before. He's one of Rafe's staff. Nothing fazes them."

"Excellent attitude." Webster raised his glass. "To better times."

Gina held up her glass. "I'll drink to that. *Sante.*"

Three drinks later after they'd talked about everything but Webster's wife, Zoe woke with a start, looked around wildly until she caught sight of her father, let out a sigh and smiled. "Papa, me want candy."

"Do you like Swedish fish?" At Zoe's startled look, Gina added, "It's candy. Here, I'll show you." Opening her jeweled evening purse on the table, she pulled out a small package of colorful jellied sweets and held them out.

"She's bashful," Webster said, as his daughter drew back from Gina's outstretched hand.

"I have a couple suckers too."

"Thucker! Me, me, me!!"

Webster laughed. "I stand corrected. Say please, Zoe."

"Pease!"

"Okay, you have a choice," Gina said, extracting two suckers from her purse. "Cherry or orange. They both have chocolate centers."

"Me wuve choclit."

She smiled like her daddy, Gina thought, the little girl's expression one of natural delight. "Good. Here's one for each hand. If that's okay with your dad."

"What do you say to Gina?" Webster prompted.

"Tanks!"

"You're welcome." The mother must have had blonde hair, Gina reflected, Zoe's frothy curls shades lighter than Webster's sun-streaked brown hair. Watching him help his daughter unwrap the cherry sucker, she noted with interest his careful folding of the wrapper before he set it on the table.

Gina pointed. "Miniature origami."

"Obsessive-compulsive tendencies. They come in handy in dark alleys around the world. Or did. I'm a home body now."

"A much nicer occupation. Having just extricated myself from a hostile environment in Rio, I applaud your choice."

"What were you doing in Rio?"

"I was looking into a money laundering scheme that was

impacting a bank in Luxembourg, i.e., fucking with their margins." She glanced at Zoe. "Pardon my language, I'm not around kids much."

"Don't worry, kids don't pay attention." Which in fact was true; Zoe was totally preoccupied with her sucker. "Was it anyone I know doing the skimming?"

"Could be. Tracking money is your *metier*, right? Ever hear of Quantitative Statistics?"

"Cyprus, Russian ties. Have they branched out?"

"Selectively. I eventually traced their new cartel partners' bank accounts, zeroed in on their pressure points, then brought in some better hackers than me to shut it down. I could have used you."

Webster smiled, glanced down at his daughter. "Early retirement."

"Anyway, my part is done"—Gina grinned—"and I'm still alive."

Webster gazed at her from under his lashes. "Letting the adrenalin drain away?"

"Trying." Running her fingers through her short, dark curls, she rested her hands on the top of her head and slowly arched her back before dropping her hands. "It always takes a few days to get all the kinks out and cut back the engines. You know that."

"How long were you in Rio?"

"Way too long. A month." She pointed at her martini. "Self-medicating."

"Been there, done that."

"And now you have something better to do." Gina lowered her voice. "She's beautiful."

"Thanks. We're getting along. She tells me what to do," he said, amusement in his gaze, "and I do it."

"Kind of like the old days when you had clients who wanted everything yesterday."

He chuckled. "Not too different. Nicer boss though. She's learning to ride."

"Seriously? At her age?"

"It gets us outside. I bought her a pony. I already had a couple Irish hunters. There are two hunt clubs near me. Nothing fancy, no red coats and shit, just some fine riding. Zoe's getting pretty good."

"I hunted in Poland when I was at university. My father's family has a place outside Krakow."

"Good for you. Nothing like some hard riding to focus your attention."

He didn't invite her to ride in Kent. He was still wary. She understood that feeling in spades. Not that she was looking for an invitation. She had all the male attention she needed, but once burned, et cetera; any hook up now was strictly on her terms. Truth and trust, faith and love had died a sudden, violent death three years ago in that Trieste hotel room.

It had also abruptly ended her career in the Mossad. She'd resigned with a terse text from a fishing boat taking her to Italy and from that day on, the line between friend and enemy had never been in question.

A small silence fell, an easygoing quiet without expectations, their former clandestine operation for Rafe in Australia having established a friendship of sorts. Then Webster smiled, nodded at her empty glass, Gina said, "Why not?" and he ordered another round.

Webster eyebrows flicked up. "So what's next for you after your down time?"

"Remember Grigory Sisani?" The clandestine world of free-lancers was incestuous and insular, a ghost society of specialized skills. "I inherited his mess, correction, agreed to unravel the transaction he left unfinished when he died."

"When he was killed, you mean. You want my advice, let it go. In that part of the world people like us aren't safe—ever. Even Sisani, one of their favorites, ended up a target."

"I'm not planning on going in country."

"Doesn't matter. Fuck with them, they'll find you." Webster frowned. "Don't give me that innocent look. You think you'll see them coming. You might not and with those guys you don't get a second chance."

She smiled. "Thanks for the advice. However, I'll be relying on the wonders of the cyber world."

"I'm guessing you'll still be seizing someone's money." He snorted. "I saw that twitch."

She smiled. "One drink too many."

"At least tell me you'll consider giving it a pass."

"I'll think about it." She picked up her drink and raised it to him.

He sighed. "Liar."

"I'll be careful. How about that?"

"Yo, Webster!" Henny shouted from halfway across the room, interrupting them and turning heads as he plowed his way through the crush to their table. Plopping down on a chair next to Webster, he flashed a smile. "Glad you could make it. You, too, Gina, you're lookin' good. Hey, that's one fine sucker, baby girl. What's your name?"

Zoe took the sucker from her mouth long enough to answer, then smiled at Henny. No matter his size and mega-personality, his wide grin was capable of charming little girls, even shy ones. "Who you?" Zoe asked.

"Call me Henny. I have a real long name that's not worth remembering. I could make you a sucker like that with chocolate in the center."

Zoe's eyes widened.

"How many do you want?"

Zoe looked up at her father, uncertain.

"Henny knows how to cook anything," Webster said. "You can tell him."

The little girl opened her arms wide. "Dis many."

"Okay, then, let's go." Coming to his feet, Henny reached over and lifted Zoe from Webster's lap.

As Henny walked away, Webster stared. "That's a first. I wonder when she'll realize I'm not around."

But Henny's head was bent low so he could talk to Zoe face to face and she was nodding to whatever he was saying as they disappeared from sight. Webster exhaled. "Jesus. The new Svengali."

"Henny has charm to spare if he chooses to use it."

"No shit." Webster blinked away his stunned look. "Two months of wariness and now suddenly Henny's her new best friend."

"One who's going to make her"—Gina opened her arms—"dis many suckers."

"Trish didn't let Zoe have candy."

She heard his first mention of his wife, saw him flinch, would bet every cent in her Swiss bank account that he hadn't known about boyfriends or much else of substance when it came to the late Mrs. Eames. "That's not so unusual," Gina casually replied, like he'd said nothing special. "Everyone's avoiding sugar these days."

"Not me," Webster muttered. "I haven't said no once to Zoe since I got back home. She wants something, she gets it."

"Again, pretty normal." Gina grinned. "And seriously, what girl wants to hear no?"

An eye-roll, a small laugh. "You're telling me I'm a

responsible dad?"

"Looks that way to me. No one else missed the first four hours of the festivities." A wry edge of a smile. "Just sayin'."

"So I don't have to go check on Zoe…you know—in case Henny left her somewhere to get another drink?"

"Nah, if he tries to leave Zoe, I'll bet she'll kick up a fuss. Twenty euros says she will."

A flicker of a smile. "That's a losing bet for me."

"I love when I'm right." Grinning, Gina checked off her win with a flick of her finger. "Now drink your drink, relax, and tell me what you're going to do when you grow up."

A faintly puzzled stare.

"You're kidding. This is my incredulous look, dude."

He shrugged. "I never planned. I just rolled with whatever life handed me."

Including your incomprehensible marriage. Gina smiled. "You have to admit, at least life handed you an impressive list of interesting activities. Most people live a routine existence; a twelve mile commute to work each day, golf on the weekends, vacation in the summer, the occasional"—

"Shoot out in an Istanbul water-front warehouse," he said, eyebrows up.

"You were an idiot."

"As if I had a choice."

Gina sighed. "I know." Webster had walked into an ambush; six against one. When the smoke had cleared, he'd been the only one alive.

"I don't miss it."

Smooth, rehearsed; she'd put money he didn't mean it. Even if people like Webster were into self-reflection—which they weren't, his life had irrevocably changed on a dime. "You don't have time to miss it," she said, kindly. "Zoe's a darling, she needs you; that's a steady job."

He offered her a slow grin. Appreciative. A wordless thank you. "Feel like dancing? It's been about a hundred years but I might still remember how."

"Sure." It was as though he wanted to touch normal again, underline what was real. His world had been shaken, nothing was the same, everything twisted and a little sad. *Join the club.* "Fair warning," she said instead, "I haven't danced in *two* hundred years. I'll probably step all over your toes."

Webster laughed. "You're pretty small, how much damage can you do?"

MEANWHILE IN THE KITCHEN, Henny set Zoe on one of the counters, and said, "Don't move. I'll get the stuff for our suckers." Turning, he surveyed the frantic level of activity in the huge kitchen and raised his voice enough to be heard in the next arrondissement. "I need ganache, spun sugar, cherry flavoring and whoever brings it to me in the next five minutes gets five thousand euros!"

The executive chef gave Henny's cheek a swat with his wooden spoon, held up his hand for silence and whether in deference to the chef's exalted position or the lure of five thousand euros, the kitchen instantly went quiet. "We still have a midnight buffet to prepare," the chef declared, "so continue with your tasks while I help *le count*. The reward money will be evenly divided amongst the kitchen staff when our work is done." Thrusting out his hand palm up, he smiled at Henny. "Trust but verify."

"Jesus, Remy, have I ever stiffed you?" They were both gambling devotees.

"Not everyone knows you like I do." Remy smiled. "Show them the money."

Swiftly counting out several large bills, Henny held them up, then shoved them in Remy's tunic pocket before lowering his voice. "The little girl recently lost her mother and is easily frightened, so *vite, vite*."

Moments later, Zoe was elbow deep in a bowl of ganache and totally absorbed in "cooking". Standing beside her, dipping from the same bowl, Henny rolled chocolate centers for the suckers and set them on wooden skewers. Since Zoe was content squeezing ganache through her fingers, Henny took the time to reheat the sugar, flavor it, and twirl delicate crystal threads around each chocolate ball. With the suckers finished, he showed Zoe how to dip strawberries in ganache and helped her arrange them on a tray with the suckers.

"Now, let's clean you up," he said, carrying Zoe to one of the large sinks, "and we'll show your daddy the candy you made." After scrubbing off the chocolate, Henny held her in the crook of one arm, picked up the tray with his other hand and transported one happy little girl back to the ballroom.

Standing in the doorway, Henny surveyed the crowded room, took note of the empty table Gina and Webster had occupied and quickly debated his options. Zoe and Webster had been inseparable since Trish's death and if anyone understood child abandonment, he was a textbook case. Recognizing the dawning look of terror on Zoe's face when she realized her father was gone, he quickly said, "I'll bet he's dancing," hoped like hell he was right, scanned the mass of dancers and softly exhaled.

"Look, over there," he said, shifting his position slightly to offer Zoe a better view. "See, your daddy's dancing with Gina. I bet you know how to dance too."

Her quivering bottom lip instantly steadied, a smile lit her eyes. "Me dance good!"

The Wedding, Etc.

"You'll have to show me how, okay?" Setting the tray on a nearby table, he leaned over so she could reach it. "Pick out a sucker. We'll bring it to your dad."

A sucker in hand, her good humor restored, Zoe patted Henny's shoulder. "Me wik you. You wik me?"

"I do. You're the sweetest little girl at the party. And," he added with a wink, "you're going to show me how to dance."

Henny didn't actually need instructions. His ancient regime family considered dance lessons de rigueur so he'd suffered through years of excruciating tea dances with associated girls' schools until he was old enough to physically threaten the dance master. Another black mark on his record, but by that time his father had remarried, his mother was on husband number three and their son's bad behavior was in the hands of his current boarding school administrator.

As they reached the dance floor, Henny glided through the swirling mass to Webster and Gina, and smoothly keeping pace with the couple, said, "Zoe's turning out to be a great cook."

Zoe held out the sucker. "For you, Papa."

"Wow, you made this?" Taking the sucker from his daughter, Webster, followed by Henny, dodged a few dancers, moved to the border of the dance floor and came to a stop. "It's perfect."

A big smile, a pat on Henny's cheek. "Him help."

"Let's go back to the table and I'll eat my sucker."

Zoe shook her head. "Me dancing."

Webster sliced a look at Henny over his daughter's head.

"Me dancing too," Henny said, cheerfully. "See you two later."

As Henny twirled away with Zoe, Webster swerved to watch them and if not for his keen reflexes Gina's toes would have been trampled. Jerking his foot back, he muttered, "Jeez, sorry, did I step on you?"

Gina shook her head. "Nope, a clean miss. Although if you'd rather watch Zoe dance, that's fine."

"Nah." Webster smiled and turned back onto the dance floor. "I just needed a second to process Zoe's startling transformation."

"Henny's enthusiasm is hard to resist. And Zoe's having fun. Try your sucker. It looks good."

A distracted look, a glance at his hand, sudden comprehension. "You want it?"

"I thought you'd never ask."

"Sorry, I forget, you're the lady who carries candy in her purse." He handed it to her. "I'm losing my touch."

"You're just busy worrying about your daughter." She put the sucker in her mouth, took it out again, said, "This is fabulous," and crunched down on the fragile spun sugar.

Webster's amused glance was exactly as she remembered, incredibly attractive, with just a touch of recklessness and teasing laughter. He was feeling better than he had an hour ago. Thanks to Henny.

"I'm glad I came," Webster said. "I wasn't sure it would be good for Zoe with so many people she didn't know, the strange place, the late hours..."

"She's having a ball." Handing Webster the used skewer, Gina swallowed the last of the ganache. "Your daughter has a new best friend. Are you jealous?"

"Of Henny?" He shoved the skewer in his coat pocket. "Of course. He's smart, smart-ass and engaging, has a complete lack of interest in what people think, and he has my daughter under his spell." Webster grinned. "Definitely pistols at dawn."

"Henny would refuse. He likes you. Seriously, it's good to have you back in the world."

"Temporarily. Monday, I go back to my farming."

Gina came to such an abrupt stop, Webster had to quickly stiff arm the back of a man about to collide with her. "Sorry." He smiled at the scowling man. "Busy place." Grabbing Gina's hand, he pulled her off the dance floor.

"Thanks, that guy would have run me over."

"No problem."

"I didn't expect you to be a farmer. You're the least likely"--

"Farmer?" He gave her a playful bow. "In the flesh."

Her liquor consumption served to kindle an insurgent interest in that magnificent flesh, his tall, athletic form sheer perfection. But off limits her more politic intellect quickly advised; Webster's friendship mattered more than wild impulse. Pointing in the direction of their table, she said, "I'll buy you a drink and you can tell me all about your farm."

"You're interested in farming?" he drawled, as they moved toward the table.

She gave him a sideways glance and smiled. "If I was hitting on you, you'd know it. I'm interested in your farm. Is that a problem?"

He shook his head. "Sorry, rusty social skills. Come over sometime and I'll give you the grand tour."

In her business, you learned to recognize tells; something in his eyes told her he wished he hadn't offered the invitation. "Call me when you get home and sober up." She smiled. "If you don't call, that's okay too. For now, just give me the beginner course in agriculture. Seriously, I'm interested."

14

The fireworks were more extravagant than those on Bastille Day, the courtyard massed with guests enjoying the spectacle, the mild temperatures only adding to the perfection of the occasion.

"You must have ordered the warm weather along with the fireworks," Nicole said, leaning back against Rafe as they stood looking skyward. "Everything's wonderful."

"I want you to be happy. That was my charge to everyone, including the weatherman," he said, lightly, his arms wrapped around her, holding her close.

She looked up and smiled. "I'm bursting with happiness. Truly."

"Me too," he whispered, sliding his hands downward, resting them gently on her stomach, realizing if what he had lasted only an hour, it would be worth it. He was at peace.

"Do we have to appear at the midnight buffet?"

Distracted by his musing, he bent low and kissed her cheek. "Sorry. Midnight what?"

"The buffet. Do we have to go?"

"No. And if you're weary of fireworks, we can leave anytime."

She shook her head. "I'm enjoying the spectacle. I'm pleased that you arranged it for me, and most of all"—she glanced up and grinned—"I'm pleased that you love me desperately."

He laughed. "How could I not?"

She turned in his arms, met his amused gaze with a faint frown, gone in a blink. "Definitely reassuring from the world's greatest living expert on"--

"I've never loved anyone before," he said, interrupting her. "So I may not always have the right words, but all that matters is you, me, our child." His voice was gentle. "Better?"

Her eyes filling with tears, she nodded.

"You're my greatest joy, Tiger." Sliding his fingers through her hair, he bent his head and kissed her. "Now, let me show you and the world how much I love you," he murmured, raising his head and turning her back toward the fireworks.

The heart-shaped explosion was a brilliant, scarlet blaze caught fast for dazzling, overdrawn moments against the dark Parisian sky.

He watched her, wide-eyed, her hands on her cheeks, breathing quickly. And when the sparkling heart faded to rosy pink and finally dissolved in the night sky, she turned, lifted her face to his and asked, half-breathless, "Did you tell them to do that?"

He dipped his head, smiled faintly. "My grand gesture."

She knew what he meant; he didn't as a rule flaunt his feelings. "I'm touched," she whispered, a tiny smile lifting the corners of her mouth. "And so deep in love I'm afraid I might embarrass you before all these people."

He grinned. "Impossible. Although"—a flicker of amusement in his eyes—"I can't speak for your mother. Perhaps we should quietly retire."

Easier said than done.

They'd not moved more than a few yards when a high-pitched voice called out, "Nicky!" Turning, they saw Rosie, seated on Dominic's shoulders, smiling and waving.

"We'll just say hi." Taking Rafe's hand, Nicole drew him through the crowd to the family. "You're up late," Nicole said, smiling at Rosie.

"*I'm* a big girl!" Rosie said, gaily. "Jimmy fell asleep." She pointed at her brother, sleeping in Dominic's arms. "He's just a baby."

"Jimmy overdid a little in the playroom," Kate said. "Rosie, tell Rafe and Nicole about the fun you had with Ellie and Titus."

"Ellie showed me how to bowl, and Titus let me play two video games with him and, we're all going to meet again somewhere"--she took a quick breath in her exuberant reply to look at her mother.

"Maybe skiing this winter or"-

"Summer vacation for sure." Rosie leaned over enough to catch her daddy's eye. "You promised I could see Titus and Ellie next summer."

Dominic nodded. "Anytime we can arrange it."

"For sure now," Rosie pressed, like children do. "You promised"—

"I said I'd talk to Melanie and I will," Dominic replied mildly, infinitely patient with his children. "You promised to email Titus for his schedule."

Rosie acknowledged her father with a beaming smile. "First thing tomorrow, Daddy."

Kate laughed. "I'm glad that's all settled." She turned her gaze on Nicole and Rafe. "We so enjoyed the wedding. It was absolute perfection. And the dazzling heart at the finale of the fireworks was so romantic, wasn't it dear?" She looked up at Dominic.

Dominic smiled faintly. "Definitely."

"It was Rafe's idea. I thought it was *lovely*," Nicole noted, responding to the palpable reserve in her uncle's voice. She smiled at Rafe. "Did someone video the fireworks?" At Rafe's nod, her smile widened. "Perfect! I get to see it again."

Aware of the undercurrent of stricture in Dominic's reply, not inclined to skirmish with him, Rafe said, pleasantly, "We were about to leave. Nicole's tired."

"Wait!" Kate exclaimed. "Let me show you the picture I took of Nicole coming down the aisle." Pulling her phone out of a small green silk shoulder purse, she thrust it at Nicole. "Look, isn't that beautiful--you, your gown, the flowers?"

As Nicole leaned over to view the photo, Dominic moved a step closer to Rafe and spoke quietly. "Did you do this to her?"

"This? You mean the baby?" A small sigh. "I thought you knew your niece better than that."

"A simple yes or no will do."

"First, I don't answer to you, and second, from where I'm standing,"--Rafe gave Dominic a quick up and down glance--"I could ask the same of you. No one would have bet a cent on you having children and now you're—what...a responsible family man? Care to explain?"

An involuntary smile. "Fair enough. I'm simply concerned with Nicole's happiness."

"It's my heartfelt concern as well." Rafe finally smiled, easy and loose. "It's called 'being in love'. Is this pointless conversation over?"

Nicole turned back. "What are you two talking about?"

"Children." A flash of a grin. "Dominic wanted to wish us well."

"I did." Standing tall and powerful, his sleeping son cradled in his arms, his wide-awake daughter scuffing the front of his bespoke suit with her sparkly shoes, satisfied with Rafe's answer, Dominic's smile was urbane and charming. "Much joy to you both."

A few moments later, after assuring Rosie she could visit them soon, Rafe and Nicole continued their passage through the courtyard throng. They were interrupted frequently by congratulatory guests, most garrulous with drink and in the case of several young women, boldly hopeful as well. As they broke free of the last of the fawning females, Nicole shot Rafe a jaundiced glance. "My rivals seem undeterred."

"Ignore them," Rafe muttered, drawing her down the gallery surrounding the courtyard. "You have no rivals."

"You were polite to them."

"I didn't want a scene."

"Perhaps you were a little too polite."

He heard the cool exasperation in her voice, knew it presaged problems. "Do you want me to go back and savage them all? I prefer a lower profile, but it's up to you."

"What if I said yes?"

"I'd do it. They're all a pain in the ass."

Her eyes opened a little wider at the sheer effrontery. "Will you be saying the same of me in a few years?"

"You're *already* a pain in the ass. I just happen to love you so I overlook it."

Eyelash-flutter. "Are we fighting?"

He gave her a faint smile. "No."

"Okay, you convinced me."

He pulled her to a stop. "I have no intention of arguing so give me a clue. Convinced you of what?"

"Despite my deep and abiding jealousy, you don't have to go back and savage those bitches."

"Christ, are we still talking about that?" He started walking again, the stairway in sight. "Swear to God, they're out of my life. I don't even remember what they said."

"They all said, *Call me.*"

He took a breath. "Sorry, I've learned not to listen." His eyes were on her for a second. "Look, I get it. You're jealous. I'm jealous. We've been over this before and knowing us, it'll come up again. But just for the record: you look at some guy the wrong way, I'll punch him out and lock you up."

She stared at him. "Ex*cuse* me?"

"Behave. That's all."

She slapped his arm. "You can't talk to me like that."

He turned to her again, something dark flaring in his eyes. "Okay, maybe I won't lock you up."

She came to a stop, jerked her hand free, and glared at him.

He thought about lying. Decided against it. Putting his brain into neutral, he came up with a smile. "Look, screw jealousy. We'll figure it out some other time. It's been a long day." He nodded upwards, toward his apartment. "How about I show you a present I got for you and promise to stop being a dick?" A fizzle of a grin. "That's me apologizing. Deal?"

"Deal," Nicole said, because she couldn't not; she loved him.

He let out a breath he hadn't realized he'd been holding. "You're stuck with me, you know that, right?"

A wry smile. "And you're stuck with a high-maintenance,

swirling mass of female hormones with a hair-trigger temper. Enjoy."

He laughed. "No problem. You're my one and only, my miracle, my little ray of sunshine." Sweeping her up in his arms, he moved toward the stairs.

"I'm not little."

"Yes, dear."

"And I'm only going to get fatter."

"Not a news flash, Tiger."

"You better like me when I'm fat."

"I'm going to *love* you, pussycat."

"Pretty soon, you won't be able to carry me."

"Wanna bet?" Taking the stairs at a run, he raised her over his head without breaking stride, ignored her wild shrieks, and reaching the top of the stairs a moment later, lowered her enough to kiss her.

"You're a wild man," she murmured against the warmth of his mouth.

Raising his head, he gave her a lazy smile. "You can reform me. *After* you open your present," he added, walking down the hallway.

"Oh, God, I don't have a present for you. I feel guilty."

He shot her a teasing glance. "You're giving me a baby. I couldn't top that if I tried. As for buying anything, what's mine is yours now."

She made a face. "Don't say that. It's embarrassing. I don't want your money, okay?"

Rather than argue the domestic legalities in Switzerland, he smiled. "Fine, more for me. Ah, here we are," he said, neatly avoiding a useless discussion. Pressing down on the latch with his knuckles, he nudged the door open with his shoulder, walked in, kicked the door shut and crossed the sitting room. Entering the bedroom, he shut the door, set

Nicole on her feet, and pointed at a green leather satchel, adorned with an enormous flower embellished bow, centered on the bed. "For you, pussycat. I hope you like it."

"What a beautiful purse! Or is it an overnight bag?" She gave him a warm smile. "It doesn't matter, it's lovely."

Cupping her shoulders, he turned her toward the bed. "Go, open it. You'll find a couple things inside."

Moving the short distance to the bed, she hiked up her skirts, sat down and began unbuckling her shoes.

"Let me," Rafe said, taking over the unbuckling. "Want me to find some scissors?"

"And ruin this gorgeous bow?" Nicole said, pulling the satchel closer. "I'll untie it."

Slipping off her shoes, Rafe dropped them on the floor, shrugged out of his suit coat, and started to toss it on a chair.

"Wait, wait, you'll crush your boutonniere!"

"So?"

"I want to press it. Don't you ever press flowers to remind you of a special occasion?"

Sure, right after he pasted pictures in his non-existent photo albums. "Not lately," he said, turning his coat lapel-side up. "It's pretty small. You still want me to take it off?"

"Would you, please?" she said, sweetly.

Her glowing smile made it less bizarre, reminded him everyone's life wasn't fast, loud and brash, that graceful leisure and pressed flowers weren't shocking or old-fashioned but perfectly normal. Removing the tiny iris, he placed it on the bedside table. Then, he carefully hung his suit coat on the back of a chair in the event dropping it in a heap would upend some other quaint ritual. Loosening his tie, he unbuttoned his shirt collar, bent to untie his shoes, kicked them off, disposed of his socks and joined her on the bed. Taking note of her continuing struggle with the bow knot, he said, "Sure you don't want some scissors?"

Purse-lipped, her brows drawn in concentration, Nicole shook her head.

Choosing to humor his wife's caprices, he leaned back against the headboard, stretched out his legs and exercised a well-mannered restraint. He didn't realize he could be so patient; he didn't realize *she* could be so patient. Until, finally, mercifully, the bow yielded to her diligent efforts.

"See!" Nicole triumphantly held up an unfurled length of white silk ribbon.

"Amazing." Although scissors or a knife would have remedied the situation a long time ago.

"If that's sarcasm it's wasted on me," she cheerfully noted. "I save ribbon."

"I'll buy you all the ribbon you want. A ribbon store if there is such a thing."

"That's not the point."

"And the point is?" he gently inquired.

"Saving the ribbon and using it over again."

There was no polite answer to such strange economy. Or any answer at all. He was speechless.

"You'll see. It's fun," Nicole said, beaming.

His darling wife never ceased to amaze him. Since his own life had been, at times, one of appreciable ennui, he delighted in her curious contents. "I look forward to a new diversion," he pleasantly said.

But she'd unclasped the satchel and her gasp of surprise saved him from further contemplation of things unknown. He watched her dip her hand into the satchel and smiled.

She took out the pieces, one by one, with various exclamations of delight, demur and astonishment and laid them on the quilted indigo bedspread.

After emptying the satchel, she sat back, took a small breath and surveyed the extravagant, costly display. "I'm unprepared for such largesse. It's slightly overwhelming." Turning to him, she brushed the back of her hand down his cheek. "I absolutely adore you. You're too good to me. Outrageously indulgent--in every way."

"But?" He'd heard the restraint in her voice, saw the polite regret in her eyes.

"It's too much," she gently said.

He leaned over and kissed her lightly. "It doesn't compare to what you've given me. Happiness, love, a child...there aren't enough gems in the world to express my gratitude. However," he said, sitting back, and acting out of common sense and meticulous good manners, "return them with my blessing."

"You wouldn't be angry?"

He didn't often see her uncertain, her blue gaze indecisive. "Of course not. It's your gift. Do with it what you like."

"I don't want to seem ungrateful, or critical...I should just politely say, thanks--but this lavish gift"—she waved her hand over the brilliant, glittering baubles—"represents an enormous sum of money. I'm not...comfortable accepting it when there are people—well...who don't have enough to eat or"—

He stopped her with a finger to her lips. "I understand, really I do. Give the money to charity instead. Do you have some favorites? If you don't, I can suggest some. Or the woman who oversees my charitable foundation could help."

Her eyes lit up and a big grin spread across her face. "You're the best, the absolute BEST! Strong and decent, patient, irresistible and I love you so much I'm shaking. See?"

"I'm not so fine, but thank you." Folding her hand in his

warm palm, he drew her close. "And remember, I want what you want. So always tell me whatever it might be." He smiled. "I'm not a good mind-reader. Okay?" He dipped his head and held her gaze.

She sniffled, nodded, whispered, "Happy tears."

"Good, so down to business," he said, in an effort to arrest her tears. "Do you have any favorite charities?"

After a couple blinks and sniffs, her voice barely wavered. "I volunteer at the food bank back home. I've been helping there since I was in high school. I can give you the name and address."

"Tell you what," Rafe suggested because he wasn't completely altruistic when it came to presents for his wife, "keep ten pieces of jewelry, I'll see that the rest are converted into cash and after I get your list of food banks to endow, I'll have checks sent out."

"Endow?"

He smiled. "People like to eat every day don't they?"

"Seriously?"

His smile deepened. "Seriously. Give me the names of say, a hundred food banks."

"Jeez, how much was that jewelry worth?"

He shrugged. "All I need is your list. In the meantime, I'll help you pick out a couple pieces."

"No you won't!"

He laughed. "I love when you're bossy."

And he watched with pleasure as she selected ten pieces, asking him twice for his opinion, otherwise making her decisions quickly.

She smiled. "I'm keeping the purse too."

He didn't say it would have been hard to find someone else with the same initials on the monogramed clasp; he said, instead, "I was hoping you'd like it."

Sitting back, her hands clasped in her lap, her smile was sweetly innocent. "So now," she murmured, "with our business concluded..."

He cast her a teasing glance. "You have expectations, Mrs. Contini?"

"Say it again. I *love* my new name."

"Mrs. Contini," he repeated, his amber gaze clear and smiling. And he silently thanked whatever twist of fate had brought her to him and made life precious. "It's our wedding night." His voice was velvet soft. "A memorable occasion."

She grinned. "Even more memorable for a man who never contemplated marriage."

"Yes," he said, this man who'd never spent more than a few hours with any woman. "You were a surprise."

Her smile was brilliant, teasing. "And you love me madly."

"I do. Along with a long list of other undisciplined obsessions." Gathering the discarded jewelry into a pile with a quick sweep of his hands, he scooped up the fortune in gems, dropped them on the carpet and turning back, gave her a wink. "I'll try not to frighten you."

Her smile was exempt from fear and tantalizing. "And I'll try not to be too demanding."

"But first." He paused long enough to gain her full attention. "This is my *one* and *only* wedding night," he said, softly, holding her blue-eyed, curious gaze, "so I thought perhaps we should have violins or"--

"Don't you dare say there are musicians next door," she whispered, casting a nervous glance at the closed bedroom door before quickly turning back to find him half-smiling. "Oh, shit, there are."

"Come on, you can't be averse to a little romance."

Tiny crinkles were forming at the corners of her eyes in advance of her smile. "No, of course not."

"Do I hear a slight *but?*"

"Let's just say we aren't all exhibitionists."

A flicker of a grin had accompanied her comment. She wasn't looking for a fight. "Just listen to one song," he coaxed, changing the subject from exhibitionists. "I found that flutist you like."

"Ohmygod, you didn't!" she blurted out.

A killer smile. "I did."

"Annie's Song?"

It was a slow smile this time. "What else."

"Oh, Lord, oh Lord, tell me to relax, am I hyperventilating, I am, oh shit, he's really here…oh jeez."

"Hey, it's all good," Rafe whispered, curling his fingers around the back of her neck and rubbing it softly. "A couple of deep breaths now, there you go…that's the way—slow and easy."

She softly exhaled and her eyebrows lifted just a little. "Is James Galway actually next door?"

"If you like." Dropping his hand, he sat back. "No rush."

He was effortlessly calm while she was freaking out. He was also sex god handsome, kind and caring, and so tender it made her heart melt. Leaning over, she took his face in her hands. "I love you, Rafe Contini, more than you'll ever know." A smile like the sun coming out. "Annie's Song? Really, truly?"

"Really, truly," he said, seamless, not missing a beat.

"Galway's version of that song always brings tears to my eyes."

His smile had a grave sweetness to it. "I know." A little nod. "He's waiting to play it for you."

Dropping her hands, she took a deep breath. "What do I

say? Tell me what to say. Oh, Lord, I'm so nervous I might faint."

"You needn't be nervous. He seems very pleasant."

"You've talked to him!"

"A couple times." Coming to his feet, he held out his hand.

Taking his hand, she slid off the bed and gave him a shaky smile. "Promise to catch me if I faint."

"Will do."

"Oh, damn, I'm barefoot—let me find my shoes."

"Sweetheart, we're both barefoot," he soothed, drawing her toward the door. "No one cares."

A second later, standing on the threshold of the empty sitting room, she looked crestfallen. "They left."

Not unless they could pilot his plane themselves. "They're down the hall. Would you like to go there or have them come here?"

"Don't ask me to make a decision when I'm giddy with delight, weirded out and in a semi-coma with shock."

"The other room's a little bigger," he said, as if only practicality was at issue. "Let's go there."

A moment later, walking down a narrow, low-ceilinged corridor, dimly lit and bordered by mullioned windows darkened by the night, Nicole gave Rafe a sideways look. "I didn't know there was another room on this floor."

"More than one. The medieval cloister house was enlarged several times so it's a virtual warren of odd rooms and connecting passages. Stairs coming up. Watch your step."

At the base of the shallow stairway, the hallway curved to the right and abruptly came to an end at tall, elaborately carved double doors, embellished with sinuous metalwork featuring fantastic, imaginary beasts.

"Wow, those are scary creatures. I'm almost afraid to go inside. What was the room's original purpose?"

Chastising impenitent nuns. The iron wall brackets and ceiling chains had been removed. "I'm not sure," he equivocated. "Natalie might know. She oversaw the restoration." Gripping the fanciful dragon-shaped doorlatch, Rafe pressed down, pushed the door open, guided Nicole in with a light hand on the small of her back and smiled at the small group inside. "Good evening, gentlemen. Allow me to introduce my wife, Nicole. Nicole, Mr. James Galway and his accompanists."

After greetings were exchanged with the world-famous flutist, his piano and violin accompanist, Rafe thanked them for their patience. "I'm afraid everything ran a little late. I hope you either enjoyed the wedding festivities or found time to rest a few hours this evening."

"Both," the pianist replied with a grin. Young and brawny he looked more like an NFL player than a pianist. "Ian and I enjoyed your mad array of liquor. James left us to it and rested this evening."

"Your staff was most attentive," Galway said. "Your housekeeper showed me to the bedroom next door. She also reminded me we'd met forty years ago at a restaurant in Budapest." He smiled. "I don't know how I could have forgotten."

Brows high, Rafe agreed. "Natalie *is* pretty unforgettable. Although, you may have come across one of her other personas. She's a natural actress."

"I wonder if she was the chanteuse. Does she sing?"

"Not that I know of. I'll have to ask her. Not that I'd necessarily get an answer." A small shrug, a smile. "Natalie's a law unto herself. Now, then, we've kept you waiting long enough." Galway was eighty and it was midnight. "It's been a long day for everyone. Perhaps your beautiful version of "Annie's Song" will suffice for a performance."

"Danny Boy, too"—Nicole glanced at James Galway. "If you don't mind."

Nicole's voice was so faint, Rafe looked at her with alarm.

"We'd be happy to play anything you like," the world's greatest flutist pleasantly replied.

"Oh, thank you! I love that song and I'm such a huge fan, although you probably hear it all the time," she said, her rare shyness replaced by her normal vivacity. "My dad always played your albums, so I came to love them just as much as he—and when he took me to one of your concerts in San Francisco I was blown away. You probably hear that all the time, too, but anyway, thanks for making my wedding really, really special." She took a quick breath. "Seriously, a thousand, million thanks."

"Our pleasure," the elderly man said, kindly. "Although, your husband was persuasive. I'm not sure he understands the word, no."

"Not in the least, I'm afraid." Nicole's smile was dazzling. "Or mostly not," she added with a playful wink at Rafe.

Pleased Nicole had regained her lively spirits, Rafe said, "Allow me to disagree. As of a few hours ago, I've become a dutiful married man."

Nicole's silvery trill of laughter made everyone smile. As did Rafe's impromptu kiss, after which he swung Nicole up into his arms in a swift, sweep of powerful muscles. "Over there, okay?" he asked. At Galway's assent, he carried his bride over to a plum-colored velvet sofa, sat, settled her on his lap and instinctively gave a nod to begin. "Forgive me." Rafe grimaced. "Old habits. Whenever you're ready, of course. We're extremely grateful you agreed to play for us."

Galway accepted the apology with a smile; preeminent in his field for so long, he understood authoritarian lapses.

A moment later, the clear, pure notes of the flute filled the room and the opening melody, *You fill up my senses, like a night in the forest. Like the mountains in springtime, like a walk in the rain...*touched Nicole's heart and tears filled her eyes. Fully conscious now how love made every smile, every casual glance or quiet word, every touch precious, she understood her world, like the song, had become infinitely more beautiful because she loved Rafe.

Holding Nicole gently in his arms, Rafe listened with wonder to a song that had never inspired either interest or emotion, and now, the lyrics not only aroused a vast tenderness, but each word inescapably spoke to him. He'd been given a gift; a woman he absolutely and entirely loved.

The ruinous sadness of "Danny Boy", the gentle finality of death and the sorrow of those left behind was in stark contrast to the sunlight and happiness of love in "Annie's Song."

Nicole openly wept.

Rafe's sensitivity to emotion still on a steep learning curve, words of comfort failed him. But pulling her close, he gently brushed away her tears, stroked the dark silk of her hair, stopped himself from saying *Let me buy you something.*

Recognizing the implications in his silence, she reached up and touched his chin with a fingertip. "It's just a beautiful song," she whispered, as his gaze flickered toward her. "Don't worry."

He softly exhaled. "I couldn't tell. One of my many shortcomings." His eyelids lowered marginally. "Understanding feelings."

She smiled. "I'll teach you."

"That's what I'm hoping," he said, his eyes warming.

As if on cue, the song ended, the performers were offered a great many thanks, and once all the courtesies had been exchanged, Rafe came to his feet with Nicole in his arms. "Whenever you're ready, someone will show you downstairs. A driver is waiting to take you to the hotel or airport. It's up to you. Thank you again, and *au revoir*."

On the way back to their suite, Nicole said, "Sorry about the tears. I probably shouldn't have asked Galway to play "Danny Boy."

"Why not if you like the song? I expect Galway always brings everyone to tears with that song."

"It was nice of him to come."

"He lives not too far from one of my homes near Lucerne, so I told him we're practically neighbors."

"He initially said no, though, didn't he?"

"Yeah, well, there are nos and there are nos."

"And you understand the difference."

"Sometimes." A politesse only; no one in recent memory had refused him.

15

After setting Nicole down in the bedroom, Rafe said, "I'm not saying your mother has no boundaries, but just in case, I'm locking us in." Turning, he walked into the sitting room, locked the corridor door, returned to the bedroom, pushed the door shut, locked it, leaned back against the door and smiled. "Fortress secured."

Nicole grinned. "Think you're safe now?"

"You gonna attack me?" A lifted brow, a twitch of a smile. "Go for it."

"I might."

He opened his arms. "Anytime. Long day, right?"

She sighed. "I don't know how you do it. Smile, make small talk, smile some more, work your way through a room full of guests smooth as silk."

"Hey." Talking her hands, he pulled her into his body. "They're all gone." At her eye roll, he added, "At least till morning. It's just us, you, me, Mr. and Mrs. Contini--there that makes you smile."

"Thanks, I love my new name. But don't forget my brothers at ten. Skateboarding."

"And don't *you* forget everyone will be gone by dinner time."

She nodded. "Hold that thought."

Knowing better than to say, I've been counting the hours since they arrived, he said, "Speaking of thoughts, how about we take it easy at first, savor the special pleasure of our wedding night"—amusement shone in his eyes at her sudden quiet--"just kidding, seriously, I shouldn't kid you." His grin broke. "It's just so tempting."

Her smile flashed, tinsel bright. "You know what *I* find tempting?" she murmured, pulling her hands free and sliding her fingertips over the soft navy wool covering his rising erection. "This, him, my personal playmate. Umm...," she murmured, pleasure swelling inside her as his dick hardened and lengthened under her palms. "I think he wants to come out and play." Her gaze flicked up. "But then he always does, doesn't he?"

Not entirely sure of her implication, he answered neutrally. "He likes you."

A tiny lift of one brow. "Likes?"

"Adores you, loves you, can't live without you," he said, smiling faintly.

She laughed. "There you go. You win the prize."

"I already won the prize. The only question," he drawled, "is how exactly I make use of the sweet, little treasure I own." He held up a finger to cut off her protest, his voice low-pitched. "I mean cherish."

"Nice save. I could give you some suggestions if you like."

He shook his head.

"Are you going to surprise me?"

His small shrug was uber sexy, flagrantly suggestive.

A blush rose on her cheeks, every sexual receptor in her

body started dancing the happy dance and turning quickly, she smiled over her shoulder. "I love your surprises. Quick, unzip me, but don't tear anything," she briskly added. "I'm saving the gown for posterity."

Her last statement drew a blank, but in the event some tradition was at stake he clarified his position as he reached for the dress zipper. "FYI, I'm wearing my suit again."

"Why wouldn't you wear it again? Careful, the bow unhooks."

At the continuing litany of instructions apropos the fragile fabric of her gown, he almost said, *Do you think I haven't taken a lady's dress off before?* And if sex on his wedding night hadn't fallen under the rarified category of *miracles do happen* he might have.

Instead, he quickly accomplished his task and with the dress satisfactorily removed, Nicole took the gown from him. Walking into the dressing room, she carefully hung up the dress, smoothing the wide straps over the padded silk hanger before turning back with a satisfied smile. "I'm saving it for our daughter's wedding."

Rather than mention they probably could afford a new wedding gown for their prospective daughter, he smiled. "What a nice idea."

"You don't understand anything," she pithily said to his suave reply. "I'll explain later. You're still dressed. Why are you still dressed?"

His dark brows rose. "I've been busy undressing you."

"Don't be reasonable. Oh, hell"--she grinned—"be as reasonable as you want as long as I come in the next two minutes."

He shouldn't have said, "Not a problem," so calmly.

Reminded of all the women in Rafe's past, as well as the pointed interest of the more recent ones at the wedding, her temper spiked. *Let it go*, her voice of reason advised. "Not a problem, because?" she said, hot-eyed with affront.

"Because you're in a hurry. What?"

"Your tone."

Lord she was cute, all hot and bothered over god knows what, and sexy as hell in that wisp of lace panties. He suppressed a smile. "Tell me what to do and I'll fix it."

"Just like that because you can fix anything?"

"I can for you. Hey, whatever it is"—and he said something he'd never said before—"wanna talk about it?"

She wrinkled her nose.

Seeing his pussycat was running out of steam, he swung her up in his arms, said, "Let's talk about it in bed," and not getting any snippy-ass reply, moved across the room.

"Tell me not to be jealous."

He almost didn't hear her. Kudos to his brain for picking up the muzzled comment. And he silently cursed the phalanx of women they'd passed through on the way to his apartment. "Don't be," he said. "I'm yours, you're mine and that's the way it's going to be. No one else, ever, till the end of time. Okay?" Stopping at the bed, he held her gaze. "Tell me it's okay, cause I'm more jealous than you."

"Okay." She sighed. "I tell myself not to be childish."

He grinned. "So, how's that going?"

"Fuck you."

"I thought you'd never ask." And he dropped her on the bed.

Before her shock had fully registered, he was pulling his shirt and tie over his head and unzipping his suit pants. "We still talking two minutes?" he asked, dropping his shirt and tie, sliding his pants and boxers down his hips. "Sexy panties, by the way," he added, stepping over his discarded clothing. "Did I give them to you?"

"Alessandra did."

"Do I get credit for paying for them?" he asked, stripping off the sheer white ribbon-trimmed panties, tossing them aside.

"I'll let you know in two minutes."

He was smiling when he swung over her, dropped between her legs and plunged deep into her slick, wet, honey-sweet warmth.

Damn, she had the world's most perfect pussy.

He almost said it.

And he might have if his head hadn't levitated slightly from his body at the sensational jolt to his brain.

She couldn't have uttered a sound if she'd had a gun to her head, the entire world suffused in a warm, golden, insanely horny glow that was literally bathing her in sensory bliss.

His lethargy was quickly replaced by an uncomplicated lust for the woman he loved beyond reason, and withdrawing with velvety languor, he drove back into her melting heat with such excruciating slowness, she opened her eyes and said, very softly, "If I wanted a chivalrous knight, I wouldn't have married you."

Curtailing his forward motion, he replied, lightly teasing and equally softly, "If I wanted peace and quiet, I wouldn't have married you. Are we negotiating degrees of force?"

"Excuse me. Did I say I'm negotiating?"

His soft laughter was a combination of charm and arrogance, his mind set, super accommodating. Also, he knew damn well how to manage his dick, she was creamy wet and antsy and if his cock had a vote, it was full steam ahead, roger that.

Brief seconds later Nicole's lush purr indicated profound satisfaction, his spectacular hard-on was buried deep, filling her so completely a hush momentarily fell on the small bed in the cloister house in Paris, France.

Then he shifted inside her, an infinitesimal movement, breathtakingly delicate. "Can you take a little more?"

Her eyes lifted to his for a shuddering moment.

And he saw pure lust.

Slipping his hands under her bottom, he forced himself deeper still, and as the first pre-orgasmic tremors spread outward in ripples from her cock-stretched pussy, she quivered, overwhelmed by the fierce pleasure, dizzy with need, her low, strangled moan manifestly desperate.

Spreading his fingers, he broadened his grip on her ass and smoothly adjusted her angle to better accommodate his dick, her expeditious timeline and the prudent/profligate equation under which he was operating. Gliding forward, her flesh slowly yielded to his cautious invasion until she gasped. He tensed, paused, was running through possible options having to do with other kinds of orgasms when Nicole sank her nails into his shoulders, hissed, "Don't you even think about stopping or"—

Breathless, frantic, her whimper turned into a soft wail.

She was racing for the finish line.

His cue to push in as far as he could go—then watching her for any sign of discomfort, push an almost imperceptible distance more.

She sucked in a sharp breath.

Oh fuck. He began to withdraw.

She clung to him. "No, no, no, no, NO!"

A pulse beat of conscious appraisal and reversing course, he gave her what she wanted, but with a tight rein on his libido, zero excess and a light, easy rhythm that touched every sensitive, trembling, restless, tantalized surface of her slick, silken sex. Then with time counting down, he increased the pressure of his hands on her bottom, finetuned his carnal choreography to further arouse and inflame and penetrated that last almost intangible measure more.

She sobbed in feverish gratitude, her nails scoring deep enough to draw blood. He winced, felt coolness sliding down his back and decided to bring this requested wham bam orgasm to an end. "Listen up, pussycat, if you want to come you're going to have to do it my way, not your way or I'm going to take my dick out and"--

Her orgasmic cry broke in high, breathless, feverish abandon, the wild scream bringing a smile to Rafe's lips; there were times she didn't mind a few orders.

And with his dick rammed into her tight little pussy, her orgasmic convulsions buffeting his cock was sensory overload to the max; the flesh to flesh contact lurid.

Raw enough to keep her screaming.

Tempered and calculated enough in his case, to appease his sense of responsibility.

When her feverish cries faded, and a hush descended, when Nicole found breath to speak, she contemplated him propped on one elbow beside her, her gaze half-lidded and still slightly dazed. "How is it I always forget how good that feels?"

"Beats me."

The softness of his tone levered her eyes open a fraction. "You didn't get a turn."

"Plenty of time." He wasn't a fan of slap dash orgasms.

Her eyelids drifted shut.

Eerily content considering he was a married man--a phrase hitherto unknown in his personal cosmos—he contemplated his go-for-broke wife who always took pleasure with such tempestuous passion and wondered what that felt like--losing control. On the other hand, the yin, yang they had going for them was fucking golden; he gave, she took, and each time, the world was brand new, dew fresh and beautiful.

So, fuck it; scratch the losing control discussion.

Moments later, feeling her way out of her pink, gauzy enchantment, Nicole murmured, "What are you doing?"

"Taking my turn."

"Where'd you learn that?"

"Hush." And he returned to gently sucking her ear lobe.

Her hips were softly moving, her breathing had changed, her low pleasure sound a soft musical hum.

A singular melody he recognized.

"Can you feel that?" Raising his head so he could see her response, he clarified. "Those little frissons sliding down to your pussy."

"Yes, god yes...it's sooo nice. Sex in the afternoon nice, or waking up sex nice, or"—

"Honeymoon sex nice."

Her smile unfurled. "Yeah."

"Pay attention. It gets better." He dipped his head.

"Wait." She put her palm on his forehead. "Seriously, where did you learn that?"

Resting on one elbow, he shrugged.

"Tell me."

"I don't remember."

"Sure you do."

"Long, boring story. I'll tell you sometime." Like never. Because it was one of those shitty stories about Maso's vice-ridden notions of child rearing. At fifteen, he'd been forced to go to a Tantric sex workshop when he would have much preferred skiing with his friends. He'd finally skipped out of the workshop early and joined Henny and Basil in St.

Moritz where there were plenty of young ladies on Christmas break who didn't care if you sucked their ear lobes or not. Although they didn't mind you sucking them in other places.

"It makes me feel all warm and fuzzy and like, super welcoming..."

"That so."

"Don't you dare smile like a goddamn know-it-all."

"Okay, but pleasure can be whisper soft too—like a barely heard song."

A sardonic life of her brows. "Are you going to teach me something?"

"I am." His voice was matter of fact, and ignoring her raised brows, he gently bit her ear lobe. "Feel those tiny flutters? See, you do," he whispered as she squirmed, little wingbeats of arousal warming her pussy. "What about this?" He ran his palm, broad and featherlight, over the swell of her breasts, her ribcage and slender waist, the smoothness of her belly, until it came to rest, warm and beguiling, on her throbbing sex.

She exhaled a low, languorous moan.

He smiled. "There's a good girl."

His deep voice resonated silken soft and proprietary through every quivering nerve in her body. Her eyelids slowly rose. "Say it again. All that soft machismo in your voice makes me super horny..."

"You don't fucking say." He slid his middle finger down her hot, slippery cleft.

A soft purr, a tiny drift of her hips, the lightest of demands in her blue-eyed gaze. "Say it again."

He smiled. "That's the key to the kingdom?"

She smiled back. "It is right now."

"In that case," he said, his deep voice silken, "be a good girl and you get a prize."

"If this is your idea of a teaching moment," she murmured, a molten heat spreading through her senses, "it rocks."

"Thought you'd like it," he said, rather than mention it was universally adored, dismissing as well, his schizoid history that allowed him the necessary expertise. "Now relax. I guarantee the payoff."

A sudden green-eyed jealous stare. "Is that a fact?"

"Cool your jets, pussycat. I had to go to a workshop a long fucking time ago before I was old enough to say no. It's just shit you don't forget, okay?"

She nodded, took a breath, then still mildly grudging, said, "If I wasn't already halfway to that payoff, I'd make you tell me all about that workshop."

"Lucky for me, you're in your usual hurry. So?"

A faint line furrowed her brow. "Do you always have to win?"

"Trust me, we both win this one."

If her sudden temptress smile wasn't a fucking green light, her next "show me what you got" command was the stamp of approval for Rafe to recreate that seminar from long ago. The added subtleties he'd picked up over the years having to do with arcane, esoteric, highly impressionable areas of the body was aesthetic frosting on the cake.

Predictably, the experience was hyper-pleasurable for his newest acolyte and after a mildly incandescent time-frame of gentle caresses and gentler touch, he targeted novel erogenous zones that quickly brought her, panting, to a wild, dizzying, flame-hot arousal. And when Nicole was so near to climax it would have been impossible to stop her, Rafe moved between her legs, slid smooth as silk deep inside her and with perfect timing guided them through a gentle, low-key rapture that gradually modulated into an unfettered, shot-of-adrenaline orgasm so awesome, they were momentarily deprived of speech.

More animated or perhaps more naïve when it came to sensation, Nicole found breath first and blurted out, "Ohmygod, that was *incredible! You're* incredible! I'm *sooo* glad I married you! In fact," she took a deep breath, "if I could needle-point I'd embroider a sampler with all the happy words like joyful, contented, ecstatic, exuberant, just to remind me how super wonderful you make me feel."

Face down on the mattress near Nicole's shoulder, Rafe's voice was muffled. A moment later, he lifted his head. "Lightning in a bottle," he repeated. "Don't forget that one."

Smiling, she reached up and touched his cheek. "I'll add that phrase. And I'll make the sampler small enough so I can take it with me wherever we go."

"Or you could just take me with you." His soft drawl was teasing. "I'll make sure you're happy every day and you won't have to learn how to needle-point."

She laughed. "Now I'm even gladder, more glad, whatever"—a tiny shrug, discharging issues of grammar—"I married you."

"Good," he said, gruffly. "Because I'll never let you go."

16

Rafe looked up as Nicole walked into his office the next morning, shut his laptop and frowned. "What the hell do you think you're doing?"

Her eyes widened in feigned surprise. "What?"

"You know damn well, what." With a flick of his finger he indicated her skateboarding garb: black sweater, black loose slacks, red and white Vans. "You could fall," he gruffly said. "Hurt yourself, hurt the baby."

She shut the door to avoid an audience; the last thing she wanted was her mother involved. "Lighten up. I'm really a good skateboarder. I never fall."

Leaning back in his chair, he stared at her. "I'm not arguing about this. You're not going."

Her blue eyes flashed with temper. "Since when did you become God?"

"A long fucking time ago," he growled.

Her back against the door, she stood silent briefly then lifted her chin. "I have no intention of taking orders from you for the next eight months. I know whether I fall or not when I skateboard, you don't. End of discussion."

Exhaling softly, Rafe gazed at her for a moment, debating his concerns against her displeasure. "You may not have fallen in the past, but that's no guarantee," he said, his voice deliberately mild.

"Say for argument, you're right, and I fall. I'm only a month pregnant. It'll be fine."

Steeling himself against his surge of anger, Rafe spoke with constraint. "Be reasonable. Why take chances? We'll bring your brothers skateboarding, show them a good time like we promised, and everyone'll be happy."

"Except me." She stood very still, her spine rigid.

"I'll make it up to you, I promise. Let's just get through today. Everyone leaves soon. Time enough tomorrow to discuss any reasonable equity you like. Right now I don't want to worry, or take risks over something as frivolous as skateboarding."

"And I'm telling you, you don't have to worry. I'm probably a better skateboarder than you."

Not likely. And he had the trophies to prove it. But a glance at the clock focused his attention on ending this argument; Nicole's brothers were due to arrive in five minutes. "Would you be willing to compromise?"

"That would involve you being unselfish." She smiled. "Are you up to it?"

"Yes, of course," he said, making another adjustment to a lifetime of selfish choices; a common occurrence of late.

"Okay, then, we'll both sit it out. My brothers won't care as long as they can skate. Harmony restored?"

"Absolutely." His smile was open, straightforward. "Thank you for your cooperation."

"*Our* cooperation."

He laughed. "Yes, dear. See, I'm learning. Marriage is teamwork."

"Hmpf," she snorted. "If I hadn't watched Dominic roll over everyone in his path for most of my life, I might believe you. But I have, so in the interests of marriage congeniality, let me remind you that I don't bulldoze easily."

His smile widened. "One of your many charms, pussycat. I look forward to a life bereft of tedium. And a life as well," he added, more softly, "where I wake up with you beside me and see you last before I close my eyes. So when I'm thoughtless, tell me."

She gave him a cheeky smile. "Thoughtless about my feelings on skateboarding? Does that count?"

He groaned. "Don't expect an instant transformation."

"I don't. Nor"—her eyes were fixed on him, there was a twitch at the corner of her mouth—"should you."

She'd never seen anyone leap over a desk, especially with such smooth, lithe grace, nor had she ever been swept off her feet so effortlessly.

"Thanks, Tiger," he whispered, kissing her lightly. "You had me worried for a second. I like you bossy, I like you standing up to me, I like you best when you're the uninhibited, willful darling who spoke to my heart when I didn't know I had one."

She sighed. "I worry sometimes. Do you think we fight too much?"

He didn't say he'd spent so many years not caring, he didn't need their love to be nice and clear, glossy and smooth. "I'll get better," he said, with the easy self-confidence of a powerful man. "And you can't fault the making up," he added with a grin. "Want me to lock the door?"

"You forget my mother and father are here," she said, drily.

"They don't have a key."

Her eyes widened. "You're shameless."

"And fast. Give me five minutes to make you smile." He didn't even flinch at the knock on the door. "Two minutes. I'm good with excuses. I saw that. You're not sure, are you? Want me to lock the door?"

"Nicole! Hurry up! Let's go!"

"Now I'm sure," Nicole said. "That was Dante and he'll be in here in a second. Put me down."

As if on cue, the door opened to her three brothers.

"Thought you could hide?" her oldest brother teased. "Not likely when we were promised prime skating."

"We weren't hiding," Nicole said, straightening her sweater, smiling at her brothers. "We're ready, right?" She glanced at Rafe.

He hesitated just long enough to make her heart lurch.

"Sure. Keir, do you want to drive one of my cars? You and your brothers could follow us."

"Hell yeah!" Keir was eighteen and car mad. He'd been struck speechless at the sight of the cars Rafe kept in Paris.

"Next time I get to drive," Dante grumbled. At sixteen, he only had a learners permit.

"If there's time," Rafe said, "I'll take you out to a private track I know and you could drive there."

"Seriously? Wow! We'll *make* time, right Nicky?" Dante turned to his sister. "You tell Mom and Dad. They'll listen to you. They're all giddy you're making them grandparents."

"What about me?" Nicole's youngest brother, Rafe, known as Buzz thanks to his toddler love of Toy Story, piped up.

"How private is the track?" Nicole asked. Buzz was only fourteen.

"It's mine," Rafe said.

Buzz's eyes lit up. "So I can drive?"

"Sure," Rafe said.

"We better ask Mom and Dad," Keir interjected.

A sharp glance, quickly shuttered; Rafe wasn't familiar with asking permission.

"I'll talk to them," Nicole said. "If it's a private track they shouldn't have any objections."

"We can set speed limits if that helps." Rafe checked his watch. "We'll skate for a couple hours, then swing over to the track if you guys get the okay." He didn't have to ask their flight time; he'd been on countdown since yesterday.

"We're lucky you married, Rafe, Nicky." Dante winked at his sister. "Good work."

"You actually weren't a deciding factor." She shot a grin at Rafe. "In fact, I might have forgotten to mention siblings so I didn't spook him."

"And I might not have cared what she said," Rafe noted, with an affectionate smile. "So long as she kept smiling at me."

Buzz made a face. "Eww, mushy."

"They're in luuuuv," Dante murmured.

"Don't knock it," Keir countered, "til you've tried it."

"Jesus, you've known Chloe since grade school. How boring is that?" All the boys were darkly handsome in a young, coltish way, but Dante had an intriguing glint in his eyes that girls couldn't resist. Going steady wasn't in the cards for him.

"You don't have to agree on girlfriends this morning. Let's go," Nicole said, taking Rafe's hand, putting an end to her brother's dispute.

"You guys know the way to the garage, right?" A second later, Rafe gave Nicole a mocking glance as her brothers disappeared down the hallway. "Am I good at diversion or what?"

"You're good at everything," she murmured, leaning into his arm. "That's why I married you."

A few minutes later, after reaching his underground garage, Rafe helped Nicole into a low slung black Aston Martin DB11, leaned down and said, "Give me a minute to go over the controls with Keir and see that security is ready to roll."

Keir had selected a yellow Maserati Quattroporte four seat coupe from the dozen cars in Rafe's garage. Seated behind the wheel, he was studying the space age dashboard.

"In case we get separated in traffic, let me put the address on the GPS," Rafe said, reaching past Keir to tap in the skate park address. "Security will follow us, but if you miss a light or take a wrong turn, you can call me or Simon. Do you have the phone numbers?"

"I have yours."

Rafe held out his hand. "Give me your phone. I'll add Simon's number. If you get lost, call, and stay in the car. Carjacking is always a possibility with a car like this."

"There was a carjacking a couple blocks from my school," Dante remarked. "It's a crime of opportunity."

"Agreed." Rafe didn't say the percentages were probably higher in some of the neighborhoods they were driving through. "Let me show you the controls and we'll hit the road."

17

Rafe's community center was in a suburb (*banlieue*) northeast of Paris. Within the *banlieue*--a pejorative for slum--a colossal concrete housing project overwhelmingly populated by recent Arab, African and Chinese immigrants dominated the skyline.

At ground level amidst graffiti-covered walls, office buildings, soccer fields, trash fires and abandoned industrial lots, the Social Frontier Community Center offered hospitality to everyone in the neighborhood. The square block, three story building housed a school, cafeteria, clinic, and food shelf, along with teachers and counselors committed to overcoming the joblessness, discrimination, and sense of isolation so common in the *banlieues*. The surrounding green space had been designed to include a playground, soccer field and their current destination, a skate park.

Even at ten on a Sunday morning, the skate park was busy. The concrete flow park combined elements of both bowl parks and street plazas, while a large indoor area served skaters in cold or wet weather.

Rafe parked in a lot adjacent to the center, followed

moments later by Keir and Simon. Ray and his girlfriend, Crissy, had ridden out with Simon and as Ray stepped from the Mercedes sedan, he raised his skateboard. "I come prepared."

Recognizing a state-of-the-art titanium board, Rafe said, "You'll have to see what our kids have made," indicating a low, garage-like building with a lift of his chin. "We have every imaginable skateboard in there."

Surveying the acres of sculpted concrete beyond the building, Crissy gave a low whistle. "That's one mammoth skate park."

"The whole area was pretty much a wasteland. Acreage wasn't a problem."

"You get an early crowd too."

"The community center is a real draw. We offer lots of services beyond recreation, a food shelf included." Rafe turned to Nicole. "I'll see that you get some addresses while we're here."

"This installation makes our local skate park look miniscule," Ray said with a faint smile.

"Our park's not exactly miniscule," Crissy noted. "Ray and his brothers built it," she explained. "It's actually pretty cool."

"This *banlieue* has a population of a million, five." Rafe dipped his head a fraction. "Hence, the size." He gestured at the low building. "Come see the skateboard shop. It's my pride and joy."

As they approached, one of the glass garage doors rolled up and a swarm of teenagers surged out in a laughing, shouting, welcoming mass.

Abruptly stopping, Rafe grabbed Nicole in a one-armed hug, held up his other hand. "Hey--slow down." He spoke in

English, the young generation bilingual at minimum. "Don't run over my wife and friends."

The wave skidded to a halt a scant foot away, excitement and curiosity writ large on every face.

"Your wedding is all over social media," a young boy with a gap-toothed grin said. "Why'd you do it?"

"She's cute," someone added.

"That's why, Waldo." A snort from an elfin blonde with spiked hair. "Open your eyes."

"What's her name?" asked a tall girl wearing a Bob Marley t-shirt, ripped jeans and combat boots.

"Nicole. Mrs. Contini to you, Keti," Rafe replied, whether teasing or not, unclear.

"Call me Nicky if you like," Nicole offered.

"Better not," a voice in the back of the crowd warned, aware of Rafe's scowl. "Rafe don't like that."

Nicole glanced up. "Come *on*." Reaching up, she smoothed away Rafe's frown. "Relax. Lots of people call me Nicky."

It took him a fraction of a second to smile. "Yes, dear."

But there wasn't a person within sight or hearing who didn't get the message. His wife was off limits for the usual mocking banter.

"Hey, Meklat," Rafe called out, rather than continue a possibly fraught conversation. "Want to give us a tour of the workshop?"

A lean, rangy kid with dark-blond hair and earphones around his neck grinned from ear to ear. "Sure. It's super rad."

Meklat and Rafe weren't the only ones proud of the workshop. All the young people pointed out their projects, as well as all the special tools and equipment in the workshop. Skateboards of every size and description lined the walls or rested, half-finished, on work benches. Racks of shoes for those not properly shod for skateboarding framed both sides of one exit, and a snack bar offered hot food for the limitless appetites of teenagers too busy to use the cafeteria in the main building.

When Rafe introduced his guests to the two world class craftsmen from Liverpool he'd hired to teach the art of skateboard construction, the sudden spike in conversation indicated a free and easy relationship between teachers and students.

Although, before long, the animated discourse was interrupted by a wiry young boy with a shaved head and a disarming smile who'd been fidgeting throughout most of the tour. "Enough, let's skate!" he yelled.

Apparently his opinion was shared by others. In seconds flat a lemming-like rush a crowd of young people poured through the doors opening to the skate park.

Rafe and the teachers exchanged knowing glances.

"Kids," Rafe said, turning to Nicole with a smile. "They're almost as impatient as you."

"I assume that's a compliment." Her voice was lightly sardonic.

"Naturally," he said very softly. "If you'll excuse us," he added, in a conversational tone, smiling at the teachers.

Taking Nicole's hand, he escorted her outside to some bleachers overlooking the skate park. Guiding her up the stairs to the top row, he took off his electric blue top coat, and spread it out on the seat. "The metal's cold. Sit here, I'll point out the popular features."

"So many kids are enjoying themselves," she murmured. "It's wonderful." She touched his hand resting on his knee. "You're doing good."

"We're trying. No guarantees. But we're hoping to give

these kids a safe environment in a tough neighborhood, along with some educational resources to help them succeed. The classic joke here is that crossing the Peripherique, the highway encircling Paris, and going into the city requires a visa and a vaccination card. I'd like to ease that crossing." He shrugged. "Glossy dreams. That aside," he quickly added, reconnecting with reality, "the skate park *is* rad. After the baby, we'll try it out."

"Lots of dreams come true," Nicole countered. "In the meantime, you're giving a chance to anyone interested. And clearly, the kids love you."

"Yeah, well, they're pretty cool kids. Most of them deserve a better life, a less dangerous one. I can relate. A war zone's a war zone, whether here or in a shitty boarding school. But fuck the angst, we're here to enjoy ourselves. Were you impressed with the workshop?"

She'd taken note of the shuttered look that appeared whenever the subject of his youth arose and tactfully picked up her cue. "It was an incredible workshop and those two guys from Liverpool are perfect for the kids. They're kind of overgrown kids themselves."

"Yeah, they live and breathe skateboarding. Speaking of skateboarding," Rafe added, pointing, "check out Dante and Keti."

Dante and the young girl in combat boots were showing off in the street plaza section of the park. He was leading, and she following his every move in a finely tuned, effortless way. Until on a particularly treacherous incline, she suddenly sailed past him, leaped up on a rail and took the lead.

Nicole laughed. "Dante's going to freak. He's used to being top dog on the rails."

"Keti has more balls than most men," Rafe said. "Jesus,

look at those two fight it out. They're neck and neck. Wanna bet on the winner?"

"Hell, no, they're too closely matched."

"Maybe he'll let her win."

"Maybe she'll let *him* win."

The faint scold in her voice tempered Rafe's reply. "You're right. Definitely too close to call."

Opportunely, Ray and Crissy walked up and interrupted a potentially controversial discussion. Holding up two smooth as silk, polished oak skateboards, Ray grinned. "I'm told these are superior to my titanium baby. We're going to try them out." Ray's brows rose. "You guys aren't skating?"

"Nah, we're sitting it out," Rafe said. "Too much excitement yesterday."

Crissy nudged Ray, and gave him a stare. "Nicole's pregnant."

"Sorry, I forgot about the baby." Ray smiled. "Take it easy, absolutely. Just holler when you want to leave. In the meantime, I'm gonna show Crissy how it's done."

Crissy laughed. "And I'm going to show him how it's done *right*."

Soon after Ray and Crissy left, a group of young boys approached. "I told Fouad you're the best, Rafe," the boy leading the pack said in French. "Come on, show him your Big Air. I got a bet goin'." He held up his hand and rubbed his thumb and fingers together, the ink on his tattooed arm vivid in the morning sun.

"Maybe next time." Rafe spoke in the same accented slang in the event Zac was his usual smart ass self. "I'm going to chill today."

A collective groan greeted Rafe's comment.

Zac gave Rafe his best sixteen-year-old, hardnose stare. "Next time, *when*?"

"When you get some manners," Rafe drawled. "How about that?"

"Okay, okay, I apologize. Please, please, *please* come skate."

"What the heck are you doing sitting up there, Rafe?" Dante asked, coming back hand in hand with Keti. "I hear your flips are sick. Give us a look-see."

"Not today." Rafe turned a warm smile on Nicole. "We're just watching."

"Ah, jeez," Dante groaned. "I saw that look. Nicole made you say no, didn't she?"

Rafe shook his head. "I'm just not in the mood."

A small crowd had formed. The teenagers all knew that Rafe never sat out when he could skate. Rash and reckless, he got off taking risks.

They also recognized that Rafe probably wasn't skating as a courtesy to his wife. Since Rafe *always* skated with them, however, they weren't inclined to be as polite. They wheedled and cajoled, made absurd promises, pleaded fervently, some dramatically begging on bended knee.

Even though most of the teenagers were speaking French, Nicole couldn't help but understand. "Go on," she finally said. "Skate with the kids. I'm fine."

Rafe held her gaze for a moment. "You sure?"

She smiled. "I don't think your fans are going to give up. Go, make them happy."

Leaning close, he whispered, "You're a sweetheart. Be back in ten minutes."

A raucous cheer went up when Rafe came to his feet, leaped to the ground and caught the skateboard Zac tossed him.

Rafe wasn't surprised it was his favorite skateboard. Zacarius Filiu was always one step ahead of the action.

The oldest of six children raised by a widowed mother, he'd been the man of the family from a young age. A brilliant student, street smart and acutely perceptive, thanks to Rafe's financial help, he'd be going to university next year.

As they walked away, Zac said under his breath, "I was beginning to think you were pussy-whipped."

Rafe laughed. "It's called love, Zac. With luck, you'll experience the feeling yourself someday."

"Merde, if it happened to you, I guess it can happen to anyone. No offense," he quickly added.

Rafe smiled. "None taken. Tell me what you've been practicing since I last saw you."

Rafe was both mentor and Pied Piper at the park, helping coach those who needed help, leading the pack of risk-takers, entertaining one and all in a breathtaking display of flips and twists and high speed tricks.

As Nicole watched a particularly eye-popping jump, two girls came up and sat beside her.

"Just so you know, every girl here's in love with Rafe."

Nicole smiled at the pink-haired teenager with kohled eyes and a smarmy grin. "Not just here."

"How'd you do it?" asked her friend with black nails, matching lipstick and badly dyed jet black hair. "What's your secret?"

"No secret. We met and just knew."

Two sets of arched brows greeted Nicole's comment, although the pink-haired girl spoke first. "No way. You must be the thousandth woman in Rafe's life. Seriously, how'd you snare him?"

"Trust me, you don't want someone you have to snare. That's a recipe for disaster." Nicole smiled. "My advice, be yourself. Then no one's ever disappointed."

A longing sigh from the little Goth. "Rafe could never *ever* disappoint."

"Yeah, he's pretty special," Nicole said.

"Keti says he'll get bored with marriage. All men do she says."

Nicole grinned. "Wanna bet?"

The two girls exchanged glances. "Nah," pink hair muttered. "Rafe wouldn't have married you unless he wanted to. He seems happy; we're glad. For both of you," she said in afterthought, offering Nicole a conciliatory grin. "Zac says he heard his old man was a piece of work who messed with his head. Did you know that?"

"Some of it. Not much. I wouldn't bring it up if I were you. That's not Rafe's favorite subject."

"You're American, right?"

Nicole nodded.

"We helped you win your freedom from England. So you owe us."

Nicole smiled at the girl's unabashed sass. "You're paying attention in class."

"Anyone who gets good grades can go to university. Rafe pays for everything. It's a cool deal, so I'm studying hard. I'm going to be an advocate. Our neighborhood could use more legal help."

Black lipstick made a smile even whiter. "I'm going to be an accountant. Aimee and I are going to be partners. *You're* never going to have to work now that you've married Rafe."

"I plan on working," Nicole said.

"Will Rafe let you?"

Nicole winked. "He doesn't have a choice."

By the time Rafe returned, Nicole and the girls had exchanged phone numbers and had promised to stay in touch.

"Elise and I aren't jealous anymore," Aimee said with a big grin for Rafe. "Even if you didn't marry us, you married a super cool lady. Well done."

Rafe's amber-eyed gaze was amused. "I appreciate your approval." Moving up the stairs, he wiped the sweat off his face with a swipe of his t-shirted arm, pushed his damp hair back with his palms. "It's bloody hot keeping up with the kids."

"But fun," Nicole said with a smile.

He gave her a sideways look, gauging her sincerity before he smiled back. "Yup."

"Nicole says she's going to work," Aimee broke in with a smirk. "Did you know that?"

Rafe shot a glance at Nicole. "That so?"

Nicole stood up and smiled. "Ready to go?" Grabbing his top coat, she held it out to him.

Taking the coat, he tossed it over his shoulder. "Your brothers will come along later." Like the discussion they'd have later about Nicole working. "Simon and Andre are going to take the boys to the track so you don't have to sit around so long. Now, get good grades, girls," he said, with a smile. "I hear there're some nice apartments by the Sorbonne."

Aimee and Elise squealed, "Yessss!" in high-pitched unison.

Quickly rubbing his sweaty palm on his jeans, Rafe offered his hand to Nicole.

As their hands touched, a smile curved Nicole's mouth. "Lord, you're hot." Her smiled widened as they descended the stairs. "As in overheated, dude. You don't need any more adulation. It's obvious everybody here adores you. Actually, it's sweet to see."

"I like to help. I'm glad I can. And I don't need anyone's adoration. If you love me, that's it, I'm content."

"Good." Nicole winked. "Because I don't share well."

"We're a perfect match then," Rafe said, with an answering wink. "Because I don't share at all."

18

Late that afternoon, Rafe closed the front door and softly exhaled. "They're all gone."

"Finally." Nicole turned to Rafe, slid her arms around his waist, rested her chin on his chest and looked up. "Was I impolite?"

He laughed. "Perhaps a little, although they're your family, so"--

"They're used to my impatience."

His gaze was amused. "I wasn't going to say it."

"You don't mind one bit if I'm impatient, do you?"

"Nope. From now on, it's just you and me, Tiger. The rest of the world can go to hell."

"Me and the baby. Don't forget that."

As if he could; he was still dealing with the shock. "I haven't forgotten, pussycat. We're going to have to start making plans. You need an OB doctor and"--

"Tomorrow we'll do that," she interrupted, not in the mood after her mother's recent litany of instructions. "We still have company, although they're all easy. None of them tell me what to do. I love my mom dearly, but she likes to give orders."

He smiled. "Do you want me to agree or disagree?"

"Neither. Let's go see how everyone's doing."

"Some might be staying. I know Jack and Fiona will. I'm not sure about Gina and Webster. His daughter calls the shots. Basil and Claudine might hide out here for a few days with her children. Her husband's unpredictable. As for me, I have a business appointment in the morning, but I'll be ready to leave for Monte Carlo right afterward."

"Perfect. I'm looking forward to some peace and quiet."

If only. Cesare was going to be troublesome. "Sounds good. Davey's going to have the plane ready in case my meeting's over early."

They found Fiona and Jack, Gina, Webster and Zoe in the downstairs reception room. Zoe was sleeping on a red damask upholstered sofa next to her dad who had his arm around Gina. Fiona and Jack were on another sofa, their feet up on the marble coffee table separating the two couches, a soccer match with the sound turned down on a nearby TV.

"You haven't gotten rid of us yet," Jack said, smiling at his cousin.

"Not a problem. Stay as long as you like. Nicole and I are leaving for Monte Carlo in the morning, but Natalie will take care of you."

"Zoe may never leave," Webster said, with a grin. "Natalie was kind enough to keep the amusement room open and fully staffed. Basil and Claudine are still in there with her kids. They're older so have more stamina. Zoe fell asleep on the merry-go-round."

"Are you tired?" Fiona held Nicole's gaze. "It's been a couple busy days."

"I might last til nine," Nicole said, with a flicker of a smile.

"That late?" Rafe teased.

"It's crazy. I sleep all the time. Who knew?"

"You should get some books on pregnancy," Fiona suggested. "Learn some of the basics so you're not clueless."

"I have a few, but not enough. Rafe wants us to start making plans, get a doctor and stuff. I take his point," Nicole noted, "but I don't see the rush."

"Says the woman who wonders why she didn't study more as she walks into a test. Fortunately, *one* of you is sensible."

"That would be me," Rafe said, drily.

"Don't worry, Fiona, Nicole's in capable hands. Rafe's been running a global corporation since his teens." Jack's gaze flicked to his cousin. "Despite Maso, right?"

His face impassive, Rafe nodded. "More or less."

Missing the suppressed fury in Rafe's voice, Fiona smiled. "That's a relief because Nicole likes to wing it, then wonders why things go wrong."

"I'm right here," Nicole muttered. "And my ears are fully functioning."

"I'm only stating the obvious. You're irresponsible."

"I can attest to that," Rafe murmured, giving Nicole a wink.

"But you don't mind in the least." Her voice was equally soft. "You're going to love being a daddy."

"Of course." Disagreeing wasn't an option.

Conscious of the small restraint in his voice, she smiled. "Don't worry, I'm certain enough for both of us."

"What are you two whispering about? Never mind," Jack quickly added at Rafe's cool stare.

"Rafe thinks I'm baby crazy." Doubt-free, Nicole spoke without compunction. "It's an ongoing conversation with us."

"I haven't reached the same level of craziness yet," Rafe said, with well-mannered grace. "But I'm sure I will."

Jack recognized the nuanced answer as politesse, wondered how Rafe was dealing with the specter of fatherhood after a lifetime of pleasure-seeking.

Suddenly, Nicole turned, flung her arms around Rafe's waist, and without a word, lifted her face for a kiss.

Rafe's smile was luminous, the love in his eyes plain to see.

When they kissed, their audience watched with wonder, the deep affection, and tenderness spellbinding.

A hush fell, everyone sorting and readjusting their disparate memories of the friends they once knew in the face of this naked display of emotion.

After a lengthy interval, Rafe raised his head, stood utterly still for a moment, then glanced around as though getting his bearings. As his eyes came to rest on his guests, he acknowledged them with a nod. "It's been a long day. I apologize for leaving you on your own, but Natalie will see to whatever you need."

And scooping Nicole up into his arms, he walked from the room.

A small incredulous silence fell.

"They didn't even know we were here," Gina said.

Having witnessed Rafe on more than one X-rated occasion, Jack knew his cousin wasn't averse to exhibitionism, but the startling intimacy of the scene stunned him. "That wasn't the Rafe I know. He's always been audacious but"--

"Nicole wanted him to kiss her so he obliged her, that's all," Fiona said.

Jack let out a long breath. "Don't kid yourself, he's not obliging."

Fiona grinned. "It sure looked like he was."

"Consider, there are degrees of audaciousness," Webster murmured, stepping into an unwinnable discussion. "Love, included."

"A new experience for Rafe," Gina noted, picking up the diplomatic torch. "But from all appearances, he's all in. I for one wish him, her, them," she quickly amended, remembering the baby announcement, "every happiness."

"I still can't believe—they're having a baby," Jack murmured with a little shake of his head.

Fiona smiled. "Despite Nicole's very public announcement?"

A sleepy little voice suddenly said, "Mer-go-round."

Webster put his finger to his lips and the room went quiet.

But the lure of carnival rides was more powerful than fatigue and a moment later Zoe struggled into a seated position, rubbing her eyes. "Me go mer-go-round, Daddy."

"Sleep a little longer, sweetheart," Webster whispered.

Zoe screwed up her face, a flush rose on her cheeks, and as she opened her mouth, it was only a question of whether she'd cry or scream.

Gina elbowed Webster and spoke the magic words. "I'll take you."

Gulping for air, Zoe began wiggling to the edge of the sofa.

"Should we have a soda first?" Standing up and holding out her hand, Gina said, "I'll bet you're thirsty."

An energetic, bobble-head nod and Zoe grabbed Gina's hand. "Me want gape fizzy."

Gina glanced at Webster. "Coming, Daddy?"

"Wouldn't miss it for the world."

Left alone, Jack turned to Fiona, his brow creased. "This wedding has been completely disorienting. It's like watching a Russian play, people coming and going in new and not so new combinations with baffling speed and no explanation, not to mention children and babies added to the mix." His voice trailed off. At Fiona's blank look, he shrugged. "Forget it. You don't know these people as well as I."

Fiona shook her head. "Just Nicole."

He grinned. "Then you're going to have to keep me grounded."

19

"Sorry, I'm late, Vincent," Rafe said, striding into his office the next morning, half dressed in jeans and moccasins, sliding his arms into his sweater sleeves. "Nicole stirred as I was dressing. So I waited until she was sleeping soundly again."

His elderly consigliere set aside his coffee cup. "Apparently, you're keeping this from your wife."

"I'd prefer to." Shrugging his shoulders into place under the navy cashmere, Rafe pulled the sweater down.

"Prefer or insist?"

With a faint grimace, Rafe dropped into a maroon leather wing-back chair opposite Vincent. "I'm not sure. But I don't want her worrying." Leaning over the mahogany table between them, he reached for a pale yellow porcelain coffee pot, poured coffee into a matching Limoges cup and set the pot down. "A false hope if Cesare goes public." Picking up a creamer, he added an inch of cream, picked up a spoon and stirred the coffee.

"It might not be to Cesare's advantage to publicize the case."

If he were sensible." Dropping the spoon, Rafe picked up the coffee cup. "He's not. He's a media whore."

"His legal team will try to control him. They're aware of the issues in dispute."

Rafe met his attorney's gaze over the rim of his cup. "My birth certificate for one." Draining the coffee cup, he set it down.

Vincent nodded. "Maso *is* listed as your father on the document."

"Nevertheless, Cesare's feeling confident for some reason. Have you discovered anything new since Saturday?" Rafe offered a plate of croissants to Vincent. "Try one. There're the best in Paris. Seriously, the pastry chef won some culinary medal." Waiting until the attorney selected a croissant Rafe did the same, set the plate back on the tray, and tore his croissant in two. Dropping one portion on his plate, he picked up a butter knife.

"I've been told your uncle considers his witnesses impeccable."

"Bought and paid for most likely," Rafe said, spreading butter lavishly on the croissant in his hand. "But even if Cesare's unearthed some affair of my mother's, it doesn't eliminate Maso as my father." Rafe smiled faintly. "More's the pity."

A small incline of Vincent's head in recognition of all that was left unsaid. "At the moment we're investigating the witnesses' background, four of them, by the way. Two I recognize." Adjusting his glasses on the bridge of his nose with a nervous twitch, the elderly counselor squared his shoulders, as though bracing himself against something disagreeable.

Leaning back in his chair, Rafe took a bite of buttered

croissant, lifted a brow as the silence lengthened and finally swallowed. "Just say it, Vincent. My armor's thick."

"Cesare's attorneys will want a DNA test."

Rafe shrugged. "I'm not altogether sure what outcome would please me most."

"If the test eliminates Maso, your problems increase."

"Noted, but we already knew we had a fight on our hands. So, until such a time as DNA proof causes us to reconsider, let's assume my uncle is trying to shake me down." Rafe gazed off into the distance for a moment before speaking in a soft, considering tone. "I was thinking I might detour to Geneva on the way to Monte Carlo. You remember Grandpere's housekeeper, Gerda. She always gave me a new book and sweets when I visited." He smiled. "The books were from Grandpere, the sweets from her. Something about those books has been flickering in and out of my consciousness. It's probably nothing, but I thought I'd walk through Grandpere's flat, perhaps jog my memory."

"Gerda's dead. You knew that, right?"

Rafe nodded. "Grandpere's valet too. Did you ever think it strange--both of them dying only a month after Grandpere?"

"Not particularly. Nils's car went out of control on an icy road, and hit another car. Both drivers were killed."

"You went to the funerals?"

"Not Gerda's. We didn't hear about in time."

"I understand you and Maso argued about a legacy Grandpere had left her."

"Maso wanted it released to him."

"How much?"

"A million five."

Rafe's brows rose. "Enough for a bet or two in the days

before Maso started siphoning off larger sums from the company. Did you give it to him?"

"Of course not. It wasn't his. It went to Gerda's sister."

"What about Grandpere's death? Why wasn't there an autopsy?"

"Neither Maso nor Cesare would allow it. I had no authority. If not for your grandfather's explicit clause in the company bylaws, I would have been sacked. Your grandfather wanted me to stay on."

Rafe smiled. "To guide me."

"I wish I could have protected you from Maso as well, but that was beyond my limited powers."

"It doesn't matter, what's past is past," Rafe said, shutting the door on his spectacularly messed up childhood with practiced ease. "Maso's in hell where he belongs and with luck, we'll send Cesare to the Devil as well. There's no bloody way he's getting my company." Rafe smiled to mitigate his rough growl. "With your help, of course."

"My pleasure," Vincent said. "Cesare was well paid for his inheritance, more than he deserved. But your grandfather wanted him out of the business. Maso may have been a sociopath, but Cesare was stupid. He would have lost the company in a matter of months."

"So if necessary, we get rid of Cesare."

"Legally," Vincent quickly said.

"Of course, Vincent," Rafe soothed. "But if the courts prove difficult, we'll have to find another way. I've already talked to Carlos. He's doing some checking for me. Don't worry, nothing untoward. But after so many years, something prompted Cesare to adopt this course. I'm curious."

"A shame your grandfather didn't leave a will," Vincent murmured. "It was common knowledge he despised both his sons. He doted on you, but you were so young. Still...

considering your grandfather's assets, it was highly unusual for him to die intestate. I've wondered at times whether he did so to protect you. Had he named you his heir…"

"Maso would have killed me. It's not as though he didn't damn near do it anyway." Rafe lifted his chin a fraction. "I've never asked. Surely Maso and Cesare *searched* for a will."

Vincent snorted. "They tore apart your grandfather's office and living quarters. It took weeks to fully restore the damage."

Leaning back in his chair, Rafe rested his head against the maroon leather and gazed at the elderly man immaculately attired in his usual banker's grey bespoke suit. "Regardless the ambiguities, Contini Pharma is mine. Will or not, birth certificate or not." He smiled tightly. "I'll personally see Cesare in his grave before I relinquish control to him." At Vincent's sudden alarm, Rafe raised his hands. "Relax, Vincent, you're absolved. I'll do the grave digging. You take care of the legalities. Two separate endeavors." His gaze shifted as the door opened and a smile lit his eyes. "I thought you were sleeping, sweetheart. Come, sit with me. I have fresh croissants and hot chocolate for you. Vincent was just leaving."

Since further discussion was curtailed, Vincent took his dismissal with good grace. "Rafe tells me you're off for Monte Carlo soon," he said, rising as Nicole approached. "It's a perfect locale to await the birth of your child."

"Rafe is being sweet to me." She smiled at her husband who'd risen and taken her hand. "He claims he doesn't have to be in Geneva much."

"As little as possible." Rafe pulled her close. "Vincent is more than happy to step in, aren't you?"

"Of course." Although the men had agreed to stay in

touch by internet and phone. A hands-on CEO, Rafe's involvement was critical.

"Thank you again, Vincent. Give our regards to Katya. Now, then, sweetheart," Rafe murmured, as Vincent walked away, "look at the pink marshmallows the chef made for your hot chocolate."

Nicole grinned. "I'm not a five-year-old who needs coddling."

"I like to coddle you. Humor me."

"Okay."

He laughed. "We're going to get along just fine." Sitting, he drew her down on his lap. "Want me to feed you?"

"Ummm...you're making me all tingly."

"Eat first. You have to stay healthy. Afterward," he said, touching her cheek with his thumb, "I'll deal with your tingles."

He was so good to her. Implausibly grateful, filled with happiness, she whispered, "Do you know how much I love you?"

"Tell me." Clear-eyed he gazed at her.

"I love you with reckless abandon, and uncontained passion, forever and ever and ever." A little tilt of her brows. "Too obsessive?"

"Not at all." Long denied love, he had a newfound respect for miracles. "Forever and ever," he whispered, dropping his head to kiss her. "Me too."

20

A few hours later, a black S-Class Mercedes rolled up to the door of Rafe's Geneva home and came to a stop. Rafe turned to Nicole. "I won't be gone long. Make yourself at home. If you'd like to go shopping, once Simon drops me off, he'll come back and drive you. He knows all the best shops."

Nicole smiled. "Why does that sound as though you've made that offer a million times before? Did they all really like to shop?"

"I thought women liked to shop," he said, rather than yes.

"Your wife doesn't. Why can't I come with you?"

He hadn't actually said she couldn't come to his grandfather's apartment, but if she did, it would require some explanation. "Come if you like. I just thought you'd be bored."

"I'll read the book I have on my phone."

There was no point in arguing. Sliding the privacy glass aside, he leaned forward. "Change of plans, Simon. Take us to my grandfather's flat."

"Sure thing." Swinging the wheel to the left, Simon was

smiling as he drove across the cobblestone forecourt of the seventeenth century mansion and passed through the electric gates. He was five hundred euros richer. Carlos had bet that Rafe would dissuade Nicole from accompanying him to his grandfather's. Cha-ching. The times they were a'changing.

Rafe's grandfather's flat was in Old Town. The medieval structure had been converted into a three story flat, with reception rooms on the ground floor and living quarters above.

Explaining he'd come to find a book his grandfather had given him, Rafe saw that Nicole was comfortable in the first floor sitting room, before taking the stairs to the library on the top floor. Coming to a halt before the towering, gothic door, decoratively framed in inlaid ivory and precious woods, he felt a rush of memories. His visits to his grandfather's home had always been an island of joy in his fractious life.

How much time had passed since he'd last come here? Quickly calculating the years, he exhaled a small sigh, a distant look in his eyes at the step back in time. Then, reminded that Nicole was waiting, he grasped the brass chimera doorknob, pushed open the door, and stood transfixed for an instant before his smile broke. The birds and butterflies on the frescoed ceiling of the vaulted room were as magical as he remembered.

The sheer beauty of the brightly painted, realistically depicted birds and butterflies had always amazed him. Much as his grandfather's boundless affection had colored his world with wonder. His visits to this room had always been his private measure of happiness: a toy chest always stocked with new toys; Gerda's cookies and sweets dispensed with a lavish hand; his grandfather's undivided attention. In fact, due in large part to that special attention, he could read by age three.

The day when Maso, himself, had brought him to his grandfather's house he'd known something was wrong. The enmity between his grandfather and father was no secret.

Dragging him into the bedroom, Maso had shoved him toward the bed and said with vicious satisfaction, "Your grandfather's dying."

"Not yet," Grandpere had snapped, struggling to sit up. Resting against his pillows a moment later, breathing hard, he'd scanned the retinue assembled at his deathbed with a prickly gaze. "Everyone out," he'd ordered in a soft hiss. "Except Gerda and Rafail."

With scowls from Maso and Cesare, a murmur of acquiescence from the army of solicitors and an understanding nod from Vincent, the entourage had filed from the room. Only then had his grandfather's familiar smile appeared. "Finally--peace and quiet." He'd patted the bed. "Come sit by me, Rafail. I want to tell you a story."

He'd been five years, four months old.

What little he recalled of the story was due to his grandfather's picturesque descriptions of pirates, black-sailed ships and hidden treasure. Had Cesare been less greedy, even those meager memories would never have surfaced. But his uncle's venal grasp had served to nudge open the door to the past and his grandfather's voice had once again rung in his ears. *Remember this story, my dear boy and remember where you liked to play under my desk. Gerda will help you remember your favorite book, and when the time comes, she'll be here to help you.* But she hadn't been; she'd died soon after, and the book's title had faded away.

Until, driven by a whisper of memory, he'd come here today.

Approaching the shelves that had once held his childhood books, he was mildly surprised to see them all in situ, more surprised at the sheer number of books in the pirate genre. With a twitch of a smile, he wondered who'd most fancied that story line, he or his grandfather?

He'd no more than pulled up a chair and opened the first book, when his phone rang. Glancing at the screen, he felt a small unease at the sight of Mireille's name. Henny's wife rarely called. Correction--she'd called him only once when Henny had gone missing for two days.

The first words he heard when he picked up were soft with anguish. "Sit down. I have bad news."

He was already sitting, but his heart lurched. "Henny's hurt."

"He just died."

It felt as though the earth had stopped; he couldn't breathe. Panic whirling through his brain, he forced air into his lungs. "I'll be back in Paris in an hour." Surging to his feet, he swiftly moved toward the door.

"No, don't. I'm taking Henny to Monte Carlo."

Rafe shivered, a sudden chill running up his spine, reminded of Henny's morbid insistence that his final resting place be on the bluffs overlooking Rafe's private beach. Henny's deep core of melancholy had been manifest that long ago night in a way rarely seen, his habitual exuberance replaced by a fucked up sense of loneliness. The hairs on the back of Rafe's neck went up. "Tell me you were with Henny."

"I'd just left for a run."

Rafe steadied himself on the door jamb, needing something solid to hold on to, light-headed at the thought of Henny dying alone.

"I was only a block away," Mireille said, each word raw

with pain, "when Henny texted me, *I feel faint. I feel like I'm dying. Love you.* I screamed, started to run and called 112." Her voice was a taut with restraint, each word a quiet measure of her grief. "I found Henny on the floor of his study. He wasn't breathing so I began mouth to mouth. The emergency crews arrived shortly after and worked over him for a long time. I don't remember anything except thinking, this can't be real, this can't be happening. He was such a vital force, so big and strong, so filled with life and love." Breaking into sobs, she whispered, "I don't know if I can live without him."

"None of us can," Rafe murmured, numb with shock, struggling to withstand the gut-wrenching sorrow. *I'll never see Henny again, never talk to him, never laugh with him, never share the good times and bad like we always did--never, never, never...the word terrible in its utter finality, suffocating.* Mireille's scream abruptly curtailed the desolation of his thoughts. "What's going on?"

"They want to take Henny away! No, no, don't *touch* him!" Mireille shrieked, her voice sharp with hysteria.

"I'll take care of this," Rafe said, tight-lipped and curt. "Put someone on the phone."

A moment later, a man spoke with a touch of impatience. "This is strictly routine. There's no need to go into a frenzy or"--

"Shut up and listen."

In rapid fire Parisian French, Rafe pointed out that he personally knew every official of note in France including the President, the Mayor and the Prefect of Police, and if they *dared* move Henny, if they so much as *touched* him, he'd see that they were all fired. And if they were stupid enough to disregard his warning, he added, his voice ice cold, he'd see that none of them ever worked *anywhere* again. "It's not a fucking idle threat. I'll hunt you down. Now put Mireille back on the phone, and get the hell out!"

"They're leaving." Mireille's voice was shaky with relief. "Thanks."

Slamming the door on his temper, he switched fast to a neutral tone. "Henny would do the same for me. Now, I'm going to call Carlos. He'll be right over and see that you're flown to Monte Carlo. Are you okay until he gets there?"

"Yes." There was a new firmness in her voice. "I'm sitting beside Henny, holding his hand. We'll wait together."

The heartrending image knocked the wind out of him. It took him a second to catch his breath and another second to steady his voice. "Kiss Henny for me. Tell him I love him. I'll meet you at my house in a couple hours."

He called Carlos next and gave him the awful news. "I don't know exactly what happened," he added. "Mireille's not in any shape to ask. I told her you'd be right over. If you'll see that she and Henny are flown to Monte Carlo, I'll meet you there. Let Basil know. He may want to fly down with you. Make sure Aleix comes along. We'll need his expertise." Ending the call, he slid to the floor, propped his elbows on his drawn up knees, put his head in his hands, and gave way to despair.

Nicole found him soon after, his harsh, peremptory commands ordering out the emergency crew, echoing down the stairs.

"Henny's dead." He didn't look up, his jaw tight.

She went pale, shocked, and saddened, knowing how much Henny had meant to Rafe. She also knew she could offer little comfort when he was in such pain. "I'm so sorry," she said, simply. "What can I do to help?"

His head came up slowly, his amber gaze blank for a second, as if needing to register the identity of the speaker as well as the words. A flicker of recognition, a breath. "There's no help, but thanks."

"If you want to talk about"—

"I can't." He held out his hand to mitigate his brusque reply and as her fingers laced through his, he squeezed them gently in unspoken apology. "We're going to meet Henny and Mireille in Monte Carlo. I have to call a few people before we leave. So…" With a heavy sigh, he freed his hand, and came to his feet. "Forgive me. My capacity for speech is limited right now."

"I understand." Although, she couldn't hope to understand, the bond between the men so intense it was impossible to fathom Rafe's sense of loss.

She waited in silence while Rafe called Simon, relayed the grim news, adding at the last, "I want to reach Monte Carlo first so I can welcome Mireille and Henny. Give Davey a head's up at the airport. We'll be down in five minutes."

Aware he'd be testing a friendship, his finger hovered over the next name on his contact list, before he softly touched it. "Henny just died," he said when Vincent answered, an undercurrent of agony resonating in his voice. "Carlos has the details. I'm going off line. I need you to take care of things."

"Yes, of course," Vincent replied. "Please accept my condolences for your loss."

"I may not"—Rafe faltered, overcome by anguish—"be in touch for a while."

"Take as much time as you need."

"This is so bloody fucked up, Vincent," Rafe muttered, his voice suddenly shot through with anger, the thought of, *Never, never, never ever again,* exploding like shrapnel in his brain. "I should have been there for him!"

"You always were, as he was for you," Vincent gently

said. "Not that it helps, my boy, but Henny knew you loved him."

"Not enough. I failed him when he needed me. I fucking failed him. Jesus..." His voice dropped to a whisper, a flood of guilt washing over him. "I'm not bitching at you, Vincent. I'm just feeling—hell, I don't know what I'm feeling. Except I want him back..." His voice failed completely for a second. "Look, I'll talk to you later." Sliding his phone in his pocket, Rafe turned to Nicole and managed a tight smile. "I'm going to apologize in advance for my lousy mood that's not likely to go away any time soon. Try to ignore me if you can." He held out his hand. "If you can't"—he sighed—"I don't know what to say."

"Don't worry about me." Nicole took his hand. "Do what you have to do." She didn't say, *Your best friend is dead, it's a nightmare,* because she didn't think she could utter the words without weeping.

"I'll probably shut down. It's my default setting. Sorry, again." He lifted his chin. "Ready?"

He was silent on the drive to the airport, memories of Henny tumbling through his mind, twisting his heart, dragging him into the deepest circle of hell. On reaching the plane, he sat up front with Davey, coming back a few minutes before they landed in Nice to see that Nicole buckled up. He made an effort to chat on the drive to Monte Carlo, the strain so obvious, she finally said, "Don't feel you have to talk, okay?"

He softly exhaled. "Thanks. I'm numb."

When they arrived at the carriage house, he escorted her upstairs, stood in the doorway to the bedroom as she dropped onto the bed and held up his phone. "I'll be in my study. I have arrangements to make before Mireille and Henny get here. Want me to give you warning before they arrive? Or I'm fine doing this myself. I can't expect you to feel"—

"Please come get me. I want to be there with you."

It took him a fraction of a second to reply, strangely touched by the thought that he had a wife who cared, who loved him. He still found himself startled at times that he was loved, the sensation doubly poignant in these grievous circumstances. If only Henny were beside him, he wistfully thought. Henny, too, had been amazed by the miracle of love. Mireille was his world, he'd always said. And now…

It hit him hard. For the first time, he couldn't fix something, when he'd always been able to fix *anything*: realign the world to his liking, move proverbial mountains, overcome daunting challenges, directly, indirectly, by sheer force of will. And now, no matter what he did, he couldn't have what he wanted. He couldn't bring Henny back.

Paralyzed with hopelessness, he swallowed back tears.

But survival mechanisms honed to a fine point in childhood intervened, dispersing the wreckage of memory, reminding him he had a great deal to do. "Carlos texted, the plane just landed," he said, crushing back the haunting regret. "They should be here in forty minutes. I'll come wake you if you fall asleep."

"Have you eaten? You should if you haven't." At his look of distress, she quickly apologized; Henny had always done the cooking when they were together. "That was stupid. Forgive me."

He shrugged, pointed to the hallway. "I'm going to give the staff some instructions. Rest if you can."

Cautious after her faux paus, she knew better than to suggest he rest as well. He was stressed, in pain and grieving. This wasn't the time for platitudes.

21

Standing on the balcony with a view of the drive, Rafe began making calls. First, he rang his housekeeper, Josephine, who ran his property and had known Henny from his youth. After extending her sympathy on the heartbreaking loss she agreed that Mireille's wishes would be their first priority. "The entire staff would like to offer their condolences as well. Henny was loved by all. They'll help with whatever you need."

"Thank them for me," Rafe said. "I'm having trouble finding words. Saying goodbye to Henny is the hardest thing I've ever had to do. I keep hoping I'll wake up and..."

"Find out it's not true. I know."

"Unfortunately"—an in and out breath to hold it together—"everyone will be here soon. Since I'm operating in a fog at times, if I forget something, remind me or take care of it yourself, okay?"

"You can leave the guests in my care, the burial site too, if you wish. Henny showed it to me once at sunrise. We were the only ones up or in his case, still up after one of your parties. He chose a beautiful spot bordered with jasmine; the view is spectacular."

"Spectacular…sounds like Henny." A quiet tenderness stirred in Rafe's voice. "I'm glad he showed it to you. Henny always said this was the only home he'd ever known." Rafe blew out a breath. "None of us gave his comments much thought. We were young, every day an adventure. Jesus fucking Christ…" he whispered, feeling a nuclear level pain.

As the silence lengthened, Josephine cleared her throat.

"Sorry." He sighed. "What's next?"

"The chef needs some directions. They can be minimal. If he has further questions, he can ask me."

"I'll call him."

"Then, if you'll see to Mireille, I can do most everything else."

"I'll take care of Mireille. Call me if you have questions."

Rafe's discussion with the chef was brief. The fact that Henny had always managed the kitchen when they were all in residence taxed Rafe's composure. He offered Josephine as his surrogate for any future matters and cutting the call short, turned to the next item on his agenda.

Simon had given him the number of the funeral director who'd handled his grandfather's burial last summer. Moments later, Rafe explained the situation to Monsieur Ribault. "My friend, Henny, and his widow are currently being flown in from Paris. Once they arrive I'd like you to deal with the burial. La Comtesse is to have whatever she desires. No expense is to be spared. She's to be accommodated in every way. Can you do that?"

"Yes, of course."

"Good. You have my address?"

"I do." Rafe Contini's house parties were legendary as

well as profitable to local businesses. A shame about his young friend.

"Then, we'll see you shortly."

Rafe's last call was to a Monte Carlo attorney he kept on retainer. Generally, LeBlanc was called if some incident during a house party threatened to turn into a scandal. Today, the issue was starkly different. Rafe's explanation was abbreviated and quickly concluded. "Since le Comte will be interned on my estate, I'd like you to take care of any necessary burial documents. If you could come up to the house, say in the next half hour, I'd be grateful."

Regardless Rafe's wishes were delivered with a polite diffidence, it was clear he didn't expect a refusal. "Yes, of course," LeBlanc said. "I'll be there in twenty minutes."

"Thank you. The gates will be open." Surveying the small convoy of vehicles currently driving through those gates, Rafe quickly pocketed his phone, walked back to the bedroom, came to a sudden stop and briefly debated waking Nicole before turning to leave.

"I'm up," she said, her voice soft with sleep. "Wait."

He swung back. "It's going to be a while before everyone settles in. Why don't you come over later?"

"Nah, I'll go with you." Sitting up, she swung her legs over the side of the bed, slid to the floor and steadied herself with her palms on the bed.

He smiled faintly. She was swaying slightly, only borderline awake, her eyes half-closed. "You sure?"

She nodded. "Give me a minute to put on my shoes."

"You don't need shoes. I'll carry you."

"That would be lovely, but no." She gave her head a shake, opened her eyes fully, quickly stepped into her red Vans and held out her hand. "There. I'm ready."

On their walk along the garden path between the

carriage house and main house, memories of the night they first met were prominent in their thoughts, but neither spoke, uncomfortable bringing up sweet memories in the midst of such sadness.

MANY HOURS LATER, after all the arrangements had been made with the funeral director, priest, attorney, florist, the chef and Josephine, after Henny had been returned to the house and was laid out in simple cherry wood casket in one of the reception rooms with a view of the sea, after Mireille had fallen asleep and Rafe returned downstairs, he glanced at the tall case clock in the corner.

Three o'clock.

"I left a nurse with Mireille," Rafe explained. "If she wakes, the nurse will tell her where we are."

Basil, Carlos, Aleix, Simon, and Nicole were on sofas disposed around the candlelit bier, keeping vigil through the night. Conversation had been desultory. There was nothing to say that hadn't already been said, no comfort to give that wouldn't sound brittle, no words sufficient to ease the pain.

Walking up to the casket, Rafe leaned over and lightly touched his friend's cheek, slid his fingers over the caption on the T-shirt Mireille had chosen. *Live Life to the Fullest* was authentic Henny. Regardless he'd had a wardrobe of bespoke suits, he'd always preferred shorts and T-shirts. He looked peaceful. His eyes were shut, his hands crossed on his chest; he could have been sleeping.

Giving Henny a fist bump, Rafe stood quietly for a moment more, wanting what he couldn't have, asking for it anyway, wanting his best friend to wake up. Heartsick at the unpalatable truth, feeling as though the world was broken beyond repair, Rafe felt an urge to scream at the gross injustice. Suppressing the impulse, he turned away, and moved toward the sofa where Nicole rested. "You changed into pajamas," he murmured. "Good idea."

His attempt at a smile was woeful. "I'm glad Mireille went to sleep," Nicole replied with the same careful blandness, shifting to make room for him on the sofa.

"Aleix finally gave her a sedative. She was completely worn out." Sitting, he gathered Nicole in his arms, settled her on his lap, leaned back against the arm rest, stretched out his legs and haunted by a sudden sense of emptiness, took a deep breath. "I've never felt this kind of pain." A muscle flicked in his jaw, his voice drained and raw. "Henny was my brother. I should have been there for him."

There was nothing to say, no help for his anguish. Stretching up, she lightly kissed his cheek, put her hand on his shoulder.

He covered her hand with his, the warmth of his palm light, enveloping, his whisper when he spoke a moment later almost inaudible. "I don't know if I can do this."

22

Materials had been requisitioned at considerable expense from a project currently underway in Monte Carlo, and scores of masons, along with an enormous crew of landscapers and gardeners had worked through the night to bring Henny's chosen site to completion in time.

A scant half hour after the last workman departed, Henny's casket was carried from a sky blue Range Rover by his friends and brought to the newly constructed mausoleum shimmering white under the noonday sun. The shrine, a miniature rendition of the Pantheon, honored a man of principled humanity, heart and, true to Roman ideals, an imperial sense of worth.

The interior was cool and shadowed, the jasmine-covered casket set on a marble base, the sweet scent perfuming the chamber. The group of mourners was small by choice. Long estranged from his family, only Henny's close friends and companions had been invited, including the local curate who'd known Henny for years. The priest cited personal remembrances, many of his stories making people smile. He spoke of Henny's buoyant spirit and his incurable zest for life, avoided tenets of piety and faith, and offered instead the grace and benevolence of God in words meant to comfort. Mireille, supported by her sister and brother who'd been flown in from Brussels during the night, quietly sobbed through the service, tears streaming down her face. And at the conclusion of his homily, the curate's protective prayer for Henny's soul brought tears to everyone's eyes.

A celebrated Romany folk singer and Henny's lover from long ago, had been tracked down late last night in Barcelona. She'd walked off the stage, stepped into the car Carlos had waiting outside and arrived by charter plane at dawn. Her eyes wet with tears, she sang two of Henny's favorite songs a cappella, her voice soft and pure in the candle light, the poignant lyrics rich with nostalgia and the ache of regret.

As her voice gently faded away, the curate offered any in attendance an opportunity to speak of their friendship with Henny. For those who responded, the common theme was Henny's unabashed passion for life. But most of the mourners were mute, too bereft to give voice to their feelings.

As the service came to an end, Mireille spoke for the first time, her voice choked. "I loved him with all my heart. I always will." Then, gathering her composure as she did in court when facing a difficult adversary, she straightened her shoulders, brushed her dark hair from her forehead and with cool clarity, added, "Thank you for coming to say goodbye to Henny on such short notice. He loved you all. He was that kind of man. Generous with his love."

Stillness fell, everyone dwelling on their own memories of Henny: his larger than life personality; his humor and good cheer; his unpretentious brilliance; his charisma that could light up a room.

"Amen and Godspeed," someone softly interjected into the silence. The affirmation quietly echoed through the chamber as each in turn offered their adieus to their friend, the gypsy songstress transforming the touching benediction into melodious plainsong, bringing the funeral to a close with a grace note of tenderness.

As the mourners dispersed they said their last, tearful goodbyes at the coffin, before walking out into the sunshine. Carlos, stationed at the door, directed everyone to a gazebo in the newly landscaped garden, remarking as they passed by, "You'll recognize Henny's menu at the funeral tea, as well as his favorite refreshments."

That Henny loved food was a given. Whether he was cooking or dining, everyone had enjoyed his amiable company in the kitchen, at a meal or both.

With Nicole at his side, and a drink in his hand, Rafe circulated among the guests, greeting everyone, stopping to chat, offering tea or sherry or something stronger, pointing out the favorite items on Henny's tea time menu as well as his taste for obscure liquors.

With melancholy a living presence, conversation languished at first, but after a drink or two, spirits eased, and the assembled company shared remembrances of Henny with tears and laughter, sympathy and affection. Even Mireille, buoyed by the fellowship and warmth of Henny's friends, had an occasional smile at some tale of her husband's humor and wit. Having married Henny after a whirlwind courtship two years ago, she wasn't well acquainted with everyone, but all Henny's friends knew she was his true love, and for that she was dear.

When the sunny afternoon gave way to sunset, the

company retired to the house. A dinner buffet with Henny's touch informing that menu as well, awaited them, with more wine and spirits to blunt the sadness. People lingered through evening, reluctant to make their last goodbyes so it was after nine when those not staying at the house began to depart. In the course of the next hour, the house guests, too, slowly drifted off to their suites.

Rafe and Carlos, standing near the drinks table in the main salon, checked their watches as the door closed on the last guest. Ten fifteen.

"And so it ends," Rafe murmured. "Thank you. You and Josephine did Henny proud." The two had managed the funeral activities that day.

Carlos sighed. "Henny deserved it--and more."

"No shit. Henny deserves to be alive. Damn it all." Rafe stopped to breathe, to push back tears. "This is so bloody fucked up." His gaze lifted, searching the room.

"Go," Carlos said, recognizing Rafe's unconscious need. "I saw Nicole walk out with the curate. I expect she's seeing him to the door. Josephine and I will finish up."

"I should thank Josephine."

"I'll relay your thanks. You're dead on your feet. Get some rest."

After a last look around, Rafe nodded. "Tell Josephine I'm in her debt. I owe you both."

"We'll collect later. Get the fuck out."

Nicole took note of Rafe's exhaustion when he walked out into the foyer and held out her hand. "The curate offers you his blessings. He says thanks to your extravagant donation, his clinic can serve the immigrant community for years to come."

It's only fucking money. "I'm glad," Rafe said, instead because she was trying to be pleasant and mentioning that very little mattered with Henny dead would be a dickhead comment. "Carlos says we're excused." He took her hand and managed a smile. "Feel like some rest?"

"My answer will be yes for the next eight months."

His shock was visible.

"Then I won't bore you with the question again," he said, recovering smoothly.

She knew better than to take issue with his forgetfulness after the events of the last two days. Nor would she have in any event. The baby had been her choice. She was grateful he hadn't objected.

"Are you as tired of talking as I?" he asked, drawing her toward a side door.

"I am. But remembering Henny was good for everyone. Sorry," she whispered, his distress instantly apparent.

"It's okay." His nostrils flared as he shoved open the garden door. "I'll be fine in a couple hundred years." He grimaced. "Maybe."

The evening was still warm, the new moon a sliver of gold, the ebony sky sparkling with stars. She bit back a comment about the beauty of the night. It didn't seem fair that the world still dazzled brightly, that life went on, that no notice was given to the crushing pain of Henny's passing.

"Don't say it," Rafe murmured, as if in sync with her thoughts.

"I love you," she said, instead.

"Thank you," he whispered, this man who needed solace when he'd never needed anyone before.

SHORTLY AFTER MIDNIGHT, Nicole came awake, realized she was alone, and left the bed. Relatively sure where Rafe had gone, she pulled on a robe, exited the carriage house, and followed the new flagstone path to the grave site.

Rafe and Basil looked up when she entered the mausoleum.

"Come sit," Rafe said with a smile. "We're talking old times and sharing a bottle with Henny." He glanced at Basil, sitting beside him on one of the marble benches lining the interior walls, a half empty bottle of Macallan 32 between them. "Basil was reminding us how we saved his ass. You were ten, right, when we showed up at that Lausanne boarding school?"

Basil rolled his eyes. "I wouldn't have seen eleven if you and Henny hadn't appeared under that window and caught me."

"Gypsy fate, man. Sure as shit." Taking Nicole's hand, he pulled her down on his lap, gave her a kiss on the cheek and glanced at Basil. "Tell Nicole how Henny found us our room that first day."

Basil grinned. "Found?" He pointed at the casket. "Henny said, 'What's the best room in this dump?' and when I told him, he winked at Rafe. 'Sounds like ours. You up for it?' I was ten, they were eleven, but fucking big for their age."

"Size never hurts," Rafe said, neatly. "Long story, short, we took the turret room from the pussies who thought it was theirs. Henny and I had been a tag team for two years by then and were pretty fucking confident we could take on anyone."

Basil tapped Rafe's arm. "Tell her why you were a tag team."

"I was nine, it was my first day of boarding school in Zurich and some douche bag upper classman was showing me around the newbies' house, giving me shit, trying to scare me. I could have told him he was years too late, but it wasn't worth the effort. Anyway, we rounded the corner of the second floor hallway and there was Henny fighting off three older kids. That was damned unfair, I thought, turned around, kicked my asshole guide in the nuts, and when he dropped to his knees, puking, I ran to give Henny a hand. With the odds substantially improved, Henny and I floored two of the bullies, and the other candy-ass ran away. Henny gave me that crooked grin of his, said, 'Call me Henny. I don't like my real name. And thanks.'"

"No problem, I told him. My old man is evil. This was easy. He stuck out his hand, I took it and that's how we became friends." Rafe took a deep breath, blinked against the threatening tears. "Life sucks," he muttered. "Damned if it doesn't."

"You need a drink," Basil said, shoving the bottle toward Rafe.

"Good idea." Rafe took it, drank deeply, handed it back to Basil and frowned. "I hope there's more."

Basil pointed at a case in the corner. "Drink up."

Nicole wasn't sure they even noticed her during the remainder of the night, both men wrapped in grief, their thoughts solely on their friend, their conversation a disjointed marathon of Henny stories: snapshot images, favorite songs, people he abhorred, those he tolerated, those he loved. By the time the sun rose, she'd heard a great deal of the long friendship between the men and while she could never hope to feel their pain, she understood a modicum of their love for Henny. They'd been The Three Musketeers in their youth, standing together against adversity. In adulthood, they'd continued that incredible closeness, their bond sustaining them in good times and bad. The good times were more frequent as they began to control their lives, the occasional bad times tempered by their deep friendship.

What they had had was rare.

Making it that much harder to lose.

As morning broke, the men rose, made some esoteric sign over Henny's casket, and promised to return. Both men were stone sober despite a night of drinking, despair a potent deterrent to intoxication.

Going their separate ways at the outdoor infinity pool, Rafe and Nicole returned to the carriage house to shower and dress while Basil retired to the main house.

23

An hour later, Rafe and Nicole entered the breakfast room and found Basil alone at the dining table, drinking his breakfast.

"Last one," he said to Rafe's raised brows. "Claudine just arrived. She brought her children to her mother's in Normandy and couldn't get away until last night. She'll be down in a minute."

Pulling out a chair for Nicole, Rafe signaled the staff lined up near a baize covered door with the faintest of nods. "What do you want to eat?"

Before she was fully seated, a young man had materialized at the table.

"Hot chocolate, right?" Rafe said, taking a seat beside her. At her nod, he added, "With lots of marshmallows, Luca. And bring us a menu."

Claudine arrived a few minutes later, and the other guests, finding sleep equally elusive, arrived in twos and threes a short time later. Rafe rose to greet everyone as they entered the room, and over breakfast, directed the conversation in such a way that Mireille and her siblings were comfortable among Henny's old friends. Rafe mentioned that before he'd first met her, Henny had warned him to be extra nice, the precaution so out of character for Henny that he'd immediately known Mireille was *the one.*

"I felt the same way." A small delight echoed in her words. "We married the next week."

"Despite the blizzard," Rafe noted, wryly. "With flights to St. Moritz grounded, I damned near died on those mountain roads."

Mireille's smile was one of gentle remembrance. "Henny never liked to wait."

"Amen to that," Basil agreed. "When Henny wanted something, it was impossible to stop him."

"Like his sudden impulse to climb the Eiger," Ganz interjected. "He was determined to drag us all with him, despite the fact we were fifteen and totally inexperienced. Thankfully, he met Madame Bardet about the same time and cooking became his passion. She saved our lives, damned if she didn't."

"In honor of our youthful stupidity, I've hung my Camp ice axe and crampons on my office wall." Rafe's brows lifted. "A souvenir to foolhardy risk."

"In contrast to calculated risk." As bodyguard, mentor, and factotum to Rafe since childhood, Carlos had dispensed that lesson well.

Rafe dipped his head. "Sometimes both."

"Henny constantly walked that line," Mireille pointed out. "He lived and breathed freedom from restraint, yet viewed the world with hope."

"A measure of his confidence," Ganz remarked.

"And his firm belief that everything was fixable. Or if not," Rafe added with a flicker of a smile, "easily resolved by force." With Mireille watching him, he amended, "Rarely used, of course."

"Such politesse." Mireille gaze was amused. "I don't know if Henny would approve."

Rafe smiled. "If you asked him to he would. He adored you."

"Yes, he was quite wonderful." Readjusting the soft tenor of her voice to a normal tone, she turned to the table at large. "Do tell me when you all met my Henny."

The conversation turned into a free-wheeling narrative of Henny's initial impact on everyone's lives, the personal stories like a litany of diary entries of time, place and Henny's singular character.

As breakfast came to a close, Carlos offered to help arrange departure flights. Mireille mentioned she planned on staying a few days; her siblings were hoping to leave that evening; Basil's schedule was subject to Claudine's and others had yet to decide.

In the course of the departure discussion, Josephine came up to Rafe and whispered in his ear.

He flinched, nodded once, his attention on the discussion otherwise undeterred.

Then, someone asked about the status of Henny's new restaurant set to open in Paris, and Mireille explained it would go on as scheduled. "Henny spent the greater part of last year planning for it, signing off on everything down to the last decorative detail. You must all come on opening night and raise a glass to Henny. *Toujours* will be his living memorial."

A short time later, the door closed on the last guest and Rafe and Nicole were alone at the table.

"Did you get enough to eat?" Rafe asked, flicking a finger at the several plates of half-finished food in front of Nicole.

She rolled her eyes. "At least for the next ten minutes. I'm constantly hungry. It's alarming."

"Nonsense, I expect it's natural. Do you want me to summon one of the staff for something more?"

"Yes, but don't." She grinned. "Even I know chocolate cake isn't a wise choice for breakfast."

"Have it for lunch." Glancing at his watch, he pushed back his chair, and came to his feet. "If you'll excuse me for a minute, I have a phone call to make. Or if you'd rather go back to the carriage house, I'll call from there."

"The carriage house if you don't mind. I'm tired as usual."

"No problem." Holding out his hand, he helped her rise. "Take a nap. You were up most of the night."

"So were you."

"I'm used to it, you're not. And," he added with a wink, "I'm not pregnant."

Ten minutes later, Rafe tucked Nicole into bed, kissed her and stood up. "Now, sleep as long as you wish. Everyone's on their own today, doing whatever they want to do. I expect the mausoleum will be busy and that's good. I'll be in my study."

Walking to the door, he turned and blew her a kiss.

But he didn't go to his study. She heard him run down the stairs, heard the front door close, suddenly recalled his flinch when Josephine had whispered to him. Not that he'd appeared disturbed in any way, having contributed to the conversation with his usual urbanity until breakfast was over. Had she been mistaken? She could ask. Although, he wasn't in the habit of explaining himself.

Give him time. They'd only been married a few days. She had to learn to adapt as well. Cooperation and understanding were the hallmarks of a good marriage. Right?

. . .

Wʜɪʟᴇ Nɪᴄᴏʟᴇ ᴡᴀs ᴛᴀʟᴋɪɴɢ herself into an obliging frame of mind, Rafe crossed the gravel drive and stepped onto a broad swath of perfectly manicured lawn. Leaving a path of faint footprints in the damp grass, Rafe entered a pergola festooned in crimson ivy, and standing under pale, dappled sunlight, called Vincent.

Vincent answered on the first ring, a touch of alarm in his voice. "I apologize for calling, but I need your authorization to deal with an explosive situation."

"No need to apologize. It must be Caesar."

"Indeed. He arrived at headquarters with a rabble of armed men and broke into the building. Security managed to stop them before they reached your office," Vincent explained, his breath coming fast, "but he vowed to return with a larger force. And we're ill-equipped for an armed attack."

"With good reason; it's Geneva, not a war zone. Hire additional security and whatever else you need. I'll have Carlos fly up to deal with Caesar. My uncle's obviously under pressure from someone or he wouldn't have acted so rashly. He's a coward at heart."

"He's in debt to some unsavory characters."

"Understatement. No one burns through money like Caesar. But our immediate issue is defense. Carlos will take over that task. I'll fly up as soon as I can--whenever that is. Fuck. Caesar's timing could have been better."

"It might be intentional."

"Perhaps, but he's too simple to have planned it." Rafe blew out a breath. "I'm fixed in Monte Carlo until Mireille leaves. Carlos will handle any further aggression. But regardless of the agency behind this hostile takeover," Rafe added, a razor edge to his voice, "neither Caesar nor his proxies are going to steal Contini Pharma from me."

"May I offer a word of caution."

"Of course, Vincent, but I'm always careful. Maso taught me well. Otherwise I wouldn't have survived childhood. Don't worry. There won't be any witnesses."

After ending the call, Rafe softly exhaled. Caesar had pretty much fucked up his plans for a next few months; he'd intended to await the birth of his child in relative peace and quiet. Instead, he had pressing concerns to address. Carlos needed orders, Nicole needed consoling, Mireille, et al, required his sympathy and/or hospitality until they left Monte Carlo.

First things first.

"Vincent just warned me of trouble in Geneva," he said when Carlos picked up. "When can you leave?"

"The helicopter's here. Ten minutes."

"Caesar and some armed thugs attacked our headquarters. Since Caesar isn't exactly a leader of men, someone has his nuts in a vise, and apparently Contini Pharma is the payoff. Hire an army, lock down the entire campus, and find Caesar. I'll come to Geneva as soon as I can."

"Okay if I take Simon with me?"

"You better clear it with Simon. He seems serious about Angelina."

"No problem. See that she has a flight home tomorrow. They were talking about doing some shopping today."

"One of the staff can take her shopping. They know the drill."

"Good. Smiles all around then. You do what you have to do here. It's not fair to leave Henny so soon. I promise no one's getting into Contini Pharma. We'll see you when we see you. Last question--with or without Nicole?"

Rafe groaned. "Don't know."

"Since I'm a totally objective observer, I do. I'll see you both in a few days."

"It may not be safe. That's the problem."

"We'll make it safe. Nicole's not going to stay in Monte Carlo without you."

"Once you find Caesar, put him under surveillance, twenty-four/seven. I'll personally deal with him. Fucker isn't going to screw up my life. It's damn near perfect and I intend to keep it that way. Ciao."

Rafe called Ganz next. "Could I meet you in the library soon? I need some research done."

"Five minutes."

Rafe was waiting when Ganz--accompanied by his girlfriend, Madeline and Ray Morgan, all three hackers extraordinaire--walked into the mammoth, high-ceilinged room housing a world class collection centered on ancient Mediterranean civilizations.

"You said research." Ganz grinned. "So I brought my assistants. You want something, we'll find it."

Rafe was seated behind a Galle art nouveau desk, his head resting against a high backed chair assembled from serried ranks of sinuous vines in polished fruitwood. His brows lifted faintly at Ganz's remark. "I like your optimism. My uncle, Caesar, has filed a claim for Contini Pharma, so I need death certificates, bank accounts, an elusive will that may or may not be registered somewhere."

"Caesar's not smart enough to file a claim," Ganz said.

"Agreed. I'd like to know who's behind this sudden yearning for my company?"

Rafe went on to explain other possible information that would be useful: most importantly, his grandfather's will, if one existed; Gerda and Nils' death certificates; Nils' accident report; both their burial sites; any relevant bank accounts; Caesar's current financial status and outstanding loans.

"ASAP, I suppose," Ganz said, "since Carlos and Simon just took off like bats from hell."

Rafe nodded. "Caesar forced entry into our headquarters building today. Not successfully, but..."

"He's not waiting for the courts to rule on the case."

"Apparently not."

"We'll set up in the computer room."

"I'll get Crissy," Ray said. "Hacking bank accounts is her specialty."

24

Rafe was tapping in a text on his phone as he walked into the carriage house. Hitting send, he looked up, and came to a sudden stop.

Nicole was sitting on the red and blue flame-patterned carpeted stairs. "Couldn't sleep?" he said, shutting the door behind him.

"Where were you?"

"Outside making a few calls."

"No you weren't. I looked."

"I had a quick chat with Ganz up at the house. By the way,"--he smiled--"that blue sweater looks better on you than me."

Dwarfed by Rafe's cashmere V-neck, the soft wool draped over her drawn up knees, her feet bare, a small strip of yellow flowered tights visible at her ankles, she looked very small on the broad, curved staircase rising thirty feet to the floor above. "Don't change the subject. Oh hell," she muttered, a tiny frown knitting her brow, "I told myself to be understanding, not bother you, or be bitchy...you have enough going on..."

"Sorry." That fretful tone meant he wasn't going to win this one. "It took much longer than I thought. I should have called."

"You should have." Her frown deepened before she took a quick breath and said what she'd been thinking for a while. "I'm not a trophy wife, okay? If you want someone to look pretty and keep their mouth shut, it's not going to happen. Not now, not ever."

"I know." He controlled the impulse to smile at the implausibility of Nicole keeping her mouth shut. "If you were a trophy wife you wouldn't be sitting there, scowling at me. You'd be upstairs counting your jewelry."

A dip of her head. "I rest my case."

"So are we done?"

Her gaze narrowed. "After you tell me what took so long."

"I had business to discuss with Vincent, and Ganz. More than I thought."

"What kind of business?"

He sighed. "You're not going to let this go, are you?"

"Not until you tell me the truth." Her eyebrows lifted minutely. "I know that's not always your first choice when something is amiss."

"Amiss?" He rolled his eyes. "That's pretty fucking tame, Jane Austen."

She sat up straighter. "I knew it!" A note of triumph echoed in her voice. "It's something disturbing. Look, I'm not going to dissolve in a puddle of tears or faint away if you tell me what happened. You don't have to protect me."

"Of course I do." The muscle along his jaw twitched, a mutinous glow lit his amber eyes. "It's the very least I can do."

"Josephine brought you a message, didn't she?" Nicole

pressed, recalling Rafe's reaction to his housekeeper's intrusion. "Whatever it is, let me help."

Jesus, as if. His nostrils flared at the enormous effort it took to suppress his first, expressly rude reply. "Look," he said, very softly, "I love you, bone deep and forever, but something's come up that could turn out to be a real pain in the ass. You can't help, I'm sorry, but you just can't. I'll deal with it. A couple weeks from now it'll be over, done, end of story." Pushing away from the door, he walked toward her. "Now give me a smile and say you'll forgive my silence."

She gave him a cool stare. "If you dare pat me on the head I'll scream."

Coming to a stop at the foot of the stairs, he ran through a quick dozen unsuitable replies before deciding on a highly edited statement of fact. "My uncle filed a lawsuit against Contini Pharma. Vincent called to let me know, Josephine relayed the message, that's all. It's not a huge issue, but once Mireille leaves, I have to run up to Geneva."

"*We* have to run up to Geneva," Nicole said, waiting with ruffled hair and an innocent gaze for his reply.

"Okay."

Her eyebrows shot up, followed by a grin. "That was easy."

Grateful the tempest was over, Rafe's voice was teasing. "Whatever you want, Tiger, just let me know."

Suddenly, her eyes were huge. "Don't ever leave me."

Leaning forward, he took her hands and pulled her to her feet. "Never." A slow headshake, an easy smile. "Never in a million years..."

FOR THE REMAINDER of the day, he avoided any further discussion of the lawsuit, choosing on the two occasions when Nicole asked a question, to reply that the case was so recently filed, he knew very little. However, he texted Ganz and Carlos, and told them not to call; he'd talk to them later. He and Nicole spent most of the day at the mausoleum with Mireille, keeping her company, talking and reminiscing, making plans to come up to Paris for the opening of *Toujours*.

Beyond the contemptible effort to steal his company, Rafe resented Caesar's crude timing. He wanted to mourn his friend in peace, deal with the rising tide of memories pressing in on all side, come to terms with his grief in a world that was shifting precariously. He didn't want to give any attention to his worthless uncle, particularly now, when he was feeling strangely unmoored.

Henny had been the very first person he'd ever relied on. They'd stood together over the years through every kind of crazy the world could throw at them, and had survived all the hassles, clear-eyed and unbreakable.

Until with one phone call, it all dissolved into a senseless waste of a life you never saw coming. The sheer, guilt-tripping hopelessness continually fizzing and crackling through his brain made him so goddamned pissed he felt like hitting something a dozen times a day.

He couldn't, of course.

He had to suck it up.

Like he had ever since he was a kid.

TEN GUESTS still remained for dinner that evening, friends of Henny's, some who knew Henny through Mireille, everyone staying to offer comfort to the widow. She was pale, her fatigue showing and when Rafe walked her to her suite soon after dinner, she thanked him with tears in her eyes. "Henny loved this home," she said. "He could always depend on you and Basil to be there for him."

"We three have been together a long time." Rafe spoke in the present tense, not yet willing to accept Henny's death. "He's with us always." Bending low, he brushed her cheek with his. "Try to sleep. If you can't, call me. I'll come over."

"I might go back to Paris soon. Talking about *Toujours* today made me anxious to finish Henny's work. He kept lists on top of lists. It'll feel as though he's right beside me directing activities."

Rafe smiled. "He'll love that. Feel free to call on me if you need anything in Paris." His smile widened. "I know how to get results."

"You and Henny both. He never took no for an answer."

"One worthwhile outcome from the Darwinian jungle of boarding school," he said, his voice gently mocking. "Now, get some sleep, okay?"

He stood in the shadowed hallway for a moment after she entered her suite, needing a second to steady himself against the unchecked rage never far from the surface since Henny's death. In the grip of a stone-cold fury, he swore under his breath, unleashing a scorching litany of expletives, followed almost instantly by a tidal wave of such utter bleakness, he groaned.

Brief moments later, with a blend of instinct and lessons learned, he flicked that switch from bat-shit crazy to seminormal, slowly inhaled, walked the length of the hallway, and returned downstairs.

Nicole rose as he entered the salon. "Mireille looked tired," she said, moving toward him. "I hope she can sleep."

"I told her to call me if she can't." Taking her hand, he smiled. "Let's say our goodnights and get out of here."

25

It was after two when Rafe slipped from the bed and entered his study next door. In the event Nicole came awake and called out, he wanted to hear her. Easing the door almost shut behind him, he crossed the room to the terrace and opening the French door, stepped outside to make his calls.

"All's quiet here," Carlos said. "The campus is secured. We have checkpoints for employees to enter and leave. Caesar's idea of hiding is the penthouse suite at the Hotel President Wilson. He has guards but we can get to him anytime you want."

"How's Vincent?"

"He's fine. He has bodyguards now but otherwise his life is unchanged."

"And Katya?"

"She understands. I told her we should have this cleared up in a week or so. Then her life will go back to normal. I didn't tell her we have a security team on her children and grandchildren too. I didn't want to alarm her."

"Have you thought of anyone who might have prompted Caesar's sudden claim on Contini Pharma?"

"No one definite," Carlos replied. "But if I had to guess, I'd say Russian mafia. Caesar's been in their pocket for years."

"Ganz is doing a search. We'll know more soon."

"How's Mireille?"

"Nicole and I spent the day with her at the mausoleum. She wanted to be with Henny."

"Understood. We're fine here. No rush."

"She mentioned she might go back to Paris and finish opening *Toujours*. But her schedule's unclear. In the meantime Ganz and crew are investigating Caesar's financial liabilities as well as looking into the particulars of my grandfather's death. I'll have additional info tomorrow," Rafe said.

"Roger that. I'll wait to hear from you."

Rafe's next call was to Ganz.

His team had made considerable progress. They'd found the death certificates for Gerda and Nils, the location of their graves and Gerda's sister's name and address. They'd discovered a discrepancy in Nils' accident report that Ray was tracking down. Crissy had unearthed six of Caesar's bank accounts, none with a sufficient balance to float his life style. He was, however, living well off an account in a Cyprus bank that was regularly replenished with wire transfers from another Cyprus bank.

"I downloaded all our searches into an encrypted file and sent it to you," Ganz said. "We're still looking for the principals behind the holding company making the transfers to Caesar. They're likely Russian."

"Ah—no surprise on his funding," Rafe murmured.

"Nope," Ganz replied. "Your uncle ran out of legitimate loan sources long ago."

"Excellent work, thanks. I'm going to have Carlos send an envoy to Gerda's sister in the event she knows something about my grandfather. It's a long shot, but Gerda may have mentioned a will, *and*, if we really get lucky and find it, Caesar's lawsuit is kaput. Although, if we don't find a will," Rafe said, a wisp of grimness like a shrug in his tone, "we move to plan B."

"Get rid of Caesar."

Rafe took a second or two before he said, "Yes. Then again, Gerda's sister might know something, and our problems will be over."

Ganz snorted. "Since when did you believe in miracles?"

"I'm trying to be aspirational."

"About Caesar? Not gonna happen. We'll nail him instead. Don't worry."

"I'm not worried, I just want this finished. I should be on my honeymoon, not fucking with Caesar's stupidity. By the way, I had to tell Nicole that Caesar filed a lawsuit against Contini Pharma, but that's all she knows. So I'll check in with you when she's not around and we'll be going up to Geneva as soon as Mireille leaves. If you need anything in the meantime, text me, otherwise I'll talk to you at night."

Returning to bed but unable to sleep, Rafe mentally ran through all his options apropos the attack on his company; adjusted and readjusted the most meritorious, discarded the high risk tactics, only to include them again...and so it went until shortly before dawn when he quietly rose and dressed.

Wearing charcoal colored slacks and a grey t-shirt, he walked barefoot into his study, sat at his desk, turned on his computer and pulled up the file Ganz had sent.

Jesus, Caesar was deep in hock to his creditors. Three yachts? Seriously? He was fucking worse than Maso. After scrolling through Caesar's liabilities and assets, the question of motivation was no longer in doubt. His creditors were calling in their debt. "Dumb motherfucker," Rafe muttered under his breath and clicked on Gerda's death certificate, then on Nils' cause of death. He was halfway through the police report of the car accident when a loud banging on the front door shattered the silence. Jumping to his feet, he shot out into the hall and raced full out toward the stairs. *Stop already, you'll wake Nicole!* Reaching the top of the staircase, he plunged down the steps in great leaps, ready to rip the brass lion head knocker off the bloody door.

As if on cue, the knocking stopped.

His adrenalin dropped ten notches. Clearing the last dozen stairs in a bound, he came to an abrupt standstill as the door slowly opened.

When Mireille walked in his brows shot up, but quickly recovering, his smile was automatic. "Morning." Holding up a finger, eyebrows pulled together, he listened then dropped his hand. "Sorry, I was afraid Nicole might have come awake. We're good." A flicker of a grin. "You're up early, la Comtesse. Would you like coffee, tea, champagne, something stronger?"

"Coffee, please." She smiled back. "If tea would be easier for you, that's fine too."

"I don't cook like Henny, but I can manage coffee. Come." He waved her toward a reception room. "Through there."

Crossing a large room filled with comfortable furniture in neutral tones to better showcase three magnificent eighteenth century Japanese screens by Hoitsu, they passed through a broad arch onto an enclosed terrace. The ocean lay beyond the floor to ceiling windows and sweep of lawn, the placid water mystical in the pale light of dawn.

"How beautiful," Mireille breathed. "The sheer size…"

"It's humbling isn't it?"

She turned and smiled. "I wouldn't have credited you with such modesty. Neither you nor Henny for that matter."

He softly laughed. "We've had our moments. Please, have a seat." Rafe indicated a long table set for breakfast with colorful Provencal print placemats and local pottery. "Coffee or espresso. I can do either. It's just a matter of pressing buttons."

"Cappuchino."

"Sounds good. Two then." Turning as he reached the small galley kitchen, he asked, "Did you sleep at all?"

"Not really."

"Same here." Pulling out two small cups, he set them on the espresso machine, and pressed buttons.

"I went downstairs, instead," Mireille said, "and prowled through the kitchen, thinking of all the wonderful times we had with Henny cooking for us. Look what I found?" She took a small, folded square of fabric from her jacket pocket and unfurled a canvas apron, once red, faded by countless washes to a soft pink, a multitude of faint stains testament to its utilitarian function.

"Ah, Madame Bardet's gift to Henny. He loved to wear that, as you can see," Rafe added with a smile, pouring milk into a pitcher, and sliding it under the steam wand. "Henny always said it recorded the history of his culinary education. Speaking of food," he quickly interjected as her eyes filled with tears, "we usually have croissants and pastries in the warming drawers. Interested?"

She nodded, gently placing the apron on the table. "It might be a good idea. I haven't eaten much lately." She flicked a finger his way. "You seem to know what you're doing."

"Coffee's a matter of survival in the morning. I don't like

to bother the staff if I get up early. Although, I'm grateful someone supplies this kitchen when I'm here." Picking up the cups half filled with espresso, he set them on the marble counter, picked up the milk pitcher, poured the hot foamed milk on top, and placed two sugar lumps on each saucer. Carrying the cups to the table, he gave her a little bow. "Enjoy. Now let me check out the food supply."

Pulling out several warming drawers, he found croissants, pastries, a vegetable quiche, bacon, sausage, and a bowl of cherries in a refrigerator drawer. Arranging them on a large platter he placed it on the table. "Josephine knows what I like. There's also some kind of chocolate flan I expect she added for Nicole if you're interested."

"Heavens no, this is more than enough." Mireille looked down for a second, then up through her lashes and taking a quick breath, said in a rush, "I'm going back to Paris today to work on *Toujours*." Her gaze lifted, met Rafe's. "And I'm here at the crack of dawn because I want you to tell me I'm doing the right thing." Her dark eyes were suddenly bright with tears. "You know Henny better than anyone. Tell me you understand. Tell me Henny would understand."

"Henny loves you with all his heart. Of course he understands. And if you want my blessing, you have it. I'll take you to Nice in the chopper whenever you wish. Davey will fly you to Paris."

She shook her head. "You needn't do that. Nicole will wonder where you are when she wakes." Her smile was teasing. "You know very well, you're focused on making her happy in an entirely smothering way."

Rafe laughed. "Is it so obvious?"

"To anyone who knew you before you met Nicole, it's glaringly obvious and, I might add, completely out of character. The fact that you don't even care who knows it, however, is typical. By the way, she's good for you. I've never seen you truly happy before."

He nodded, unable to wish her the same good fortune, pained no soothing remedy or miracle existed to restore his friend to the land of the living.

"We had two wonderful years," Mireille murmured, taking note of both his pain and discomfort. "Many people never have what we did." She picked up her coffee cup and raised it. "To that once-in-a-lifetime love. We're lucky, you and I. And at least for the moment, I'm done crying. I'm going to take Henny with me when I go and finish what he started." She smiled. "I'm already packed."

They both made an effort to speak of mundane matters as they ate, drank another coffee and waited for a decent hour to wake Rafe's pilot.

When a distant clock somewhere in the house struck six, Mireille said, "Do you think Davey would mind an early call?"

"Not at all." After calling Davey, Rafe had one of his staff bring Mireille's luggage to the helicopter, and escorted her to the aircraft parked on the lawn.

Davey had preceded them, and leaning out the aircraft door, greeted Mireille with a smile. "Henny's going to be pleased you're going to Paris to finish his passion project. It's all he talked about lately."

"You have to promise to come to the grand opening."

"Absolutely." The pilot caught Rafe'e eye. "We'll bring up the whole crew, right?"

"You can count on it." Turning to Mireille, Rafe bent low and brushed her cheeks in a farewell kiss. "Now call me if you need anything at all, okay? I'm available twenty-four/seven."

Mireille chuckled. "You might be sorry you said that. But

don't worry, if I need your help, I won't be shy. And I'll be back soon." She patted her jacket pocket that held the apron. "Henny's coming with me today."

"He wouldn't have it any other way," Rafe murmured. "You're making Henny happy. I'm glad."

Davey offered Mireille a hand ascending the ramp, then followed her inside, gave Rafe a wave and shut the door.

Pulling the ramp back from the chopper, Rafe retreated a few yards to avoid the backdraft when the rotors came to life. Moments later, the helicopter lifted off the lawn, picked up speed as it gained altitude, and banking to the right, made a wide sweeping turn toward Nice.

Buffeted by poignant memories and a crushing sense of loss, Rafe stood unmoving, until the chopper disappeared from sight.

Another part of Henny was gone now, taken to Paris by his wife. It felt as though his friend was slipping from his grasp. Shutting his eyes briefly, he took a deep breath, exhaled. *Fuck, life was unfair.* Not that he had time to actually grieve now, thanks to his bonehead uncle.

He had a battle to win.

If only Henny were here in his familiar, backup role, life would be sweet.

He said as much to Henny on his flying visit to the mausoleum. *I'm going to miss you beside me in this fight or any fight. Wish me well, mon ami. Au revoir. I'll be back soon.*

26

Returning to the bedroom, Rafe dropped into a chair opposite the bed, and waiting for Nicole to wake up, checked his emails on his phone, answering some, deleting others, skipping over those that needed data.

"Have you been there long?"

He looked up, took in Nicole's heavy-lidded gaze, her voice softly woozy. "Go back to sleep. It's still early."

She blinked, took a breath. "What time is it?"

A glance at his phone. "Going on seven. Seriously, there's no need to get up yet."

"You're dressed."

He smiled. "Go to sleep." He held up his phone. "I have emails to answer."

Her brows slid upward. "I so dislike orders."

"Then might I *suggest* you go back to sleep," he gently said.

Her independence politely acknowledged, she lazily stretched and blew him a kiss. "Can't, I'm awake now. And

Mireille is always up early for breakfast. In fact," she said, starting to rise, "I'd better hustle."

"Mireille's on her way back to Paris. Davey's taking her."

She fell back on her pillows. "*That's* why you're dressed. You should have wakened me."

"She wouldn't let me." At Nicole's squinty-eyed look, he added, "We agreed you should sleep."

"Is that so."

"Pretty much, yeah," he said. "Look, don't get mad. It was fucking early as hell, I didn't see any point in waking you when you sleeping soundly. And she didn't tell me she was leaving until—later. Sorry."

A sharp glance. "We're going to have to discuss you making decisions for me."

"Could we do it in Geneva?"

Nicole sat bolt upright. "You were just waiting for me to wake up so we could leave. Why didn't you say so?" Tossing aside the covers, she threw her legs over the side of the bed, slid to the floor and moving the short distance to the chair, flashed him a wide smile. "I'm of sturdy stock, Contini. I don't need pampering."

His gaze traveled slowly down her nude body, then up again, a twinkle in his amber eyes. "I don't know about sturdy, sweetheart, but you're becoming spectacularly, jaw-droppingly curvy. Come here." Pulling her down on his lap, he tucked her into the warmth of his body and circled her with his arms. "And I'll pamper you if I wish. Seriously, a few hours one way or the other doesn't matter." Dipping his head, he kissed her nose. "I want you and baby to be healthy."

"Don't worry, I'm always healthy." She could have said, *You look as though you haven't slept in days*. Instead, she brushed the faint shadow under his eyes with a fingertip, and felt a surge of tenderness. "Let's go now. I'm wide awake. And I promise if I feel tired, I'll sleep on the plane."

"You sure?"

She nodded.

"I'll have someone pack for you. We"—

She lifted her finger from his mouth. "I know how to pack." Sitting up, she flashed him a smile. "Give me ten minutes."

He grinned. "You're one of a kind, Tiger. Most women take an hour to put on their makeup, not that I'd know," he quickly added at her raised brow. "Strictly rumor."

She winked. "Smooth."

His thumb gently stroked the back of her neck. "And lucky as hell to have met you."

"Kismet for sure." A smile lit up her eyes. "Aren't you glad I stumbled into your stateroom?"

"Glad times infinity. I don't like to think of the odds," he murmured. "Scary shit."

"But everything worked out," she brightly noted, "right?"

"Absolutely."

"And now we're on our way to Geneva sooner than you thought. Is Carlos there? I heard he left."

His smug sense of well-being took a hit as the gravity of his problems resurfaced. "Yes, he is. Would you like help dressing?"

The change in subject was meant to arrest further questions so she politely resisted asking for full disclosure. "You're the fashion expert. Pick out something."

Lifting her from his lap, he set her on her feet. "Any requests?"

Moving toward the dressing room, she half turned and smiled. "Just make sure it's comfortable. Nothing tight."

"You're going to need a new wardrobe soon."

Her reply was muffled as she reached into the closet for her backpack and turning, she dropped the bag on a chair. "I'm going to be packed before you get your ass out of that chair," she called out, reaching for the drawer that held her underwear.

Seconds later, her feet left the ground.

Swinging her up into his arms, Rafe gave her a big smile. "FYI, pussycat, I'll always be faster than you. On the other hand, you'll always be a whole lot prettier than me and for that I'm super grateful. And oh, yeah, in case I haven't mentioned it lately, I love you like crazy. You *and*--the baby," he added, softly.

Wrapping her arms around his neck, she tilted her head back so her blue-eyed gaze held his. "I love you always and only," she whispered, "and I love that we're going to be a family."

For a clarifying moment the word, family, sent a chill down his spine. But a second later that small faltering shock had steadied and he was able to reply with genuine warmth. "It's perfect. I've never really had a family. Thank you for giving me one."

As for the member of his dubious family threatening his personal and professional life, uncle or not, Caesar had made a huge mistake.

He wouldn't get a second one.

27

Simon was at the Geneva airport, sitting behind the wheel of a black Mercedes sedan parked on the tarmac just short of the landing strip when Rafe's Gulfstream G650ER set down. As the plane came to a stop, Simon stepped out of the car, shifted his shoulders to settle the holster under his left arm, buttoned one of the two buttons on his bespoke tweed jacket, and walking toward the aircraft, waited for the cabin door open.

"Good to see you," he said, a moment later, taking Nicole's backpack from Rafe at the base of the ramp. "Glad you could get away."

"Everything worked out," Rafe said, turning to help Nicole descend the last few steps to the ground, putting his arm around her to protect her from the wind. "How's traffic?"

"Not bad. We should have you home in twenty minutes. Morning." Simon smiled at Nicole. "Sorry for the cool temp. Rain's on the way."

"No problem. Rafe found me something warm to wear," she said, indicting her colorful Missoni sweater dress with a flick of her finger. "And"—she put her palm on Rafe's t-shirt clad chest-"I have my heater with me."

"Anytime," Rafe murmured, "but let's get you out of the wind." Moving the few yards to the car, he helped her into the back seat, turned to Simon and spoke in an undertone. "Is Carlos at the house?"

Simon nodded, his voice equally soft. "He's waiting to talk to you. Caesar had some reinforcements come into town last night."

"Tell him I'll see him as soon as Nicole is settled in."

"He figured. Uneventful trip, I hope," Simon added in a conversational tone, taking the top of the car door in a loose grip.

"Yes, trouble free." Sliding into the back seat, Rafe smiled at Nicole as the door was shut behind him. "Feel like breakfast?"

"You mean over and above what I ate on the plane?"

"No worries, you're eating for two."

Resting her head against the sleek black leather, she gave him a dazzling smile. "I didn't know you could be so tactful."

"And I didn't know waiting for a baby could be so filled with promise. Every day's a new experience." Leaning over, he kissed her cheek. "Thanks, pussycat."

"It *is* different, isn't it?"

"Understatement." There was something in his voice she hadn't heard before—a tentative flicker of uncertainty. "We have a helluva lot to learn."

"We're not *all* novices," she said with a smile. "Six kids in my family remember? And don't give me that skeptical look. I've babysat all my life."

How does one politely say, *But this is* my *child.* "In that case, I stand corrected," he said, smoothly.

She snorted. "As if. But it doesn't matter what you think. I'm on solid ground here. You might give orders a hundred times a day, run an international corporation and have gazillions, but I know babies." She gave him a warm, crinkly smile. "So there."

He laughed. "Such self-confidence."

"Practice." She squeezed his hand. "Come on, it's going to be fine, better than fine. Our baby will be perfect. He'll be a pink, chubby version of you as an infant, he'll sleep through the night, rarely cry and play video games at six months."

"Please, no video games until at least age four. And he might be a she with blue, blue eyes like you and the cutest smile and an adorable personality she inherited from me. Hey...don't punch so hard, you'll hurt yourself," he murmured, grabbing her fist, bringing it to his mouth and kissing her knuckles. "Seriously though," he whispered, his breath warm on her fingers, "it wasn't only your bikini-clad body that blew me away the first time I saw you, it was your sass and audacity." He smiled. "Definitely life-altering."

Leaning her head on his shoulder, she glanced up and whispered, "God, I love you."

"I love you more and that's never going to change."

"Swear." She knew Geneva wasn't a pleasure trip.

"I swear." He sighed. "As soon as this dispute with my uncle is settled, we'll go back to Monte Carlo and wait for the baby. Just you and me."

BUT CARLOS WAS STANDING at the front door when they stepped out of the car and the radioactive world preempted any considerations of an idyllic future.

"I need a minute," Carlos said, his voice mild.

Rafe nodded. "Let me show Nicole into the breakfast room first. I'll meet you in my study."

Nicole patted Rafe's arm. "Go, I'll find my way."

"Nonsense. Carlos, tell her this isn't a crisis."

"Not at all." A quick nod. "Enjoy your breakfast."

"Come, sweetheart," Rafe said, taking her hand. "This way."

They walked through several splendid reception rooms, and intimate salons, a small reading room, a paneled, coffered chamber with a large display of medieval armor, the enfilade of rooms characteristic of Baroque architecture.

"Do you collect armor?"

"It came with the house."

"Can I redecorate?"

"Of course. Do whatever you like. I'm sure some museum would appreciate the Duke of Savoy's armor collection."

"I don't want to redecorate."

He turned to her with a smile. "Just staking your claim?"

She grinned. "Sorry, I couldn't resist. This place is humongous."

"I like the location."

"Because?" Why did men speak in short cryptic sentences?

Security. It's surrounded by ten foot high walls. "Great lake view," he said instead, standing aside so she could enter a light-filled room overlooking not only Lake Geneva in the distance but a garden bright with colorful fall flowers. "This is one of my favorite rooms. You can see the sunrise if you're up early."

"It's gorgeous, the whole house, palace, whatever...is magnificent." When she'd been here before she hadn't had the grand tour, only the mini tour between the entrance and Rafe's apartment upstairs. "How many rooms are there?"

"I've never counted. Ask Chomak. He was the major domo when I bought the place. He knows everything down to the last piece of furniture in the attics."

"Have you seen the attics?" She raised a brow. "I only ask, because you seem a bit vague about"--

"I saw them once. Chomak wanted to show me a leak in the roof."

"I assume he didn't do that again," she said, her mouth twitching in a faint smile.

"I can be polite if I have to." Pulling out a chair for Nicole, he waited for her to sit. "I suggested he call someone with more repair expertise. Now, if you're done needling me," he drolly murmured, taking the chair opposite her at the small table, "allow me to point out that Chomak and I get along despite my indifference to housekeeping details. I like him. He may or may not like me. I can't tell. He's old school, well-bred, refined. We muddle through. So when and if *you* need anything related to the household, redecorating or otherwise," he said, "Chomak's the person to ask. Ah, here we are. Good morning, Chomak. May I introduce my wife. Nicole, Chomak. Chomak's in charge of this establishment."

The tall, trim, elderly man in a dark suit, and striped bow tie, bowed faintly. "May I offer everyone's congratulations on your nuptials, sir. And present our good wishes to your lady."

"Thank you. We're pleased, life couldn't be better. Although, Nicole is a bit peckish this morning. What do you suggest?"

"Perhaps hot chocolate with marshmallows, berries

from the Orangery with cream, a warm doughnut and a small serving of scrambled eggs with smoked salmon."

"Did you say warm doughnut?" Nicole murmured, a hush in her voice.

"The cook just finished rolling them in cinnamon sugar, Mrs. Contini."

"OhmyGod, yes please." She thought about asking him to call her Nicole, but regardless she'd seen any number of major domos at her Uncle Dominic's homes, Chomak was infinitely more intimidating.

"Thank you, Chomak. Why don't we start with doughnuts?" The moment Chomak had said hot chocolate with marshmallows, Rafe knew his ever-efficient major domo had coordinated with Paris and Monte Carlo. "Bring a plate. I'll have some too. And coffee for me."

Waiting until the faintly aristocratic Chomak had left the room, Nicole giggled. "I feel like I'm a long way from Kansas. It's a kids' movie," she explained to Rafe's questioning gaze. "And the noble Chomak is slightly alarming like the wicked witch in the movie."

"No need to be alarmed. He politely overlooks my wild ways. You on the other hand are honey sweet. He'll adore you."

"Flatter me if you will, but seriously, does he ever smile?"

There was a beat before Rafe spoke. "I'm sure he does. Want to sit on my lap?" he asked, grinning broadly. "I'll protect you."

"Do I dare?"

He laughed and held out his arms. "Come here and we'll find out."

Not a flicker of emotion crossed the major domo's face when he returned to the breakfast room to find Nicole on

Rafe's lap. Setting the tray on the table, he silently arranged cups of hot chocolate, coffee, a plate of doughnuts and pots containing additional chocolate and coffee in front of the couple. "Mrs. Gladis will have the rest shortly. Is there anything more?"

"No, thank you, Chomak."

"Tell her the doughnuts are delicious," Nicole said, a dusting of sugar on her lower lip. "Absolutely perfect."

Chomak nodded. "Yes, Ma'am."

"Umm...perfect indeed," Rafe whispered, kissing her sugary mouth as his major domo exited the room. "And super sweet..."

During breakfast, Rafe ignored the clouds gathering on the horizon, the critical lawsuit, the dangerous reinforcements Caesar had called in and allowed himself to delight in the small joys and goodness of their life together.

There were perfect moments even today.

28

He didn't, however, argue when Nicole said, "You've been polite long enough. Go see Carlos. I'll be fine. I have stuff to do."

But his eyes widened slightly at the last.

"I know you're more familiar with models and privileged bitches that don't do anything but shop and gossip, but I prefer useful activities. I've always wanted to write a screenplay, and I have time now until the baby's born. So I'll find a quiet corner somewhere and write."

"There's a laptop upstairs in my bedroom."

"I'm going to write long hand."

Another flare of surprise quickly suppressed. "You'll find paper in the desk in the library."

"There, you see, I'll be busy. Take your time, do what you have to do, if I get tired I'll take a nap."

"How the hell did I find such a perfect wife?"

She grinned. "Actually, I decided I wanted *you*, and I always get what I want."

He laughed. "Is that a fact?"

"Yup. You were caught well and good and you didn't even know it until it was over, the fat lady had sung, done deal."

He could have argued about who had caught whom, his possessive instincts apropos Nicole, imperious, monopolistic and not open to debate. But he only smiled and said, "Here I thought I was completely jaded and cynical and find out I was naïve instead. How clever of you."

She looked amused. "Clever women don't offend you?"

"One particular woman doesn't. You make me happy. An impossible task until you came into my life." His smile flashed. "But then you're not easily daunted," he said, the pensive note in his voice eliminated with his smile. "Speaking of intrepidity and resolve," he added, interested in shifting the conversation to less sensitive subjects, "don't forget your food bank project. Isabelle Tansy will help if you wish."

"Oh good. I wasn't sure you still wanted to spend money and I didn't want to ask or be presumptuous or"--

"It's my wedding gift to you, pussycat. And at the risk of reviving an old argument, my money is your money, there's plenty to go around, okay?" Affection warmed his gaze. "So, do you want me to call Isabelle and tell her to come over?"

Nicole hesitated for a fraction of a second, uncomfortable with Rafe's largesse, recognizing, however, that her unease paled to insignificance against the pressures he was confronting. "If you think she won't mind."

He smiled faintly. "She won't."

"Okay, then. And thank you again for your generosity."

"Not a problem. What time?"

"I don't know, one, two. But if she's busy on such short notice, tell her anytime at all is fine."

"I pay her handsomely not be busy when I need her. I'll tell her one. Let Chomak know where you'll be."

A bewildered look. "How do I do that? The house is a maze."

"There's an intercom in every room, usually near the door. Press the button, and start talking."

"Jeez, I have a lot to learn about living the plutocratic life." She wrinkled her nose. "Or not...no offense."

"None taken. Do exactly as you please so long as you're within shouting distance." He grinned. "That's my only request. We good?"

She nodded, smiled, gave him a quick kiss. "Thanks for understanding." Leaning back slightly, she offered him a comparable understanding. "Now you're excused to go and take care of whatever was making Carlos frown. Just make sure you come back to me in one piece."

"I may not be going anywhere. I just have to check on the progress of the lawsuit. If I'm still around, I'll come find you when Isabelle arrives. She runs the Contini Foundation with efficiency and heart. You'll like her."

Nicole winked, recalling mention of her the day she met Rafe. "As much as Silvie's husband liked her?"

"Probably more. Isabelle won't have her defenses up with you." Lifting Nicole to her feet, Rafe stood. "Now if you need anything, me included, hit the intercom by the door. Love you, pussycat." He brushed her cheek with a kiss. "See you soon."

Nicole stood in the bright, sunlit room, papered in a miniature yellow rose pattern fashionable in the mid-nineteenth century, her feet cushioned by the plush green silk Tabriz carpet, and watched the man she loved walk through a twelve foot high doorway framed in gilded wood, the difference between this charming room and the issues facing him, stark. Perhaps, perilous.

She wasn't naïve.

Despite Carlo's disclaimer, Rafe wouldn't have left Henny and Monte Carlo if the matter hadn't been urgent.

She also knew he wanted her distant from whatever troubles were plaguing him, and if she was virtuous she'd observe his wishes. But virtue had never been her strong suit. And she loved him and wanted him safe.

Perhaps Isabelle knew something.

29

After a quick call setting up Nicole's meeting with Isabelle, Rafe walked into his study, acknowledged Carlos, Simon, Davey and Vincent with a brisk nod and said, "I understand Caesar brought in reinforcements last night. How many?"

Carlos stood up, about to vacate Rafe's desk chair when Rafe waved him back down and dropped into a chair next to Vincent.

"Twenty men, ex-military," Carlos replied. "We have them under surveillance. They're in a rental property not far from here."

Rafe's brows arched high. "How far exactly?"

"Two blocks." Simon pointed toward the lake.

"Christ, Caesar's an idiot," Rafe muttered. "And now his problem is my fucking problem." Leaning forward, he rested his hands on his knees, a muscle ticking in his cheek. "Since no one seems to be waiting for a verdict in the court case,"—his voice was soft with distaste—"why don't I have a talk with Caesar. Offer him more than he'll get from his mafia creditors, guarantee him protection which is more than his criminal associates will do. He's weak and scared. He'll take the deal. Then the bogus court case goes away, and we're done playing bloody defense."

"There's a possibility Caesar's even more terrorized by his handlers," Carlos noted. "He may not deal."

"I'm not giving him a choice. Either he agrees or I'll personally send him to Hell. What? Jesus, it's not as though anything about this shit storm is legit." Rafe put up his hands, a growing impatience in his voice. "And before anyone brings up the legal niceties, consider...we're facing another assault—from fucking two blocks away. That puts my wife in danger. Do you think I give a flying fuck about Caesar?"

"No one's arguing legalities," Carlos said, quietly; ex-Basque separatist, ex-French Foreign Legion, ex-mercenary, his view of the law was flexible. "But it might be useful to identify Caesar's masters so we can better defend against them."

Rafe dropped back in the chair, his narrowed gaze on Carlos. "Do we have time? With a strike force down the block?"

"*Should* time allow, Rafail," Vincent interjected, softly, "Gerda's sister, Annali, would like to talk to you. She finally returned my call this morning."

Rafe's eyes cut sideways to his consigliere. "Where is she?"

"Outside Montreux."

"Call her. We could be there in little more than an hour."

Vincent left the room to make his call. He didn't want to risk the men's conversation being overheard.

At the soft click of the door closing, Rafe slid upward from his lounging pose, and surveyed his companions, his amber eyes somber. "We all agree the threat is imminent?"

Carlos nodded. "No argument there."

"What do we have in numbers on Caesar's side?"

Carlos gaze swung to Simon. "Last count?"

Simon paused for a second, doing the math in his head; field logistics second nature to a man who'd fought in hellholes around the world. "With the latest arrivals, forty-two."

Rafe frowned. "And our team?"

"Thirty. We've sent for more," Davey said. "A flight's coming in from Marseille this afternoon. Want me to get the chopper ready for a trip to Montreux?"

"We'll wait for Vincent, but hopefully yes. Caesar's fucked up my life long enough." Rafe's voice was flat. "I want this over."

"It's not really Caesar," Carlos pointed out.

"Well, whoever the fuck it is, they're crazy--going to war in Geneva. It's ludicrous. That said, we do what we have to do. Starting tonight." Rafe looked up as Vincent walked in.

"I told Annali you'd be there before noon."

Rafe came to his feet. "I'll let Nicole know that I'll be gone for a few hours. Davey, call the airport. Ten minutes. At the door."

Remembering Nicole had seen the library on their previous visit, he took the stairs at a run, hoping she'd decided to work on her screenplay there. Absorbed in the grim task of planning an attack in an oppressively tight timeframe, he strode down the hall oblivious of his surroundings, shoved open the double doors into the library and felt a wash of relief. Nicole was at the large partners' desk, her head down, intent on her writing. And safe.

"How's the screenplay going?"

Startled, she glanced up. "Jeez, talk about well-oiled hinges. My compliments to Chomak's management skills. And to answer your question, it's going well, thank you."

She lifted a sheet of paper from the desk and smiled. "I like your monogramed paper. Very posh. Is your meeting over?"

"Not quite. I just came to tell you that I'll be gone for a short time. Vincent found someone who knew my grandfather and the information they have might be helpful to the court case, so we're flying to Montreux. Offer my apologies to Isabelle. I would have liked to have seen her." He smiled. "Don't miss me too badly. Any questions, Mrs. Contini?"

An arched eyebrow, a grin. "How much do you love me?"

"You're my life," he said, softly.

Tears sprang to her eyes.

He crossed the room in a few swift strides, and lifting her into his arms, whispered, "Hey, hey...don't cry. I never want to see you sad."

"I'm not sad." She blinked away her tears, sniffled. "Really...I cry at anything or nothing nowadays. Hormones. Sorry."

"No problem." He kissed her gently. "Until I figure this out, you're going to have to let me know when you're crying for real so I can fix it. Okay?"

"Gotcha," she whispered, his blanket kindness nearly giving rise to another flood of tears.

"Do I get to read what you've written when I come back?" Rafe asked, in an attempt to steady her quivering lip.

"No!" Her tearfulness vanished in a flash, her eyes wide. "I mean—not now...maybe later, or like somewhere down the road—later when, oh hell..." Her voice trailed off, she flushed to her hairline in such obvious discomfort Rafe gently said, "My fault, I shouldn't have asked."

She shook her head. "No, I mean, yes, you can ask." Taking a quick breath, she blew it out, and gave him a faint smile. "And of course you can read it. Just wait a few days until I have a few more pages to show you."

"Take your time." A day, a year or ten, it didn't matter, he wanted to say. "I'm just pleased you have something interesting to do," he said, instead, kicking the chair away from the desk, sitting down and settling her on his lap. "And if you'd rather keep your work private, that's fine. Also, speaking of interesting, if you need a little variety--somewhere down the road," he added with a teasing grin, "you're always welcome to join me at Contini Pharma. I'd be more than happy to have you aboard."

She nibbled on her bottom lip, temporizing for so long her answer was obvious before she spoke. "I appreciate the offer, really I do," she said, choosing her words carefully. "And I don't mean to be ungrateful, nor overlook my chemistry degree I should probably put to use." She smiled. "Who am I kidding?"

"Don't look at me. If you'd wanted to, you would have applied for graduate school. Still, my offer holds. You have the background."

"A career in business doesn't appeal to me." She tucked her hair behind her ear, a spark of nervousness in her eyes. "Do you mind?"

"Not in the least. Do anything or nothing at all, whatever makes you happy. Writing a screenplay is unquestionably fascinating. No argument there. However"—he grinned.

"What?" An alertness in her gaze.

"You do have an appointment today so I take back my "nothing at all" comment."

"Jeez, is that all. You scared me." *Like this whole bloody trip scares me.*

"My apologies. Would you like Chomak to bring Isabelle to the library when she arrives. Or would you like to visit with her elsewhere?"

Nicole contemplated the several furniture arrangements

artfully disposed for conversation, the precious books from floor to ceiling, the well-stocked drinks table. "This is very nice. And I can offer Isabelle a drink. Does she drink?"

"Ask her. I don't know."

"Really, you don't know? You aren't personally acquainted with the woman Emilio found so intriguing?"

"I never mix business with pleasure."

"But you don't mind if I work at Contini Pharma?"

He smiled. "That's different. You're my darling wife."

Their eyes met.

A heart beat passed.

Nicole spoke first, her voice hushed. "Who knew, right?"

"Who indeed?" he said as softly. There were still times when he was astonished they'd found each other.

"We must live right."

An eye roll, a quirked grin. "I couldn't possibly comment."

She slugged him, he pretended it hurt, and as she threaded her fingers through his hair and drew his face down, he politely waited when he couldn't recall ever waiting for any woman other than Nicole. And for a fleeting moment he existed in a bubble of pure happiness separate from the dangers swirling around him.

"You know that shouting distance thing you mentioned?" she murmured. "I need you *just* a little closer." She gently tugged. "If you don't mind..."

Her breath was warm on his mouth, her smile close and warmer still. "Don't mind at all." His mouth brushed hers, soft as velvet. "You're the best thing that ever happened to me." His kiss was butterfly light, no more than a teasing caress at first, the gentle pressure slowly increasing by tantalizing degrees until a feverish heat flickered and shimmered through their senses, coiled deep inside, flowed over their nerve endings in sweet temptation.

"Mmmm," she purred, shifting slightly on his lap.

Recognizing the familiar pleasure sound, the subtle movement of her hips, he swiftly calculated time, distance, critical urgency, deliberately ignored the adverse equation for a second...two...three, before raising his head and issuing a sigh. "They're waiting for me downstairs."

"I know." She would have liked to pretend that Vincent, et al waiting downstairs was perfectly normal. Her smile took effort. "Hurry back."

"That's my girl." Lifting her from his lap, he set her on her feet, stood, and gently framing her face in his palms, bent low and kissed her. Straightening, he kept his voice deliberately bland. "This won't take long. Give my regards to Isabelle."

She nodded, tense and unblinking.

She looked so frightened, he almost didn't go.

But his deadline was unrelenting. "I'll be back in three hours," he said, an almost impossible undertaking. "I promise."

Then he left without touching her.

He had his limits.

On his way downstairs, he called Isabelle.

"I just have a minute," he said when she picked up. "I won't be here when you come to see Nicole, so a few instructions. Don't mention the assault on headquarters. And Nicole is not to leave the house. If she suggests going out, make some excuse. Caesar has men two blocks away."

"Do you want me to stay with her until you return?"

"Please, if possible. She talked about taking a nap, so use

your discretion there. I don't know whether she has suspicions beyond what I told her about Caesar filing a lawsuit, but she seems frightened. Do what you can to reassure her." Having covered the length of the hallway, he moved swiftly down the main staircase. "A last item. She's overly concerned with spending money on the food banks. Ease her mind on that score. There's no budget. Make sure she understands. I gotta go. I have a chance to checkmate Caesar."

"Good luck."

"Thanks." Although in his experience you made your own luck. "Hopefully, the food bank project will serve as a distraction from whatever's worrying Nicole. See that she gets everything she wants and more. She's way too polite about spending money. Ciao." He ended the call without waiting for an answer. Carlos was holding the front door open, the car was outside, its motor idling.

30

Shortly after eleven, Davey landed the helicopter on a grassy field northeast of Montreux and the small party made their way up a slight incline to a two story wooden farmhouse set against tall, soaring pines in the foothills of the Alps. The gray, weathered exterior was punctuated with tall windows framed in an unusually exuberant green trim, the windows otherwise empty of life, an unearthly quiet in the air.

"They know we're coming?" Rafe murmured.

Vincent nodded. "Annali was cautious, though, when I spoke to her. She said she'd debated even returning my call."

"She definitely lives off the beaten path." Simon surveyed the surrounding countryside with a critical eye. "And that single lane road visible from the air is largely invisible from the ground."

"The farm was in Annali's husband's family," Vincent explained. "She inherited it after he died."

Rafe shot him a look. "So she hasn't always lived here?"

"No, she and her husband lived in Montreux until his death."

"When was that?"

"Nearly twenty years ago."

Simon flicked a finger at the farmhouse. "You're saying she chose to move to this secluded place rather than stay in Montreux?"

Vincent inclined his head. "So it seems."

"You'd need a helluva good vehicle to get in and out of here in winter," Simon noted. "Even then access would be uncertain."

"If all goes well we'll get everyone's questions answered,"--Carlos glanced at Rafe-- "and finally put Caesar in our rear view mirror."

Rafe smiled. "Wouldn't that be grand. I'll be back in Monte Carlo by nightfall." Entering the small covered porch sheltering the front door from winter storms, he knocked on the inner door and waited. Several moments later after no response, Rafe turned to Vincent. "Call her. Tell her we're here."

"Try once more. If no one answers I'll call."

A sharper rapping this time.

Still no results.

"I'll go look around," Davey said, turning to leave, only to swivel back at the faint echo of approaching footsteps.

A hush descended, everyone listening to the measured tread drawing near. When the footsteps came to a stop on the other side of the door, Rafe raised his index finger, signaling quiet.

The first sharp metallic click came as no surprise. The second lock unbolting was equally unremarkable. At the third and fourth lock unsnapping, glances were exchanged.

The fifth brought eyebrows up. And as the sixth bolt slid free, Davey murmured, "That's fucking caution."

"The cause soon to be determined," Rafe said under his breath. "Be respectful now, no sudden moves, weapons out of sight." Stepping back as the door began to open, he stood perfectly still while the door swung wide. *"Bonjour, Madame."* His French was as polished as his flawlessly tailored grey slacks and Saxony tweed jacket. "I'm Rafe Contini." Masking his surprise at seeing a slender, well-dressed, older lady quite different from the Gerda he remembered, he dipped his head faintly. "You must be Annali Rochat." He offered her a smile that never failed to get a response. "It's a pleasure to meet you."

His smile wasn't returned.

Instead she looked him over from head to toe, her steely gaze moving to take in the men behind him with the same sharp scrutiny before she stepped aside. "Come in—just you...not your men." And without waiting for an answer, she turned and walked away.

With a nod to his companions, Rafe followed the grey-haired, ramrod straight figure in a Prussian blue silk dress he'd bet was designed in Paris, disappear down the shadowed hall.

The dim hallway opened into a sunny drawing room as surprising as the lady of the house, its simple elegance pure Biedermeier. The polished wood floors gleamed, sheer white curtains framed a bank of tall windows, the pear and cherry wood Empire furniture upholstered in striped silk evoked a more graceful era. But *most* surprising, was the unmistakable aroma of genuine happiness from his youth: Gerda's cookies.

"You had some questions?" Annali Rochat stood motionless in the center of the room, her expression shuttered, her hands clasped before her, her pose and demeanor, resolutely defensive.

Lost in fond memories of visits to his grandfather, Rafe was oblivious to all but the long ago fragrance. "Gerda used to bake those cookies," he said, a surge of exhilaration catching him off guard. "They were my favorites."

The ensuing silence was so protracted, Rafe's whimsical good humor deflated. "I'm sorry," he said, conscious of his hostess's cool gaze. "You were saying?"

She stared at him, her expression suddenly stiff with displeasure. "Your father came here twice and threatened me. Did you know that?"

"No, I didn't," Rafe said. "I sincerely apologize. In my defense, Maso may not have been my father." He shrugged. "Sorry, that hardly matters. You shouldn't have been subjected to his violence. Period."

"Fortunately, I'm not easily intimidated." She held his gaze. "But my sister lived in terror of your father, Maso… whoever he was. He was a monster."

A muscle flickered in Rafe's jaw. "Yes, he was that and more. I hope he wasn't the cause of Gerda's heart attack."

"Not directly."

With the high color on Annali's face, he didn't know if he dared press the point of Maso's visit. "If you don't mind me asking," he ventured, delicately, "why *did* Maso threaten you?"

She sniffed. "He wanted Gerda's inheritance."

"Did he get it?"

She gave him a look of astonishment. "Of course not. Your grandfather left the money to my sister, I was my sister's heir, it was beyond his grasp and I told him so in no uncertain terms. The second time he barged in with ruffians, the commanding officer of our canton police force happened to be visiting. Otto made short work of your father and his henchmen. We do not suffer monsters *or* thieves here."

He would have paid to see that exchange. Repressing a smile, Rafe said, "I'm pleased his threats didn't work. Maso liked to prey on those he perceived as weaker than he."

"That was his mistake."

Also the reason Maso had brought muscle with him the second time, Rafe reflected. "In contrast to Maso's intrusions," he said, with calculated gravity, fully aware he was here on sufferance, "I've come to *respectfully* ask for your help. My uncle is threatening my ownership of Contini Pharmaceutical. I'm hoping you might have some information from Gerda that would confirm my legal right to the company."

Annali frowned. "I'll listen, but I can't promise anything."

Accepting the small opening he'd been given, he explained the problematic lawsuit in broad strokes: Caesar's sudden claim to Contini Pharma; his own vague memories of a childhood book; his grandfather's admonition to rely on Gerda; the very slight hope that a will existed. "It's unlikely you know much about my grandfather's death," he finished. "But you did say you wished to see me so even a remembered word or two might be useful. Or if Gerda had discussed or hinted at a will those references could be meaningful."

Annali gave him a nod so slight he may have imagined it.

"Sit. Would you like coffee?"

"Yes, thank you," he said, sitting on the nearest chair before she changed her mind.

Crossing the room, Annali stopped before a cream

colored door, turned and nodded as if conceding a point. "You don't look like your father."

"I know." Rafe smiled faintly. "It pleases me. A will, of course, would be even more gratifying."

She opened her mouth to speak, changed her mind, then opened the door, and walked from the room.

Almost immediately, muted squabbling erupted from behind the door, the muffled sounds of dispute continuing unabated until just moments before Annali reappeared, carrying a tray. "I put milk and sugar in your coffee without thinking," Annali said. "Habit I'm afraid."

"I prefer it that way, thank you," he said with the same casual disregard for what had clearly transpired in the room next door. Then with the blink of an eye, his attention was arrested by the sight of chocolate cookies on the tray being held out to him. The years fell away, and if he closed his eyes, he might have been five again. "I knew I'd smelled them," he said, deeply moved.

"Take two," Annali said. "They're small."

He glanced up. "Gerda used to say that to me."

"It must be a family saying. Please, help yourself."

Lifting a coffee cup and saucer from the tray, he set it on a small ebony-inlaid table beside his chair, and experienced a flood of nostalgia as he picked up two cookies rich with hazelnuts, cherries, and chocolate and set them on the saucer. "If possible I'd like this recipe before I go. My wife is fond of sweets. I don't know if you heard, but I recently married."

"Yes, we heard." Sitting down opposite him, Annali smiled for the first time. "Your wedding made the news. Congratulations."

"Thank you." He cocked his head at the first person plural pronoun. "You don't live alone?"

Taking a leisurely sip of coffee, she swallowed before answering. "No. Now, what might I do to help."

At her sudden offer of aid, her enigmatic reply lost relevance. "I was wondering whether Gerda ever mentioned a particular pirate story, a title, perhaps a description of a scene. I vaguely remember a book with treasure and sailing ships. My hazy memory suggests that Gerda was to provide for the gaps in my memory when I came of age, but her unexpected death…" His voice trailed off for a moment. "It must have been devastating for you. I recently lost a close friend." He took a deep breath, forcibly pushed away his grief and managed to keep his voice steady. "Obviously, a will giving me control of Contini Pharma would be the Holy Grail. I can only assume if my grandfather wished Maso to inherit the company, he would have filed a will, or left it with his lawyer or banker. Since he didn't, I suspect it was to protect me. Had I been named, heir—well…he knew his sons. As for Caesar's sudden claim, it's without merit. He was paid for his share of the company years ago."

"I've heard some of this from my sister. Still, your uncle chose to file a lawsuit? Do you know why?"

"He's run up debts he can't possibly pay. Contini Pharma is the means to satisfy his crippling obligations. And in muddying the waters of my paternity he hopes to prevail."

"Your grandfather must have found his sons a burden," Annali said, voicing her disapproval with a humorless smile.

"I'm afraid so. My consigliere, Vincent Weiser, knows all the sordid details."

A sharp gasp from behind the door brought Rafe's head up.

"Gerda always spoke of Vincent with fondness," Annali said, unfazed. "I understand he was close to your grandfather."

"Yes." *If she was feigning deafness, he could too.* "He's been my mentor and friend since childhood. He'd like to meet you today if possible."

She put up a finger. "I still have a few concerns."

"Ask me anything."

"How much danger does Caesar pose to me? If Maso found this house, Caesar could as well. And he has more to lose than Gerda's inheritance," she finished, studying him intently.

"I doubt Caesar knows you exist. He left the company long before Grandfather died. I can put a security team in place to protect you. And you needn't worry for long. I expect to bring this lawsuit to an end shortly."

"You can guarantee my safety?"

"Absolutely, no question." The ensuing silence suggested her decision was still in dispute, so he undertook to give additional guarantees. "I have upwards of fifty men in Geneva protecting my properties. You may have them all if you wish. I'll hire more."

Her slight frown cleared. "I'm sure a lesser number of men will suffice for us, but thank you for your generosity." She gazed at him for a moment in silence.

Rafe was about to ask what more he could do for her when she abruptly came to her feet, walked to the door she'd entered before, opened it and turned to him. "My sister, Mr. Contini."

Rafe stared at the woman who appeared in the doorway, wondering if he was hallucinating or haunted by a ghost from his past. Whether he was imagining things because he wanted to.

"You've grown, Rafail."

The sound of Gerda's voice warmed his soul, reminded him viscerally of those blissful afternoons with his grandfather, turned this glorious phantasm into flesh and blood. Quickly coming to his feet, he went to the woman who represented rare moments of happiness in his life and took her hands. "You look the same," he said, softly, standing back a little to scrutinize her against the remembered image from the past. "*Exactly* the same." Small, rotund, exuding good cheer without the least effort, her flowered dress and colorful apron definitely not designed in Paris. He looked down on her from his great height and smiled. "Perhaps...a little shorter than I recall." His eyes closed for a second, then opened. "*Magnifique*," he whispered. "You're still here. I'm not dreaming."

Gerda shook her head. "You're not dreaming, my boy. Come now," she added, gently squeezing his hands before letting go and gesturing at a table. "Sit. Tell me what I can do for you."

"Maso and Caesar tore apart Grandpere's apartment looking for a will so Vincent is of the opinion the company"—

"Is yours. He's right. I witnessed your grandfather's will."

"Excellent." The single word was deliverance, relief, a chance for a settlement. "Vincent was right after all." His smile unfolded. "Would you mind if he came in? He'll be thrilled to see you."

"I'd love to see him."

Crossing the room in swift strides, Rafe reached the entrance to the hallway, shouted for his friends, then swung around, beaming.

The decades disappeared, and Gerda was reminded of the cheerful, young boy who was the world to his grandfather...and now needed her help.

When the men entered the drawing room, Vincent greeted Gerda warmly, the others were introduced and everyone expressed their delight at Gerda's return from the grave. Once all were seated at the table, an onslaught of questions erupted.

"Hey, hey, point of privilege," Rafe said, raising his hand to fend off the flurry of inquiries. "First, tell us how you managed to facilitate and maintain this subterfuge for so long?"

To no one's surprise, Annali answered, her air of authority unmistakable. "After Nils *accidental* death," she began, with a slight lift of one brow, "Gerda feared for her life. Thanks to our friends, Dr. Kulik, who signed the death certificate, and, Andrei, who oversaw the private funeral and burial, Gerda's sudden *death* raised no suspicions." Annali surveyed the group. "You have the death certificate I presume." At a nod from Vincent, she went on. "We chose this farm for obvious reasons--remoteness and inaccessibility. And here we have remained."

Rafe looked at Gerda. "You suspected foul play in Nils' death?"

"Without a doubt. Nils had raced in Le Mans as a young man. There wasn't a car he couldn't handle. I knew Maso was behind his death. Somehow, the fact that we were witnesses to your grandfather's will had come to Maso's attention, so...we became obstacles in his path."

"When Maso died, we debated coming forward," Annali interjected. "But Caesar was still a threat. And you'd been at the helm of the company for years without hindrance—so..." She raised an eyebrow as if to say, *You understand?*

"You did the right thing," Rafe said. "However, once this lawsuit is dismissed, there's no further need to hide."

"Provided Caesar is neutralized," Carlos cautioned.

"That won't be a problem." Rafe smiled at the women. "If we don't find a will, I'll buy off Caesar. He can be managed." Rafe didn't mention Caesar's mafia cohorts would require a different kind of persuasion, but that too could be managed. "And once Caesar is no longer a danger," he said in extraordinary understatement, "you'll have to come to Geneva or Monte Carlo and meet Nicole." His grin was pure joy. "We're going to have a baby. Another reason," he added, firmly, "I want Caesar dealt with quickly." He took a breath, forced to admit beneath this happy reunion lay a labyrinth of danger. "A few questions more." Turning to Gerda, he apologized for having to ask, mentioned time was an issue. Didn't mention this war with Caesar had to be brought to an end before the mafia's hired guns hit the streets.

Gerda's answers were clear in some cases: the will, stitched into the binding of Howard Pyle's *Book of Pirates,* was in one of two locations; uncertain in others: Maso's search may have disturbed its locale.

"It doesn't look like a children's book," she added. "It has a leather binding and marbled boards. Your grandfather selected it because it was one of your favorites and he thought the nondescript binding might escape notice."

"Ah, yes--that title. Now that you've mentioned it, I recall Grandpapa repeating it to me."

"I'd be happy to come back to Geneva and help you find the book."

"No, no, not just yet," Rafe said. "Let the lawyers do their work first."

It was a lie.

He didn't have time for the lawyers.

Exchanging a quick glance with his friends, he pushed back his chair and rose to his feet. "Thank you for your help. We have a good idea where to look. I'm afraid we have another appointment this afternoon, but we'll stay in touch.

A security team will be here in two hours. Don't worry about a thing."

Annali met Rafe's gaze. "You'll let us know when it's safe."

"I will." Bending low, he gave Gerda a hug. "I'm so pleased you're alive and well. It's awesome." Brushing her cheek with a kiss, he stood upright, his smile matching the warmth in his eyes. "A few days, a week at the most, you'll have your lives back."

Polite goodbyes were exchanged and a moment later, Rafe's party exited the house. Within minutes, their helicopter was airborne.

As the sound of the rotor blades grew faint, Annali leaned back in her chair, and spoke in a considering tone. "It's more than a simple lawsuit if fifty security men are required to insure a successful outcome."

"Nothing is ever simple with violent men like Maso or Caesar." A flicker of dismay crossed Gerda's face. "A shame they're not both dead."

"The boy appears competent."

"Indeed," Gerda said with a bit of a smile. "He could read at three, took over the company in his teens, graduated university at nineteen, increased Contini Pharma's net worth a hundred-fold over the years and"—

"You love him."

"Who wouldn't." She'd followed Rafail's life on the internet, but now, after all these years, it was time to step out of the shadows. Rapping the table top, Gerda said, briskly, "We have to find that will for Rafail." She came to her feet like a shot. "I'll get the car. Bring Daniel's old hunting rifle."

Annali looked at her with disbelief. "Good God, Gerda, be sensible. I'm happy to go with you, but a weapon? Is that necessary?"

"Of course it's necessary. You heard Rafail. He's hired fifty men." She might be willing to defer to her sister in things that didn't matter. But Rafail mattered. "Hurry." She was already halfway across the room. "And don't forget the ammunition. It's in the linen closet."

About to ask why the ammunition for the hunting rifle was in the linen closet, Annali suddenly found herself alone. "*Mon Dieu*," she exclaimed, shocked at Gerda's willful disregard for planning. But the sound of the kitchen door slamming brought her to her feet and she turned her attention to Gerda's requests. Collecting her husband's hunting rifle, she tossed the large supply of ammunition hidden behind the sheets into a duffle bag, and slipped into her bedroom to fetch the revolver concealed under the magazines in her bedside table.

While she'd never mentioned it to her sister, Maso's first visit had shaken her. She'd purchased the Linebaugh revolver against future visits from the man she viewed as deserving of a fifty-caliber round to the head.

Not that she'd ever admit to being faint hearted.

To give into fear was to abandon your principles.

Tossing the handgun into the duffle bag, she zipped the bag, picked it up, grabbed the rifle, walked out of the bedroom and a few moments later, exited the house.

Gerda was behind the wheel of the thirty-year-old black Rolls Royce Daniel had purchased when the private bank he managed had had a particularly good earnings year. Opening the car's back door, Annali deposited the duffle bag and rifle on the floor, closed the door, walked around the back of the Phantom VI, opened the front passenger door, settled onto the rose colored leather seat, drew the door shut and glanced at her sister. "Watch your speed." She indicated the items in the back with a flick of her fingers. "We don't want to be stopped."

"Don't worry. Two elderly ladies in this ancient car—we look harmless. And I must say, I'm feeling almost giddy to *finally* be doing something!" Gerda turned a glowing smile on Annali. "Didn't he look just wonderful? Tall, handsome, sweet as ever."

"Yes, he did, my dear. He looked quite wonderful. Like a cinema star."

31

In the same vein vis a vis Rafe Contini's *wonderfulness*, Nicole discovered that while Rafe may not have noticed the woman who ran his charitable foundation other than in her role as director, the reverse was decidedly not the case.

Within minutes of meeting Isabelle Tansy, it was apparent that she was, if not in love, totally infatuated with Rafe. Her conversation was replete with "Rafe says", or "Rafe thinks", or "Rafe prefers", every observation delivered with a knowing smile, a little nod, even a tender sigh on occasion signifying the depth of his compassion.

The situation might have been awkward if Nicole hadn't chosen to be gracious. But assured of Rafe's love and devotion, she could afford to be magnanimous.

Also, beyond extolling Rafe's superior qualities, Isabelle's comprehensive grasp of the Contini charities...and more definitively, food banks, was truly remarkable. Nicole listened with genuine interest to Isabelle's broad acquaintance with charities around the world. As the chairwoman of a cultural exchange program focused on promoting dance in schools, Isabelle had traveled widely. "Thanks to my trust fund I was able to indulge a pet project," she said, with false modesty and a brief downcast glance that was obviously rehearsed.

"Kudos to you and your generosity," Nicole said, sincere in her praise of Isabelle's charitable impulses.

A delicate pause. "Thank you, one does what one can."

"You gave of yourself more than most," Nicole said, ignoring Isabelle's shortcomings as an actress. "It was very kind-hearted."

"Papa always said we must give back and helping others is so *deeply* fulfilling."

Isabelle's portrayal of Lady Bountiful was wearing. "Tell me how you came to be the Director of the Contini Foundation," Nicole said, looking for a temporary lapse in the drama. "Rafe thinks highly of your work." It was true; there was no reason not to tell her.

"It's a pleasure to work for him. And so I said four Christmases ago at St. Moritz when out of the blue Rafe offered me carte blanche at the Contini Foundation." She smiled. "I'd known him forever and he was such a dear...so caring and considerate--an absolute prince. How could I refuse?"

Nicole was fully aware that Rafe's appeal to women in general and Isabelle in particular, had less to do with his princely beneficence and more to do with his stark good looks, bad boy reputation and colossal fortune. But rather than introduce a note of reality into the conversation, she made another fresh start. "Perhaps we should begin making a list of food banks? I have a few favorites in my neighborhood back home. I'm sure you do as well. Would you like a drink before we begin?"

"I'd *love* a drink."

There. Candor at last. "Forgive me, I should have asked before," Nicole said. "Let me ring for someone. I'm not sure what we have."

"Don't bother." With a wave of her perfectly manicured hand, Isabelle rose from her chair. "I know what I want."

So do I. The subtext this afternoon was clear. As for any information Isabelle might have about the lawsuit, her loyalties were clear; it would be useless to ask her. "If you can't find what you need," Nicole said, politely, "let me know and I'll call for help."

"I'm sure Rafe has what I like," Isabelle purred.

Nicole smiled, rather than yield to her inner bitch. And frankly, she couldn't help but feel a little smug as she watched the tall, willowy blonde, dressed in pale pink cashmere, glide away in a dancer's flowing gait. Despite her cover model perfection and eagerness to please, Isabelle had never been able to engage Rafe's interest.

While her husband's appreciation of beautiful women had been confirmed by any number of glossy tabloids the decade past, Nicole knew it took more than beauty to truly interest him. Self-assurance, the ability to say *no,* strength to withstand a challenge captured his attention; personal qualities she liked to think she possessed in abundance. While the magical lightning flash that had bewitched them both the first day they met could only be characterized as a Twilight Zone moment.

"There now, the perfect drink." Isabelle held up her stemmed glass, the lavender liquid sparkling as she glided back. "An Aviation."

Abandoning beguiling memory, Nicole looked up. "What a lovely color. You found everything?"

Isabelle smiled. "Yes, even freshly squeezed lemon juice.

Rafe has a wonderful staff. Now, then," she said, sitting across from Nicole, setting her drink down on the low table separating the green leather Chesterfield sofas and drawing her laptop near, "let's start with your neighborhood food banks."

Isabelle keyed in swiftly, adding Nicole's names, then hers, asking for Nicole's preferences when she ran through a number of sites from various cities. She drank one drink, then two as they worked, keeping up a steady conversation about seasonal items, menu options, shipping problems at various locations, her expertise amazing. A fact Nicole was more than willing to commend. "I'm in awe," Nicole said. "You have all this information at your fingertips."

"Rafe mentioned you were interested in food banks, so I did some research. He likes answers when he asks questions."

"Well, thank you for doing the research. I really appreciate it."

Isabelle glanced up, questioning Nicole's sincerity. Surprised to see genuine warmth in her eyes, she jettisoned her cynicism. "You're entirely welcome. It's my pleasure." Although, she peevishly thought, why wouldn't Nicole be warm and gracious? She'd won the billionaire lottery. But what really pissed her off was that Rafe, who'd never spent an entire night with a woman, had actually *married* Nicole. Draining her drink in one big swallow, she stood up and said, tight-lipped. "Give me a minute. These are so delicious. I can't resist."

Isabelle was on her fourth drink when Chomak came in with a tea tray. After pouring tea for Nicole, he replenished Isabelle's drink, then stood to one side awaiting further orders. After several moments, he coughed gently.

Nicole looked up. "Sorry, Chomak. Thank you," she said, nodding her head like Rafe had at breakfast. "That will be all." As the door closed on Rafe's butler, Nicole smiled at Isabelle. "I come from a large family without help other than a housekeeper. Chomak takes some getting used to."

"Staff should be invisible. Relax. You're doing fine."

Picturing Mrs. B, who was not only visible, but unapologetically outspoken, Nicole gave a little shrug. "I warned Rafe I may not assimilate. His lifestyle is quite a change." Leaning over, she pushed the tiered plate with delicate sandwiches and pastries toward Isabelle. "Please, help yourself."

"I'm fine, thank you." Isabelle held up her stemmed glass, newly filled with icy lavender liquor.

"I'm afraid I'm hungry all the time." Nicole selected a tiny salmon sandwich. "Rafe reminds me I'm eating for two. It's sweet of him to humor me." Isabelle, along with a number of other Contini Pharma employees, had been at the wedding. Nicole's pregnancy was no secret.

After finishing off the sandwiches, Nicole noticed Isabelle studying her with mild disbelief as she reached for a lemon tart. Rather than comment on Isabelle's liquor consumption, Nicole held up the colorful pastry and smiled. "Here's hoping Rafe still adores me when I'm fat." And she popped the bitesize pastry into her mouth.

Isabelle's smile was forced. "I'm sure he will. Rafe has perfect manners."

Not with Japanese rope. The lurid imagery unceremoniously leaped into her mind, and after a brief fit of coughing the pastry went down. "Yes, I've noticed that," Nicole replied in a near normal tone.

"Noticed what?" Rafe asked, walking into the library.

"We're remarking on your excellent manners."

A flicker of his brows at such obvious bombast, his voice in contrast, smooth as silk. "You don't say. My mother thanks you." Surveying the laptop on the table, as well as several spread sheets, he nodded at the ladies. "It looks like you've put together a plan."

Nicole's smile was dazzling. "The project turned out to be much more expansive than I anticipated, but Isabelle said you approved. I can't thank you enough! Show him what we did, Isabelle." Her gaze swung back to Rafe. "You're an absolute angel, you know."

Rafe laughed. "You're easy to please, Tiger. Seriously, though, I'm glad you're helping some of the food insecure populations." Waving off Isabelle's offer of a spread sheet, he sat beside Nicole, wrapped his arm around her shoulders, leaned in, and kissed her cheek. "It's good to be home."

Something in his voice brought her gaze up. "You're back early."

"I missed you." A pulse beat at the base of his throat, his smile for public consumption. "Are you about done?" His gaze swiveled to Isabelle and it was an order no matter how softly put.

"Yes we are." She closed out her laptop, shut the lid, gathered up the papers in a neat stack and came to her feet.

"Thanks so much for helping me set up the food bank accounts," Nicole said. "I'm incredibly grateful." Glancing up at Rafe, she added, "Isabelle knows just *everything* about food banks."

Rafe smiled at Isabelle. "We appreciate your expertise."

He held his wife with such tenderness, she wanted to scream. "It was my pleasure," Isabelle said, instead, each polite syllable a sham.

"You'll let us know when the checks go out?" Rafe spoke in the purposeful tone he used at the office. "And send a spread sheet to Nicole." He smiled at his wife. "You can monitor the progress if you like."

"I'd like that."

Rafe looked up, gave a nod to Isabelle. "Someone will drive you back to headquarters. Again, many thanks for your help. If you have any questions, give us a call."

A few moments later, the door closed on Isabelle.

Swinging Nicole up onto his lap, Rafe dropped back against the tufted leather, pulled her close and softly sighed. "It's been a long fucking day."

Reaching up, Nicole brushed his cheek with her fingertips. "Are you okay? You sound tired."

His gaze slanted downward and met hers. "I'm fine. My schedule's crap, that's all. Things will quiet down soon."

"I don't suppose I can help."

"Not really." He shut his eyes briefly, opened them and gave her a twitch of a smile. "I want to wrap up this lawsuit. So…I'm asking a lot, but if you could be understanding"—he drew in a breath—"for another day, maybe less, we'll be out of here."

"Seriously?" Sitting up, she framed his face in her hands and held his gaze. "We get to go home?"

He covered her hands with his, nodded. "Word of God."

She kissed him hard, a hotspur, tumultuous reaction to his promise, wanting to believe him so badly she refused to question him further. Sitting back a moment later, she slid her hands free, looked at him gravely. "Tell me what to do and I'll do it."

"I might be gone for a few hours tonight. I don't want you to worry. Carlos, Vincent, Simon and Davey are going with me. We're meeting with Caesar's lawyers, trying to reach some settlement." It was as close to the truth as he could manage. "I don't have to leave until seven, so I'm all yours till then."

She glanced at the tall case clock in the corner.

He gave her the barest hint of a smile. "Whatever you want, Tiger. You're the boss. Oh, shit," he muttered at the message ping on his cellphone. "Give me a minute." Pulling his phone from his jacket pocket, he quickly read the text from Vincent: Annali had called. She and Gerda were on the road to Geneva. Don't send a security team. Rafe texted back, Thanks, then sliding his phone back in his pocket glanced down and smiled. "Business. Nothing that can't wait." His smile widened. "Want me to lock the door? Or are you in the mood for a little more privacy?"

"The thought of Chomak standing outside a locked door might be disconcerting." She smiled. "Mood wise."

"He can't get in."

"Some of us are less exhibitionist than others," she murmured.

He recalled circumstances where she'd not been so shy, but he had no intention of arguing over something so trifling when he was facing what he was facing. "Our bedroom then. Want me to carry you?"

But while making love he found his thoughts straying to his meeting with Caesar, the potential for things going wrong, the possibility of not surviving. Not that he hadn't planned for any and all eventualities; he wasn't reckless. But there were always unknowns.

Perhaps it made him more gentle than usual, or made his kisses sweeter, or prompted him to bring her to orgasm so many times, she finally let out a happy sigh, and gave him a smile so filled with joy, he couldn't help but smile back. "Remember I'll always love you," he said, very softly, the dangers in the night ahead stark.

"Till the end of time..."

His breath caught in his throat, every word filled with new intent, the travails of the world unspoken. He ran a thumb over the softness of her bottom lip, his amber gaze beautiful. "Yes—till then."

32

At seven fifteen, Rafe and Carlos entered his grandfather's townhouse through the mews in back.

"They haven't found anything yet?" Rafe said, moving swiftly across the cobbled courtyard.

"Last I heard."

Rafe shot him a raised eyebrow.

"A half hour ago."

"It doesn't matter," Rafe said gruffly. "We visit Caesar tonight, with or without a will." Reaching the back door, he held it open for Carlos, followed him in and striding down the servants' hall, took the stairs to the entry hall at a run. After greeting the two men at the front door, he asked, "Is everyone upstairs in the library?" and at their affirmative reply, raced up the curved staircase to the third floor. The library door was open, the floor stacked with books, some shelves empty, others filled with books returned haphazardly.

"Maso and Caesar disturbed everything," Gerda said with a scowl. "Vincent did what he could but there are huge sections of books out of order. Going through this disarray is"—she blew out an exasperated breath—"time-consuming." She waved to her left. "We've finished that wall. The book has marbled papers in turquoise, wine and cream, the binding is wine colored. Start anywhere."

"Thanks for coming down to help," Rafe said, "but if we don't find the book, it's not critical. I plan to see Caesar tonight regardless of the search results."

And so it went the next hour. Even with extra men called in to aid in the search, the key book was not found.

Rafe wasn't surprised. It would have been more surprising if the book had surfaced after the almost complete destruction of the room years ago by Maso and Caesar. According to Vincent, wall paneling had been ripped off, paintings wrenched from their frames, drawers tossed and broken into splinters, the floor carpeted with trampled books. He smiled faintly, contemplating their obvious failure when it came to demolishing his grandfather's desk. It stood, then as now, a half ton island of rock-hard walnut in the middle of the room; the seasons of the year carved in bas relief on all sides with the virtuosity and intricacy characteristic of Renaissance goldsmith work. Even the walls of the foot well were elaborately embellished. As a child he'd hide under the desk while his grandfather would pretend he couldn't find him. How many times had he traced the carved panels with his fingers: the boar hunt; the harvest; the winter pruning of the orchards; the ships sailing into port. He stiffened. The *ships*...

Pulling out his phone, he slid his thumb over the glass, brought up the flashlight and moved toward the desk. "I might have something."

His voice was a blend of optimism and incredulity, with a spark of sharpness that swung everyone's glance his way.

"Under the desk," he said, acknowledging his audience. "I used to play there. I remember ships." Pulling out the high-backed, ornately carved desk chair, he dropped to his knees, dipped his head and passed the light slowly over the carvings—abruptly stopped and sucked in a breath. There. Center left—three ships, sails aloft, exquisitely carved from black walnut, the entire scene dark as night.

Dropping onto his back, he slid under the desk, ran his fingers over the ships as he had as a child, tracing the outlines with slightly more pressure than he had then, the surface of the polished wood solid under his fingers across the entire panel until he reached the main mast top sail on the largest ship. He felt the wood give, felt his pulse spike. *Take it easy,* he cautioned himself, breathing in slowly, exhaling even more slowly. *The desk is five hundred years old, wood shrinks, a section of carving can loosen.*

Having steeled himself against false hope, he spread his fingers, set his palm on the top sail, took a breath and pushed firmly. At the faint click, he jerked his hand back, and watched in wonder as a seamless door swung open.

His heart pounding, he reached inside a velvet-lined compartment, touched the slick surface of a book and knew it was marbled papers before he pulled it out and saw the vivid colors.

At that instant, his grandfather's words came flooding back, his voice a low murmur in his ear. *Remember where you hide from me. Remember the sails are hidden too.*

Sliding out from under the desk, Rafe came to his feet, held up the book and smiled. "*Grandpere's* hidden treasure. He must have changed his mind at the end or perhaps"--

"He didn't trust anyone but you," Gerda said.

"A shame I didn't remember what he said."

"It was a lot to expect. You were only five."

Rafe smiled. "On the other hand, Maso didn't find the will, so he couldn't destroy it." He turned the book in his hand. "You think it's really here?"

Gerda nodded. "I'm sure."

Pulling the chair back, Rafe sat at the desk, set the book down and examined the leather binding. This pirate book was one of his favorites. "I'd rather not tear it apart. Do you think we can steam the end papers?"

"Tick tock," Carlos said, softly sardonic.

Rafe looked up and smiled. "That sounds like a no."

Carlos pointed at his watch. "Find the will, blow up Caesar's claim." He smiled. "You can give him the news in person."

"It's just a single sheet of paper," Gerda said.

"Be my guest." Rafe came to his feet and turned the chair.

Gerda found a letter opener in the desk drawer, carefully plucked out the stitching on the leather spine, loosened the binding, slid the point of the opener under the marbled papers on the front board, eased up one corner and smiled. "There it is."

With billions at stake, collective breaths were held and all eyes were trained on Gerda as she gripped one corner of the concealed sheet between her thumb and forefinger, and carefully slid it free. "Here," she said, holding it out to Rafe. "It's yours."

Taking the single sheet of paper, Rafe quickly scanned the document: the notary seals; the two signatures of witnesses; his grandfather's signature written in a bold script across the bottom of the page. Then his gaze returned to the top line where his full name, Rafail Clement (after his grandfather) Contini, was followed by the words, sole beneficiary of Contini Pharmaceuticals. "Contini Pharma's mine," he said, very softly, looking up a moment later, and smiling. "It's a good feeling. A *great* feeling." He softly exhaled. "I didn't really think we'd find it." He grinned. "Thanks to everyone we actually did. Now, to inform Caesar and then"—he blew out a breath—"I can get on with my life."

"Don't forget Caesar's creditors and newest recruits," Carlos said.

"The new recruits will be taken care of soon. The furnace repair men went in this afternoon without mishap. Caesar's creditors will have their lawsuit dismissed, as for the others," he said, giving Carlos a telling look to end any further conversation about their opposition, "I'm sure they won't be an issue." Turning to Gerda and Annali, Rafe smiled. "I'm truly indebted to you. Please, stay here tonight. I'll send a car for you in the morning so you can come over and meet Nicole. I'd invite you now, but I'm not going home until I talk to Caesar--and that might take some time."

"We'll be very comfortable here. I lived in this flat for twenty years," Gerda said. "It's like home."

"Perfect. There's a small staff downstairs. If you need anything, they'll take care of you. I told them you'd likely be here for dinner. Please take advantage of *Grandpere's* wine cellar. Vincent walled up the good wines to keep them safe from Maso, but they're available again. The Chateau Latour '61 might be a good choice tonight. We certainly have reason to celebrate." Rafe gave them a small, ceremonial bow. "I can't thank you enough. Your help was invaluable."

"It was our pleasure. And it's wonderful to be back, and know that your grandfather's wishes are fulfilled." Gerda glanced at her sister. "We couldn't be happier."

"Indeed, it's a felicitous occasion. However," Annali said,

briskly, giving her sister a pointed look, "these young men have things to do tonight."

Understatement. "Yes, beginning with Caesar. He won't like my news. But with a little diplomacy and a good deal of money," Rafe said, drily, "I expect he'll come around. Out of an abundance of caution though"—he held up the will--"I'm going to leave this here." He placed it in the desk drawer. "Don't worry, the flat is secured." A quick smile. "*Au revoir* until tomorrow."

Minutes later, Rafe and Carlos were in the mews, conferring with the group of men who would assist in the operation against Caesar. The new recruits lodged near Rafe's house would be dealt with easily, thanks to the spurious furnace repair that afternoon. The mercenaries housed in the vicinity of Caesar's hotel would be first rendered technically incommunicado and then, dispatched. The good news had been given to Vincent. He'd pick up the will before court in the morning.

Now, all that was left was the visit to Caesar.

And for that, Rafe and his team had the advantage of surprise.

With the preliminary hearing on the lawsuit scheduled for ten a.m. tomorrow, no one was expecting a confrontation tonight.

33

The Hotel President Wilson was built in 1962 during the existential threat of the Cold War. The Berlin Wall had gone up the year before, the Cuban Missile Crisis reached flash point during construction and the doctrine of mutually assured destruction, MAD, was the only deterrent to nuclear war between the US and the USSR. During those tumultuous months, while school children practiced survival drills by hiding under their desks, an underground passage was dug between the hotel and the Banque Nationale de Commerce a block away.

When the hotel manager, Mr. Christophe, received a call on his cell phone and a man's voice said, "I'm in the wine cellar," he immediately knew who it was. After a quick glance at his assistant through the open door to his office, he replied in his normal obliging tone. "Let me check that for you. Give me five minutes."

Coming to his feet, he buttoned his blue suit coat, took an electronic key card from a locked desk drawer, walked through the door of his office and offered his assistant a smile as he passed by. "A small matter, Miss Bonneau. I'll be back shortly."

He took the elevator down two floors, stepped out into the subbasement, walked down a climate controlled corridor, took a key from his waistcoat pocket and opened the door to a wine cellar containing five million euros of fine wines.

Rafe rose from his chair when the manager walked into the tasting room, and smiled. "Thank you for your swift response, Ari. You know Carlos." He gestured at Carlos who was seated beside Simon and Davey. "Simon and Davey are here to lend a hand."

The men exchanged greetings. "Your uncle has heavy security, inside and out," the manager said, taking a seat at the table. "You know that, I expect."

Rafe nodded. "That's why we came in underground. *And* why I need access to the private service elevator. Also, if the surveillance cameras and magnetic sensors in the penthouse suite could be turned off for a short time, I'd be grateful."

"No problem. I'll take care of it. The monitors are next door. Here's the elevator key." Ari took the key card from his pocket and slid it across the table with a warm smile. "This reminds me of old times."

Rafe grinned. "Except, this time, I'm not bringing up a bevy of beautiful women. As in the past, though, it's definitely going to be a surprise." The Royal Penthouse Suite had served as a favorite party venue for Rafe and the men had become good friends. While Ari was a devoted family man and until recently Rafe was not, they'd shared, among other things, an interest in wine and baccarat, and had often indulged those pleasures in this exact room.

"Your uncle's patrons are covering his expenses here. His

newest bankers are, as you doubtless know, gangsters. I'm assuming his debts caught up with him. Not that it's sobered him. He's still as pompous as ever. In fact, when he checked in, he was boasting about a lawsuit that would make him a titan of industry. Your name came up." Ari smiled faintly. "I knew I'd be seeing you."

Rafe grimaced. "My uncle made a deal with the Devil this time. I'm here to advance him the funds to settle his debt and get his neck off the chopping block."

"I didn't get the impression he understood he was at risk."

"He's a fucking head case, that's why. But luckily, he understands simple arithmetic. I'm going to see if I can make us both happy."

Ari frowned. "You four aren't doing this alone? No offense to anyone's skill set, but Caesar has a full security team up there."

"If I know my uncle, his security team is outside, not inside. And this is just a friendly visit. Not that Caesar deserves a lifeline after trying to steal my company, but I figure the less people hurt"—Rafe shrugged—"why not?"

Ari looked at Carlos. "And you?"

Carlos's eyelids drifted lower. "I hate loose ends."

Rafe smiled. "Come on...carrot first, stick later. I'm going in with good intentions. The rest is up to Caesar."

"You're going in solo?" Ari's eyebrows shot up.

"Unless Caesar's had a personality change, he'll be alone. Trust me, I know his fetishes. He doesn't like hired help around." Coming to his feet, Rafe flashed a smile. "Let's get this over with."

Ari looked at Rafe with concern. "You have a weapon at least."

"Uh-uh. Even if I wanted to kill him, murder's messy.

There'd be an investigation. It could be trouble for you, possible trouble for me, problems I'd like to avoid. This is just a courtesy call."

Carlos snorted. "Waste of time with that asshole."

"Humor me," Rafe drawled. "I'm feeling charitable."

Moments later, entering the private service elevator to the Penthouse Suite, Rafe held the door open with one hand, and handed the key card to Carlos. "If you don't hear from me, come up and save my ass."

"Roger that. Don't be gone long."

"I don't plan to. I make my offer, Caesar either takes it or not and it's over. Ten minutes tops." Rafe released the elevator door, and it slid shut.

"We go up in five," Carlos said, checking his watch. "Caesar might be Rafe's relative, but he's not mine. And he's a treacherous, double-dealing prick."

As the service elevator opened on a hallway leading into the kitchen, Rafe experienced a feeling of déjà vu. How many times had he escorted a throng of beautiful women through these doors for a party with his friends? He'd lost count. Europe's largest and most expensive hotel suite at 81,000 euros a night was quintessential party turf: 18,000 square feet, twelve bedrooms, twelve baths, multiple living rooms, a library, panoramic views from the top floor, a wrap-around terrace, a Steinway grand piano, a billiards room, an executive board room, a dining room seating thirty, bullet proof windows, armored doors, private elevator, an ensuite gym and personal chef and butler on call.

Mindful of time constraints, Rafe dismissed fond memory and a moment later, stood in the kitchen, listening to the faint sound of music. *Christ, fucking Wagner. Caesar and Maso both had shitty taste.* Steeling himself against his least favorite music, he moved cautiously through the intervening room, his senses on alert, listening, in particular, for voices.

Caesar might *not* be alone.

There was always that chance in a million.

But Caesar was playing to type tonight, Rafe understood, as he came up to the billiard room. He was alone.

Stopping in the shadows just short of the doorway, grateful for the ear-splitting music that had muffed his approach, Rafe silently observed the scene.

His uncle looked half in the bag, as usual, red-faced, enormously fat, sweat beading his bald head, his open neck silk shirt stretched over his stomach, his slacks so wrinkled they looked as though he'd slept in them. He was playing billiards, and cheating, that too as usual, moving the ball to a more advantageous position before each shot. A cue in one hand, a bottle of single malt in the other, he shuffled around the table, setting down the bottle, taking a shot, picking up the bottle, drinking a long draught, repeating the cycle a couple more times before he leaned over the table for a bank shot. His back to Rafe.

Entering the salon, Rafe walked to the Bang and Olufsen entertainment center, shut off the music, crossed the small distance to the billiard table and said, "How's it going, Caesar? I haven't seen you for a while."

His uncle had raised his head slowly when the music stopped, but his alcohol-blunted brain synapses required a three count before reality registered and a second more for the shock to snap open his bleary eyes. Jerking upright, he dropped the cue stick, stumbled back, caught himself on the table, and snarled, "How the fuck did you get in?"

"Easy, easy...relax," Rafe drawled. "I'm just here for a little chat."

"You better talk fast," Caesar muttered, turning, "cause you're a dead man when I call in my security."

Rafe grabbed his shoulder, hauled him back, his fingers dug in hard. "I wouldn't recommend you do that. Got it?" His amber eyes were stone cold. At his uncle's faint nod, he said, "Now, listen up, I have a proposition that'll save your ass."

Under the best of circumstances, Caesar's restraint was nominal; after nearly a bottle, it was MIA. He wrenched his shoulder free. "Screw you. I'll don't need my ass saved. I'll see you in court tomorrow. Now get the fuck out," he growled, giving Rafe a shove.

Grabbing Caesar's wrist, Rafe jammed his thumb into the nerve, heard a sharp gasp, then leaned in so close he smelled hot, rank sweat. "I forgot to mention, the will turned up. I'm *Grandpere's* sole beneficiary, so you can forget about court tomorrow." He opened his fingers, took a step back. "It's over."

"You're a bloody liar!" Caesar spat, his face flushing a deeper shade of red.

Rafe sighed. All he wanted to do was slam the door on this clusterfuck once and for all, go home, live a normal life. "Look, it's not all bad news. I'll cover your tick with your Russian creditors, get you out of hock and set up a trust to keep you in gambling chips. Tell me what you owe, I'll have it wired to your creditor's bank and you can keep drinking your life away. Come on, whaddya say?"

Caesar paused a moment, then smiled slyly. "You're bluffing. You didn't find a will. There never was one. That's why you want to buy me off."

Rafe's jaw clenched, the temptation to wipe the smile off Caesar's fat face, intense. "I don't bluff," he said, his voice taut with restraint. "Make up your mind."

No reaction for a second, then a shrug fueled by single malt and bravado. "There's no way my father left his company to a five-year-old kid."

What the hell, he tried. "Your call," Rafe said, "but you should have taken the deal." He turned to leave.

"You think you can walk in like you own the world and threaten me!" Caesar screamed. "I'll have you know I have powerful friends who can destroy you! They'll cut you up a piece at a time! You'll beg them to kill you!"

Rafe came to a stop, took a breath, thought about ways to murder someone without leaving fingerprints. Fought the urge; Caesar wasn't worth the trouble. *Keep walking.*

"Maybe I'll have your wife kidnapped, too," Caesar shrieked, his voice tight and excited, alcohol and bitterness feeding his fantasies. "And when that kid of yours is born, I'll make sure it suffers every day as long as"--

Wheeling, Rafe launched himself at Caesar, willing to rip Caesar's throat out with his teeth to shut him the fuck up. Hurtling forward, his fingertips grazed the cue stick on the table. Snatching it up, he balanced it for a nanosecond, slid his palm upward to gain the most torque and slammed it down on Caesar's head with such fury it plowed a furrow in his skull.

The fierce jolt almost lifted Rafe off the floor, clots of brain matter splattering his face went unnoticed, his predator's gaze tightly focused.

For an instant Caesar's face was distorted with surprise, his mouth open, eyes wide, blood pouring down his face from his split forehead, then he toppled forward, his face bounced off the corner of the table and he landed on the carpet with a thud.

Tossing the cue stick, Rafe dropped to the floor, jammed his knee into the center of Caesar's back, got a grip on his head, pulled it up, leaned down and whispered, "No one touches my wife and child."

Then dragging Caesar's head back, he gave it a sharp twist, heard the neck snap, released his grip and watched the head slip to the floor. His breathing rough, he stared for a moment at the widening pool of blood staining the pale, yellow carpet.

Fuck you. And fuck your brother.

Exhaling a long, slow sigh, he tamped down the rush of cruel memory; he wanted Maso and Caesar gone from his life. *Go away, I'm done with you.* It was at last, he thought, coming to his feet, the absolute end. Bending over, he picked up the bloodied cue stick.

"Good work," Carlos said from the doorway. "I was afraid you'd decide to give him a pass."

Rafe turned. "He threatened Nicole." He didn't mention the threat to his baby. Caesar's words had chilled him to the marrow, the evil he'd endured as a child still swirling in his brain.

"He was more stupid than I thought. Give me that cue," Carlos said, coming up to Rafe. "We have to clean this up. Davey, gloves for everyone."

Davey had more than gloves. He'd brought a duffle bag with supplies. When they left, the scene had been sanitized and tidily arranged. The laws of physics dictated the flight of the whiskey bottle, its momentum carrying it a dozen feet past the point where Caesar's head hit the table. A replacement cue was positioned where it would have dropped if Caesar had, indeed, stumbled. Whisky was sprayed on Caesar's shirt front in a fan of droplets that corresponded to his lurching fall. And finally, an untied shoelace served as a conspicuous clue to the fatal accident.

The murder weapon was brought to the basement and

after taking a saw to it, tossed into the incinerator. "That was practically petrified wood," Carlos muttered, shutting the incinerator door.

"The billiard table's from the 1930's. Good quality craftsmanship, some rare African woods, perfect tensile strength." Rafe stripped off his bloody t-shirt and smiled. "Sometimes the gods are on your side."

After everyone washed up in the laundry sinks, the key card was left where Ari could find it and he was informed that the penthouse surveillance could be rebooted, sans the billiard room if possible. Returning through the underground passage, the men waited for Simon to pull up the car to the Commerce Bank then walked out.

Simon drove them to a quiet street, and parked while Carlos and Rafe made calls. After a cryptic conversation, Carlos slipped his phone back into his pocket and waited for Rafe to finish.

"Problem solved," Rafe said, sliding his phone into his pocket. "A ventilation problem produced fatally high levels of carbon monoxide in that house near mine. No survivors."

Carlos smiled. "I heard some terrorists in a safe house blew themselves up. Amateurs building explosive devices never ends well."

"That only leaves the guards outside Caesar's door," Rafe noted. "I expect they'll split once they find the body. Caesar was the mother lode. His creditors are going to want heads."

"Those we have. They're just not breathing anymore."

34

Rafe showered and changed clothes at the mews. As his teams reassembled there, he personally thanked everyone; his own men and those who'd been hired after the attack on Contini Pharma headquarters.

"We'll continue to monitor the situation for another few weeks," Rafe explained. "The Russian mafia funding my uncle's lawsuit may or may not go away quietly. We'll have to wait and see. Carlos's in charge. If you need anything from me personally, he'll let me know. I'm taking my wife back to Monte Carlo tomorrow." He smiled. "I'm extremely grateful to everyone for making our return trip possible. Her safety was always my primary concern, and as of now, it's no longer an issue. In fact," he said, grinning widely, "thanks to you guys, I might actually have a honeymoon."

Simon drove Rafe back to his house, dropped him off at the rear gate, waited while he tapped in the code, opened the heavy oak gate, walked through and shut it behind him.

Resting for a moment, his back to the solid wood, Rafe allowed the adrenaline pulsing through his body to slow.

His gaze on the exterior façade of his Baroque palace, he took note of the few lit and mostly unlit windows, the darkened servants' entrance, the play of shadow and moonlight on the curvilinear architectural detail and smiled, pleased his wife was inside, tired but grateful to be home after a brutal brush with his hellish past. Pushing away from the garden gate, he moved down the garden path, entered the house through the conservatory, and took the back stairs to his dressing room. Opening the door, he slipped inside, softly closed the door and glanced at the set of six clocks displaying time zones on the opposite wall. Christ, it was nearly two.

Standing motionless for a second, he listened intently. Good. No sound from his bedroom.

Moving to a wardrobe wall, he opened a door, took pajama pants off the shelf, stripped off the clothes he'd put on at the mews and stepped into blue flannel pajama bottoms. Looping the tie at his waist as he walked into his bedroom, he came to an abrupt stop. "You're still up." Pulling the bow tight, he raised one brow. "You should be sleeping."

And you should have been home hours ago. Nicole set her book down, told herself to be reasonable even though it was two in the morning. "The story was engaging. Oh hell," she muttered, jettisoning reasonableness in seconds flat, "I can't remember most of what I've read, I've been so worried. Where have you been? It's really late."

"Sorry, I should have called." A conventional answer; the truth was impossible. Moving toward the palace-size four-poster bed in the palace-size room, understanding that discussing the evening's events was out of the question, Rafe took pains, instead, to avoid controversy. "By the time I realized my uncle's lawyers weren't going to leave without a big payday, I was afraid if I called I'd wake you up. Caesar's people bitched about every fucking penny, every stupid comma and clause. I practically fell asleep listening to the mind-numbing minutiae. But hey, it's all over. We get to go home tomorrow." Smiling, he dropped onto the bed, leaned back against the elaborately carved headboard, and pulled her into his arms. "What do you think of that, Mrs. Contini?" Dipping his head, he kissed her cheek. "Feel like going home?"

She broke free of his embrace, sat up and looked at him squarely. "You mean it? Seriously? You not just trying to pacify me cause it's two in the morning and you don't want to argue so you'll say any"--

"Hey, stop." Taking her face in his hands, he held her gaze. "I mean it, okay? My business in Geneva is finished. We go home tomorrow and wait for the baby to be born. That's it. That's all we have to do. I'll make sure you eat well and get plenty of rest and you can smile at me once in a while and make me happy. Swear to God, nothing but sunshine and happiness from now on. How's that? We good?" So he might have been lying a little, but it was mostly true. They were going home and if anyone came after them, the fucking gates were locked and well-guarded. The odds of a happy ending were definitely in their favor, and if anyone knew Monte Carlo odds, he did.

In addition he was perfectly willing to augment those odds with force if necessary. His Monte Carlo security team had been increased substantially, his electronic monitoring had been cranked up to infinity and new facial recognition soft-wear had been installed inside and out.

"Yeah, we're good." Nicole swallowed, started to say something, stopped, gave him a shaky smile, then whispered, "I was so worried..."

"It's all over," Rafe said, gently. "No more late nights for me." But her eyes were tearing up, so he gently drew her back into his arms. "If you're not too tired, I've been thinking about baby names. Do you have any preferences?"

"Are you trying to distract me?" She glanced up and squinted. "Of course you are."

"Of course I am." He liked her ability to pivot and move on. "Come on, indulge me," he said, smiling. "Give me a name."

"Englebert."

He laughed. "With a name like that, we'd better teach him to fight. How about a girl's name?"

"Althea."

"I like it."

"Jeez, you're really on your best behavior tonight. Are you hiding something from me or rather, *what* are you hiding from me?" Narrow-eyed, she watched him, weighing his response.

"Neither." His innocent gaze couldn't have been improved on by angels on high. "Please, I don't feel like arguing or debating whatever the fuck is making you look at me like that. I'm just glad to be back. I'm even more pleased to be holding you in my arms and you having my baby makes me happiest of all." He sighed. "Look, could this wait? It's been a helluva long day."

"Oh God, I'm sorry. You're exhausted and I'm badgering you. Forgive me. I have to learn to be more understanding. Call me on it when I'm not, okay?"

He smiled and shook his head. "Not a problem, Tiger. I like you just the way you are. Talk to me though. Tell me what you did after I left, or give me the plot of your book, let me know how the baby's doing. Anything at all, the fucking weather report, your newest play list; I don't care. I just want to hear the sound of your voice." He needed reminding that a world existed beyond the corrupt and venal, that here and now, by a stroke of luck or an extraordinary conspiracy of fate, he felt warmed by love and human tenderness.

"Chomak brought me chocolate cake and milk after I went to bed," Nicole began, understanding the raw simplicity in his request, wanting to offer him comfort. "He said you'd left orders. The tray had a white linen placemat, with an embroidered border of peach-colored roses, the same color as the roses in the vase on the tray. You picked those out too, Chomak said. He smiled when he said that. I hadn't seen him smile before. He likes you, doesn't he?"

"He might, but I suspect his smile was for you." Rafe touched her cheek with his thumb. "You're adorable, pussycat. How could he not smile?"

"The chocolate cake was divine and the milk was icy cold. He said you'd ordered that as well. You're going to spoil me."

"Yes, I am. Was there enough frosting on the cake?"

She shifted slightly in his arms, her gaze wide. "Don't say you insisted on the exact depth."

He smiled. "I may have mentioned you liked frosting."

"If you're going to be so incredibly sweet to me, I'm going to have to do everything I can to make sure our baby is strong and healthy."

"I'll help."

"I know."

A small silence fell and then he smiled. "You make me happy." He touched her mouth lightly, the pad of his index finger an almost imperceptible pressure. "Don't ever leave me."

"I won't." One downy brow went up a notch. "And?"

"I'll be staying," he said, a bad boy grin crinkling the

corners of his amber eyes. "Absolutely, surely, no doubt about it. Now tell me about the book you're reading." He needed a diversion from the formidable array of enemies taking up space in his brain; would they accept their defeat and fade away? Or would they respond with reprisals? Try to kill him and those he loved.

"It's a biography of a medieval Portuguese princess."

He looked surprised for a moment, then concentrated. "That's off the beaten path. What year?"

"She married in 1095, they're not certain of her birth date. My minor was medieval history, so I was pleased to find the book in your library."

"Ah--a chem major with some fun on the side," he said, approvingly. "So tell me about this princess."

"Her name was Theresa. She was the daughter of Alfonso VI of Castile and was married to Count Henry of Burgundy, a crusading knight in service to her father. Her dowry included the fief of Portugal, recently won from Moslem Spain. She and her husband continued to wage war against the Moors, hoping to gain enough land to lay the foundation for a kingdom. Even after her husband died in battle, Theresa led her soldiers on campaigns and in the lull between wars, surrounded herself with poets, musicians and lovers. Strong, independent women, particularly medieval women, interest me. In order to survive in that powerfully male world, a woman had to be smarter, more strategic and resilient than her opposition. In fact,"—Nicole looked up and smiled. Rafe was sleeping. Apparently, medieval history wasn't as fascinating to him as it was to her. More likely, his lack of sleep the last few days had finally overcome him.

Fortunately, they were going back to Monte Carlo tomorrow. And now that the crisis that had brought him to

Geneva was resolved, his schedule should be less hectic. She could press him for details apropos that resolution, but disclosure had never been his strong suit. It was enough that they were going home, more than enough. It was heaven.

She closed her eyes.

35

Early the next morning, Rafe slid out of bed without waking Nicole. Quickly dressing in navy slacks and a white crew neck sweater, he went in search of his cook to arrange a lunch menu respectful of Nicole's tastes. Mrs. Gladis greeted him with surprise; he'd never been in her kitchen.

"I'd like to go over a menu for lunch today." His smile was bland, as if he commonly oversaw her menus.

"Certainly." Aware of his late return last night--household gossip being what it was, she suggested, "Perhaps coffee and a slice of apple strudel while we talk?"

"That would be great. Thanks."

Taking note of his examining gaze surveying the large, white-tiled kitchen, she gestured at a table near the windows. "Please, have a seat."

As he moved down the wide aisle between the counters, he greeted the kitchen staff with a smile and a good morning, stopping for a moment at the pastry chef's station to admire a clafoutis, the custard tart brilliant with cherries. "With pits?" Rafe's raised brows seconded the query.

"But of course," the young pastry chef said. A traditional dessert of the Limousin region, the pits were thought to give the fruit more flavor.

"Excellent. I wonder if we might have a fresh one for lunch."

The chef admired the deferential tone from a man who had the sublime confidence and jungle instincts of a powerful, billionaire CEO. "Not a problem, sir."

Rafe's eyes widened for a moment at the honorific, but too tired to correct the needless courtesy, smiled instead. "My wife will be pleased."

Sitting at the table a moment later, Rafe leaned back in the chair and shut his eyes. He was looking forward to sleeping more than a few hours at a time. A week would be nice.

"There now."

Opening his eyes, he smiled at Mrs. Gladis as she placed a tray on the table and began setting out their coffee and strudel. "It's been a busy few days," he said. "I'm looking forward to"—

"Less commotion?" The house had been filled with extra security.

A normal workday, the company of my wife. He smiled. "Yes. My thanks for dealing with the added entourage. My wife and I leave directly after lunch, so your duties will lessen somewhat. But Carlos and a few of his men will stay." He dropped two sugar lumps into his coffee.

"It's not a problem. We're equipped to handle a large number of guests. You must be pleased your schedule has freed up."

Rafe glanced up from stirring his coffee. "Yes...very much."

Her employer looked and sounded weary. She knew

Caesar Contini had become a problem, but hadn't he always been? Since her father had served as steward to Clement Contini, she knew all the rumors. "Tell me what you had in mind for lunch," she said, wanting in however small a way to ease Rafe Contini's burdens.

"You remember Gerda, don't you? She and her sister are coming for lunch. Although," Rafe said with a small smile, "my main concern is for my wife. I want her to have foods she enjoys."

"I understand." The cook had come to work for Rafe when he'd first purchased the house. Over the years, none of the staff, she more than any, had ever thought the young man who ran his grandfather's company with masterful competence while living a life of scandal would succumb to love. "Why don't I begin with a few choices for each course," she said, finding the concern for his wife that had brought him to her kitchen for the first time, touching. "Then you tell me if Mrs. Contini would approve."

By the time the menu was finished, Rafe had had three cups of coffee, two slices of strudel and at Mrs. Gladis' suggestion, a small omelet with chives.

Pushing away from the table, Rafe smiled. "Thank you for breakfast and your expertise on the menu." He came to his feet. "And thanks to the excellent coffee, I'm fully awake. Now, if you'll excuse me," he said, with a dip of his head, "I have some calls to make."

Taking the stairs to the ground floor at a run, he swiftly strode to his study, dropped into a chair, punched in Carlos number and said, "Tell me the latest."

"The body hasn't been officially discovered yet. But according to Ari, Caesar's security team is gone."

"As expected. Good. Text me when the authorities arrive."

"I will. None of the mafia made an appearance. We're monitoring those still in the city, but with their ranks sizably reduced, any operations are, at least, temporarily hampered."

"After the court hearing today and some cost/analysis calculations, Caesar's creditors may decide to write off their losses."

"Possible. They have to be aware that they're seriously screwed."

"As are their future options. Deprived of Caesar as front man, they don't have standing in court. Keep me in the loop. I have to make a quick call to Vincent, then get back to Nicole before she wakes up."

"Best case, we have a few days to regroup. Enjoy your honeymoon."

Rafe heard the twitch of humor in Carlos tone at the last. "In the event it's short."

"Yes, that."

"Consider me warned." Rafe was as clear-eyed as his personal bodyguard when it came to his enemies. "I'll have Nicole back in Monte Carlo by mid-afternoon. After that, Caesar's goons can go fuck themselves."

"Agreed. Your place there is locked down."

"Tighter than the proverbial vulgarity of your choice," Rafe replied, a new lightness in his voice. "I'm counting the hours till we're out of here."

"Call me from the airport. The security teams at your house can be reassigned."

"Will do." Rafe glanced at the clock. "Hey, I gotta go."

"Pussy-whipped."

Rafe laughed. "The quid pro quo is damned fine, and to that point, *Ciao*."

His call to Vincent was brief. Everything was in order.

There wasn't a scintilla of doubt how the court would rule. As with his previous call, Rafe said, "Text me when the ruling comes in."

He called Gerda last and arranged a time for her and her sister to be picked up. He also explained that he'd kept most of the particulars of the lawsuit from Nicole. "Everything's so messed up, I simply told her I had to deal with some issues here in Geneva. If she asks questions about the lawsuit, you needn't be duplicitous. I don't mean that or"—

"Annali and I will be discrete if we can," Gerda said. "Don't worry."

"Thank you. Nicole means the world to me. I don't want her worrying unnecessarily."

As it turned out the conversation over lunch didn't require censoring. After meeting the two women, Nicole smiled and with undisguised excitement, instantly said, "You don't know how *thrilled* I am to talk to someone who knew Rafe as a child. Tell me *everything!*" Then her swift litany of questions began: What did Rafe look like? Was his hair long or short? Did he laugh easily? She'd heard that he could read at three. Was that true? How young was Rafe when Gerda had first seen him?

"He was a week old," Gerda began, "sturdy as a little oak, cute as a button, with a full head of dark, silky hair, and lovely, big eyes."

"I knew it, I knew you were a beautiful baby," Nicole said in a rush, flashing Rafe a smile. "Tell me, how he looked when he laughed. Sorry," she added with another quick smile for her husband. "I'm trying to picture you as a baby."

His small sigh was indulgence.

Understanding Rafe's sigh was also permission, Gerda went on to explain about his early reading and the games Rafe and his grandfather had played: children's board games; chess when Rafe had left babyhood; a verbal game of numbers she could never understand but one that had made Rafe laugh and clap his hands, and made his grandfather smile. "I think it had something to do with music as well." She turned to Rafe. "Do you remember?"

"I do. It was a puzzle with numbers for notes and chords, the sum a line of music."

"You amaze me," Nicole said, softly. "You always have."

He smiled. "As you do me, darling. Now I think we might be boring our guests. Are you about finished with questions?"

Since her interrogation had lasted through several courses and the cherry clafoutis was being served, Nicole graciously acquiesced. "Thank you *so* much, Gerda. My apologies, as well, for my persistence, but Rafe and I just met three months ago and he's the most reticent man I've ever met"—she shot Rafe a cheeky grin—"particularly when it comes to his personal life. So when I find someone who knew him when he was young, well"--she threw her arms open wide—"how can I resist asking every little thing."

"You could have asked me," Rafe said.

"Ha! As if you'd tell me."

"You may not have remembered much of those early years anyway, Rafail," Gerda politely interjected, aware that he'd not interfered with his wife's interrogation when he could have cut it short on some pretext. In fact, Rafe's affection for his wife was obvious. Understanding some of the trials he'd undergone as a child, Gerda was delighted that Rafe had found love. And no one could doubt he was loved; Nicole wore her heart on her sleeve.

As the visit came to a close, the women were invited to Monte Carlo, and agreed to come once the baby was born.

Soon after, Rafe and Nicole escorted the ladies to a car waiting outside and said their goodbyes.

"So," Rafe said, turning to Nicole as the Mercedes sedan passed through the electric gates, "are you ready to go back to Monte Carlo and pull up the drawbridge?"

"Do fish swim?"

He smiled. "Last I heard." Raising his hand in a slight gesture brought another black Mercedes purring to life in a corner of the courtyard.

Nicole looked up and winked. "You run a smooth operation."

"Mostly normal routine. Davey's waiting for us at the airport." A moment later as the car came to a stop, he opened the back door and helped Nicole in. "We're finally going home, Simon." The smile in his voice was conspicuous as he slid in beside Nicole and pulled the door shut. "How's that sound?"

"Damn good. I have some vacation time coming."

"We all do. And if you want to set some records to the airport, I'll pay the fines."

"Gotcha. Hang on."

Rafe put his arm around Nicole as Simon accelerated through the gates, smoothly swung right and stepped on the gas. "You don't mind a little speed, do you?"

"Nope," she said, turning slightly in his arms. "The faster the better."

He gave her a lazy smile. "I've heard that once or twice before."

"And you'll hear it again real soon."

"Awesome." His smile was tantalizing. "Two hours, Tiger, and we'll be on our honeymoon."

"For how long?" Her smile was candy sweet. "I only ask because your life is more complicated than mine."

"The complications are gone, so our honeymoon is as long as you want; a year or two, ten. You decide."

A little frisson of pleasure ran up her spine at the prospect until her voice of reason sensibly stepped in. "Don't forget the baby in between."

"I doubt that'll be possible," he said, drily.

"Oh, God, you're not going to be pissed again about me not telling you."

"No, not at all," he said, understanding what was required of him. "I'm looking forward to the baby."

"Oh, good," she said, blowing out a quick breath. "Me too. I can hardly wait to see what he or she looks like. You were absolutely darling according to Gerda. Do you have baby pictures I could see?"

"My mother might have some."

"Seriously, you don't know?"

He looked at her. "Haven't a clue. It's not a guy thing or at least not in my world." *Survival topped his list from his earliest memories.* "I bet you have photos, though. You'll have to show them to me some time," he added, changing the subject. "Did you have pigtails?"

"Do I look like Pippi Longstocking?"

"From your expression of disgust, I'm guessing not... whoever Pippi is."

"She was a fictional girl with pigtails who led an adventurous life. It sounds as though *your* adventure reading leaned toward pirate stories."

"I wish. I was thrown into boarding school at nine, and the word, adventure, took on a stark reality."

"God, sorry, I always forget. Speaking of babies, do you think our baby boy will inherit your size?"

He appreciated her admirable sense of retreat. "For the

record, I want a girl, so keep that in mind. And I don't care about size."

"For the record," she repeated, "it's a fifty-fifty crapshoot. You'll have to take what you get. But I'm betting on a boy."

This wasn't the time to bring up his misgivings about having a son and failing him as he'd been failed. Not that he gave undue significance to psychic ghosts, but a girl would eliminate the risk of repeating bad behaviors. It was a matter of hedging his bets. But ever courteous, he said, "Whatever you choose to give me, pussycat, will be perfect."

"Such finesse."

He smiled. "I'm in a super good mood. We're going home."

36

Once Nicole was seated in the plane with a magazine and cup of tea, Rafe excused himself. "I'll give Davey a heads up. Tell him we're ready to leave." After relaying the message to Davey, he stood in the cockpit and gave Carlos a call. "We'll be airborne in ten minutes. You probably heard, but Vincent texted me that the court ruled in our favor. No surprise, but still, it's a fucking relief to have it over. Now, it's only a question of whether the Russian mafia withdraws."

"We'll have a better idea in a few days."

"Keep me informed."

An hour later, Rafe's Gulfstream landed in Nice. Simon pulled up the car Rafe kept at the airport and forty minutes later they reached Monte Carlo; the trip two hours, door to door. As Simon drove away and they walked up to the carriage house entrance, Rafe took Nicole's hand and pulled her to a stop. "I think the time has come for me to carry you over the threshold like a proper bridegroom." Her expression unreadable, he looked at her, a small smile on his lips. "Is the tradition *passe*?"

"You're romantic."

"You didn't know that?"

"I thought the word frightened you."

"Nothing frightens me," he said, calmly. "Now humor me, Tiger. For the first time, this feels like a real home."

"It does, doesn't it?" Her voice was hushed. "This will be my first home, you know...married I mean"—she looked up, her eyes velvety blue and warm with affection—"to you."

"Your only marriage by the way," he said, careful to soften his voice in order not to give offense. "I wonder if we should have a photographer memorialize the occasion?"

"I don't think I'll ever forget."

At the small tremble in her voice, he quickly shoved open the door, hoping to arrest her tears and swung her up in his arms. "Me neither," he whispered, dropping a kiss on her nose, raising his head and taking a small breath. "I've never done this before, nor will I again, so" he smiled—"do I have your attention?" He paused and at her mute nod, quietly said, "At"—he lifted his arm enough to see his watch—"four o'clock, October seventeenth"—his deep voice dropped to a murmur—"my darling wife and I begin our honeymoon. And I promise our life together, under sunshine and starry skies"—a boyish smile, touched with sweetness—"will be forever happy." His amber gaze revealed the depth of his love. "Ready?"

"Oh dear...tell me not to cry," she sniffed, her eyes wet with tears.

"Cry all you want. I'm here to wipe away your tears." He grinned. "You have to say, ready, though or I can't move."

She laughed as he intended. "Yes, yes, ready!"

He crossed the threshold of the home that had always been his refuge, and in good times, a place of joy. But now it was truly a home with a wife, a prospective child and a love he never could have imagined. Fate had taken a hand, or instinct, or some preposterous stroke of luck and he'd finally reached landfall. "Welcome home, Tiger. We'll show the baby around later," he said, in a casual conversational tone to stay Nicole's tears, "and decide on a room for a nursery."

"Next to ours," she instantly replied, firmly--and tearless.

"Ah, of course," he said, kicking the door shut. "You see how much I have to learn. Now what's on your schedule?"

As if turned out, they spent their first few hours home in a cozy domesticity unique to both their lives, yet curiously satisfying; as though they were accustomed to deciding where a cradle should go, or a crib, whether to have the room next door to their bedroom painted mint green or butter yellow. Or whether, perhaps, the dressing room should be converted into a nursery.

He took pleasure in her excitement as she chose one thing or another, and found it beguiling when she'd look up to make sure her decision was agreeable to him. As if he'd ever say no. "I defer to you in all things having to do with babies," he said. "Consider me your neophyte partner. Tell me what to do and I'll do it."

She laughed. "Give me a moment to absorb the enormity of your compliance."

His eyelids drifted lower, amusement in his gaze. "A qualified compliance, pussycat."

"As if I didn't know," she said with a grin. "Honestly though, I appreciate your offer." Speaking to the personal privacies he protected from intrusion, she added, softly, "Thanks for being understanding. A baby needs *both* parents."

He absorbed the gut punch, took a quick breath and smiled. "You can count on me. I won't fuck this up." *Oh shit.* "I mean I'm committed to being a good dad--from day one."

"I know you will be. You're already so good to me." She smiled. "And babies are so sweet you can't help but love them."

He had to change the subject; it was blowing a hole in his life-long defenses. "Maybe we should go online and order some baby furniture. How about it?"

By the time they'd furnished the nursery, selected the name of a local painter, decided on birth announcements cheerfully characterized by Nicole as, "Syrupy in an artfully wonderful way," he'd regained his equilibrium. But he was on guard now against future parenting minefields.

They had an early dinner, an earlier bedtime that wasn't entirely about sleep, and once Nicole was blissfully satisfied and sleeping soundly, he dressed and went to find Simon and Davey.

Meeting in the computer room at the main house, they double checked the security operation with the evening crew, held a brief conference call with Carlos in Geneva then went to spend a few hours with Henny.

Seated in the mausoleum, a drink in hand, the men talked about their lost friend, their memories comforting and poignant, amusing, even heartening at times as they remembered joyous events they'd all shared with Henny. As midnight approached, Rafe drained his glass of Macallan, set it down on the marble bench and came to his feet. "I don't want to leave Nicole for long." Moving to the simple white marble sarcophagus in the center of the room, he placed his hand on the cool stone, his gaze on Henny's favorite Rilke quote carved into the marble: "Let life happen to you." Raising his head, he whispered, "I miss you, I always will. Remember that." Drawing in a breath, he absorbed the unforgiving sorrow. "Till tomorrow, *mon ami*."

37

Nicole was coming awake when Rafe walked into the bedroom, carrying a tray with her breakfast.

She smiled. "Good timing."

"Thank you, we try," he said, using the royal we with ease. "Sit up and I'll put this in your lap."

"I just love orders the minute I wake up."

Damn that was a luscious little pout, all sleepy-eyed and sexy as hell. "I know what kinds of orders you like, pussycat. We can talk about that later," he said with a grin. "Right now you have to eat." Picking up a t-shirt draped over his arm, he held it out. "Don't argue, okay? Just put it on."

She smiled. "I could say since when, but"—

"You don't want to get cold."

His drawl held a slight edge. She took the offered T-shirt.

While she slipped it on, he made a mental note to see that sleepwear or a robe was always within reach since he planned on continuing this morning routine until the baby was born. Nicole's voluptuous nudity would test a monk's virtue. And a monk he wasn't.

Unfolding the legs on the tray, he set it over her lap.

"Sorry, no coffee, but you have hot chocolate. Caffeine is restricted in pregnancy. Intense exercise too. Swimming is acceptable. I'm sure the list will expand as I become better informed. How are you feeling? Rested I hope. That's another thing—eight hours of sleep is compulsory."

Her eyes narrowed slightly. "Don't tell me you're going to do this for the next seven and a half months."

"Okay, I won't tell you."

Really, you don't have to. I'm super healthy"--her brows lifted—"independent"—

"Semi-independent. The baby's half mine. You're all mine, but I'll try to share so you won't scowl at me like that."

"Don't you have work to do," she grumbled. "I heard you run a company with twenty thousand employees."

He'd been up for three hours already; his company had been given his full attention. He was taking a break. "You're not interested in my heartfelt devotion?"

She looked amused. "I'm impressed. You're learning new words."

"All in the interest of conjugal harmony, sweetheart. Tomorrow's word is adoration or soulful, maybe oogamy depending on whether"—

"Oh God—stop." She was smiling.

"Okay. Eat now or would you like me to feed you?"

"You know what I'd like?"

He grinned. "After you eat, I promise. I don't have a conference call until ten. Now, hot chocolate first or a mango smoothie? Some strawberries? Or these crepes with an egg, butter and syrup on top?"

She wrinkled her nose. "Eggs and syrup? I don't think so."

"Come on, you don't know how good it is. Try a bite." He grinned. "Want me to play the airplane game?"

"Jeez, you bulldoze a lot?"

His company was one of the most profitable in the world, so yeah, he did. "I'm just concerned for your health," he said with a super sweet smile, "and for the baby too. According to gestational guidelines, nutritional requirements are more important than ever now."

She stared at him for a moment, her mouth pursed. "Guidelines? Requirements? Did you hire a nutritionist?"

"No." *He'd hired three--twenty-four hour coverage. Just in case.*

"Look, I know how to eat well, okay? It's practically a religion in San Francisco. I know what I'm doing."

"Good. That's settled, then. Now try the crepes."

She rolled her eyes. "You're not gonna give up are you?"

"Come on, just try. If you don't like them, we'll send them back."

A moment later Rafe suppressed a smile as Nicole glanced up after swallowing her first mouthful and murmured, dreamily, "Ohmygod...those flavors are *heavenly.*"

Instead of saying, *I told you so,* he held up another forkful, and spoke in a light, cajoling tone. "Here we go, pussycat. Another airplane coming in..."

She giggled. "You don't seem the type for baby games."

Nor was he, but he understood the concept of *whatever works.* "I like taking care of you. Indulge me."

"I can help take care of you too, you know," she said, softly.

Discussing his beliefs apropos of who took care of whom would have been counterproductive, so he politely said, "Perfect. We'll help each other. Now let's finish this breakfast."

After eating most of the food, Nicole finally shook her head.

"Just a couple more bites of strawberries."

Nicole put up her hand. "No, no and *no*."

"You did well," Rafe said, mildly. "The baby and I thank you." Setting the tray aside, Rafe turned back with a smile. "Want to give your food a little rest? I'm not going anywhere for a while."

"Or we *could* take it slow."

He laughed. "So far I haven't had much luck slowing you down, but I'll do my best."

He undressed quickly, a mild source of irritation she overlooked because there were better things to consider than his wild past when he was stripping. Damn, he was beautiful; classic features, stark cheekbones, fine straight nose, the slight tilt to his amber eyes a remnant of some eastern ancestor. Her gaze slid lower to his broad shoulders, his taut, hard stomach—she softly inhaled as he came upright--his tatted erection huge and navel high. "I'm not sure slow is going to be possible. That"-she pointed—"is one serious aphrodisiac."

"Speaking of aphrodisiacs"—he kicked aside his sweats —"I can see your nipples through that T-shirt. Do they want to be sucked?" Smiling, he took in the rising peaks pressing against the soft cotton. "Apparently so. Take off your shirt."

"Or?" An automatic response to orders.

"Or maybe I'll jack off while you watch," he murmured, curling his fingers around his rigid cock.

A half second debate, a glance at his massive dick, and pulling off her T-shirt, she hurled it at him. "Jerk."

"Sorry, I shouldn't tease you," he said, walking over the T-shirt and moving toward the bed. "I do apologize. Would you like to hit me?" Stopping bedside, he opened his arms. "Punch hard."

She sighed. "Nah, I'm not mad anymore. Short fuse, sorry. Personality flaw."

"Uh-uh, my kind of personality; cheeky, audacious. I like it." He sank to his knees, touched her arm. "Seriously, my fault anyway. Now come a little closer and I'll suck on my tits."

She held up a finger. "I don't want to be a trouble-maker, but they're only half yours. You can suck on your half."

Suppressing a smile, he said, "Appreciate it." Her give-no-quarter posture was charming and optional depending on how badly she wanted something, i.e. sex. He understood. "Put your hands on my shoulders. I'm going to move you." Lifting her in a smooth show of strength, he swung her around, so she was sitting on the side of the bed, her legs straddling his body. Then slipping his hands under her bottom, he drew her closer. "They're really showy, getting bigger all the time," he murmured, sliding his fingertips over her flamboyant breasts. "Fucking beautiful." Then his gaze lifted to hers, and he lightly touched each nipple with an impressively feather-light stroke. "Feel that?"

"Clear down to my tippy toes," she said on a suffocated breath, the evanescent tingle like a match to tinder, flame hot lust streaking downward with dizzying speed. "Is there more?" she whispered, half-breathless. "You have to say yes."

"Yes, always yeses for you," he gently said, and balancing her plump, expanding beasts on his fingertips, lowered his head, and unhurried, kissed first one taut crest, then the other, delicately, repeatedly, with a barely there pressure until she was breathing fast and starting to squirm. Stopping with his lips resting lightly on a jewel hard nipple, he glanced up, quickly debated her impatience versus delay and deciding she was still manageable, drew the stiff, rigid peak into his mouth, with a slight, exacting pressure. A dilletante's austere sampling; a connoisseur's trifling coercion.

Nicole's soft moan was gratitude and approval, a spiking bliss curled downward, melting, hot and delicious, into every glossy, overwrought nerve in her pussy, desire flaring, liquifying. Tightening her grip on his shoulders, she arched her back, and pressed against his mouth, craving more of the delicate, shimmering splendor, the sense of expectation acute.

Sensible of her rising arousal and his husbandly obligations, Rafe's fingers closed firmly on Nicole's resplendent breasts, and increasing the pressure of his mouth, he sucked and nibbled, lightly bit and teased each stiff peak until she was feverishly whimpering.

An audible, recognizable ask.

He closed his teeth on one engorged nipple, softly enough not to do harm, firmly enough to leave marks, calculated to shock; one hundred percent guaranteed to hot wire every libidinous nerve in her body.

She squealed at the fierce lustful jolt, the tenuous pain/pleasure tremor sheer ecstasy, the high-octane, full-on hit to her pussy like a drug to an addict. Clutching fistfuls of hair, she dragged his head close, then closer still, wanting more of the brute, scorching rapture.

Being smothered by a huge, opulent breast wasn't all bad, but his darling wife had expectations that involved some effort on his part, so he eased a finger between his nose and her tit, and shoved her back enough so he could breathe. Also, fully aware she was at that semi-hysterical, give-it-to-me-now state where delay was iffy, he sucked her nipples, hard, hard, hard, slid two fingers into her drenched pussy, stroked her favorite erogenous zones with targeted subtlety, and listened for that tell-tale catch in her breath.

Wait, wait, wait—and....yes!

Quickly now--G-spot, clit, fingers and thumb with one hand, adjust his grip on her breast with his other hand, and suckle her nipple with enough force to stretch the sensitive crest. Then, having attenuated the soft flesh to the max, he bit down roughly.

Her orgasmic scream exploded, and despite the hellish ringing in his ears, he smiled. She was so fucking easy to get off, sweet-as-candy innocent for all her sass and swagger; a radical change from his vice-ridden past for which he was profoundly grateful. Her innocence called for a tamer sexual repertoire with limited crazy shit, but *c'est la vie*. She liked simple pleasures, orgasms any which way--that's it, she was happy. And strangely or weirdly considering his seriously fucked up carnal history, if she was happy with semi-vanilla, he was too.

To that end, he politely waited—ignoring the ringing in his ears--until her last spasm died away, her screams wound down and her painful grip loosened on his hair. "Just a FYI," he said softly, understanding she was still coming down. "I'm moving you."

He didn't expect an answer, nor did he get one. Coming to his feet, he carefully lifted her, swung her into the center of the bed, and covered her with the blanket. "You good?"

Nicole's blissful purr was sweet content.

"Rest now."

Her eyes half opened, revealing a sliver of blue flame. "Don't want to."

He hesitated for selfish and unselfish reasons.

"There's time until ten." She smiled. "In case you were wondering."

"Sure?"

A quick lift of her brows. "I am about me, so if it's not too much of an imposition for *you*," she drawled.

He was smiling when he glided into her liquid warmth, her soft, breathy moan warming his shoulder, her gently pulsing pussy welcoming, his low, deep growl testament to the exquisitely tight friction. And once he was fully ensconced, his dick buried deep, he moved in a slow ebb and flow, penetrating and withdrawing gently at first, then not so gently, alert, as always, to her impatience; and when, in her frankly confessed state of addiction she quickly reached crisis point, he plunged in a compelling depth more, politely waited for her first orgasmic ripples to slide up his erection, waited a nanosecond more for her overwrought scream to arrive, then without missing a beat, with a libertine's experience and a lover's joy, he came with her in a noisy/quiet, perfectly coordinated climax.

Sometime later, her lashes lifted, and she whispered, "Thank you very, very, *very* much..." The husky note in her voice matched the shimmering heat in her eyes. "Don't go just yet."

"I'd stay if I could," he murmured, brushing her mouth with a kiss. Giving the bedside clock a glance, he debated his responsibilities for a fraction of a second before withdrawing. *Nine fifty-five. Even Nicole wasn't that fast.* "Sorry, Tiger, I gotta go." Bending low, he kissed her. "A dozen people are waiting for me." With a biceps swelling push up, he swung his feet off the bed, stood in a smooth ripple of muscle, reached for his sweats, and pulled them on. "It's going to be a few hours. Do you want me to call someone over from the main house?" He didn't keep permanent staff at the carriage house.

Tamping down her feverish desires, she took a steadying

breath. He had people waiting for him; it was time to be mature and accommodating. "Don't bother anyone. I'm fine." She blew him a kiss. "I'll work for a few hours, too." She pointed at a small desk set against the wall. "It's a perfect place to write."

"I know it's our honeymoon and I *do* apologize," he said, picking up a grey T-shirt from a chair, pulling it over his head, slipping his arms into the sleeves and letting it fall over his ripped torso. "But this is something Vincent can't handle. I'm really sorry."

She shook her head. "Don't apologize. I understand." She was navigating their honeymoon waters with equal politesse.

He smiled. "This takes some getting used to, doesn't it? Just you and me."

"Tip toeing around each other, yes." She grinned. "I was raised in a large family though and you learn to create space for yourself. Otherwise, you'd be swallowed up whole. What I'm trying to say is I don't mind being alone."

"Good. I'm used to being alone, too."

"So I don't have to entertain you every minute?"

He laughed. "Jesus, talk about a perfect marriage. Maybe we should light some candles to make sure the gods stay on our side."

She held up crossed fingers. "Do you have a chapel here?"

"Yeah, I'll show you later. It's in the main house." A quick glance at the clock, a grimace. "If you need something, I'm next door in my study. Come get me."

"Something?" she purred.

"Behave," he muttered. "If I don't sort out this conference call, I'll lose a ton of money." But he didn't move. He waited because he loved her more.

"I shouldn't tease you. Now, *I'm* sorry. Go."

"If I can get this group to cooperate, I might finish sooner. If you're bored, come and sit in on the conference call."

Her smile was dazzling. "Not on your life. I have a screenplay to write."

He chuckled. "Let me know when I can read it."

"Right now, it's at the don't-hold-your-breath stage."

"Fair enough." He held up his hand, three fingers visible. "Worst case, I'll see you for lunch at one."

Their honeymoon continued apace in the same satisfying pattern: breakfast in bed; a walk together when possible; work time; a shared luncheon, more work, then an evening of companionship and pleasure. And after Nicole fell asleep, Rafe visited Henny.

Not that their schedule was firmly fixed. It was subject to Nicole's impetuous nature, seething hormones, and lustful cravings, all of which Rafe viewed as awesome opportunities. He'd never turned down sex in his life so obliging his wife's ramped up libido was no imposition. In fact, he chalked it up to another instance of their admirable marital compatibility.

38

And so it went, their life together one of perfect harmony.

Nicole was busy with her screenplay, writing and rewriting, then writing some more.

Rafe handled Contini Pharma remotely with the help of a dozen critical employees he'd imported from Geneva and installed in the main house; occasionally he flew to Geneva to deal with problems face to face. Nicole chose to stay home the second time he went. Rafe was back before dinner. He'd missed her.

Nicole pregnancy was uneventful, thanks to Rafe's close supervision, or perhaps despite his close supervision. They continued to mind their manners and behave civilly to one another on that score. "It must be love," Nicole said, six weeks into her health regimen, smiling at Rafe across the breakfast table. "I'm trying hard not to be snappish."

Rafe laughed. "I've never been so circumspect in my life. You understand, I tell people what to do a hundred times a day, and have for a decade or more." Reaching across the small table, he touched her cheek lightly. "I'm polite to you because it matters, because I love you, because I don't want you unhappy."

"Same."

"Do you want to walk outside when we're done? The sun's out today." It had rained the past week.

She grinned over the rim of her hot chocolate cup. "Do I have a choice?"

His mouth twitched into a half smile. "Would a choice of times do?"

"I'll go if you'll carry me."

He hesitated. "I will, of course, but you should walk thirty"—

"Minutes a day, yes I know." And she had even on rainy days, Rafe's gym impressive.

"I'm sorry," he said, quietly. "Am I impossible?"

She shook her head. "We both are. I called the doctor."

He sat up in his chair, sudden warmth in his amber eyes. "Thank you." It had been a small matter of contention after he'd given her a list of local obstetricians. She'd balked at his preemptive authority.

"I go in tomorrow. Would you like to come with me?"

He found he had to swallow before he answered and wondered how it had come about that so simple a request could touch him so profoundly. He smiled and nodded. "I'll drive you." The last of Caesar's Russians had left Geneva. Carlos would be back in Monte Carlo by the end of the week.

"You don't usually drive."

"I want to be alone with you." He smiled. "On this auspicious day."

. . .

The female doctor Nicole had chosen met them in her office.

It was a small room with one large window facing the Mediterranean, white marble on the floor, some holograms of bicycle touring on the white walls, red, high tech fabric on ergo chairs, a slab of plexiglass on chrome legs for a desk. The whole room could be hosed down by a cleaning crew in under five minutes.

But more striking was the doctor's youth; Rafe momentarily questioned the list Aleix had given him. He would have preferred a more experienced physician.

"Please, sit." Dr. Gabriella Moncur waved at the chairs in front of her desk. "I like to meet new patients informally. If you'd care to tell me a little of what you're looking for in a doctor, I'll explain our services and we can go on from there."

"At the moment, my husband is annoyingly concerned with my health," Nicole said. "I'm hoping you can assure him I'm healthy"—she smiled at Rafe—"and then we can both relax."

"I'll be able to give you a definitive answer once I examine you." The doctor's voice was neutral. "And it's not unusual for a husband to be concerned."

Rafe's concern at the moment was the doctor's credentials. She looked much too young to have the expertise he required, particularly with her feet in red sneakers, her hair in long braid down her back and the logo on the t-shirt she wore more appropriate for a gamer. "You were recommended by Aleix Rovira," he said, his tone, in contrast to the simple statement, rife with doubt. "Have you been in Monaco long?"

"I was born here. Aleix and I were in school together at the Sorbonne. He was the rock star med student, but you probably know that. He's your personal physician." She knew who and what Rafe Contini was: powerful, wealthy, familiar with wielding authority. She also knew what he was asking. "I assure you, I'm quite competent." *She and Aleix both had been rock stars.*

Nicole punched Rafe's arm. "Jeez, mind your manners." Her gaze swung to the doctor. "Please forgive my husband. He worries about me."

"I do. Please accept my apologies, Dr. Moncur." Rafe smiled at Nicole and said very, very softly, "Is that better?"

Nicole smiled back.

And for a moment the young couple before her was lost to the world, unaware of anyone else. Gabriella felt uncomfortably like a voyeur, or a witness to an alien universe; surely this wasn't the Rafe Contini of scandalous repute.

A moment later, Rafe took Nicole's hand in his, turned to the doctor and said, simply, "We're still on our honeymoon."

"And enjoying it immensely," Nicole added with a wide smile. "Actually, I wouldn't have even made an appointment this early except Rafe was so insistent. You were, don't say you weren't"—she smiled and patted Rafe's cheek—"even if you didn't actually say the words."

He laughed softly. "Yes, dear."

"Anyway," Nicole said, turning to the doctor, "that's why we're here now today...instead of...well--later." She grinned. "You see the immense pressure I'm under."

Rafe Contini's wife was as unconventional as he, but definitely more outspoken; his cool restraint was conspicuous. "It never hurts to get baseline information in terms of your health," the doctor diplomatically pointed out. "We'll just check your vitals today, and monitor your progress in the coming months. The appointments aren't particularly demanding."

"See," Rafe said, quietly. "Told you."

Nicole wrinkled her nose. "I'm doing this for you, you know. My choice would have been to wait."

He leaned in close and whispered, "I'll make you a deal."

The doctor cleared her throat.

Rafe looked up. "We're keeping you waiting aren't we?"

No embarrassment or actual apology for his actions, Gabriella reflected, simply an acknowledgement of her schedule.

Pulling Nicole to her feet, Rafe straightened the crisp white collar on her blue wool dress in a small, protective gesture, then turned and smiled at the doctor. "We're ready whenever you are."

Rafe held Nicole's hand during the exam, calmly watching, not speaking unless spoken to, closely attentive to the procedure and Doctor Moncur's instructions; giving Nicole a smile and a kiss when it was over.

The doctor's verdict: Nicole couldn't have been healthier.

"Now will you relax?" Hopping off the exam table, she smiled up at Rafe. "I'm perfect."

"Yes, you are," he said without reservation.

"So you'll relax?"

Understanding, no, was unacceptable, he said, "I'm sure I will." Turning a half step, he extended his hand. "Thank you, doctor. I'm grateful for your expertise and enlightenment."

"You're welcome." His handshake was firm, his smile cordial, his affection for his wife startlingly genuine; the man in the tabloids entirely absent. "My receptionist will make your next appointment--unless you have any more questions."

"No, we're fine, thank you," Nicole interjected, and taking Rafe's hand, lifted her gaze to his. "Can we go now?"

About to say something, Rafe deferred to his wife. "Yes, of course. I'll wait at the front desk while you change."

But after following the doctor into the corridor outside the exam room, he stopped her with a light touch on her arm. "If I might have a few minutes of your time. I have some questions."

She turned to face him, her eyebrows lifting slightly. "I gathered as much. How may I help you?"

"I'd like some information about the hospital, particularly about the suites and birthing rooms. Could they use some retrofitting or new equipment, upgrades, that sort of thing? As a trustee of Geneva University Hospital, I'm familiar with their facilities, but Nicole wants to have the baby in Monte Carlo, so"—he lifted one shoulder in a small deprecatory shrug—"here we are. I'm not suggesting the local hospital is deficient in any way, only that I'm unfamiliar with its operation. So if any improvements are needed, I'd be more than happy to finance them. And if additional staff would be helpful to you, I have access to any doctor you'd like, whether from my research labs or elsewhere. Simply give me a name or names, and I'll see that they're flown in." The last was a brief declarative sentence without inflection, as though arranging other people's lives was commonplace.

"That won't be necessary, but thank you for the offer."

He hesitated for a small space of time. "You're sure?"

"I'm sure," she said, politely.

"Well, should you change your mind, let me know." Then his voice dropped in volume and he spoke more slowly so there was no mistaking his intentions. "It's absolutely essential that Nicole's delivery be flawless."

Well, that was a bit intimidating. Not to mention, he was literally towering over her, broad and powerful, his gaze unflinching. "You're concerned for your wife," she said, her voice deliberately mild, dissent, apparently, a rarity in the world of billionaires. "I understand."

"There's nothing I wouldn't do for her."

No matter his words were simply put, that was a holdback-the-tides promise; she didn't doubt for a minute he meant it. "Let me assure you the hospital is excellent, the delivery rooms first rate, the Monaco royal family chooses to have their children there."

"Ah...I see."

It was a provisional reply; regardless the royal family's endorsement, it might not be good enough for his wife. "You're more than welcome to visit the facility," she offered, "and see for yourself."

"Unfortunately, that's not my area of expertise." He was trying to keep his breathing calm; he wasn't getting the answers he wanted.

She met his cool gaze. "Why not have Aleix advise you, have him take you on a tour of the hospital. I'm sure he could address your concerns. I can only promise that your wife will have the very best care. She's young, healthy, the baby's healthy. There's no reason to worry. If you have any other questions, feel free to call me. The nurse will give you my numbers."

He was being politely dismissed; he had to admire her nerve. She and Nicole should get along well. "If you'd give me the hospital administrator's number too, I'd appreciate it," he said, evenly, making the necessary adjustment since Nicole wanted this doctor.

"Certainly."

"I'll have Aleix call you for the numbers."

By the time Nicole arrived at the front desk, Rafe had made her next appointment. He'd also talked to Aleix who'd promised him a meeting with the administrator tomorrow morning and with that he'd have to be content. Rafe held out his hand. "Ready to go home?"

She gave him a mildly sardonic look. "Yes, and you owe me."

"Gladly." Nicole had seen the doctor; he was grateful. Leaning over, he kissed her on the cheek, ignored the surprised scrutiny of everyone in the waiting room and lowered his voice. "It would be my pleasure to pay you back..."

"Hey, we're on stage," she whispered, the sudden silence in the room palpable.

He smiled. "Can't I adore my wife?"

Reaching up, she pulled his head down, murmured, "What the hay, I don't know anyone," and kissed him lightly.

He returned her kiss with equal delicacy and at some length and when they exited the doctor's office, whispers and spellbound comments exploded behind them; some touched with envy. Not all husbands were so romantically inclined.

A few minutes later, they were standing at the clinic entrance, waiting for the valet to bring up their car.

"That went well I thought," Rafe said, in a modulated social voice.

"Easy for you to say. No one was prodding you."

He frowned. "Did it hurt? If it did, I'll go back and speak to the doctor."

"Nah, there's nothing she can do about it anyway. And hey," she added, lightly, "it's over for a while."

"A month." Aware of her apprehensions, he watched her.

Nicole glanced up, smiled. "Do not rain on my parade right now, okay?"

"What appointment?" he said, serenely.

"There you go--a well-behaved, super agreeable husband. Let's do something fun when we get home."

"Such as," he drawled.

Her smile was playful. "Use your imagination."

"Don't have to with you. It's always the same."

"I'm just nice enough not to tax your imagination. You're welcome."

Nothing sexual taxed his libertine imagination, but it wouldn't be appropriate to mention that right now, or ever, now that he was married. "Kind of you to ease the strain," he murmured, bending down, kissing her cheek, straightening at the familiar soft roar of the twin turbo, V-8, 641 horsepower motor. "Ah, here's our car."

"Sweet ride," the young valet remarked, walking around the front of the black Lamborghini SUV, checking out the owner who needed an armored car.

"Thanks," Rafe said, handing the man a tip. "The suspension is prime, good for these mountain roads."

And required for the extra weight. But the valet just smiled and opened the passenger door, waited for dude to help the lady in, buckle her seat belt, and give her a kiss. *Wow, love. You didn't see that often with the rich and famous.*

Rafe stepped away and the valet shut the car door.

Moments later, Rafe drove away from the clinic. Simon and Davey pulled out of a no parking zone, and dropped in behind the SUV.

The valet thrust out his hand to his car parking partner. "See. Told you they weren't in that No Parking zone by accident," he said, shoving a ten euro bill into his pocket. "And the dude gave me a fifty coming and going. He can afford bodyguards."

Rafe took note of the Mercedes in his rear view mirror, security a fact of life, as it would be for his child. He'd have to see that Carlos began preparing a team for the baby. Reaching out, he brushed Nicole's cheek with his fingertips. "Thanks for going to the doctor. I really appreciate it."

"I know." She turned and smiled at him. "That's why I did it."

There'd always been women—more than anyone would ever need--and now, Nicole only had to smile at him and he felt like the luckiest man in the world. He didn't even try anymore to understand the difference one woman could make in his life; he simply accepted the magic. "I'll have to do something for you in return," he murmured.

She gave him a wink. "You already said you would."

"Something more then, something special."

"Hmmmm..."

He laughed. "Go for it, it's an open-ended offer. Whatever you fancy."

"How do you feel about financing a movie?"

His brows shot up, a nanosecond passed. "Sure, no problem."

"Jeez, I was joking. What's wrong with you? You can't just say yes like you're buying a beer."

"If it's something you want, I can. Look," he said, softly, "making you happy makes me happy. And I've never been truly happy before--never, not once in my entire fucking life before I met you. So don't tell me I can't buy you something," he muttered. "I can buy you any damn thing I please."

"Hey, relax." She touched his arm lightly. "I take it all back."

He softly exhaled. "Sorry. My past left a few scars. I'm recovering though." He shot her a look that was pretty much sugar-coated sweetness wrapped in silver moonbeams. "Just give me time to mellow out."

She smiled. "It's not as though I'm the most easy-going person in the world either. But we love each other. That's all the matters. We'll deal with our testiness like we always do…"

"With sex?" He was smiling again.

"That works for me," she purred. "Can you drive a little faster? I love making up."

But, twenty minutes later, as they walked into their bedroom, Rafe swung Nicole up in his arms, walked to the bed, set her down and said, "Give me a brief rain check." Pulling up a heavy upholstered chair, he dropped into it, leaned back, stretched out his legs and looking up from under his lashes, met her puzzled gaze. "I need a minute to process the doctor visit." His voice was soft, diffident. "I'm still struggling with the bewildering, semi-explosive before and after emotional tumult. Everything is suddenly strange and off center, transformative, irreversible"—he took a steadying breath—"overwhelming."

"And the baby's no longer a hypothetical, but"—

"A mind-blowing reality that takes my breath away," he said softly, his hushed tone authenticating his feelings. "So"—his brows creased--"I find myself facing a future that's no longer predictable, but fluid, involving an infant that belongs to me *and* you, together, collectively…world without end." Slowly inhaling, he exhaled as slowly, a hint of doubt in the shadowed depths of his eyes. "I know you've always been around babies, you're confident in your abilities, but"—

"You've never been around babies?"

"No. Never. Titus is the only child I know and he was almost five when my mother married Anton."

I'm sorry, she thought, his words poignant somehow for a man who had everything. "Are you afraid?" she asked, although he didn't look afraid. He looked self-possessed lounging at his ease, lean, yet powerfully muscled, the hard contours of his legs evident beneath the fine black wool of his trousers, his broad shoulders under the soft black cashmere sweater relaxed, his large hands resting gracefully on the chair arms.

"No," he said, economically, having learned long ago to deal with fear. "It's just that the world is different now, life is different"—he shrugged, his innate reticence being tested by this need for an explanation—"and what I'm feeling is... unsettling--in a good way," he quickly added at her slight frown. His smile appeared, boyish and warm. "Every priority I've ever known has shifted. I was wildly unprepared, that's all. But fuck it," he abruptly said, dispatching his odd vulnerability with a natural evasion, a teasing smile in its place. "I'm done being weirded-out. I apologize for wasting your time."

"Don't apologize," Nicole said, charmed by Rafe's admissions. "Your world has changed. It's only natural for you to feel slightly unnerved."

He hesitated, then more frankly than he intended, said, "*Very* unnerved if you must know. On the other hand"--sliding upright in his chair, he gave her a brilliant smile--"I'm also enormously pleased about the baby—joyful, happy, *alarmingly* happy...so screw the rest." Leaning over, he began untying his black suede shoes. Barefoot a moment later, he looked up from under a fall of dark hair loosened from its moorings at his nape, and back on familiar ground, said, softly, "What would you like to do first..."

"Do you have a dungeon here?"

There was a sudden stillness to his face, his breathing

controlled. Then he sat back and said, "No. Would you like me to outfit one?"

How pleasantly he'd spoken, she thought, as if such outfitting was a simple task. "Have you one somewhere else?"

He looked startled, then amused. "Why the sudden interest in coercion?"

"I just thought dungeons were a fashionable fetish for billionaires."

For a moment he debated his answer, not sure it was a subject he cared to pursue; decided it wasn't. "I'm no authority but I suspect billionaires with dungeons are the exception rather than the rule." He smiled. "Feel free to correct me if you know differently."

"As if." Her mouth twitched into a sexy grin. "Feel like some improv?"

"Sure." Reaching down, he picked up a shoe and began unlacing the silk cord laces.

"What are you doing?"

"Improvising."

"I don't want anything strange, okay?"

"No problem." Dropping the lace-less shoe, he picked up the other one and eased the tie through the grommets.

"I mean it."

With his fingers swiftly sliding the cord free, he spoke without looking up. "Understood."

"Why am I getting the feeling you've done this a million times before?"

Dropping the second shoe, his amber gaze came up, warm and cloudless. "Make up your mind. Or change your mind. I'm more than willing to accommodate you."

"I don't want to be the millionth and one, that's all."

He sighed, sat back, let the silk corded laces slip from his fingers to the floor. "I don't want to fight. Tell me what you'd like to do?"

"Damn you." A small fretful sound, heated, impatient. "I don't know, or I don't know for sure, like—absolutely, positively."

His mouth lifted in the faintest of smiles. "Give me a hint."

She pointed. "What were you going to do with those laces?"

"Tie your wrists." He shrugged. "Go from there."

"Go where?"

He dipped his head and looked at her from under his long lashes. "Want a roadmap?"

"If it looks like the path in Candy Land, not Dante's Inferno."

"Candy Land?" he said, mildly.

"A children's game."

"Ah." He'd assumed it wasn't the candy land of drugs but with sex it was best to clarify. "Then, no to both. You're my sweetheart. I'm here to make you feel good."

"You see, that's the problem. I want you to make me feel good, but the fact that you're so goddamned sure you can pisses me off." A tick of a smile. "Not completely though."

"Then it's up to me to resolve your uncertainty." *Never a problem, but this was no time to point that out.* "Maybe we're both a little weirded out today," he said gently. "Why don't I go slowly, you stop me if something's not right and we'll see what happens."

She softly exhaled. "I adore you, you know."

"It's a mutual admiration society, pussycat." He smiled. "I didn't know it was possible to love someone as much as I love you."

"To absolute pieces."

"That and more..." *He had more to lose too with a wife he loved to a frightening degree and a baby on the way. Fuck.*

Rafe's gaze was suddenly empty of feeling and Nicole spoke lightly, wanting to distract. "Are you going to amaze me with those shoelaces?"

A curtain dropped, the blankness disappeared from his eyes, amusement in its place. He picked up the laces from the carpet, his dark hair hanging in his eyes, his mouth tilting in a smile. "Prepare to be amazed."

He knew how to play this game. With the unconscious expertise one would expect from a man who had a unique interest in sexual bondage, Rafe quickly twined and knotted the laces into makeshift handcuffs. Coming to his feet in a flexing of honed muscle, he moved the few steps to the bed and extended the looped cords on his upturned fingertips. "Hold out your hands." At Nicole's doubtful gaze, he added, "The ties that circle your wrists are slip knots. You can release yourself whenever you want. I'll show you."

Her concerns addressed she slid her hands through the loops.

After tightening the wrist bonds, Rafe placed the loose ends of the laces in her palms, curled her thumbs and forefingers over the braided tips and glanced up. "Just pull and you're free. Okay?" His smile was indulgent.

She took a breath. "So far."

"If you don't like something, we'll stop." Lifting her higher on the bed, he eased her down, and slid a pillow under her head. "Arms up," he murmured, and guiding her bound hands to the headboard, hooked the short span of cord between her wrists to the acanthus leaf molding. Straightening, he gazed down on her. "Comfortable? Warm enough?"

She arched her back ever so slightly, felt the soft tug on

her wrists, the irresistible rush of desire spiraling downward. "Comfortable? Not exactly. But tautly expectant." Her lashes rose infinitesimally; he saw the heat in her eyes. "And warming nicely."

A lazy smile. "Good to know."

The watchfulness of his gaze gave her a moment of unease, obliterated a heartbeat later by a blaze of carnal need so sharp-set and ravenous, her voice trembled when she spoke. "Don't--look at me...like that."

He blinked, dropped his gaze to her wrists and spoke of mundane matters. "The ties aren't too tight?"

"What if I said they were?"

"I'd loosen them."

"So, I could give you orders?"

He shrugged. "Or I could offer you a few suggestions--things you might like in terms of gratification."

His voice was uber mild; he could have been commenting on the weather. But he wasn't and the polite attention in his eyes was strangely unsettling. "I don't know. Maybe. It depends."

"On?" He knew where this was going even if she was unsure.

"My mood, your mood." She grimaced. "Degrees of power and authority."

He smiled. "You're overthinking this. I know what you like."

"While you're a completely unselfish observer?"

"No, pussycat, but your pleasure comes first." After years of selfish pursuits, a little self-denial was no imposition. "Now, I'm going to sit down." He pointed at the chair. "Come see me."

A tiny crease appeared between her brows. "How would I do that?"

"I showed you." Turning, he walked away.

"Hey," she muttered, jerking on the wrist restraints. "Untie me."

He dropped into the chair. "Do it yourself. You know how your pussy likes me taking charge. It gets all hot and creamy."

"Does not." Even as she spoke, self-willed and unruly, said pussy turned liquid.

"Sorry, my mistake," he murmured, recognizing the sudden shift in her breathing.

"Fuck you," she said, annoyed at his bloody composure.

"All in good time." He leaned back in a lazy sprawl, his long legs stretched out before him, his pose one of infinite patience.

Damn him, she sulkily thought, that casual arrogance was obscenely arousing, as was his erection swelling under the soft wool of his trousers.

Aware of the focus of her gaze, he smiled the quick dazzling smile that always reminded her of the first time they met. "They're simple slip knots, sweetheart. Humor me."

She found herself smiling back, her temper dissolving. "I'm assuming you'll make it worth my while?"

"Did you ever doubt it?"

She rolled her eyes. "Smug bastard. The stories are legion."

He put up his hands, frowned. "You're my wife. There are no more stories."

She flinched at the steel in his voice.

"Oh, shit, now I've frightened you. I'm so sorry." He began to rise from his chair. "Let me untie you."

"Sit down!" She smiled at his quickly suppressed shock

and when he calmly obeyed, she added, "Maybe we'll take turns giving orders."

He never engaged in useless polemics. He only said, "If you need help with the ties let me know."

Following his instructions, she quickly freed herself, slipped from the bed and moving toward him, stopped at his raised hand.

"Undress for me first."

She smiled. "What if I say no?"

"You wouldn't climax as quickly." Their sexual history was occasionally one of small battles and testiness, but in this novel moment sweet with expectation, his wife deserved more. She deserved all he knew in the way of pleasure. "Forgive me. Old habits." Leaning forward, he took her hand and drew her between his legs. "Let me undress you."

"Quickly."

He glanced up, his fingers on her collar button.

She laughed. "That look. Should I add a please?"

With a flick of his fingers, the button slipped free. "You continue to surprise me," he gently said, moving to the next button. "Not a complaint, an observation only. By the way, you look like a prim and proper young lady in this unornamented dress with a little white collar."

"No doubt the reason you picked it out for the doctor appointment."

His gaze came up again, followed by a twitch of a smile. "Too theatrical?"

"It's also easy to put on and take off with these buttons down the front which comes in handy for doctor appointments and"—she tapped his cheek—"slam bang sex."

Taking his cue, he slipped his hand under her dress, slid his middle finger past her lacy underwear, pushed it palm deep into her sleek, glossy pussy and at her soft gasp, whispered, "Just checking the time table."

Grabbing his hand, she held it firmly in place and eyes shut, hissed, "It's go time. Undress me later."

"No can do."

Her eyes snapped open, flaring indignation plain to see. "You have to!"

Sliding his finger free with ease, their strength hopelessly mismatched, he sat back, and looked up. "Compromise?"

She stifled her initial, hot-headed reply because his goddamn erection was huge, close enough to touch if she dared-- his cool regard a deterrent—and bottom line, a compromise might be acceptable if fast and furious somehow featured in it. "Sure," she said, not really meaning it when she was melting inside.

He smiled. "Why don't I believe you?"

"You want the unvarnished truth?" Bending over, she slid her hands under her dress, pulled her panties down, let them drop to the carpet and stepped out of them. She pointed at his crotch, her smile tight. "Now, not later. That's my compromise."

"I need your dress off."

That ultra-soft command, his utter stillness annihilated her free agency, effaced any thought of independence, raised the lust level in her body to a mindless fever pitch. Her hands were shaking as she began to unbutton the remaining buttons.

"Here, let me," he murmured, recognizing the perilous state of her arousal, lifting her hands away and swiftly unbuttoning. "Think of chocolate cake." Looking up, he smiled into her startled gaze. "Focus on something else you like."

She shivered. "I can't. I need you, him"—a quick dip of her head—"both, now, now, *now!*"

With stunning speed, he pulled the last button free, brushed the silk-lined dress down her arms, picked her up from the blue wool puddled at her feet, whispered, "Spread your legs," and dropped her on his thighs. Unzipping his trousers, he slid his palm under her ass, raised her enough to guide his dick into place, and watched her plummet down his rampant cock with a small, incoherent cry that turned into a blissful sigh as she came to rest, deeply impaled.

Understanding the minutia of sensation, he held her lightly in place for a languorous moment before flexing his hips upward with the precise degree of defensible force, at the same time she abruptly moved downward and for a taut, suspended moment in time, dying of pleasure was more than a poetic phrase. It was diamond-bright and feather-light and fragile with wonder; a shocking sensation to a man who hadn't been shocked in years. Nicole's whimper abruptly displaced rarified sensation and Rafe immediately responded, giving her what she wanted, slowly at first, then more insistently, with increasing wildness as she clung to him overwhelmed and frantic, desperate. Until with timely competence and finesse, he delivered the soul-stirring satisfaction she craved in an explosive climax so deep felt and prolonged, so unbearably raw, that joining her at the last was like touching the stars.

Neither spoke for lengthy moments, their heartbeats pounding in their chests, their breathing rough.

"That," Rafe said, at last, his heart still beating like thunder, "was—incredibly fine."

She nodded, still caught up in the sweet, warm wave of astonishment, her body softly humming, cross currents of melting bliss and shimmering arousal swirling down her nerve endings, softly pulsing in her liquid, scented pussy.

Since those soft pulsations were flickering up and down his demonstrably rising erection, he said, softly, "Too soon? Or would you like some help?"

His voice was deep, whisper soft, knowing. Selfishly, she no longer resented his experience. Selfishly, she said, "Yes, please."

He kissed her gently, and rising from the chair without dislodging her, moved the few paces to the bed, leaned over, placed her on her back and withdrew from her body.

Her eyes flew open.

He smiled. "Give me a second to get my clothes off."

"One, one thousand..."

He laughed. "Okay, five seconds."

But he managed to undress in less time and smoothly lowering himself between her thighs, was welcomed with warm, engulfing arms, a lush, opulent smile, and the most tantalizingly, demanding pussy he had the good fortune to own.

To *call* his own he silently amended.

There were rules now.

Standards of husbandly behavior that precluded ownership.

No matter how well-intended his husbandly behavior, however, his proffered satisfaction quickly morphed into a passionate interlude of new and alarming sensations. Perhaps they were both compelled by subtly altered sensibilities, by restless impulses, by the new and radical changes in the ordinary rhythm of their lives. Or maybe one of them was, and the other, simply wildly receptive. But ever generous in his love, Rafe also gratified and appeased Nicole, with finesse and languor, with shuddering frenzy and necessary caution, ultimately at the dazzling climax, with pulse pounding intensity and an unbearable rapture that touched them both with joy.

Because on this propitious day, life had turned a page.

His conversation with Henny that night was the kind of full disclosure he'd always freely shared with his dearest friend. Pouring himself a drink, Rafe took a seat on one of the mausoleum benches, swallowed a mouthful of whisky and raised his glass. "Hey, Henny, I have news. We saw the OB/GYN today and it's fucking real, not a maybe or a possible, but an actual, undeniable, sure-as-the-sun-rises-in-the-East fact...I'm going to be a dad. You know how I've never liked to wing it, always planned ahead, loathed surprises, and now, shit, here I am in the unprecedented position of playing catch up. Not that I'm not pleased about the baby, don't get me wrong, I'm fully on board, resolved to help in any way with the pregnancy, looking forward to June." A nervous energy suddenly registered in his voice. "A goddamn life-changing June. Christ." He paused for a moment, lips pursed, then said more softly, "Not that we haven't learned how to adjust on a dime coming from our fucked-up families." Another short pause, followed by a shrug of dismissal, habitual to the subject of fucked-up families. "Anyway, I wanted you to know. I knew you'd understand. You always have. To friendship." Raising his glass, he acknowledged Henny with a nod, then brought the glass to his mouth, and drained it.

"Ask Mireille about"--

At the sound of Henny's voice Rafe choked on the whisky, the rest of Henny's comment muffled by his paroxysm of coughing. Finally catching his breath, he dropped the glass on the bench and reached the sarcophagus in two long strides. Bending low, his voice animated with excitement, he said, "I heard you, Henny--clear as day, fuck it was beautiful...you sounded absolutely the same. But ask Mireille what? I missed that."

He waited, ears strained, his heart beating like a drum, scarcely daring to breath for what seemed endless moments. Then dropping his forehead to the cool marble, he whispered, "Please, Henny, say it again. Please, please, let me know you can hear me."

But only silence prevailed; a sad, wistful silence.

Finally standing upright, Rafe scanned the chamber, hoping for the impossible—hoping to see Henny. But reality eventually intervened, followed by bitter despair and resting his hands on the sarcophagus, he swallowed hard before he spoke. "Don't forget, I'm always around in case you want to talk to me again. Anytime, okay? I miss you."

But on his walk back to the carriage house, Henny's voice was a continuous echo in his mind, the sound familiar and spot on in every nuanced intonation, the startling episode contradictory to everything he'd ever believed in, but so unspeakably awesome, he couldn't help but smile. His faith in the mystic or the occult, or rather his lack of faith, had been an established fact until a few moments ago when he'd clearly heard Henny speak. "Ask Mireille..."

Shit, his pulse rate spiked at the certifiable out-of-body experience. So next question: dare he call and talk to Mireille? Would she think him delusional? Did he care? How the hell late was it? He glanced at his watch. Christ, it was late. Then again, Henny had been clear in his instruction; call Mireille. Coming to a stop just short of the carriage house door, he pulled out his phone and hit Mireille's number.

"I apologize for calling so late," Rafe immediately said. "Did I wake you?"

"No, my sleep is fitful. I was watching TV."

"How are you feeling, other than missing Henny, I mean, like in general, do you ever"—

"You sound strange, not to mention you're calling at two a.m.," she said, kindly, on the cusp of asking him if he'd been drinking.

Understanding the underlying message in her voice, he said, "I'm sober. But I do have a good reason for sounding strange. Henny just spoke to me."

"He *did?*" Her excitement vibrated through the phone. "Tell me every word, every *single* word he said!"

"He said clear as day, 'Ask Mireille about', at which point I choked on my whisky, so I didn't hear the rest. Do you have any idea what he might have wanted me to ask you?"

"I'm so happy he talked to you! But why wouldn't he, you're his dearest friend."

She didn't sound upset or unnerved. He'd been concerned about mentioning the incident with Henny when she still was deep in mourning, afraid he might disturb her. "You're not surprised? Has Henny spoken to you?"

"Of course, I talk to him all the time. Isn't it just like Henny not to wait," she added, brightly. "But I'm sure he wanted you to be the first to hear our grand news."

Rafe stopped breathing.

"I haven't mentioned it to anyone yet," she continued more quietly, "because it's still very early, and unlike my bold and audacious Henny, I'm fearful of tipping the fragile balance of life inside me."

"A baby," Rafe breathed, sitting down heavily on the front stoop, thrilled, dazed, delighted but mainly ridiculously happy that his child and Henny's would be friends as he and Henny had been. If the universe had ever turned full circle and a gift of celestial wonder had been granted, the birth of his and Henny's child was that ultimate mercy. "Thank you for telling me." His voice was velvet soft, his mind quickly calculating the weeks since Henny's death. "When did you know?"

"I first began to suspect two weeks ago, but I didn't dare hope because even though we were rash and impetuous under the romantic spell of your wedding, the percentages for conception that night were practically nil."

"So you were surprised."

"No, my first reaction was a tenuous joy, followed by a fierce hope that Henny had given me a child."

"You should have a doctor there with you," Rafe said, his voice suddenly crisp with authority. "I'll see that you have one on site or at least close by. You know Henny wants me to take care of you. That's why he talked to me."

She laughed. "Do I have a choice with both of you bossing me?"

Rafe laughed for the first time when thinking about Henny. "We all know the answer to that. I'll check with him on his preferences, you do the same and between the three of us we'll get you the very best doctor. Deal?"

"Yes, deal," she softly said. "But I'd like to keep this *entre nous* until I'm completely sure. I couldn't bear to share my sorrow with the world if something goes wrong."

"I won't tell anyone. You have my word," he said, firmly. "And nothing's going to go wrong. Henny and I won't let it, okay? This is a miracle of awesome proportions, and I promise, everything's going to be fine. Guaranteed." His voice was resolute. "Now try and sleep," he added, more softly. "I have to be in Geneva in two days. I'll stop in Paris on my way back with a list of doctors for you."

"You're a dear."

"Nope, Henny's in charge. I'm just here to do his bidding. I'll see you in two days. If you have anything you need me to bring, just let me know."

"I'll call you if I do. Thank you."

"My pleasure. Jesus, this is unbelievably good news. I'll see you in two days. Ciao."

Entering the house, Rafe strode into the reception room, dropped into a chair and started waking up several of his employees. He needed a list of top OB/GYNs in Paris, from his Geneva labs, or anywhere in the world by ten the next morning with appropriate contact people and phone numbers.

A half hour later, he went upstairs, slipped into bed beside Nicole, and recognized with new-found clarity that life isn't always rational, that reality can appear in all guises and best of all, despair can be tempered by the brightest of promises…a tiny, new life.

Warmed by a deep contentment, he fell asleep with a smile.

39

The next morning, after breakfast and a walk with Nicole, Rafe spent an hour at the main house engaged in Contini Pharma business before leaving for Monte Carlo with Aleix.

Simon was waiting at the main entrance and gave them a wave as the two men entered the Mercedes. "I thought you may have forgotten."

"Sorry," Rafe said. "There's always a last call from Geneva. Can you get there in time?"

"Probably."

"Good enough for me." Rafe turned to Aleix. "Should we call...what's his name, mention we might be late?"

"Henri Guimond. No, I planned on a possible delay." Aleix smiled. "Knowing your busy schedule in the morning."

"Ah--Nicole's schedule, you mean. Smart. You heard, Simon? Take your time. By the way, Dr. Moncur knows you," Rafe said, turning back to Aleix. "You didn't mention that."

"We were classmates. That's why I know she's the best."

"She called you a rock star. *I'm* aware of your brilliance, which is why you run your own research lab at Contini Pharma. But it was gracious of her to compliment you."

"She was being modest. We both took firsts. She was a scholarship student, in addition to working on the side, so it wasn't really a fair competition."

"With a trust fund you didn't have to work."

"Money eases life's burdens," Aleix said, with cool sarcasm.

"Some, but not all, as you and I both know." The men had lamentable childhoods. "Dr. Moncur said she was born in Monaco," Rafe remarked, returning the conversation to a more benign subject.

"Her father's a croupier at the casino. It's a good income, but he has four other children, so…"

"It's not enough."

"Gabriella's helping her family"—Aleix held up his hand—"before you say it, don't. You'll offend her if you offer her money for giving Nicole special attention."

Rafe sighed in acknowledgment. "I already received that message. She made it clear she was an independent woman."

"Speaking of women, did you notice the other OB/GYNs on the list were men?"

Rafe grinned. "Shit, you know Nicole better than I."

Aleix shook his head. "You're just not in the habit of paying attention because the women in your past only smiled and said yes."

"Until now. Not that I'm complaining--on the contrary. Doctor Moncur, on the other hand", Rafe muttered in a low grumble of discontent, "is stubbornly intractable, even when I pressed her on the hospital facilities. Which is why"—

"I'm your tour guide today. I figured."

Sensibly dismissing intractable doctors, the gravity of Rafe's expression altered to a more familiar urbanity. "So, tell me, is this Guimond likely to be amenable, open to negotiation? How well do you know him?"

"Only vaguely. He's a physician but never actually practiced. His father was the hospital administrator before him, so he was groomed for the position. Managing donors is his major function."

"Rafe smiled. "Are you suggesting I allow myself to be managed?"

"No, I'm just pointing out his skill set. Monaco is a donor-rich environment. And he's good at what he does."

"I don't see a problem then," Rafe said. "We simply have to agree on a price for what *I* want."

"And what is that, exactly?"

"A hundred percent guarantee Nicole's delivery will be perfect."

"Impossible."

"I don't acknowledge that word." Unfamiliar with defeat, Rafe knew any dilemma was open to a solution. "I also understand the positives are in Nicole's favor: her youth and good health; Moncur's expertise; the hospital's excellence. What I'm trying to avoid is any risk, however remote, that something or someone fails. I want that threat eliminated." He'd lived his adult life largely oblivious to rules and the conviction in his voice was sharp and clear. "What I need from this visit today is some fucking guarantees. Capiche?"

Aleix realized there was no satisfactory answer, short of a miracle, to such an incredulous condition.

But then Rafe wasn't expecting a reply.

His last statement had been in the way of a fiat.

. . .

The Wedding, Etc.

WHEN THE MEN entered his office, Dr. Guimond rose from his chair, moved around his desk, and approached them with a smile.

He had the look of a prosperous banker, and, as CEO of a profitable hospital in a nation of billionaires, the positions were perhaps interchangeable. His grey hair was well cut, his double breasted navy suit, bespoke, his trim, middle aged physique a testament to his trainer and a healthy diet; his only adornment a half million dollar watch.

Having done his research on Rafe Contini prior to the meeting, Dr. Guimond's smile was reminiscent of a private banker welcoming a new client, albeit one dressed in glen plaid slacks, a black t-shirt and handsome smoke grey pseudo work boots. Putting out his manicured hand, he looked Rafe in the eye like any cultivated CEO, and said, "It's a pleasure to meet you, Mr. Contini. I understand you're interested in our hospital."

"I am." Rafe shook his hand. "Thank you for agreeing to meet us on such short notice. As Aleix mentioned, my wife and I are expecting our first child. I'm interested in seeing that she has the very best accommodations. I understand you might be willing to help."

"Of course." In a cartoon, the doctor's eyes would be displaying dollar signs. "Let me show you our maternity wing."

The addition was recently built and Dr. Guimond was proud of it. He pointed out all the latest equipment, the luxury suites and birthing rooms, the large staff in attendance. He answered Aleix's questions concerning delivery room protocols, in particular those utilized when multiple women were in labor. He waved off offers of additional equipment since the delivery rooms were new and he assured Rafe numerous times that the health of the mothers and babies was their primary concern.

The tour complete, Rafe said, "If I might see the corner suite again. I think my wife would like the view."

Moments later, Dr. Guimond stood in the doorway of the large space while Rafe walked around the room, ran his hand over the marble window sills, stood for a moment gazing out on the azure Mediterranean, trailed a fingertip down one of the brightly patterned curtains, then turned around and mouth pursed, contemplated the floor for so long the hospital administrator felt a potential donation slipping away. Finally looking up, Rafe's expression cleared. "I'd like to have the suite redone, new furniture, paint, flooring, lighting, et cetera, so everything is fresh. I'd also like to reserve the suite until my wife's due date in June. Would you be amenable? And if so, what would you need for a remodel and reservation?"

"Twenty million."

Rafe's brows rose in swift surprise. He'd just built a wing for the Geneva University Hospital so he understood construction costs. Then again, the room would be unused for several months and he wasn't here to quibble. "Very well," he said. "When can we start?"

A potential loss was suddenly a win. In local parlance, Contini had covered the bet—and without demur. Not always the case with billionaires. Some liked to play it safe or beat down the price out of habit, others, like Rafe Contini, apparently, cared little about money. "You may start at your convenience."

"I'll have the twenty million wired over within the hour and have a designer here tomorrow to draw up some plans." Rafe extended his hand. "You've been very helpful."

Standing in the hallway a moment later, Dr. Guimond

watched the two men walk away and thought like a punter would, *I should have asked for more.*

FIVE MINUTES LATER, Simon was driving away from the hospital, Rafe was on his phone, giving instructions to one of his accountants to wire twenty million to the Princess Grace Hospital, in care of Dr. Guimond, while Aleix, lounging in a corner of the wide back seat, marveled at the startling transformation of his friend from degage playboy to devoted husband in a few short months.

As though to put a fine point on that husbandly devotion, Rafe ended his call, turned to Aleix and said, "Done. The money's on its way. Thanks for your expertise. I wouldn't have known what to look for. Tell me Nicole's going to be safe there."

"Yes, she is." There was no other answer for Rafe's faint frown. "You needn't worry."

"I will, of course," Rafe said, his smile polite. "But thank you for your reassurance."

"This must be a first," Aleix quipped. "You finally found something you can't control."

"We'll see." Rafe wasn't about to argue. He knew what he could and could not do. "Now, should I send for Odile in Paris or do you think we can find a competent designer here?"

40

"The hospital's maternity wing looked pleasant, warm colors, comfortable furniture," Rafe said, smiling at Nicole over the luncheon table. "You should take a look sometime."

"I'll see it when I have the baby." Rafe had mentioned at breakfast that he was going to visit the hospital.

"No interest at all? Not even a little curious?"

She grinned. "How do I say this diplomatically? Fuck, no. Or if you'd like a longer explanation," she added at his slightly raised brows, "everyone with half a brain knows that labor is a pain, literally. Why would I want to remind myself of that before I have to? I'll deal with it when the time comes, but until then--sorry." Her blue eyed gaze was direct. "Any more questions?"

He laughed. "Hell, no."

"Good." Her smile was sunny. "I love when you agree with me."

Apparently he'd be making the decisions on the hospital suite remodel. He'd bring Odile down from Paris. He liked her taste, and if she took over the project, his involvement would be minimal.

"On a more pleasant subject," he said, spooning up some bouillabaisse broth, "how's the screenplay going?" Since Nicole favored the soup, the nutritionists approved, and he ate anything, it was a luncheon staple.

"Pretty darn good. Do you want to read it?"

He glanced up at the excitement in her voice, set down his spoon and leaned back in his chair. "I'd love to read it. You sound pleased." His voice was softer now. "Did it turn out the way you wanted?"

"I think so, or hope so..." She pushed up the sleeves on one of his sweaters—her preferred clothing choice of late--rested her forearms on the table and met his gaze with a slight grimace. "When you do as much rewriting as I did, it's hard to be absolutely sure about anything anymore. But *I* like it. You'll have to tell me whether you approve."

Touched by her unusual indecision, his smile was teasing. "Don't tell me the Princess of the Universe is interested in my approval?"

"Screw you." She stuck out her tongue, suddenly grinned. "Oh, all right. Be kind though."

"Come, on, Tiger," he said, very softly, "you can do no wrong in my world. If you like it, I'll like it, okay? I have a couple meetings this afternoon. I'll read it afterward."

"Remember, it's a first effort," she said, tentatively.

"I know."

"Don't expect perfection."

He'd never seen her so uncertain. "I'll make you a deal," he said, his smile indulgent. "Don't expect perfection from me and I'll not expect it from you."

"Damn," she said, feeling a glow of elation at his tantalizing smile, "I thought you could do anything, anywhere, anytime, that you were the consummate achiever."

He shook his head, his gaze drifting over her face. "That's you, pussycat, capable of anything, remarkable in every way."

"God, I love you," she whispered, her happiness a tangible thing.

"I love you more," he softly said, echoing the quiet mantra of his heart.

The sound of someone clearing their throat interrupted the private moment and glancing up, Rafe waved in the young man from the doorway. "Dessert has arrived," he said, with a little lift of his brows. "What did you order today?"

"One of my favorites." Nicole's smile was enchanting. "Warm strawberry tart."

A moment later, the young man, set the desserts before them, put a small bowl of Chantilly crème on the table and glanced at Rafe.

"We're fine, now, Luca, thank you. Tell the chef the bouillabaisse was exceptional."

"Yes, it was wonderful," Nicole added. A moment later, when they were alone once again, she exhaled softly. "I always feel like I'm in a restaurant."

Rafe shrugged. "Since neither of us can cook, and we like to eat..."

"I should learn to be comfortable with your staff."

"I'm sure no one notices your qualms, but take your time. Most of the staff have been here for years and"—

"They've learned to overlook more than my unease."

"Yes. And before you say it," he added, "those days are over. If we have parties they'll be"—

"Sedate affairs."

He laughed. "I'm not that old yet, but at least the

company will be acceptable. At the moment though, I'm content with no company at all. Your call, of course; I don't mean to be selfish."

"I'm selfish too. No company, just you and me."

"Goddamn paradise," he said, softly, reaching across the small table to touch her hand, his gaze warm with affection. "I don't know what I did to get this lucky, but I love you, pussycat…more than anything."

Her eyes filled with tears. "Sorry, I cry so easily now, but I love you so."

He'd risen to his feet the moment he'd seen her tears, and moving around the table, lifted her from her chair, sat in her place and held her close. "Don't cry, there's no need to cry, I'm here, and always will be." He kissed her lightly. "That's a promise, or warning or threat, whichever you prefer."

She giggled, looked up with a smile. "I'm equally possessive, just a reminder."

"I wouldn't have it any other way." A shocking comment from a man who, brief months ago, would have found the concept unthinkable. "And I adore you for it."

His phone rang; he ignored it.

"Answer," Nicole said. "I'm done being weepy. Really, answer."

"It can wait. See, it went to voice mail." Pulling out his phone, he set it to vibrate, and slid it back into his pocket. "Now tell me what's the baby been doing today?"

"Putting on weight." She touched the slight rise of her belly.

"She's not very big yet," he murmured, placing his hand gently on her stomach.

"Eventually, *he's* going to be big like you."

He chuckled. "Yes, dear."

"Are you patronizing me?" she whispered, a mischievous light in her eyes.

"If it gets me a kiss, you can have any answer you want." He half smiled. "You see how accommodating I can be."

"Just a kiss?" Her voice was velvet soft. "Is that all?"

He sighed. "It is for now." His phone had been steadily vibrating in his pocket. "Someone's not satisfied with voicemail. Sorry."

"Don't be; lunch is over." She exhaled softly. "See, I can be accommodating too."

"Thanks for your understanding. Some new research is gearing up and everyone has questions I'm expected to answer." He exhaled a small rueful sound. "You're sure you're okay, now?"

He was so damned sweet and polite. "I'm sure."

"As soon as my meetings are over, I'll come back, and read your screenplay."

She gazed up at him with a smile. "Don't worry, it'll wait. You don't have to read it today."

"I want to. Just give me a couple hours. Would you like me to carry you upstairs?"

"Yes, but you don't have to." Her voice was touched with playfulness. "I've been walking upstairs by myself for years."

"But I'm here now," he said, mildly. "Why should you have to?"

"In that case, I won't even consider it."

"That's my girl." A flashing grin. "Dare I say, my sweetly compliant girl?"

"Only if you think we're living in the nineteen fifties."

He recognized that politely quarrelsome tone in a woman and rising to his feet, shook his head. "Sorry--a momentary lapse of judgment." He didn't say there were times when she was more than ready to be compliant; a pointless conversation other than in the heat of the moment. Instead he spoke of the man they're hired from a drug startup in Denmark, a celebrated wunderkind, he added, as he carried her from the sunny terrace room, and strode through the reception room to the entrance hall and stairway.

As he swiftly mounted the stairs with ease, Nicole was impressed with her own personal wunderkind's brute strength and power--again, as usual; her senses instantly responding with a rush of wild, carnal cravings. She should ignore temptation—there wasn't time, Rafe's schedule oppressive--but a dizzying need chose not to recognize purer motive.

"Chair or bed?" he said, walking into the bedroom.

"It depends what you have in mind."

His gaze snapped down at the breathless hush in the voice, the raw provocation.

Her hand went up. "Sorry," she said, quickly. "I didn't mean that."

She did, of course and he debated how he could please her in a compressed time frame. Both of his meetings were global conference calls that were difficult to postpone. He took a small breath. "I'll stay if you like."

Recognizing the extravagance of his offer, understanding the pressures he was under, Nicole forcibly tamped down her wayward impulses. "Don't be silly, go," she said with a little flutter of her fingers. "You're busy. I'll see you after your meetings."

He almost said, *Do you want your vibrator,* decided, instead, to avoid the subject, gently laid her on the bed, pulled up the snow white cashmere blanket at her feet and covered her. "Two hours, maybe less," he said, tucking the soft fabric under her chin. "Then you'll have my undivided attention. Deal?"

She winked. "I'll make a list while you're gone; a long one."

His smile flashed and leaning down, he kissed her. "Definitely intriguing," he said, coming upright. "I'll hurry." A moment later, he paused, his hand on the doorknob, his smile as lazy as his drawl. "I might have some ideas for your list, so save me a couple lines."

She reacted to his deep voice and silken promise with a quicksilver, flaring lust and looking up, would have said, "Stay."

But the door softly shut and he was gone.

MINUTES LATER, Rafe entered the conference room at the main house, took his seat at the table, and acknowledged his colleagues with a brief nod. "Is everyone prepared?" Without waiting for an answer, he signaled for the video connection to be booted up. After greeting those joining them via video, he offered a few succinct comments apropos the scheduled topics then proceeded to direct the agenda at a headlong pace. Despite the forced momentum during both conference calls, Rafe politely listened to each report or data point, answered every question and made all the necessary decisions with a crisp rigorousness. But the instant the last video shut down, he was on his feet. "I apologize for my haste today. If anyone has any questions, call Vincent. See you all tomorrow."

"He's good." The recently hired director of their new drug study nodded at the figure disappearing through the doorway. "Talk about well-informed. He didn't hesitate over any decision."

"He's been doing this since he was fourteen," Rafe's decade-long personal assistant noted, pride in his voice.

"With a privately held company, that's not necessarily a guarantee of competence," the comptroller remarked. "We've all seen pampered offspring fuck up a company."

The PA, an employee of Contini Pharma for as long as Vincent, closed his laptop with a snap. "Not this company. Rafe's a bloody genius and the financials prove it."

"A genius who also happens to be in love with his wife," one of the female managers murmured. "Check the time. It's only three-fifteen."

There wasn't a man at the table who was foolish enough to comment on love with the widely divergent gender views on the subject. While those who'd known Rafe prior to his marriage were fully aware only months ago he wouldn't have recognized the word if it was lit up in flashing, twenty foot high letters on his front lawn. *Since* his wedding, they'd had to readjust their views apropos Contini Pharma's CEO and that tender emotion.

"It just goes to show that love can zap anyone," an accountant said, blandly.

"No shit." Despite the security tech's expressionless face, the weight in his voice prompted a moment of loaded silence; everyone thinking, *Life's a mystery.*

Entering the carriage house, Rafe shut the door and dialed a personal shopper in Rome who occasionally handled purchases for him. "Nicole's waiting for me," he said when Alessandra answered. "So I'm in a rush. Do you have time to jot down a couple items?"

"First item?"

He smiled at her efficiency. "Send me twenty Cucinelli

cashmere sweaters. Nicole's wearing mine in this early stage of pregnancy. She says they're comfortable. I was thinking some colors other than the dark shades I usually wear would better suit her. And maybe some comfortable tights if there is such a thing."

"Maternity tights?" The indecision in his voice at the last was obvious.

"I don't know; that's the problem. She has reservations for some reason."

"I'll send some; you don't have to give them to her. I'll also send a couple other things she might like when she's in a more girly mood. Dresses she can wear anytime, loose fitting, swingy, casual."

"Perfect. That avoids arguments about maternity clothes. Bottom line though, I don't care what she wears. She looks great in anything."

"A man in love," Alessandra murmured.

"A *lucky* man in love."

"How nice for you. She's very beautiful." Alessandra was at the wedding. "I'm pleased you found happiness."

"Me too," he said, simply, rather than *I could have gone through my entire life without knowing her.* That accident of circumstance always made his heart skip a beat. He took a small breath. "As usual, thanks for your help," he added, his composure restored. "I'm in Monte Carlo and I need everything ASAP. You're a sweetheart. Ciao."

He was halfway up the stairs when he remembered another unresolved issue. Retracing his steps, he walked into the reception room, moved to a chair in the far corner so his voice wouldn't carry upstairs, and sitting, tapped a name on his phone.

"Hey," he said when Aleix answered. "I have a slight problem."

"Better than a major one."

"Actually, this might be in the semi-major category. I talked to Nicole over lunch and she's totally uninterested in seeing the hospital until it's absolutely necessary."

"That's not so unusual. A certain amount of disquiet, if not actual fear is pretty common during pregnancy. Most women understand labor is intense."

"Yeah, that's what she said. So what I need from you is to find a super competent OB/GYN and pediatrician who are willing to come here say, in April, stay at the main house and arrange for whatever supplies and equipment are required in case of an emergency delivery. Since we're twenty minutes from the hospital, I'd feel more secure if we had backup on site. I dislike unknowns. Maso fucked with me for so many years, I'm hard wired against potential threats."

"We both learned self-preservation young. I'll find you what you need."

"Thanks. And keep it confidential. You can text me with any questions."

"Do you think Nicole should know? It might reassure her."

"I'd prefer she go to the hospital. I'm not sure I want to give her an alternative. She can be stubborn."

"Understood."

"I'm not being a controlling prick. I'll tell her eventually. At the moment, I'm just avoiding controversy. I gotta go. Nicole's waiting. You know my requirements, now. I want the best."

"I assume money isn't an issue."

"Of course not, it's for Nicole. Let me know as soon as you find them."

. . .

Moments later, Rafe cautiously opened the bedroom door, saw that Nicole was sleeping, and noiselessly moved to the desk. Picking up the screenplay, he quietly lowered himself into the chair still in place beside the bed, and began reading.

An hour later, her voice soft with sleep, Nicole murmured, "You're back."

"I'm done for the day." Rafe smiled and with a backward stretch of his arm, set the screenplay on the desk. "Did you finish your list?"

"Did you finish that?" Nicole pointed at the manuscript, an inquisitive lift to her brows.

"I did. It's good. It's really good."

"You say that as if you didn't expect it."

He smiled. "I didn't know what to expect. You sounded hesitant. And I have to admit"--his expression was amused—"your uncertainty threw me. I didn't think it possible. One question, though. Why am I a farmer?" She'd written their love story, and done it wonderfully.

"Duh. So no one knows it's us. That's why I'm a server who works part time in your olive groves helping a botanist with her research. Did you know some blight is decimating the olive groves in Italy?"

He grinned. "I do now."

"Did you like the happy ending? We win the lottery. Do you believe in luck?"

He looked at her from under the downward drift of his lashes. "Obviously. Or I'd never have met you."

Her smile could have been seen from outer space. "There, you see? Fate, pure and simple."

Fate pushed in the right direction. Once they'd met, it never had been a game of chance--not even close. "Were you ever a server?" he asked, rather than debate how many angels could dance on the head of a pin.

"I was for a while--at a frou-frou restaurant. Actually, it was Dominic's restaurant. My mother wanted me to have a job while I was in high school, you know, to teach me responsibility. But seriously, I liked it and I was good with customers."

"I'll bet." Young and pretty, the men, for sure, liked her.

"Don't be snarky. It wasn't like that at all. It was fun."

"Sorry, male bias. Forget I said it."

"For your information, Mr. Quick-to-Jump-to-Conclusions," she said with a small moue, "the only reason I wasn't a server longer was because I had a chance to volunteer at our local foodbank. That job was beaucoup more fulfilling than serving people who ordered hundred dollar entrees and drank five hundred dollar bottles of wine. Okay?"

"Absolutely, pussycat, I stand corrected. We good?"

"We're always good." She grinned. "And I thank you for it. You indulge me."

"My pleasure," he said, his voice subdued, having Nicole in his life like winning the lottery every day. Both pleased and grateful he could further indulge her, he said, "Now back to your screenplay. I know a couple directors. Want me to call them?"

She pushed herself up into a seated position, wide-eyed. "Do you really?"

He adored her flashes of naivete, the little glimpses of a girl from a normal family. It warmed his new-found soul to be reminded of a world that was good, even benevolent, where contentment and joy was not only possible but expected. "Yes, really," he said. "Basil's a documentary film maker and I've been to the Cannes Film Festival with him countless times. He knows everyone so I've met quite a few directors, any of whom would be more than happy to take advantage of your brilliant, clever screenplay."

"Is it really clever? You're not just being polite? You can tell me if you are, I'd understand—I mean why wouldn't you be polite? We're married; you're practically obliged to say something nice. Don't just smile, dammit, like I'm a child to cajole or I'll throw a tantrum. Say something!"

"It's brilliant and clever. Why would I lie?"

"So I don't feel bad, so you don't feel bad"—she smiled —"so I don't cut you off."

"That'll be the day. You can't go more than a few hours without sex."

"I can too."

"Wanna bet?" he lazily drawled.

"Now you're just messing with me." A pettish note shaded her voice.

"Uh-uh. I'm offering you a little wager."

A small stabbing jealousy struck her at his glib tone; the legions of women in his past contributing to that assurance. "You think I can't resist you?" A flush of temper pinked her cheeks. "For your information I'm not like the thousand women you've known who spread their legs without so much as a—stop grinning, damn you, or I'll get out of bed and punch you."

"Or I could join you in bed and fuck you instead."

She fell back against her pillows, shut her eyes and softly moaned. "Jesus... that fuck you comment landed right on target--literally," she breathed. "Oh, god..." Restlessly shifting her hips, she absorbed the shuddering bliss, the hot, frenzied delirium, the rapture melting deep down inside. Raising her lashes as though they were weighted, her eyes half-shut, sulky and restive, she whispered, "I'm not sure...I like this—uncontrollable...need."

"Why don't I make sure you do?" His voice was low, rich with suggestion and enticement. Loosening the ties on his boots, he quickly pulled them off, slipped his socks free, rose from the chair and covered the distance to the bed in two long, strides. Pulling aside the cashmere blanket, he lowered himself between her legs with a lithe, supple grace and resting his weight on his forearms, smiled and said, velvet soft, "I know exactly what you like, pussycat"—his mouth touched her cheek in a brushing kiss—"even without a list."

Her sudden smile was pure sass, her temper gone as quickly as it had risen. "You might want to look. My list is clever and brilliant, too."

The laughter in her eyes was artless, her voice playful, her beguiling sensuality freely offered. In all the years, with all the women, he'd never before known sex with laughter; it was a revelation. His grin was teasing. "So not only will I be fucking a clever, brilliant screen writer, but I have a script to follow. Show me."

"It's under the pillow."

His brows rose infinitesimally as he read, but after setting the sheet of paper aside, he only said, "In that order? Or randomly."

"Surprise me."

She'd said that the first time they'd met, about a drink, or not exclusively about a drink he'd translated, wanting what he wanted.

"You remember," she said.

His expression softened. "I'll remember it all my life."

"Everything changed that day."

"Yes, you brought me love"—he released an almost invisible breath—"and a peace I'd never known."

She brushed his forehead with a fingertip in a consoling

gesture, saw his expression alter, chameleon-like, turn charming.

"I'm thinking random," he casually said, back in the moment, quickly scanning the list again. He took note of item six: Kama Sutra, followed by a question mark. He could have asked what the question mark meant but decided against it. She had said, "Surprise me."

So, he did, his recall of the Kama Sutra impressive.

She was deeply grateful; he could tell by her orgasmic screams.

He climaxed more quietly, but with equal frequency and gratitude.

And because he was loved and in love, unselfish and skilled, that afternoon in Monte Carlo, the phrase, *a match made in heaven,* took on a substantive, passionate, sweet and joyful reality.

41

Two days later, on a Saturday, when the Geneva employees were gone for the weekend, Rafe was lying on the sofa in the reception room answering emails from locations around the world. An ex-pat employee in Mumbai mentioned he was going home for the holidays, reminding Rafe that Christmas was fast approaching. Turning his head, he glanced at Nicole. "Do you have any idea what you'd like to do for Christmas?"

She looked up from the baby book she was reading. "I don't care so long as I'm with you. Did you know there's a difference between French and American parenting?" She tapped the book.

He was the last person in the world to have a useful opinion on parenting. "No, I didn't know. Do you have a preference?"

"Probably not, but it's interesting."

He smiled. "You'll be a great mother, no matter what you do." She'd been reading widely on babies and parenting. Since he hadn't received a specific answer to his earlier question, he asked again. "Do you *want* to make plans for

Christmas? Your mother's been calling more than usual lately."

She sighed and set her book aside. "You noticed."

"How could I not? Your mother called four times yesterday. What's going on?"

She gave him a fretful look. "Mom wants us to come to San Francisco for Christmas."

"And?"

A rueful grimace. "I keep telling her I don't know, because I don't know."

"What don't you know?"

"It's just that I like being here with you. Am I being selfish?"

He smiled. "Probably."

She gave him the finger.

"On the other hand," he said, mindful her rude gesture was only half-hearted, "we could be selfish and polite at the same time. We could fly over for Christmas Eve and Day, then come back here and celebrate the New Year alone." He gave her a considered look. "Completely alone; I always give the staff two weeks off for the holidays."

"If that's what you want, sure, okay."

"Such enthusiasm, my little hermit. Look, we have our own house in San Francisco, so it's not as though we'll have people underfoot every second."

"You're right." Two words full of doubt. Then conscience-stricken, she uneasily added, "I hope you don't *mind* me being a hermit. Have I disrupted your social life?"

He laughed. "That's a tame word for the life I led. And no, you haven't disrupted anything that matters. I'm content to never see another living soul outside of work so long as I can come home to you."

"And the baby."

"Yes, and the baby."

Her brows rose. "You're going to have to adjust, you know."

He nodded. "I know, don't worry." Conscious of his vast ignorance of pregnancy and infants, he'd been asking questions of Aleix, doing some reading of his own. "Speaking of adjustments, if we see your family at Christmas, you can let them know you're having the baby in Monte Carlo. You haven't told your mother, have you?"

She softly sighed. "I'm avoiding it. It's sure to turn into an endless and potentially unwinnable argument."

Unwinnable wasn't in his vocabulary. "Want me to tell her?"

"Would you?" she breathed, her expression brightening, her smile dazzling. "In that case, Christmas in San Francisco would be awesome!"

He gazed at her, quizzically. "Really? That's been the deterrent? Talking to your mother?"

Nicole rolled her eyes. "To say my mom's persistent is putting it mildly. I would have been on edge the entire Christmas visit, waiting for her to ask where I was going to deliver, or looking for the right opportunity to give her the bad news."

"Lucky I'm here," he pleasantly said, the dilemma easily solved. "Want me to talk to your mother before we go, so you can relax?"

"Ohmygod, yes!" Throwing her arms open wide, she smiled and fell back in a sprawl. "See--I'm relaxing already!"

Amused and gratified at her dramatic mood shift, he rolled off the sofa in a smooth uncoiling of muscle, walked over to her chair, and picked her up. Carrying her back to the sofa, he lay down, and easily shifting her in his grasp, lowered her, face down, over the length of his body. "Now here's the plan," he murmured, lightly stroking her back. "I'll call your mom when you're not around so you don't have to freak. I'll be super nice and take all the blame, tell her you're having the baby here to please me. If she's pissed at me, I'll add her name to the list. But I doubt it'll come to that. I'll be Mr. Tactful."

"Jeez, talk about lifting a weight from my shoulders. Seriously, I can't thank you enough––really, to infinity and back. I so dislike confrontations—don't look at me like that —I mean with my mom. With you, it's different. I like arguing with you. It's more like foreplay"--she grinned--"like tempting the Devil, and I mean it in the nicest way," she added, dropping a kiss on his nose. "You're hotter than hot and so damned sexy, sometimes I think I could come just looking at you."

He grinned. "Thank you but we're off topic. Why is it so hard for you to talk to your mom? Give me a clue."

"I like my independence, you know that."

"You don't fucking say."

She smiled back. "You don't mind one single bit. It's one of the reasons we get along, why I adore you." She sighed. "It's more complicated with my mom; years-and-lame-ass-memories more complicated. I always get the feeling that I'm disappointing her when I disagree, or that somehow I'm transgressing an unspoken rule." Rafe's brows rose at the word rule and Nicole acknowledged his response with a small smile. "Unlike your personal philosophy, I might add."

"Ours," he corrected, his sudden smile, teasing. "I found your audacity charming from the first."

"Good, unfortunately"—another sigh—"it's a problem for some people. Including my dad when he hears I've upset my mother. He protects her from the slightest controversy.

Anyway, if at all possible, that's why I avoid arguing with my mom."

"I get it," he quietly said. "Why rock the boat?" But he marveled at what was defined as controversy in the Parrish family; a far cry from the warzone of his childhood. "It's nice of your dad to protect your mother. I understand completely. I'd do the same for you. So I'll just inform your mom about the plan to have the baby born here, and let her know we'll be in San Francisco for Christmas and any and all trauma will be resolved. When we get back we *could* go up to my chalet in the mountains. It's beautiful there, even if we don't ski."

"I like to ski."

His smile was fleeting. "Then you'll enjoy skiing next year."

"Hey, for your information, I'm a skilled skier. I never fall."

"Good for you."

"Seriously? You're going to tell me I can't ski?"

"I just did."

She laughed. "Damn, you're fun. You're the big, bad wolf, and I'm Little Red Riding Hood trying to outmaneuver you."

"You're not going to win on this, pussycat." Her presence in his life was like breath to him; jeopardizing that was unthinkable. "My place is only accessible by helicopter when the snow gets deep, the closest hospital fifty miles away should you fall and hurt yourself or the baby. I won't take the risk."

"Oh, very well."

Suppressing his surprise, he smiled. "Thank you."

"Now that I'm agreeable," she purred, all sass and cheek, "do I get a prize?"

His dark, showy lashes drifted downward fractionally. "I'm sure we could work something out."

It turned out to be a Saturday afternoon of simple and not so simple pleasures and when Nicole fell asleep, he left to make his promised call to her mother.

42

Walking into his office next door, he glanced at the clock. Another half hour and he could call. Dropping into his desk chair, he booted up his computer and answered some of the unending emails while keeping an eye on the time. Ideally, he'd finish talking to Mrs. Parrish before Nicole woke.

At precisely nine a.m. Pacific time, he punched in the phone number and the housekeeper, Mrs. B. answered. Identifying himself in case she didn't recognize the caller ID, he asked to speak to Mrs. Parrish, and met a dead silence. At the lengthening silence he almost said, *It's none of your business why I'm calling, and I can outwait you,* but the housekeeper gave in first.

"I'll get Mrs. Parrish," she said, grudgingly.

"Thank you," he replied, well-mannered. But he couldn't help but smile at the picture of Mrs. B, with her shocking red hair, tie-dyed hippy clothes and drill sergeant personality, vetting Nicole's high school boyfriends. That would have been a helluva gauntlet. One that apparently continued to this day, his position as husband to the family's eldest daughter, not yet fully sanctioned.

Several moments later, Nicole's mother came on the line, half-breathless. "Oh, dear--don't tell me Nicole's--been hurt?"

"No, she's fine. Actually she's taking a nap now," he politely added. "Nicole said you were wondering about our holiday plans so I thought I'd give you a call and let you know we'll be in San Francisco Christmas Eve and Christmas Day."

"Why didn't Nicole call?" A short, suspicious pause. "Are you sure she's all right?"

"She's in perfect health, sleeping a little more than usual but otherwise well. I just told her I'd call you after I finalized our flight plans," he lied in the interests of his wife's peace of mind. "We'll arrive early morning on Christmas Eve. I imagine we'll be at our house by nine, so whatever your schedule is for the day, just let us know. Nicole also mentioned you'd asked about her delivery plans, so I offered to pass along that information as well. She's decided to have the baby in Monte Carlo, to please me I think. It's very kind of her. Once Nicole's home from the hospital, everyone's welcome to come and see the baby."

"You're running interference for her, aren't you?" Melanie's tone was abrupt and disapproving.

"Yes, I offered to step in." His voice in contrast, was temperate. "Nicole dislikes controversy, particularly on the subject of her delivery. I agree with her. She's the one having the baby; she should make the decision. I hope you understand."

"I see."

If the sharp belligerence in those two words rang true,

Mrs. Parrish didn't see at all, nor did she mind letting him know. On the other hand, he had no intention of arguing about Nicole's decision to have the baby in Monte Carlo. "Nicole's really looking forward to Christmas in San Francisco," he said, changing the subject. "In fact, she said that seeing her family again would be awesome. I couldn't agree more."

"You're very diplomatic." It wasn't a compliment so much as a nice blend of passive/aggressive temper and sarcasm.

"I simply want Nicole to be happy." That everything else was white noise, he chose not to mention.

"Nicole seems *very* happy whenever I talk to her, thanks to you, no doubt." A sliver of a pause, then Mrs. Parrish's voice lost its hard edge. "I don't suppose she'll change her mind."

"About having the baby in San Francisco? No. Nicole's intentions are quite firm." He hoped that was plain enough because discussing personal issues, particularly with a semi-stranger wasn't something he chose to pursue. "Now, if Nicole's siblings have Christmas lists, please email them to us. We'll enjoy shopping for them."

"Nicole doesn't shop."

I hadn't noticed," he said, rather than debate an issue Alessandra could very well handle for them. "We'll figure it out. Until Christmas then?"

"Don't be extravagant."

A muscle in his jaw flexed. "If you send the lists, it shouldn't be an issue." As the mother of six children, giving orders must come automatically. "We'll see you in a couple weeks."

"Thank you for your call." A tight-lipped courtesy.

"No problem. Ciao." If she didn't hang up by the count of ten, he would. On eight, the line went dead. He softly exhaled, and thanked whatever spirits had taken a hand in the conversation; at least open hostility had been averted.

He laughed.

Fucking low bar, but hey, it was over.

43

On Christmas Eve morning, Simon turned the Mercedes S-Class sedan into the driveway of their San Francisco home. Rafe had bought the house sight unseen last summer, had put Nicole's name on the title and while she loved it, she'd also chided him for what she called an extravagance. He, on the other hand, saw the house as a practicality. It was two blocks from her parents.

"Look," Nicole said, nudging Rafe beside her in the back seat as their car came to a stop. "We have a welcoming committee." Her nine-year-old sister, Ellie, was on the porch steps.

Glancing up from a phone call, Rafe murmured, "Talk to you later," and turning to Nicole, smiled. "Nice welcoming committee. I like the Santa hat."

Ellie was running toward them. Putting her hand out like a traffic cop to the second Mercedes turning into the drive, she darted in front of the car.

"Good thing we have trained drivers," Rafe said, drily,

watching the front end of the second Mercedes nosedive as the driver braked hard. "Reckless must run in your family."

Nicole shot him a grin. "I married you, didn't I?" Ellie was pounding on Nicole's window. "Gotta go."

"I'll give security a head's up." Leaning past Nicole, he reached for the door handle. "Give me five."

Ellie was not only pounding on the window, but hopping up and down and waving a sheet of paper with the intensity of an airport employee waving off a plane about to land on the wrong runway.

Nicole stepped out into a minor outburst.

"Finally! At last! I thought you'd *never* come! I've been waiting and waiting! Because *look*!" Ellie shouted. "We have an extra-special, super busy schedule"—the paper narrowly missed Nicole's nose—"for *two whole* days!"

"Let me see," Nicole said, taking the paper from Ellie, giving her a hug then holding her at arm's length. "Holy, moly, you've shot up again. You're going to pass me up soon."

Ellie drew herself up and straightened her shoulders. "I grew an inch since September. Mommy says I'm going to be tall like Dad. What *took* you guys so long? You said nine and it's way, way past."

"We had a delay landing—something about winds." It was almost eleven. "Sorry, have you been here long?"

"Since *seven*," Ellie said, with a cartoonish eye roll. "But Grace gave me breakfast and I watched TV for a while then Jorge said you were on your way so I came out here and I've been waiting *patiently* ever since," she finished in a breathless rush.

Nicole had no idea who Grace and Jorge were but Ellie made friends easily, and obviously they'd taken care of her. "I wish I'd known you were waiting; I'd have called Mom to let you know we were delayed. But hey, we're finally here. Let's go inside and you can tell me all about the holiday agenda." With a glance at Rafe who was talking to his security, she pointed at the house and at his nod, took Ellie's hand and walked toward the front door that was already swinging open.

"Rafe told Grace to make breakfast and Jorge and their kids are helping too," Ellie offered, every word buzzing with enthusiasm. "I already had some French toast, but I might eat again. Are you hungry? Grace has croissants and smoothies if you want and tons of other good food and like a *real* menu. Are you excited about opening presents?" she asked, her voice going up a notch or two. "*I* sure am!"

"Me too," Nicole whispered, squeezing her sister's hand as they approached the front door held open by a slender woman dressed in jeans and a Clean The Oceans t-shirt, her blonde hair pulled back in a ponytail.

"Welcome." The woman smiled. "I'm Grace." She hadn't known what to expect from a billionaire's spouse, but this young woman dressed in a man's oversized sweater, tights and flip flops didn't fit the celebrity ideal of trophy wife. No makeup, no bling, no attitude, but definitely a beauty; that fit the billionaire criteria.

"I'm Nicole, pleased to meet you." Nicole smiled. "It's a lovely day isn't it?"

"As usual," Grace said, pleasantly. "But you grew up here so you know that. Breakfast is ready whenever you wish. It was so warm today we set up a table on the terrace."

"Thank you, but I'll wait for Rafe." Nicole wondered if this family Ellie mentioned was live-in staff. She should pay more attention but Rafe usually took care of things and it was way too easy to let him. Assailed by a twinge of guilt, her conscience-stricken reverie was almost immediately broken by a sharp tug on her hand.

"Come *on!*" Ellie proclaimed in ringing tones, pulling Nicole toward the living room, and dereliction of duty issues were swept aside by more agreeable pursuits. "You have to see the Christmas tree! I helped decorate it with a whole bunch of super cool artists! Tons of other people have been here too, doing all kinds of stuff!"

Lord, she really was the world's worst housewife, Nicole decided; she hadn't inquired once about preparations for their visit. Then again, she thought with an inner smile, she had a husband who could do anything and he didn't mind a slacker for wife--at least in management skills. She wouldn't cede him the ground completely; in other areas she was infinitely capable, even impressive.

"See, see! Look!" Ellie's voice was high-pressure giddy.

Jerked to a stop on the threshold of the living room, Nicole stared, awestruck. A tall—it had to be twenty feet high—exquisitely decorated, brilliantly lit tree stood center stage in front of the windows overlooking the bay.

"I put every single ornament on the bottom until I couldn't reach any higher even on tippy toe!" Ellie cried in her high decibel Christmas voice, running toward the tree, and pointing in little jabs. "See—there are lacy ones, and tiny toys and musical instruments and angels, and little, bitty animals that look so real you can't believe it!"

Nicole felt Rafe's presence behind her, felt the light, skimming kiss on her cheek.

"Do you like it?" he murmured.

She half turned and smiled. "It's magical..."

"It's our first Christmas," he said softly, wrapping his arms around her, drawing her back against his solid warmth. "I wanted it to be special. This tree was on a Victorian Christmas card, one of hundreds I looked at, maybe thousands. I am currently an authority on Victorian Christmas customs," he added, drolly. He didn't say, until this year, he'd given little thought to decorations or trees or Christmas in general, his past holidays focused primarily on revel and carouse.

"My compliments on your research; the result's not only special," Nicole said, softly, "it's breathtaking." The huge, soaring tree was dense with glittering ornaments, twinkling lights, and a festooning of Victorian excess typical of the era. While the colorfully wrapped presents massed at the base in artful, tumbled disarray added the perfect grace note to the picturesque tableau.

"I already found *all my* presents!" Ellie's screams echoed in the high ceilinged room. "Want me to show you?"

Bending, Rafe kissed Nicole's cheek and whispered, "Go. Christmas is for children."

Nicole glanced up, and grinned. "Speak for yourself." Moving away, she added in a carrying tone, "I'm coming, I'm coming! Oh my goodness, isn't that an enormous package! I wonder what in the world it could be?"

Taking advantage of the interruption, Rafe beckoned to a tall, russet-haired man standing in the doorway to the dining room. As he came up, Rafe spoke softly. "Tell the cook we'll have something to eat in ten minutes. And will you see that the people in the guest cottage have a menu? Thanks." He smiled. "I'm Rafe. Did I talk to you or someone else?"

"Jorge. You talked to me."

"The tree's magnificent. Many thanks. And thanks as well for finding people willing to work over Christmas. I know that's not easy."

"My wife's doing the cooking and our son and two daughters are helping out."

"Excellent. I appreciate your assistance. How do you know Alessandra?"

"We met her years ago in Nice. We have a sailboat and cruise during our off times."

"What type of craft?"

"An Amel 54."

"That's a beautiful cruiser."

"We like it."

"So where are you off to next when time allows?"

"Bali."

"Stay at my place if you like. I'll give you the details before we leave."

"Super." Jorge put out his hand. "Thanks."

"Not a problem," Rafe said, shaking his hand.

Jorge raised his chin a fraction. "The tree upstairs is decorated per your instructions."

"Perfect."

"I'll go and see that breakfast is ready. Enjoy."

Their brunch was abbreviated since Ellie was insistent they leave. So with apologies to Grace, they ate quickly and followed Ellie's skipping progress the two blocks to her house.

After his recent phone conversation with Nicole's mother, Rafe braced himself as he entered the Parrish home. Instead, he was pleasantly surprised to be greeted with welcoming smiles and hugs from everyone.

He was even more pleased to see Nicole's delight at being home. He'd not seen her in such an effervescent, lighthearted mood before; asking and answering questions without reservation, chatting brightly about the baby, giggling over familiar family jokes, and before long, being dragged off by her mother and sisters.

Looking back, Nicole raised her eyebrows in query; Rafe gave her a reassuring wave. He was perfectly capable of making small talk. After years of talking to strangers at business functions, he'd honed the art of bland conversation to a fine art.

"Nicole tells me you restore Chris Crafts," he said, turning to Nicole's father. "Are you working on one now?"

"*We're* working on one now," Keir and Dante said in unison, shooting quick glances at their father. Their father's inner sanctum workshop was private and not often breached.

Matt Parrish smiled at Rafe. "Want to see it? I have a workspace downstairs and like all addictive collectors I assume everyone's dying to see my runabouts." He was graciously offering access to his new son-in-law. "We're working on a 1929, 22 foot Cadet now."

Rafe smiled and nodded. "Lead the way."

The designated space encompassed most of the lower section of the house and was completely devoted to a state-of-the-art workshop. And in the center of the eighty foot long area was a mahogany runabout partially sanded down.

"Wow, it's a beauty," Rafe said, walking up to the speedboat and running his hand over the starboard gunwale that had been sanded clear. "It looks like this operation is almost entirely hand work."

"Yeah, that's what makes it fun. Seeing the sleek frame and raw bones appear once the dirt and debris is gone. This one had been sitting in a barn in Monterey for seventy years. There's some rot but not much. Want a beer? Is it too early for you? I have juice, water, bottled espresso, if you prefer."

"Beer's fine, thanks."

"Get us a beer," Matt said to his sons. "You boys can share one. It's a holiday."

The men and boys retired to two old sofas that had been pulled up near the boat, for times such as this, Rafe suspected, to admire work done and contemplate work yet to do. Keir and Dante kept up a running commentary on their progress, Matt occasionally offered a relevant observation, and Rafe answered the few questions directed his way —those, mostly about his yacht. It was common knowledge Nicole had met him at a party onboard last summer.

They were on their second beers when Melanie called out from the top of the stairs, her voice animated, "Don't forget about us up here! Buzz just arrived with the florist and the holly! Everyone has to help decorate!"

The boys groaned.

"Hey, none of that," Matt warned. "Your Mom likes everyone to pitch in, so we're going to do that with a smile. Right?"

Two sighs. "Okay, Dad."

"How big a smile?" Dante quipped.

"As big as the one you give Gemma Forbes when she comes over," Matt said, drily.

Dante laughed. "She's worth it. Decorating?" He grimaced. "Not so much."

Matt gave his wild son a chiding look. "It's for your mom. Behave."

"Okay, okay. I *love* decorating."

"I'll need a tad more sincerity upstairs," Matt said. "Now go help your mother."

As the boys raced away, Matt paused for a moment just short of the stairway. "Before we go up, I want to apologize for Melanie's occasional obstinacy. I understand you were playing defense for Nicole on that phone call. It's none of our business where Nicole has the baby and so I told Mel, but both Nicole and her mother can be stubborn." He smiled. "You've noticed."

Rafe grinned. "Just a little. But I want Nicole to be happy," he added, quietly. "I hope you understand."

"Of course. You two kids live your lives, don't worry about us. Whatever you do is your business. Mel eventually comes around; sometimes it just takes a while. I'll deal with that. Now, we'd better get upstairs or the decorating will never get done. I'll be ready for a stiff drink when it's over. I keep telling Mel, hire someone to decorate the house, but she thinks it's a family activity, so"—

"Whatever makes them happy," Rafe finished with a smile.

"Good man," Matt said, slapping Rafe's shoulder. "You already know the secret to a successful marriage."

Rafe added his help to the all-hands-on-deck activity that secured the holly garlands in great swags over the windows and doorways, along the mantle and credenza, above the divider between living room and kitchen; the task accomplished with much laughter, and recall of past Christmases, including a minor disaster having to do with mistletoe. Apparently, at one of their Boxing Day parties the local minister had been accosted. Granted he was good looking everyone agreed, but that one of his most stiff-necked female parishioners was the seductress had raised eyebrows. Since then, the mistletoe had been hung in clear public view.

During the bustle of decorating that afternoon, Rafe occasionally felt as though he were standing apart, like a visitor to an alien world. He'd never seen such a warm, affectionate family Christmas. The festivities were a stark departure from his Christmases in the opulent world of the glitterati, where holidays were spent at luxurious ski resorts, five star hotels or private clubs, and the amusements, unlike the cozy merriment today, were profligate; boredom the ultimate sin.

At Nicole's touch, he quickly glanced over. "Sorry." A quick blink, the unpleasant past banished. "Did you say something?"

"You okay?" He'd looked right through her for a second.

"Yes, fine." Rafe smiled. "I've never decorated before," he added apropos nothing, his voice carrying the same emotional weightlessness. "You were saying?"

He wasn't going to bare his soul, Nicole understood, familiar with his moments of withdrawal. Sliding her fingers through his, she smiled. "I said you're going to love our punch. Come on, I'll show you how it's done."

Once everyone had gathered around the kitchen table, the ritual punch making commenced; the much-spattered recipe card had been passed down through Matt's family, its origins veiled in the mists of Venetian history. Since the region bordering the Adriatic Sea had been under the hegemony of Venice during the height of the Republic, Rafe recognized all the Croatian liquors. He'd taken Nicole to his island in the Adriatic last summer and they exchanged silent smiles as each liquor was poured into the silver punch bowl.

Just as the sugar cubes floating in the punch bowl were set aflame, Dominic, Kate, Rosie and James arrived. Like a two-year-old dynamo Jimmy was in the lead, wiggling out of his jacket as he ran through the living room, Rosie following more sedately, unbuttoning her quilted vest, their parents, hand in hand, bringing up the rear. Bending over to pick up Jimmy's jacket discarded on the carpet, Dominic tossed it on a chair, said something to Kate that made her smile and coming to rest in the doorway to the kitchen, they ignored their son's high pitched rendition of "Santa tuming to town," and wished everyone a Merry Christmas.

But a moment later, Jimmy scrambled up on a chair, screamed, "Fire!," and reached toward the flame. Releasing Kate's hand, Domenic lunged forward, grabbed his son off the chair, and spoke to him quietly.

Everyone ignored the toddler pout, the puff of protest and moments later, when Domenic deposited his son back on the chair, Jimmy said, "Daddy me make deal." He glanced back at his father and smiled.

In the interim Rosie had taken off her red velvet vest, hung it on a hook by the back door and was standing by Ellie, the girls deep in conversation.

Putting his arm around Kate, Domenic smiled and softly said, "Ready for a drink? I might have a couple."

"I might have more." She winked. "I believe you said you were babysitting tonight?"

He laughed. "Drink away. I like you tipsy."

"I like you any way, anywhere, anytime," she whispered. "So don't go far."

"Not a chance, Katherine. You're mine," he said, softly, his blue eyes grave.

At the sudden chorus of "Good King Wenceslas" breaking out, they smiled at each other.

"You should be more sociable," Kate teased.

"Yeah, that's me. But, for you"—he grinned—"I'll be neighborly. Let me get you a drink."

The punch was a big hit as always, a non-alcoholic version available for the youngsters. Mrs. B set out an array of hors d'oeuvres on the kitchen counters and everyone ate and drank punch, shared Christmas stories, exchanged gossip, until the children's patience wore thin. Fortunately, dusk came early because tradition required at least a hint of darkness before presents could be opened. Amidst much whooping and hollering, the children ran into the living room, and took their places before the tree, while the adults followed and found comfortable seats.

The present opening was wildly exuberant, the children ripping open their packages, shrieking and exclaiming in age-appropriate delight over each gift, then quickly searching for another package to open, their raucous glee a lively reminder of the heightened joy the season inspired in the young.

Rafe and Nicole sat together on a sofa, observing the children's pleasure, sharing intimate smiles, cocooned in a warm, golden bliss. Squeezing Rafe's hand from time to time, Nicole would whisper, "Thanks for smoothing the way so we could come home."

"My pleasure, Tiger. Having fun?"

She'd beam and snuggle in closer, her smile rich with satisfaction. "Best Christmas ever…"

Like a treasure found, he thought. "Yes, best ever."

Once the last gift had been opened and admired, and the children were getting rambunctious, Christmas Eve dinner was announced. It was served informally in the kitchen, the Italian feast a collection of recipes from Parrish ancestors. Mrs. B had been cooking for days with help from Dominic's restaurant staff at Lucia and the large kitchen table was groaning under the weight of sweet and savory delicacies. The punch gave way to distinguished wines and Rafe made a note to contribute some next year, including reserve wines from his vineyards. Dessert was a hybrid *Buche de Noel* with a tiramisu base, the richly decorated jelly-roll a favorite of the children when they were young and now a perennial Christmas treat.

It was an evening that filled hearts with love, warmed spirits, and reminded those who needed reminding that the companionship of family was priceless.

As the younger children grew fatigued, a slow leave-taking ensued. Jimmy was asleep in Dominic's arms, Rosie holding Kate's hand and leaning against her mother, Rafe and Nicole, their coats on against the night's chill, stood hand in hand near the front door. The conversation was one of thanks and quiet contentment, of punch and wine languor, of promises to see everyone tomorrow.

After exiting the house, Kate and Nicole paused for a moment in quiet conversation. Leaning toward Rafe, Dominic spoke softly, his voice amused. "Welcome to the family. You didn't bolt. I admire your courage."

"No courage required," Rafe said, equally softly. "This is paradise. And having been to Hell and back, I know the difference."

"Amen to that." Dominic glanced at his son in his arms then looked up. "It makes one grateful." Responding to his wife's hand on his arm, Dominic quickly turned. "You're ready then?" Swiveling back, he smiled at Rafe and Nicole. "We'll see you tomorrow."

Rosie suddenly looked up, drowsy-eyed. "Bring that book on polar bears, Nicky. Don't forget."

"I won't." Nicole waved. "See you guys."

44

As they walked in the door, Nicole glanced up.

"They're gone," Rafe said.

She smiled. "Are you a mind reader?"

"Don't ever play poker, Tiger." He pulled her close with one arm. "Also," he said, kissing her cheek, "I'm selfish. I want you all to myself. I told Grace to leave something for breakfast in the refrigerator so we don't starve."

"Thanks on both counts." She grinned. "Now, ta tum, drum roll please. Wanna see your presents?"

"Yup, but while we still have our jackets on, come out on the balcony for a minute."

"Sounds mysterious."

He shook his head. "Just a little surprise." Taking her hand, he drew her through the living room to the balcony doors.

Moments later, standing on the balcony overlooking the bay, he typed a short text, sent it, and slipped his phone back into his jacket pocket. Then gently cupping Nicole's shoulders, he turned her to the right. "Look."

A blaze of Christmas lights appeared two hundred yards

out in the ocean, the colorful brilliance forming the words, "Merry Christmas, I Love You," in ten foot high letters along the entire length of an oil tanker.

"I tried to have my message installed on the Golden Gate Bridge but hit a road block," he said, a note of amusement in in his voice. "The bureaucracy wouldn't budge."

"You're crazy—in a very nice way," she said, swinging around and wrapping her arms around his waist. Coming up on tip toe, she waited for him to dip his head then kissed him softly. "It's the most splendid present I've ever received," she murmured. "It's wonderful and sweet and thoughtful and I love you more than anything in the whole wide world, the universe and beyond."

"Good," he said, holding her close, careful not to frighten her with the obsessive nature of his love. "You're my happiness, my life…I'm mad for you." He smiled to dismiss the sudden uncompromising intensity in his tone, and added more casually, "Ready to see some trinkets I bought for you?"

"This is more than enough. In fact," she said, "it's stupendous."

"Humor me, Tiger. I've been waiting a long time for a real Christmas."

She knew better than to remark on the melancholy note in his voice. "On second thought," she said, smiling, "I'd adore some trinkets."

"There you go, a woman of immense tact."

He knew she thought, but the moodiness was gone from his eyes. She winked. "We try."

He laughed. "I thank you for your good manners." And lifting her in his arms, he carried her inside, up the stairs and on entering their bedroom, walked to the windows before setting her down. "Take a last look. The tanker is anchored in a shipping lane."

Nicole turned, her brows lightly raised. "And you're bending the rules."

"Just a little." His voice was lazy. "It's Christmas. I figured we had ten, fifteen minutes before someone complained." He pulled out his phone, tapped in a text, gave her a smile. "Time's about up."

"Take a picture. Then I can admire it at my leisure."

He did, hit send, and as the Christmas message immediately dimmed, put his phone away. "Now, come see our little tree." Taking her hand, he walked across the room, and pulled up two chairs before a table with a small tree on top. It was decorated simply with fairy lights and tiny, red boxes suspended from its branches.

"A different theme." Glancing up, Nicole smiled. "Do you have hidden decorating talents?"

"Uh-uh, this is purely functional. Although," he said, softly teasing, "I have other kinds of hidden talents I'd be happy to show you...later."

She glanced up, a half-smile on her lips. "Ah--a future delight..."

"Or a new experience," he silkily murmured. "Your favorite kind."

"Or yours."

He smiled. There was no polite response when he'd run out of new sexual experiences years ago. Nor did he wish to recall that wasteland of his life. "Why don't we finish this discussion after we open some presents?"

She was beginning to recognize that tick along his jaw. "Of course," she quickly agreed. "Let me get my presents."

Returning a few moments later with her carryon, she sat down and took three packages from the bag. Holding out the largest package, she smiled. "Merry Christmas. I hope you like it."

Her smile was bright and beautiful, enchanting; he was a lucky man. Taking the package from her, Rafe sat and after briefly admiring the metallic green gift wrap and bright red bow, began to untie the silk bow.

"Hurry."

He looked up, saw her eyes all aglow and was tempted to tell her he'd never received a gift from a woman before. With the perfunctory nature of his female liaisons, if and when gifts were dispensed, his staff dealt with it.

"Jeez, you're slow," Nicole said, interrupting his moment of reflection, grabbing the package from him. "Let me do that." Pulling off the bow, she ripped off the paper and dropped it on the floor. "Here." She handed the gift back with a captivating grin. "Enjoy."

Holding up green knit fabric, he let it unfurl and a V-neck sweater materialized. "My favorite style," he murmured, giving her a smile. "I *will* enjoy it, thank you. I like the color."

"It's called gunpowder green. How's that for conjuring up all kinds of historical incidents? Cool, hey? Now, try it on!"

The excitement in her voice immediately brought him to his feet and setting the gift down, he pulled off the sweater he wore and tossed it aside. "You must have shopped online." She rarely left the house and if she did, he was with her.

"Au contraire." Her eyes sparkled. "I made it."

About to slip the green sweater over his head, he stopped and stared. "I didn't know you knit."

Her gaze was sweetly innocent. "That's because I wanted it to be a surprise."

"What others skills are you hiding?" he asked, with a teasing lift of his brows.

She threw her arms open wide with a flourish. "I'll have you know I'm a woman of vast accomplishments."

"Indeed." His voice was whisper soft; she was all that was good in his life.

Gazing up at him from under her lashes, she made a tiny twirling motion with her index finger. "Put the sweater on. Or if you're going to stand there half naked, come a little closer," she said, low-pitched and sultry, "and we'll unwrap gifts later."

"Uh-uh." He shook his head, his smile warm. "I'm like Ellie. I have a schedule."

"Mine might be better," she lazily murmured.

"We'll talk about it later." His soft drawl denoted a later of his choosing.

"Excuse me?" Cool, slightly fractious.

His grin was instant, warm and boyish. "Consider me completely at your disposal--as soon as I try on this sweater." And in a few economical moves; head, arms, hitch of his shoulders, the sweater slid down his sleek torso. Stretching his arms, he measured the sleeve length and gave her a thumbs' up. "My compliments, it's a perfect fit. How did you do it?"

She suddenly smiled. "Don't look so surprised. I copied the one you had on."

He shook his head. "You're truly amazing, Tiger. I feel bad. I just bought stuff. I should have built you a desk or bookshelf, made you a watch or something."

She didn't doubt he could do any of that, but disagreed with his self-reproach. "Look, you have a company to run while I have nothing but time on my hands. There's no comparison. Now, I have two more presents." She grinned. "So look interested or I'll pout like Jimmy."

He laughed. "I am so fucking interested--word of God." Aware of Nicole's lack of patience, he ripped open the wrapping on the larger package and discovered an eight by ten framed photo of his yacht, the sky above it ablaze with a flash of lightening. Nicole had written across the top: *Sometimes you just get lucky.*

"It's true, you know," she said, softly, as he ran his fingers over the inscription. "If I hadn't been lost in the meandering corridors of your yacht"-

"And if you hadn't stumbled into my stateroom." He took a deep breath, thinking how destitute his life would have been. "This goes in a place of honor on my desk as a reminder of my good fortune. Thank you," he said, quietly.

"I get the shivers sometimes, thinking how close I came to missing you." Shaking away a shudder of fear, she blew out a breath. "Nuf about that, though. You're here, I'm here, it's Christmas, and," she said with a grin, "you're never getting away. Also, apropos nothing, Keir added the lightening to the photo. He's awesome on Photoshop."

"I'll have to thank him," Rafe said, matching her casual tone. "It's marvelous. This memento is very special."

"Yes, it is. It's the day I found you." She smiled and blew him a kiss. "Now, open that last little one." Sitting up, she leaned forward, a pink flush rising on her cheeks.

He slid his finger under the flap of the silver envelope covered in Christmas stickers, opened it and pulled out a card. Nicole had written in green ink, *You can pick out the name for our baby.* He looked up and smiled. "Thank you, sweetheart. It's very considerate of you." Rising from his chair, he set the card under the little Christmas tree, unhooked a tiny red box from a branch and walking back, handed it to Nicole with a small bow. "Your turn."

Pulling off the ribbon, she lifted the lid on the box and took out a small roll of paper. Uncurling it, she read Rafe's small, tight script. *You're doing all of the work. You name the baby.* She laughed. "Apparently, some negotiations are in order."

"Or I could arm wrestle you. Loser names the baby."

"Are you implying I can't win?"

"Consider the physical differences," he murmured, a smile in his voice.

She pursed her lips. "I still could win. It's not all about size."

He looked at her from under half-lowered lashes, constraint in his gaze. "Why don't you open another present," he said, rather than debate the impossible.

"Don't change the subject. I'll have you know I won lots of arm wrestling contests at Stanford."

"With men?"

"Of course, with men."

"Ah."

"What the hell does that mean?"

"It means I'm trying not to argue."

"So you're saying they let me win," she said, a fiery little heat in her voice.

He exhaled, his brows rose fractionally. "I could ask you if you slept with any of them, but I really don't want to know. Now, I have some other things you might like." Turning to the tree, he pulled off several little red boxes, sat down and handed her another one. "Try this one."

"Is the argument over? Am I to be obliging?"

For a moment he didn't know if that was remonstrance

or teasing. Then she smiled and he answered her with a flashing grin. "Is it possible?"

"Of course." She took the present from him, her smile playful. "I'm always obliging when someone's giving me gifts."

"Someone?"

Her eyes widened, slightly. "Seriously, you're jealous? I thought we got past all that."

"Tell me who the someones were," he said, tersely.

"There weren't any. I told you before, I never stayed long enough. It's only you, it's been only you from the first, and it always will be only you."

The crease that had formed between his eyes, eased and his slow smile was full of grace. "Thank you," he said, softly. Taking a small calming breath, he wondered whether his violently possessive feelings would ever dissipate, knew the unfortunate answer, and opted for distraction. "Are you going to see what's inside?" he asked, nodding at the gift Nicole was holding.

When Nicole opened the box along with several more in the next few moments, she found written promises in the same small script on little curls of paper: a certificate for unlimited baby clothes at a shop she loved; one for a photographer to film the baby for the entire first year; a uncertain offer of baby jewelry if she liked from Cartier; Alessandra's phone number, answered day or night, for whatever clothes she might want; a list of nannies (open to discussion) he'd added, knowing his wife; and last, an offer that was greeted with a scream of delight. Fiona would be taking over the food bank program from Isabelle Tansy.

"You're an absolute dear, darling, completely loveable man of my dreams. How did you *know?*"

He would have had to have been deaf, dumb and blind not to know.

Two weeks ago, Nicole had walked into the conference room at the main house and found Isabelle seated *way* the hell too close to him. Busy on his laptop, he hadn't realized Isabelle had stayed behind when the others left until he'd looked up as the door opened, saw Nicole's face and suddenly noticed Isabelle was about to kiss him.

He'd jumped up like a shot, strode across the room, grasped Nicole's hand and taking her away, apologized up, down and sideways for first, Isabelle's presence (she'd arrived uninvited, ostensibly with a new proposal) and second, for her atrocious behavior. Nicole had graciously accepted his explanation and he'd seen that Isabelle was flown back to Geneva immediately.

"I thought you'd be more comfortable with Fiona," Rafe said. "After a little persuasion, she agreed to my proposal." He smiled, recalling Fiona's initial businesslike approach to salary negotiations to which he responded, *I'll pay you anything,* ending the discussion. "She claims she can do most of the work long distance, and on occasion, she'll fly over to discuss details with you in person. You said Fiona was in the graduate program at Stanford in Business Analytics, so I thought who better to help you out?"

"She still thinks you're available you know."

There was no need to question the subject of Nicole's statement. "She doesn't anymore," he said, his voice dry as dust.

"Would you think me childish if I asked whether"—

"Isabelle no longer works for Contini Pharma," he said, flatly. "And don't even consider feeling sorry for her," he added, aware of Nicole's sudden unease. "She has a fucking trust fund, her severance was more than she deserved and

The Wedding, Etc.

you know as well as I, she'll land on her feet, preferably at some company run by a man with a sizeable balance sheet."

Nicole smiled. "You can be very persuasive."

"Fucking A. Do you know how many women there are like Isabelle who think wealthy men are just dying to have someone tell them how great they are? Don't answer that." He held up his hand and pointed to his wedding band. "There's only one woman for me, now and always. Could we stop talking about this?" His conversation with Isabelle had been irksome, he'd abruptly cut her off and turned her over to Vincent.

"Yes, gladly."

Rafe blew out a breath. "Thanks. Now, on to more pleasant topics; call Fiona when you have time. She said she'd be looking for an excuse to get out of the house."

"I'll invite her for breakfast."

"Sounds like a plan. Fiona's actually enthused about helping you."

"I suppose you're paying her a fortune."

"I wouldn't say that." It wasn't a lie, the word, fortune, fluid.

"That's super evasive. I'll have to ask Fiona."

"I thought salaries were personal."

"Oh, God, you told Fiona not to tell me." Nicole grinned. "I'll have to see if she breaks." Leaning over, she kissed Rafe's cheek. "But either way, I adore you for spoiling me. *For getting rid of the bitch.* I'm sublimely, insanely, blissfully happy with my new foodbank director."

And so the holiday continued in unblemished perfection. Breakfast the next morning was a marathon talking-a-mile-a-minute with Fiona while Rafe sat back and listened in amazement to a mercurial, warp speed shift of topics, gossip, and reminiscences. Fiona agreed to meet in Monte

Carlo in a month and she left just before they were scheduled to go to the Parrish house. Christmas dinner was another incredible feast, conversation never at a loss with so many at the table, and the afternoon was occupied with assembling children's toys and visiting. As twilight approached, after a round of promises to stay in touch, everyone dispersed: Rafe and Nicole left for their flight home, Dominic's family was going skiing in Aspen, the Parrish family was off to Hawaii for New Years.

After an overnight stay in Monte Carlo, Rafe and Nicole flew to Geneva, then took a helicopter to Rafe's chalet near Val d'Isere in the French Alps. The couple who staffed his home had the fires lit in the fireplaces, food prepared and after greeting them at the door, returned to their cottage in the valley below. In terms of an idyllic interlude, the isolated chalet couldn't have been more peaceful and snug. Rafe and Nicole spent long hours in bed indulging their senses, sweetly, then not so sweetly, in turn, ardently and tender, breathless, seething, delirious, savoring every carnal pleasure with delight. And the interim between Christmas and the New Year passed in sumptuous, cozy content.

They arrived home January second to a sunshiny Monte Carlo and a new year, their sense of well-being, matchless.

45

The Grand Opening of *Toujours* was on Valentine's Day. Not only was the date an *homage* to what had been Henny's all-consuming passion at the time of his death, but a symbolic nod to the love he and Mireille had shared. And to a few of Mireille's close friends, Rafe included, her timing had also been contingent on her passing the crucial three month milestone of pregnancy. Now at four months, the risk of a miscarriage had lessened, and feeling more secure and confident, she was ready to share her news with the world.

The restaurant was full, a milling crowd taking advantage of the stupendous buffet and well-tended bar, Mireille holding court and greeting her guests in a corner of the main room bordered by low planters lush with pale daffodils and forsythia.

As Rafe and Nicole moved through the crowd and came within sight of Mireille, Nicole gave Rafe's arm a nudge. "Do you see what I see, or am I jumping to conclusions?" Mireille wore a slender red silk gown that revealed the slight rise of her tummy.

"No, you're right."

"You knew!"

"Yes, but she didn't want anyone to know until—well, until she felt the baby was no longer at risk or at less risk." He pulled Nicole to a stop. "I'm sorry, sweetheart, but I gave her my word I wouldn't tell anyone. And this child is in the way of a miracle to her, to me as well…as if Henny lives on," he said, his voice whisper soft at the end.

Reaching up, Nicole brushed Rafe's cheek with her finger tip. "I understand. I'm so happy for her—and you. I know how much you loved Henny." Her sudden smile was one of delight. "This is truly a night for celebration."

"It is, thanks, Tiger." Rafe pulled her close, dropped a kiss on her nose and grinned. "Our kids will be friends. What do you think of that?"

"I think there must be beneficent gods watching over us. Consider me a convert to that unknown glory."

He laughed softly. "No kidding, serious magic. Now, come on," he said, taking her hand, "let's go say hello to Mireille and you ladies can compare baby vibes."

"Such as our son's constant kicking."

Rafe gave her a wink. "Or our daughter's love of dance."

"You're in for a big surprise, Contini." Nicole winked back. "Just sayin' cause I'm always right."

"Yes, dear," said the man who bent the world to his will. "Absolutely."

After chatting with Mireille for a few minutes, Rafe withdrew, leaving the women to talk undisturbed. They shared their experiences of the first trimester, discussed baby names, and extended offers of assistance if either ever needed a friendly ear or some issue of pregnancy prove overwhelming.

Not that Nicole had ever experienced the latter feelings

with her irrepressible personality and good health. But should that day come, she'd welcome the offer of help.

Aware that many other guests were waiting to speak to Mireille, after mutual promises to stay in touch, Nicole left to find Rafe. He was talking to a group nearby and welcomed her into the conversation. Since he knew everyone, in the course of the evening she was introduced to a blur of people, many of the men Rafe's close friends, the male banter familiar to her—having been raised with three brothers--and highly amusing. Less amusing were the overly-friendly females trying to flirt with her husband. However, Rafe was deft at avoiding opportuning women and retreated from their advances with ease, apologizing to Nicole each time until she finally said, "It's all right, sweetheart. They don't have a chance."

"Not in a million years," he whispered, leaning in and kissing her ear. "I'm yours, you're mine, end of story."

The Grand Opening turned out to be a truly celebratory evening with lively conversation, excellent food, fine wines and a feeling that if at times everything in the world was unsettled, here, tonight, life was balanced and manageable and touched with grace.

On the drive back to the cloister house, Nicole glanced up and said, "You're going to watch over Mireille, right?"

"I am. I have a little already. Mireille's sister will come to stay with her soon and she has a phalanx of doctors currently on speed dial. In a couple months, a doctor of her choice will take up residence in her apartment." He smiled faintly. "Henny's orders."

"I figured," she said, unsurprised by his answer. The mausoleum was Rafe's late night home. "I'm so glad you're here to help her."

It took him a fraction of a second to answer and his voice

was husky when he said, "Me too." Pulling Nicole into his arms, he said more casually, "You looked beautiful tonight, pussycat. Like a sparkly fairy princess."

"Thanks to Alessandra," she murmured, glancing up. "She had this made for you, didn't she?"

"I thought a blue and silver beaded gown would suit you. I was remembering that glittery dress you brought to my place that first night."

"The one you tore?" she lightly noted.

He grimaced. "I'm so sorry about that." He sighed. "It was asinine."

"No problem. I can hold it over your head forever." She grinned. "Perennial leverage."

He laughed. "Be my guest. But I've reformed. Consider me a model citizen now that I'm about to have a child."

She gave him a jaundiced look. "I'm not actually looking for a model citizen for a husband."

"Okay."

She pulled away, and stared at him. "Okay, just like that? No additional contrition or explanation?"

"I was being agreeable. But if you want an additional apology, consider it done. If you want an explanation, I'm not good with those."

"Okay."

"Thanks."

"No problem."

The shorthand conversation was a mark of their indulgent love, like the warm smiles they exchanged and the increasingly heated kisses that followed.

When the car came to a stop at the cloister house and Simon stepped out and opened their door, he had to clear his throat to gain their attention. "Anytime, kids," he said, "or I could just shut the door."

Rafe glanced at him, narrow-eyed. "Good idea."

46

The next few months passed in balmy seclusion with little of the outside world impinging on their pleasure, their daily affairs only moderately managed by Rafe. Nicole was more than content with the simplicity of their lives. She was in good health, good spirits, working on another screenplay, devoting time to the food bank charity, knitting baby sweaters for the coming fall, sleeping a lot, spending time with the man she loved. Although, she viewed Rafe's unusual restraint with curiosity and faint amusement; for a man of unhindered habits, his model behavior was extraordinary.

A prescient observation, as it turned out.

For with June approaching, Rafe's model behavior came under increasing pressure.

"At least let me show you the hospital facilities," he proposed. "So there won't be any surprises."

Nicole smiled. "I trust you." She placed her palms on the swell of her belly and winked. "*We* trust you. You said the hospital was excellent. There's no need to angst."

"Too fucking late," he grumbled. Fighting to control his

The Wedding, Etc.

temper, he took a calming breath and looked at her from under his dark lashes. "You're way too casual about this, Tiger."

"And you worry too much. I'm super healthy. The doctor reminds you of that fact each week when we go in. Relax."

"I'll try," he answered, conceding the moment to her, rather than prolong an unwinnable argument.

But he'd learned long ago to make contingency plans, that lesson mastered as a child. Life was precarious; taking chances was a losing bet. He never gambled when it mattered. And no one mattered more to him than Nicole.

As Nicole's due date drew near, the doctors at the main house were tasked with giving Rafe twice daily updates on their readiness. He also had a driver parked outside wherever Dr. Moncur happened to be—twenty-four/seven--with orders to carry her bodily out to the car if necessary. The birthing room at the hospital with a staff of private duty nurses was on alert.

All was in order.

And so it went until five eleven p.m. June sixteenth.

Rafe was just finishing up a meeting in the main house conference room when his phone vibrated in his pocket. Pulling out the phone, he read the text.

I need you!!!

"Nicole," he said, to the table at large, and leaping up, raced from the room, panic drumming through his brain. Sprinting full out down the ground floor corridors, he signaled the driver stationed outside Dr. Moncur's office with a pre-arranged text, dashed across the pool room, shoved the outside door wide, and rocketed down the garden path to the carriage house. Thrusting open the front door, he froze for a second at the sight of Nicole lying inert at the base of the stairs in a horrifying pool of shimmering, blood-streaked fluid.

At her side in a flash, he dropped to his knees, gently gathered her into his arms, and rose to his feet. Retracing his steps as swiftly as possible without jarring Nicole, his mind was convulsed with a whirlwind of disquieting questions. How long had she lain there? Why hadn't she texted him sooner? God in Heaven, why was there blood on the floor?

Her eyes fluttered open as he moved down the garden path. "It hurts like crazy," she whispered, a flicker of fear in her voice. "Make it stop."

"That's why I'm here, pussycat," he murmured, keeping his tone reasonable with effort, swallowing his apprehension. "Two minutes and your pain will be gone. Want me to count?" he added, lightly teasing, hoping to distract her. "One, one thousand, two, one thousand"—

Her giggle quickly turned into an anguished moan, the stricken sound slowly diminishing...fading away completely a second later as Nicole went limp in his arms.

Rafe blanched beneath the bronze of his skin, his heart pounding against his ribs. None of the books he'd read had mentioned the potential of collapse, or life-threatening possibilities like blood, or Nicole's ashen face and dangerously faint breathing. Dammit, he should have *insisted* they go to the hospital a week ago and wait there for her labor to begin. Fuck, fuck, fuck. And now his precious wife was unresponsive and pale as death. Reaching the pool room doors, he backed into them, shoved them open and spinning around, broke into a run.

Shouting for the doctors in a thunderous roar, he raced through the ground floor hallways, terrified, feeling powerless, the thought of losing Nicole shaking him to the core. Even while understanding the hypocrisy; he'd always been dismissive of religion, his prayer, simply put, came from his heart. He offered the gods all he possessed if they would keep his wife and unborn child safe.

Rounding the last corner leading to the newly outfitted birthing room, he witnessed an answer of sorts to his prayer; both onsite doctors were running toward him.

"I found Nicole—collapsed...and in pain," Rafe panted, gasping for breath as the doctors reached him and turning, ran alongside him. "She...needs--pain meds."

Responding to Rafe's voice, Nicole whispered, "Help..."

"Only a second more, sweetheart. The doctors are here."

"Let's see what stage of labor we're dealing with first," the OB/GYN said, following Rafe into the birthing room. "We don't want the meds to slow down labor."

"Fuck that," Rafe snapped, kicking the door open. "Do something!" Shutting his eyes, he looked up a second later and added, softly, "Please."

The doctor nodded at a nurse. "Nitrous."

While a nurse ran to turn on the equipment, Rafe carried Nicole to a high tech bed fitted out with hand loomed linen sheets from some village in Normandy Alessandra favored. Lowering Nicole to the bed with painstaking care, Rafe gingerly adjusted the pillow under her head. "I apologize for the mattress," he murmured, as her eyes fluttered open and she scanned the space age apparatus she was lying on. "It's not as soft as a normal bed."

She gave him a shaky smile. "Always prepared, aren't you? You should have been a Boy Scout."

"Who says I wasn't?" he lightly replied, stifling his alarm as a nurse cut away Nicole's blood-stained tights. "Now, try and relax." He brushed her hair off her forehead with exaggerated care, as if the slightest touch might cause her discomfort. "You're going to feel better soon. They're getting you something for the pain." He forced himself to speak calmly despite the fresh blood on the sheets. What the fuck was going on?

Quickly refocusing, he listened to the doctor's instructions for the nitrous oxide. "You or your wife can hold the mask and she can decide when she needs to inhale. It fits over the nose like this." The OB/GYN placed the transparent mask over Nicole's nose then stepped back to make room for the two nurses who were clasping the last snaps on Nicole's gown, while a third nurse was unfurling a warming blanket at the foot of the bed, and a fourth was taking Nicole's blood pressure.

Standing on the other side of the bed, Rafe took over from the doctor. "Inhale, sweetheart, hey, hey, slow down. There, that's the way," he said, holding the mask in place, grateful Nicole had even a modicum of relief from her suffering. "Good girl, nice and easy now."

"If your wife had come in sooner we would have had other options for pain," the doctor noted, "but at this late stage, nitrous gas is the best alternative. It reduces anxiety and promotes a feeling of wellbeing, makes the intensity of the contraction easier to manage." The doctor nodded. "As you see." Nicole's breathing was more normal, relaxed. "Also, inhaling thirty seconds before the start of a contraction, gives the best results."

"I'll pay attention," Rafe promised, not sure Nicole was capable of timing her contractions when she was in agony.

"You're doing very nicely, Mrs. Contini," the OB/GYN said, pleasantly. "I'm glad you arrived in time."

Rafe shot a quick, questioning look at the doctor.

"You'll see your baby very soon," he said.

With the nitrous having temporarily mitigated the brutal assault on her senses, Nicole looked up and met

Rafe's gaze. "Soon, hey?" She smiled. "I was trying to wait until tomorrow, so we'd all have the same birthday."

"That was a real nice of you, sweetheart," Rafe murmured, returning her smile. "But it looks like baby doesn't want to share a birthday."

"I thought I could tough it out." She sighed. "I'm an idiot."

"No you're not." His gaze was affectionate. "You're my little Wonder Woman." He smiled. "You think you can do anything."

"Instead, I screwed up," she muttered. "Sorry, by the way--I won't see that hospital room you were talking about."

"It doesn't matter." He lightly caressed her cheek with his fingertips. "I'm just glad you're feeling a little better?"

She nodded, then sucked in a breath and stifled a scream.

He quickly slid the mask over her nose. "Inhale, deep breath, slowly, slowly." Glancing at his watch, he decided he'd have to more alert and pushed the button on his stop watch function. A few minutes later when the contraction ended and Nicole was half-dozing, Rafe glanced at the doctor and spoke quietly in French. "Why is there blood?"

"It's nothing to worry about," the OB/GYN replied in an undertone.

A faint scowl. "Explain."

The doctor was describing how the sac containing the amniotic fluid was a membrane with blood vessels when the birthing room door swung open and a brisk voice said in English, "So what have we here? Are you going on without me, Nicole?"

Dr. Moncur strode into the room, shrugging out of a denim jacket. Handing it to one of the nurses, she moved to the bed, shot a quick look at the stained sheets before she leaned over Nicole and smiled. "You were supposed to call me when your labor started."

Nicole grimaced. "I probably should have."

"No probably about it. Luckily your husband has some brains. Nice setup here." She'd heard about the twenty million birthing room remodel at the hospital. Obviously this state of the art facility signaled Rafe Contini's aversion to taking chances. With a nod to the two doctors, she said, lightly, "Good duty, Francois, Louis?" Turning to Rafe, she raised one brow. "Nothing but the best, right?"

Rafe could have said, *Including you,* but he spoke softly in French instead. "Is this bleeding normal?"

Dr. Moncur did a little seesaw of her hand and replied in the same language. "The amniotic membrane may have torn a little, but at this point it doesn't matter. Should the placenta be a problem later, I expect Francois has taken that eventuality into account." She cast a sideways look at the OB/GYN, a tall, handsome fellow with sand-colored hair and a youthful face.

He smiled and you could tell that they were more than friends. "Twenty units in the refrigerator, Gabi."

"There you see, Mr. Contini, all is in hand." She spoke in an undertone to her colleagues now that Nicole was resting between contractions. "What do we have for dilation?"

"The baby's moments away from crowning."

She turned back to Rafe, one brow aloft. "You almost had an unattended birth, Mr. Contini. Now put the mask back on your wife, another contraction is about to begin. I'll wash up and get ready."

Nicole screamed during the entire next contraction despite the nitrous. "Sorry," she whispered when it was over, panting softly, her brow still furrowed.

"Scream all you want." Wiping the sweat from her face with a wet cloth, Rafe smiled. "You're doing fine."

She gave him a sardonic look. "Wanna trade places?"

"I'm so sorry," he whispered, bending to kiss her cheek. "That was seriously unfeeling of me. Tell me what to do and I'll do it."

"You can feed the baby at night. I'll sleep."

"No problem."

She winced. "Uh, oh"—she swore under her breath—"shut your ears."

She screamed almost continuously during the last few contractions. And once the baby was born and the torment finally stopped, she jerked the mask from her face, tossed it aside and exhaled a great sigh of relief, every shredded, tortured, lacerated nerve in her body singing hallelujah. "So," she said, still slightly winded, looking up at Rafe with a grin, "did you get your girl?"

He smiled. "You win. It's a boy."

"Ha! Told you! Show me."

"Louis is checking him out. He's beautiful. You were awesome, sweetheart," he whispered, leaning over and kissing her tenderly. "They still have to finish up a little." He didn't say he wouldn't relax until someone assured him his wife's mysterious bleeding was over. "Then we're going to get you in fresh clothes, put clean sheets on the bed, so bear with us. I'll bring the baby over in a few minutes."

In pursuit of perfection, Rafe had had the doctors and nurses run through numerous rehearsals of any birthing possibilities, scenarios, and contingencies. Even the doctors had overlooked their egos and cooperated since Rafe was paying them a fortune.

Soon, Nicole was pronounced in excellent health by Dr.

Moncur with her usual brusqueness, and a sharp-eyed glance at Rafe. "You can rest easy now, Mr. Contini."

"Thank you," he quietly said, and put out his hand.

While Moncur's handshake was not precisely bone-crushing, it was damned close. "I don't have to tell you to take care of your family, do I?" she said, a hint of amusement in her eyes.

He grinned, his spirits sky high. "No." He dipped his head in polite acknowledgement. "We're going to be just fine."

"See that Nicole comes in for her six weeks check-up." Turning to Nicole she wagged her finger. "No excuses, now."

Nicole grinned. "I have a feeling someone will see that I get there."

"Good. *Au revoir*, everyone. I'll stop by tomorrow."

Short minutes later, the numerous rehearsals proved fruitful. Nicole was washed and dressed in a white eyelet nightgown Alessandra considered appropriate for a new mother, the sheets were replaced with crisp new ones, and Nicole was resting against the raised bed, sipping ice water.

Louis, a short, grey-haired, world-renowned pediatrician with a weathered face from following butterfly migrations on his holidays, was smiling as he handed Rafe his son. "Congratulations, Mr. Contini," he said in French. "You have a big, healthy baby boy—he's almost five kilos." His brows arched upward. "Your wife will need rest."

"We have a large staff and I'll care for my son until Nicole recovers."

The flicker of surprise in the pediatrician's eyes was marked.

"Children shouldn't be raised by strangers," Rafe said, softly.

"Ah, I see. I applaud your commitment," Louis noted,

reassessing his presumptions on billionaire lifestyles, or at least one particular billionaire. "Well then, I'll leave you to introduce your son to his mother."

As previously arranged, the doctors, nurses and staff withdrew to give the new parents privacy.

Standing beside the bed a moment later, wearing a clean t-shirt taken from the closet in the room, his swaddled son in his arms, Rafe smiled down at his rosy-cheeked wife. "Ready to see perfection?"

"Yes, yes, yes!" she exclaimed, setting down her glass, smiling up at her husband and son.

Bending low, Rafe placed the baby in her arms.

"He looks just like you," she whispered, awed by her son's beauty. "His dark hair, those little winged brows, that perfect nose."

"His eyes are blue, like yours."

"They'll change," she said, decisive and sure. "Now let's get this blanket straitjacket off and count his fingers and toes." She began unfurling the soft white blanket.

"Don't babies like to be swaddled?"

"I don't know about you, but I sure don't."

He had no suitable answer other than to suggest the majority of baby authorities disagreed.

"Well, they're wrong," Nicole said, calmly. "Oh, look, he has little rolls on his arms and legs. I love plump babies."

"He's slightly over ten pounds."

"Perfect," she said, as if she hadn't recently suffered unmercifully in part because her son was not a small baby. "Don't you just love their little fingers," she purred, kissing her son's tiny fingers, one by one. And as the silence lengthened, she glanced up, took note of Rafe's blank expression and smiled. "Don't worry, you'll figure it out. You just give them what they need. Food, sleep, clean diapers, kisses...lots of kisses."

He took a small breath. "I can do that."

"Of course you can." She smiled. "You're super capable."

He would have readily agreed in the past, but with a newborn son, he was facing the great unknown. Untutored and ignorant, the smattering of child development books he'd read, aside, he was relatively clueless.

"I'll be asking a lot of questions," he said, "so bear with me."

"Of course, ask me anything, anytime...well, don't wake me up at least the first week, unless it's an emergency. In fact, I'm going to close my eyes for a couple minutes. Is that okay with you?" she asked, bundling the baby back into his blanket. "I could sleep standing up."

"Sleep as long as you want. I had Aleix develop some organic baby formula in case we wanted it, so if—what are we going to call him? Calling him baby seems dismissive in a way."

"You decide."

"Come on, it's a joint effort."

"When I wake up, okay? My brain's fried. Look, baby's tired too. He's almost sleeping."

"Fine, when you wake up," he murmured, leaning over and picking up his son. "Now do you want anything? Something to drink? Eat?"

She pointed at her water. "I'll eat in a couple hours. Right now, all I want to do is sleep."

After giving her a kiss, he walked over to the windows, and discovered that his son wasn't sleeping but studying him with a wide, blue-eyed gaze. "Welcome to the world, little one," he said, his deep voice gentle. "I don't know if you can see me, they say you can't this young, but you can hear me I know…and this I promise you: You will know only kindness in this world. No one will ever harm you." Taking a small breath, he dismissed the bubbling cauldron of crazy that had been his childhood, and said, very, very softly, "I swear on my life…you will be loved."

"What did you say?" Nicole murmured, opening her eyes.

"I told baby I love him." He glanced over to the bed and smiled. "His mommy too. I also told him I'd find him a unicorn somewhere, and if he wants a race car when he's young, we're going to need some guidelines."

She squinted. "You didn't say all that."

"We have this ESP thing going," he lightly replied.

"A unicorn and race car? You're going to spoil him."

"For sure."

"Apparently, I'm going to have to be the disciplinarian."

He grinned. "Go for it."

She laughed. "Does that mean I'm going to have a fight on my hands?"

"Nah, I never fight. Now go to sleep. I'll entertain baby."

"I kinda like Leo if you don't mind." She held his gaze, her brows raised.

"You mean for a name?"

"Yeah, then we don't have to keep calling him baby."

He smiled, thinking it was a big name for a baby. "Leo, as in King of the Jungle?"

She nodded. "I don't necessarily see the name in such heroic terms, but baby's going to be big like you and strong and brave and all the rest. Okay?"

"It's nice. I like it."

"You pick the middle name." Her smile was tender. "I'm guessing you might have a preference."

He nodded and found he had to swallow before he

answered. "Thank you, sweetheart." He smiled. "Leo will have two strong names."

"Three." She grinned. "I've noticed the surname Contini commands a certain authority."

"Shit, maybe we're wildly over-projecting. He's only a tiny baby."

"Come on, we both have more self-confidence than we need. He's bound to have inherited oodles."

"Really, is that how it works?" Rafe teased.

"Damn right. I have spoken, now go do something. I'm going to sleep, but don't let me sleep long. I don't want to miss anything."

Nicole was truly exhausted though and when the doctors poked their heads in the door a short time later, Rafe put a finger to his lips before beckoning them in. Leo, too, had fallen asleep so mother and baby's vitals were checked without waking either patient.

Aleix came in to offer congratulations a few minutes after the medical team left and the men quietly visited another half hour before Leo woke.

Contemplating his son's little mouth restlessly twitching, Rafe said, "Get me one of those bottles of formula from the refrigerator." He lifted his chin. "Over there. Leo might be getting hungry. There's a bottle warmer on the counter. I'll change him while you're doing that." At Aleix's astonished look, Rafe grinned. "You don't know how many videos I watched. Change diapers first then feed the baby. It's a fucking rule."

Rafe's first diaper change was less than perfect, but Leo didn't seem to mind, staring gravely up at his father as if to say, "We both have a lot to learn."

"Maybe there actually is ESP," Rafe murmured, "because I think I heard you. Now, want to try some formula compliments of Contini Pharma's research labs and new organic farm?"

The baby didn't actually voice his approval of the baby formula, but he drank the entire six ounce bottle so it was a tacit approval.

"It appears our formula has your son's endorsement," Aleix noted, taking the empty bottle from Rafe. "The thousand acre organic farm and herd of cows and goats won't go to waste." Discarding the bottle on the counter in the small kitchen, he returned to his seat, grinning widely. "Aren't you the picture."

Rocking his sleeping son in a chair selected by Odile to accommodate his size, Rafe smiled back. "You don't have to say it. For someone who's seen it all, done it all, been everywhere, including sundry tours of crazy town…I never knew life could be this sweet."

"I'm happy for you. It's a nice change."

"Fucking A. Speaking of change, I actually prayed today for the first time in my life."

Aleix nodded. "I'm not surprised. I talked to Francois. While Nicole wasn't in absolutely dire straits, this facility came in handy. I'm glad it all went well."

Rafe tensed, exhaled, let the jolt of fear subside before he said, "Yeah, me too."

47

When Nicole woke, a brief discussion ensued.

She wanted to return to the carriage house.

Rafe, only recently restored to a modicum of tranquility after the terror of Nicole's delivery, wanted her to wait another few days. Here, in the main house, with the doctors close at hand.

She shot him a gimlet-eyed look. "Are we going to argue about this?"

He shrugged. "Could we do it quietly?" He pointed at the cradle. "Leo's sleeping."

"I don't need all this monitoring," she said, waving her hand to encompass the array of medical equipment near the bed. "I feel perfectly fine."

Sitting at the foot of her bed, Rafe pointed at some frozen numbers on an electronic screen. "Your blood pressure's still low."

"It's always low."

"Leo's so tiny. I'd be more comfortable with Louis near."

"The carriage house is only three minutes away."

"Look," he said, trying to keep the exasperation from his voice, "I'm a novice at all this. Humor me."

"Jesus, *I'm* not a novice. I know what I'm doing."

He sighed rather than remind her of the recent near disaster when she clearly *didn't* know what she was doing. "Want to compromise?" He had no intention of discussing this ad nauseam and he could move the doctors into the servants' quarters at the carriage house. Nicole wasn't aware the apartments existed. "I'd prefer you and Leo stay here at least four days," he said, opening the negotiations. "As a precaution."

"Four days? Are you crazy?"

"Probably, but I worry."

"You don't have to. I feel great, super, a hundred percent. But if you *insist* on compromising, I'd be willing to go back to the carriage house tomorrow."

"The day after."

"Okay, but I'm gonna bitch the whole time," she muttered.

He grinned. "I'll get earplugs for Leo."

Her gaze turned assessing. "You think you can protect him from every little crisis and adversity? You can't."

"Sure I can," he said with utter calm.

She held his cool, amber gaze for a deliberate moment and understood it was entirely possible he could...and more likely, would. The realization checked her briefly. But she, also, more practically recognized that losing a very small argument in a totally grand life wasn't actually losing. "So tell me," she said, with an indulgent smile, "how long have you been like this? Doing exactly as you please, no-holds-barred?"

"A long time," he said, his voice arid.

His instant slide into solitude was startling. He immediately disengaged; his eyes went blank, the sudden silence palpable, as if a door had closed with a bang.

She'd obviously triggered comfortless memories. Shit. In an effort to distract him from his morbid thoughts, Nicole lowered her voice to a teasing murmur. "Once I'm back in blooming health and feeling my usual awesome self, perhaps you could show me some of your no-holds-barred skills."

A small startle reflex passed across his face, and he sat perfectly still for a moment, staring at her, before his smile slowly unfolded. "My pleasure, pussycat," he murmured, velvet soft and obliging. "You tell me when. I'll mark my calendar." Then dipping his head, his voice turned whisper soft. "Thank you for reminding me what's important in life."

"Not the past."

"No. You and Leo. Here and now." He stared at her from under his lashes. "When I forget, remind me."

She could see what effort it took for him shed the insidious melancholy of his past, the bonds oppressive. But benevolent in her love, she wished to offer him at least temporary relief. "When I've fully recovered"—she grinned—"I have my own unique ways of reminding you of the here and now."

He laughed. "I'm sure you do. I look forward to your full recovery with lively fucking interest." Then his expression sobered. "You make every day perfect, Tiger. You're my ground zero for happiness...my magnetic north."

Her smile was beguiling. "And you're mine..."

VERY LATE THAT NIGHT, after dinner had been served and the remains cleared away, after Nicole had nursed Leo twice and had fallen asleep watching a program on TV, Rafe turned off the TV and sat by the bed until he was certain she was sleeping soundly. Quietly rising to his feet, he grabbed a bottle of formula from the refrigerator, slipped it into his pants pocket along with an extra diaper, gently wrapped Leo in a blanket, lifted him from his cradle and walked out.

The summer night was tepid after the heat of the day, the stars brilliant in an inky black sky, the quarter moon sufficient to illuminate the path to the mausoleum.

Entering the dimly lit interior, he walked to the sarcophagus and spoke softly. "It's three o'clock, Henny, so I can't stay long, but I wanted you to meet Leo. He has your name as his middle name—just so you know. When Leo gets older, I'll tell him about some of our youthful escapades, some, the operative word; others are best forgotten, right?" At the thought of all he and Henny had gone through together—the good, bad and indifferent—Rafe's voice dropped low. "Jesus...I miss you." Slowly inhaling, he carefully modulated his tone. "At least our kids will be friends. I'm stoked about that. And we'll sit here for a little while in case you want to talk."

Moving to one of the benches, with Leo cradled snugly in the crook of his arm, Rafe leaned back and quietly exhaled. It had been a helluva day, intense, terrifying--ultimately joyful. Letting the silence and the jasmine scented air wash over him, he shut his eyes. Whether the perfumed fragrance or location was impetus to his thoughts, a rush of whimsical memories of Henny and his friendship flashed through his mind, and as if his son's birth colored the narrative, the review was solely of good times and laughter. It was a pleasant end to a chaotic, watershed day and before long, Rafe's breathing slowed, exhaustion overcame him and he slept.

. . .

AT THE FOOTFALL, Rafe came awake with a start.

"Sorry, sir, I didn't know anyone was here." An elderly gardener, holding a basket of jasmine was silhouetted in the open doorway.

Rafe blinked. "What time is it?"

"Four thirty. I can come back later."

"No, please, come in, Gaston. I'm just leaving." After a quick glance at his sleeping son, Rafe came to his feet. Moving past the sarcophagus, he offered Henny a silent goodbye and coming to a stop just short of the gardener, he raised his son toward the light. "Meet my baby boy. Leo's just a few hours old."

"Congratulations, sir. We should plant a tree for him."

"Would you? I'd like that." Rafe smiled. "Something he can climb when the tree gets bigger."

"Yes, sir. You were mighty young the first time you climbed too high."

"I remember. You brought a ladder to save me."

"Aye. We'll do it again I don't doubt for your boy."

"I expect so. My wife likes it here."

"You'll be stayin' a bit more than in the past then."

Rafe grinned. "It looks that way. We'll have to set up a playground for Leo."

"I'll have Ramon come and see you."

"Do I know him?"

"He came on board last year. He designed that astonishing garden and parkland in Morocco."

"Ah, yes, I remember--a fantastic concept." Rafe shot a glance at his son. "You hear that, Leo? Ramon will create a fairyland for you to play in."

As if talk of playgrounds was of interest, Leo began to rouse, snorting and snuffling, twitching his little shoulders, his eyelids fluttering up and down in that half-dormant state between sleep and wakefulness.

Henri stepped aside. "You'd best get back. After five children and eight grandchildren, I know you don't have much time before the crying starts. Give our good wishes to your missus."

"I will thank you. Come and see me in a couple days. We'll decide on a tree," Rafe added, stepping out into the pale morning light. "Bring Ramon with you."

Blinking against the brightness, Leo scrunched up his little face in readiness for a wail, took a deep breath and had just opened his mouth when Rafe, hastily said, "Wait, wait, kiddo! We're gonna make tracks to a fresh bottle or your mommy." Lengthening his stride, Rafe kept talking with enough brio and urgency in his voice to arrest Leo's cry until they'd almost reached the birthing room.

"I hear you!" Nicole called out, pushing herself up into a sitting position on the bed as Rafe walked in. "Come to Mommy, sweetums." She smiled and held out her arms. "What time is it?"

"A little after four thirty. I can give him a bottle if you'd prefer."

"Don't bother, I'm awake now. You look tired," she murmured as Rafe placed Leo in her arms.

"Nah, I'm good. We slept a little."

After Leo was happily nursing, Nicole glanced at Rafe sprawled in a chair beside the bed, his tan linen slacks rumpled, his white t-shirt no longer pristine, his sandals kicked off, and despite his disclaimer, his fatigue showed. "You should nap," she said. "Even for a short time. I'll watch Leo."

He shook his head. "Maybe later."

Since she couldn't very well *make* Rafe sleep, no more

than she could make him do much anything unless he chose to, she asked instead, "Did Henny like Leo?"

Rafe smiled. "He loved him."

"I hope you explained that our children will have play dates galore."

"Yeah, we talked about that." Arching his back, Rafe stretched then dropped his hands and slid lower on his spine. "We're both on board--new generation, same friendship." The simple admission brought a faint smile to his face. "That'll be nice."

"How is Mireille? She must be getting close to her due date."

"I talked to her two days ago. She was feeling fine. The doctors are giving her good reports." He grinned. "And unlike you, she's already checked out her hospital suite."

"Hey, all's well that ends well. And I'm practically home here." She made a little moue. "Tell me you don't mind."

"I don't. You're right, it's better to be here." His brows rose fractionally. "Since everything went well."

She wrinkled her nose. "Can we not talk about this?"

He mimed locking his mouth.

"May I say on a happier note," she said with a dazzling smile, "it's June seventeenth. Happy Birthday!"

Shoving himself up in the chair, Rafe softly exclaimed, "Jesus, I forgot." He'd show her the Land Rover SUV with a built in cooler and custom baby seat he'd bought her later. "Happy Birthday, Tiger. We'll have to have a little celebration."

"After Leo settles down for the night."

Rather than say, *That's not gonna happen,* Rafe smiled and said, "Good idea."

48

After a restless afternoon and evening, Leo finally fell asleep near midnight, and Rafe and Nicole celebrated their birthdays quietly with a bottle of champagne.

"We almost missed the seventeenth," Rafe said, saluting Nicole with his flute. "Happy Birthday, sweetheart. I don't know about you, but this is my best birthday ever. Thanks to you and Leo. Cheers." He drained his glass.

"It *is* pretty great," Nicole agreed, her smile warm as the sun. "We're very lucky, you and I." Her voice was soft at the last.

If this moment could have arrested in time, Rafe would have frozen it in amber, marking as it did the quintessential perfection of his life. His beautiful wife, arrayed in a frothy blue dimity nightgown and ensconced on a nearby chaise longue, was smiling at him. His precious Leo was peacefully sleeping in his cradle. He was happier than he'd ever been in his life, more than he'd ever thought possible, perhaps more than he deserved had he been a humble man. "I love you, Tiger," he said, quietly. "I love you more each day, every minute and second. And yes, we are, undeniably, the luckiest people on the face of the earth."

She smiled. "Are we tempting fate with such smug presumption? Should we be more modest?"

"Modest...really?" He looked amused. "Is that more admirable?"

"I'm sure you wouldn't know," she murmured.

"I hope that wasn't sarcasm because you know damned well you'd be bored to tears if I was fucking modest or reserved."

She grinned. "Okay, so your wild and reckless ways may have intrigued me just a little when we first met."

"Ya think?" he drawled. Holding up his hands to arrest her heated response, he added, softly, "Seriously, you were a dream come true...the beautiful, brilliant, warm-hearted woman I'd been waiting for all my life."

"Oh, jeez, now I'm going to cry," she whispered, blinking furiously. "And you know how Leo responds when I get emotional...then my boobs start leaking and"—

"I fucked up," Rafe murmured, leaping to his feet, covering the small distance between them in two strides and lifting her into his arms. "Sorry," he whispered, swiftly moving away from the cradle. "Next time I get romantic, I'll put it in writing."

Framing his face in her hands, she said, "Shhh," and kissed him. "What you said was wonderful and sweet and I love you more than anything. You and Leo both."

He smiled. "We're a team."

"Tell me you're glad I did what I did."

"Very glad."

"For sure now? You're not just saying that to be nice?"

"No. I rarely say things to be nice."

"You do for me."

"Yes, correction, I do for you, but not in this instance. I really am happy about Leo. He's perfect in every way. Like that beautiful poem you wrote for my birthday."

She grinned. "Goddamn, I'm good aren't I?"

His smile was amused, indulgent—resolutely tender. "Yes, you're the very best in every way; wife, mother, sweetheart, lover, genius writer. How's that?"

Her brows came together. "You better mean it."

He laughed. "I mean it. Seriously, hand on my heart. And I'll bring your present around tomorrow." He'd already given her the key to the Range Rover. Also, a check for her movie. She'd balked at the amount, as expected, and he'd answered, as planned, that if she preferred, she could pay him back with her profits. "Now, go to sleep," he added, moving toward the bed. "I'm still on night shift. I'll wake you for Leo's morning feeding."

"God, I feel guilty. You're tired too."

"But you're still recuperating," he said, lowering her to the bed. "Don't sweat it. Leo and I get along great. He's teaching me baby talk, and I'm showing him the constellations in the southern sky."

"Are you going outside?"

"I hope there isn't a correct answer."

"Well, bundle him up at least."

He gave her a look.

"Sorry."

"No problem. And just to put your mind at ease, he'll be bundled up to his chin in cashmere."

"Isn't that hard to wash?"

A quick lift of his brows at her quaint concern over laundry. "Since neither of us wash clothes it's not hard at all." As a matter of fact, Josephine had hired two ladies from Normandy who were familiar with lace making and linens (both requiring careful washing) to handle Leo's laundry. "Now sleep. Leo will be up again before you know it."

"Yes, sir." She smiled. "I can hardly wait until you give me orders again, you know the kind"—

"Hold that thought because I'm not a eunuch, okay?"

"Sorry, again. Six weeks isn't so long."

This was one of those times when the truth wouldn't fly. "Not at all," he graciously replied. "It'll be over before we know it." And at base, he was willing to wait more than six weeks if necessary. Love and sex were two different things and he understood the distinction better than most; sex as entertainment had been his trademark for a decade--with only ennui and dissatisfaction to show for it.

As if the new spirits of change were pulling the strings, Nicole had no more than fallen asleep when Leo woke.

Quickly picking up his son before he cried, Rafe changed Leo's diaper—the process slightly improved in terms of execution and fit--then dressed him in a fresh onesie, bundled him up in a clean blanket and after grabbing a bottle from the frig, went outside to admire the night sky. Walking through the gardens near the sea, Rafe pointed out Libra and Lupus south of the equator and turning, showed Leo Ursa Minor, the Little Bear, its brightest stars forming the Little Dipper. And when in time Leo reached the end of his patience, Rafe sat on a bench overlooking the Mediterranean and fed him his bottle.

Once the bottle was empty and Leo was sleeping, Rafe returned him to his cradle and both father and son slept until dawn.

And the second day of Leo's life began.

He was bathed by his parents with many smiles and much splashing then dressed, fed, and wide awake after his long sleep, calmly tolerated his medical checkup. The adults had breakfast, took turns showering and dressing, and tag teamed care for their son in a schedule that would become the norm in the coming days.

Late that afternoon, in a moment of calm, Nicole said, "I should call my parents."

"I'd offer to do it, but they'd rather hear from you. Tell them I'll send a plane to San Francisco to fetch them."

When Nicole's mother answered, she was given the good news and invited to come see her new grandson. "Rafe said he'd send a plane for you."

"Tell him not to bother, we'll come with Dominic. Kate is as anxious as I to see the new baby. Not that the men aren't, but"—

"I know, Mom, we're just more gushy. Come anytime. I'm feeling fine."

"Let me check with Daddy and Kate, but I expect we'll be there in the next day or so."

After a few minutes more of conversation devoted to Leo's wonderfulness, Nicole's mother promised to let them know their flight plans as soon as they were arranged and said goodbye.

Nicole smiled at Rafe. "Now, call *your* parents."

Rafe did, accepted their congratulations, assured them they were welcome anytime and after ending the call, turned to Nicole. "Give me a minute. I'm going to see if Costa can come down and handle the crowd."

Walking into his study next door, Rafe phoned the event planner. When Costa picked up, Rafe said, "My apologies up front, but I need you in Monte Carlo for a few days. Is that possible?"

"When?"

"Now. My son was born yesterday, the entire family is

about to descend on us and Nicole and I are both busy taking care of the baby."

Busy taking care of the baby. A phrase he never thought to hear from the legendary player, Rafe Contini. Always politic, however, Costa graciously offered his congratulations. "And I'd be happy to help," he added. "I should be there in a few hours." It meant having one of his lieutenants oversee the engagement party tonight for an ancient regime family in Chantilly, but Rafe Contini merited his full attention for any number of reasons, not least the fact that he'd given him a fortune over the years. That Costa genuinely liked him as well carried considerable weight and the opportunity to see Rafe Contini *busy taking care of the baby* was an aberration not to be missed. "Do you know how many guests?"

"I don't. Our parents, an uncle and his family, several children, we'll do a head count once you get here. You should have a day or so to organize before they arrive."

"Any idea how long they're staying?"

Rafe sighed. "Hopefully not long, but I haven't a clue. Neither Nicole nor I are looking forward to company, but under the circumstances"—

"We'll see that they're kept busy. After they ooh and ah over the baby, we'll offer them a full gamut of activities to amuse them."

"Good. I'm counting on you, Costa. Text me your arrival time and I'll have someone at the airport in Nice to meet you. Ciao."

Walking back into the room, Rafe smiled. "Costa will be down in a few hours. He'll take care of everything. All we have to do is"—

"Be polite?"

"Close enough." He grinned. "I was going to say test our

social graces. Seriously, though, you don't have to exert yourself. Everyone understands that you're still fatigued. I'll deal with our guests. And Costa assures me he'll have enough activities to entertain everyone."

"You told him about the children."

"I did in general. I'll give him a full run down of ages when he gets here. Now, don't worry about a thing. Costa, along with Josephine, is in charge."

"That's a relief. My energy levels are super low."

"No surprise, pussycat. You went through hell. But I'm here, Josephine is familiar with a house full of guests and Costa is an expert on hospitality. You don't have to do anything but rest." He smiled. "I'll take care of Leo."

She grinned. "You know you're perfect, right?"

"I wish. But our life will be perfect again in"--he tapped his wrist watch—"say a three, four day visit, at most ninety-six hours and they'll be on their way back home."

Nicole rolled her eyes. "That's a long time to keep smiling."

"Look, let's shoot for a two day visit." Seriously, he'd push them out the door himself if necessary. Come to think of it, he'd talk to Dominic and Gora. Men understood short visits as well as keeping their wives happy. They'd cooperate.

Problem solved.

49

Two days later, their guests arrived.

In the interim, Rafe and Nicole had moved back to the carriage house, Leo had been installed in his nursery next to their bedroom and Nicole was feeling stronger. They'd been arguing about Nicole doing too much and undermining her recovery but constraining his wife had proved fruitless, so Rafe had had the doctors moved into the apartments downstairs.

At the moment, Rafe was at the main house greeting the families before escorting everyone to the carriage house. Costa was hovering in the doorway to Rafe and Nicole's bedroom, his phone to his ear, listening, while surveying the room with a practiced eye, checking out every detail from the numerous bouquets to the seating, scanning the small arrangement of drinks and refreshments on a side table, confirming with a glance that Nicole was comfortable resting against a bolster of pillows on the bed. She was looking radiant in a flower print, floaty sundress, the small emerald hoops in her ears a gift from Rafe that morning.

She waved at Costa. "Tell him I'm being good." Rafe

hadn't wanted her on her feet entertaining a room full of guests today. Regardless he'd spoken quietly, his stern expression had merited her consideration, and honestly, she still was feeling far from normal. Yielding to Rafe's common sense hadn't been a hardship.

Putting his phone away, Costa smiled. "I already sent him a picture. And if I might use a hackneyed, but in this case, fitting phrase, you look absolutely glowing."

Nicole swept a hand downward and smiled. "It's my sunflower dress. Alessandra always knows what's appropriate in terms of central casting."

He could have disagreed; Nicole's beauty would shine equally in sackcloth. "Alessandra does have an eye," he said instead, conscious of his employee status. "Now I'll be out in the hallway while your family's here. If you become fatigued, just give me a glance, and I'll whisk everyone out of the room posthaste."

"Thank you, Costa. I may take you up on your offer if people stay too long." He was not only cordial to a fault but so incredibly efficient she understood why Rafe relied on him.

Costa looked down at the text on his watch. "They're on their way. Should I close the door to the nursery so the noise doesn't wake Leo?"

"Would you? He just went to sleep."

"Leo's a darling," Costa said, moving into the room. "And his resemblance to his father is stunning."

Nicole grinned. "Rafe can't deny paternity."

Softly closing the nursery room door, Costa smiled. "Nor would he want to." Although, the Rafe Contini he'd once known would have written a check to the prospective mother and walked away. That's if he'd made such a blunder in the first place, which he never had.

"I don't suppose you believe in magic?" Nicole remarked.

Nicole's dazzling smile made it tempting, *had* been tempting to the former hardcore playboy once impervious to both female smiles *and* magic. "I'm not completely averse to the notion," Costa replied, diplomatically.

Nicole laughed. "Men--ever practical." Then her voice dropped. "You know, Rafe was dumbfounded by love at first, caught totally by surprise. What do you think of that?"

He was tempted to say Rafe wasn't nearly as surprised as he'd been. "I think your husband's a very fortunate man."

"We both are," she said with a nod. "Twilight Zone lucky, that's a fact."

"Ah, there they are...I hear them. If you'll excuse me." Walking out into the hallway, Costa recalled Rafe's recent orders that had nothing to do with luck and he wondered whether his employer had ever been surprised by anything. "I don't want Nicole or Leo unhappy," Rafe had said in the quietly peremptory tone of an autocrat. "So I need you to help see that nothing untoward happens during this fucking family visit." Rafe had shrugged. "Sorry, but you get the picture."

Costa had smiled. "These guests will be easier to manage than your former friends and acquaintances."

"No shit. Thanks for the reminder. Although," Rafe had added with a grimace, "Dominic Knight and my stepfather are unknowns."

"I've always found the mitigating influence of a loving wife deterrent to fractious men."

Rafe's brows had lifted marginally. "Present company included?"

"I've known you a long time and it's clear your current life has given you much more satisfaction than the entertainments in your past. You are a man in love."

Rafe hadn't immediately answered and when he'd spoken, his voice had been a velvety murmur. "Is it that obvious?"

"As glass, sir. Now, tell me the children's ages," Costa had interjected. "And I'll bring in appropriate video games and movies. We'll need a lifeguard on duty at your beach. I expect someone knows how to sail your small catamaran. And together with Josephine and the chef we'll arrange a menu suitable for young and old, including picnic fare for any outings."

And that had been the closest Rafe and Costa had ever come to personal comments.

AT THE SOUND of voices in the stairway, the cadence light-hearted and effervescent, Nicole sat up a little straighter in bed and half smiled at her reluctance to have guests. That's what came from loving her husband and son to an ill-mannered degree; she resisted widening her social circle. Understanding discourtesy wasn't an option though, she took a deep breath, put a smile on her face and braced for the family onslaught.

The youngsters ran in first: Jimmy, Rosie, Titus and Ellie; followed in turn as though in age sequence by Buzz, Dante and Keir; Isabelle was coming later in the month with Jack. Then the adults entered the room, with Rafe last, smiling at her from behind everyone, and blowing her a kiss.

How did he know she needed that kiss?

She relaxed, her smile assumed a genuine sincerity and when her mother immediately said, "Oh dear, you look tired," Nicole replied, serenely, "With good reason, Mom. Leo weighed over ten pounds."

Everyone offered congratulations as well as gifts for the

new baby, one of Rafe's staff passed around champagne, and the ensuing conversation turned almost exclusively on Leo. Very shortly, the sound of so many voices, particularly the high-pitched tones of the young children, woke the baby, and at his first cry, Rafe swiftly walked toward the nursery. "Give me a minute and I'll bring Leo out."

Regardless his casual tone, it was clear he didn't want assistance. And whether Nicole's mother missed the nuance or ignored it, only her husband's hand stayed her forward movement. Melanie looked up, Matt raised a brow, she hesitated a moment, then smiled.

And any hint of disturbance was averted.

Rafe returned a few minutes later, carrying Leo. Suddenly conscious of the crowd, Leo's eyes opened wide and lying utterly still in his father's arms, he calmly regarded the roomful of people staring at him.

"Meet your family, Leo," Rafe murmured.

"Baby!" Jimmy screamed.

Leo freaked; his arms flew out wide, his little face turned red and puckered up a second before he let out a howl.

Covering the distance to the bed in three swift strides, Rafe deposited the crying baby in his mommy's arms, whispered, sardonically, "That went well," dropped a quick kiss on Nicole's cheek and straightening, smiled at his wife's wink.

Dominic, having quickly picked up Jimmy, was speaking quietly to the pouty faced toddler.

Rosie and Ellie had come up to the bed, and were watching Nicole begin to nurse Leo. "May we sit on the bed?" Ellie asked in a near whisper.

Nicole smiled. "Sure. Rafe lift the girls up."

After lifting Rosie and Ellie onto the bed, Rafe stood, indecisive for a moment, taking in the maternal tableau. He wasn't entirely comfortable with people looking at Nicole's boobs, regardless her dress was only partially unbuttoned and Leo's head concealed a good deal. But his wife was unfazed, and aware of her strong opinions on breast feeding as perfectly natural, he remained mute. He just hoped he wouldn't have to punch someone out if and when Nicole decided to nurse Leo at a restaurant and a customer took issue. Since that wasn't an immediate problem, he opted for a stiff drink and went to talk to his mother.

50

"I thought you might prefer something stronger than champagne," Rafe said, handing his mother one of two glasses of Macallan 32 whisky he'd poured. "Two ice cubes, a twist of lemon, the way you like it." Taking her champagne glass from her, without turning, he held it out behind him, assuming correctly that one of his staff would take it from him. "Sorry about the venue. It's a little crowded in here but I wanted Nicole to be comfortable."

Camelia smiled. "So diplomatic, Rafail, when you and I both know I shouldn't be standing in this corner." She lifted the glass a fraction. "Dutch courage. Thank you."

"It's not a problem. No one's noticed." Regardless his mother had been Miss World before her marriage and understood the limelight, she was shy at heart. "What do you think of Leo?"

"He's beautiful." Camelia beamed. "He looks exactly like you as a baby. But, of course, I'm prejudiced. I'm sure Melanie sees a resemblance to Nicole. Oh, heavens, look, Nicole's handing Leo to Anton."

Rafe turned. "Now there's a sight to behold," he said, drily, dropping his glass on a nearby table.

"He's your father."

Rafe's head swiveled back with a snap. "*What?*"

"Anton's your father," Camelia repeated, her voice trembling slightly.

"My *father?*" Rafe half expected his mother to correct him.

"You don't know how many times I wanted to tell you but I couldn't think of a way without jeopardizing—well... everything." Not a clear yes, but a yes. "I'm sorry."

Sorry? That was a word you used if you bumped into someone, or forgot a name; it was patently inadequate in this cataclysmic instance when the world as he knew it had exploded. Rafe shot a glance at Gora, then turned back to his mother and wondered what would have happened if he hadn't inherited her dark hair and amber eyes. "Jesus...are you sure--you're sure, fine, okay--got it." Sweeping aside the blast debris clogging his brain, he ran his hands over his face and still mildly shell-shocked, tried to reorder his life on the fly. "I'd always promised myself I'd cut my throat if I ever turned out like Maso." He met his mother's gaze. "You should have told me."

"I didn't dare." Draining her drink, Camelia set the glass on the window sill and hesitated a moment more before she spoke. "If Maso found out you weren't his son," she said, her voice barely audible, "you know what he would have done."

"He probably would have killed me."

"Us. He would have killed us." She looked down for a moment then lifting her gaze, added with a kind of apologetic restraint, "I also remained silent for a less lethal reason. You loved your grandfather's company, you had from a very young age. You'd sit beside Vincent, watching and listening, asking questions when any other child would have been at play. And as you became more involved in the company"—

"And Maso became more psychotic."

"Your role in Contini Pharma took on a new urgency," Camelia said, quietly reflective, as though reliving the byzantine nightmare. "And if Maso died—a real possibility with his vices--Caesar would have been incapable of taking over. You loved the work, the employees and they loved you; everyone expected you to take charge someday." She studied his face for a moment. "Truth wasn't an option. Or survivable."

"Contini Pharma would have ceased to exist for me," Rafe noted, the significance of his mother's statement clear. "We might have as well."

"No might about it." A whip sharp murmur.

"So we both learned to watch Maso," Rafe said. "His eyes, not his words, his body language. You never let down your guard."

"No, never." She lifted her shoulder in a faint shrug and the diamonds in her ears caught the light. "If only I'd known about Clement's will."

"No one did except Gerda. If Maso had suspected she was alive, he would have found her, forced her to tell him where the will was and"—

"He would have destroyed them both," Camelia finished. She looked off in the distance for a moment. "I've often wondered," she murmured, refocusing on Rafe, "if I'd chosen a different course, whether our lives would have been easier. Since that ideal construct never materialized, it became instead a matter of endurance." Her voice dropped to a whisper. "Anton was my tower of strength all those years."

Rafe didn't wish to hurt his mother, but the thought crossed his mind that it may have been better for them both if she'd taken him and walked away. On the other hand, examining what might have been was a willful waste of time; it changed nothing. "I'm glad you had someone to rely on," he said, kindly.

"At least in your early years you had Clement." Camelia smiled. "He adored you."

"And *Grandpere* did what he could to protect me," Rafe replied with an answering smile rather than offend his mother; mentioning all the years of Maso's punishing presence would have been churlish.

She nodded, grateful for his understanding. God knows she had regrets enough for both of them. "Anton did what he could to protect us too," she said, recalling times when she'd phoned him in a panic. "Not openly, of course, but within the scope of his limited powers, he helped."

Perhaps while Maso lived, Anton's powers, apropos them, had been limited; that was no longer the case. After marrying his mother, Gora had become an integral part of their family. Last year he'd come to Thailand, walked into an armed compound with the fifty million for Rafe's ransom, saw that Rafe was freed then personally executed Zou, the man who'd imprisoned his son. It made one question the concept of limited powers no matter the time frame.

And now the retired Mafioso, Anton Georgescu, known to the world as Gora, newly identified as *his birth father* was half a room away, gently holding Leo. Fuck if life didn't occasionally hit impressive levels of crazy.

"Anton never wanted me to tell you."

Rafe turned back. "Because?"

"He didn't want you to lose Contini Pharma."

"Had he always known he was my father?"

"No." Her face softened. "If he'd known, he would have immediately taken matters into his own hands. It was too dangerous with Maso's rages and paranoia. I was terrified you'd be hurt if things went wrong." She flinched. "And you were hurt anyway," she said, a strain of guilt in her voice.

"We both managed, Mum," Rafe gently replied. "It wasn't your fault. When *did* Anton know?"

"Soon after Maso died, I heard Anton's wife had passed away in Istanbul. So I called and told him you were his son. Before that, any future for us would have been impossible. He'd married into a dangerous family."

Even though Rafe had been aware of the extent of Gora's mafia connections, he was less naïve than his mother about what was and was not possible; the clusterfuck of his childhood had made him not only a cynic, but immune to orthodoxy. Nothing was impossible. His mother, by some miracle, had remained surprisingly innocent and unworldly despite the hellish years of her marriage. "Fortunately, we passed through all those turbulent years relatively unscathed," he said, bland and consoling. "Thanks in large part to you." Abruptly turning at the sound of a male voice singing in Romanian, Rafe stared. "I don't believe it. He's singing to Leo."

"Anton and I were both in the church choir when we were young. He has a wonderful voice."

"We have a lot of catching up to do," Rafe murmured, amused and impressed. "Are you going to tell Anton or should I?"

"I will, dear. He's going to be displeased at first. He never wanted the taint of his former life to sully you. All he ever wanted was for you to be safe and well and happy, and now you are all three are you not?"

His smile was effortless. "Yes, Mum, I am."

. . .

LATE THAT EVENING, after most of the guests at the main house had retired for the night, and Rafe had taken his leave of those still visiting in one of the reception rooms, he found Gora waiting for him on a garden bench beside the path to the carriage house.

"Sit for a minute," Gora said, extending the invitation with a slight lift of his hand. "Your mother said she talked to you."

Rafe smiled at the tall, lean man with close-cropped salt and pepper hair, stark features and a quiet assurance. Well-dressed in black linen slacks and a soft gray shirt, Rafe recognized his mother's favorite tailor.

"Your mother dresses me now," Gora drawled, taking note of Rafe's raking glance. "Little of the village peasant remains," he said, his tone amused.

Rafe grinned. "You indulge her. Although knowing mother's fondness for Herr Gruen, she probably had a persuasive argument. Since I'm being spit up on or burped on several times a day, I'm reduced to shorts and t-shirts," Rafe said, sitting down beside Gora. "Hello, Father." He held out his hand. "Mother's news was a pleasant surprise. I wish I'd known long ago."

Gora's hand was large like Rafe's, his grip firm. "I, too, wish I'd known. Perhaps Maso could have been managed better, sooner," he added, gruffly.

Rafe didn't question Gora's definition of managed. "I think Mother felt she had valid reasons for reticence."

"Your mother was always much nicer than I," Gora said, softly. "She suffered needlessly, you did as well." A muscle flicked in his jaw. "I'll go to my grave with the guilt."

"Don't. It's over. The world is awesome now. Fuck the past."

Gora responded with a wry smile. "Survivors' euphoria?"

"Who the fuck knows--or cares? I have a wife and son I adore, a mother and father I cherish and a company I revere. What more could I want? I'll answer that. Nada. Zilch."

His guilt aside, Gora understood that over the years, in some small and not so small ways only he was privy to, he'd helped make this young man who he was: strong, resilient, determined. He'd done it for Camelia without knowing her ultimate gift would be out of all proportion to his assistance. "If I might make a small request"—Gora's eyelids lowered slightly--"in this world of perfection." His tone was faintly apologetic. "Out of an abundance of caution."

"You. Cautious?" Rafe's grin was mocking.

"Occasionally." Gora's voice was non-committal. "Call it a personal favor if you prefer."

"I'm listening, but the answer is yes in advance. What is it?"

"For the sake of your mother's reputation, I'd rather not announce that I'm your father. Camelia would be labeled an adulteress—if such old-fashioned terms still exist. Regardless though, her reputation concerns me. I'd prefer not unnecessarily risking it. You're my son in my heart and to those close to us. The rest don't matter."

"Perhaps you should run this by Mother. She may not agree."

"I'd like you to help explain it to her. Perhaps the argument that my mafia past discredits Contini Pharma would be the most effective. Such rumors could be damaging to the company."

"You know very well your past is irrelevant. You already engage in Contini Pharma business and nobody cares."

"But I took part as your mother's husband, not your father. The changed status impacts your mother as well as you."

Rafe smiled. "Mother's respectability is beyond reproach while my life of excess had always been notorious and no one ever gave a shit. Money's power; you know that. However, I'm more than happy to present your arguments to Mum, but I'm guessing before I'm halfway through my comments she's going to stop me and ask, 'Did Anton send you?'"

Gora sighed. "I'd appreciate it if you'd at least try. Camelia's still very much like the young girl I fell in love with years ago in our village. She doesn't deal with scandal as well as we do."

"Are you sure? Mother survived Maso."

"That's because she has a deep core of strength. Also, the heart of a lioness; she did whatever was necessary to shield you from the worst of Maso's viciousness."

Rafe went pale. "Tell me that's not true."

"I don't know all the details," Gora lied. "But I know Maso lived too long. I should have done something sooner." He'd been unforgiving in his final act of justice for the woman he loved.

"Jesus." Rafe's nostrils flared. "How did Mother do it?"

"Your mother had undaunted courage and the will to live. Poverty was a fact of life in the small village of our youth; you learned to survive." He sighed. "If only your mother and I could have been together years ago. It was always our dream, distant and more often than not, hopeless, but like the Holy Grail, a never forsaken quest."

"Christ, talk about all of us going through hell. Maybe

we should hire a live-in therapist to smooth out all the jagged edges and vandalized psyches."

Gora's cool grey gaze rose. "You're going to disclose the agonies and struggles you endured to a stranger?"

Rafe grimaced.

"I wouldn't dare," Gora said, simply.

"So we're both averse to therapy. What about mother?"

Gora shrugged. "Ask her."

Rafe smiled. "That sounds like a no."

"Not necessarily. She's happy now, that's all I'm saying."

"So why bring up the hellacious shit."

Gora's nod was infinitesimal. "Why push if you don't have to, that's my motto."

"And if you have to?" Rafe said softly.

"You know as well as I do, then you fucking push. Hard." A quick lift of his brows. "A lesson you learned long ago."

Rafe drew in a breath before he spoke, his tone, softly intense. "I don't want Leo to ever experience that."

"Nor do I. With Maso dead and my former life relinquished, with love and happiness animating both our lives, it's time to leave the grim, too often tiresome past and take comfort in the peaceful present."

"Yes, in spades," Rafe said, quietly. "Nicole makes it all possible. Sometimes I have to beat back my alarm thinking of all I would have missed if not for her."

"Your mother and I always knew," Gora murmured. "The world just got in the way."

A small silence fell, both men conscious of all that had transpired to bring them to this point where love and contentment were not just words for other people. Where they, too, were allowed happiness.

Uncomfortable with public displays of emotion, Rafe spoke first. "The baby might be up by now."

"Yes, it's late," Gora said, understanding emotional reticence; a necessity in his former profession. "Go, Nicole needs you."

Walking away, Rafe thought how good it felt to be needed by someone you loved with mindless joy. He smiled at the last adjective; an anomaly in his formerly disciplined life.

He was still smiling faintly when he walked into the carriage house bedroom, his smile widening at the sight of his wife and son waiting for him in bed.

"We couldn't sleep," Nicole said. "We miss you."

His eyes went shut briefly, an overwhelming feeling of peace inundating his senses. "Thank you," he softly said.

51

The next morning after breakfast, Rafe took the opportunity to speak to Dominic and Gora in private. He'd no more than begun his explanation when Dominic held up his hand, said, "Would tomorrow do?" and shot a quick look at Gora.

"Tomorrow's fine," Gora agreed.

And with male succinctness, the issue was resolved.

The following afternoon when Rafe entered the carriage house bedroom after seeing their guests off, Nicole offered him a dazzling smile. "Hurrah! They left sooner than I expected."

"Gora and Dominic had business appointments."

"And Dominic dragged my mother away. Thank you."

"Don't thank me. Thank your uncle. He had a tight schedule."

"Okay."

"What?" Although he wasn't sure he wanted to know; she'd just winked.

"Nothing. I just really appreciate you."

He smiled. "And I appreciate you. Could we change the subject?"

"Of course." She didn't know what he'd done to get everyone to leave so quickly but she owed him. And if he didn't want to talk about it, fine. "I think Leo said, 'Mama', while you were gone."

"Come on, he's just a week old."

"You'll see when he wakes up."

"In that case, I wait to be amazed."

As it turned out, Leo's "Mama," was part gurgle and part drooling bubbles, but Rafe politely agreed his son had spoken because he loved his wife, and she was captivated by Leo's clever vocal efforts.

"Told you," she said, grinning.

Leaning over, Rafe kissed mother and child. "Definitely a genius," he murmured, and straightening, added, "I was thinking about taking Leo to the main house for an hour or so. Do you mind? There's a meeting I shouldn't miss."

"He might be fussy."

"I'll bring a bottle and diaper." One brow went up and his smile appeared. "Do we have your permission?"

"Is Contini Pharma being compromised without your hand on the wheel?"

He'd didn't mention he'd been in regular contact with Vincent. "It would give me a chance to show off Leo," Rafe pointed out instead. "In addition"—he grinned—"I could check that Contini Pharma isn't veering off course."

"By all means go. But I'm more than willing to keep Leo here while you attend the meeting. You've done more than your share of babysitting the past few days. Seriously, go."

"I *do* want to show off my son."

His words were softly put, and inexpressibly tender. "In

that case, I'm sure Leo will do you proud," Nicole replied, lifting the baby, holding him out.

Leo not only went to work with his father for a few hours that day, but the practice became habitual. Rafe supervised meetings with Leo either sleeping in his arms or in a small crib that had been brought in. More often than not, Leo was content to calmly observe the activities from the comfort of his father's lap and occasionally if he fussed, Rafe walked him without interrupting the flow of business. The baby even politely accepted his bottle from one of the women from time to time; he had his father's charm. Soon, the conference room was as familiar to Leo as his nursery.

Nicole took advantage of her new leisure to rest. By week three, she was completely recovered, and the rhythm of the small family's life had settled into an established pattern. Rafe was managing Contini Pharma with the help of his small, on-site staff, Nicole was exercising when she could, writing a page of screenplay in odd moments, occasionally discussing food bank concerns with Fiona, otherwise devoting her time to her newborn son.

Leo had zero complaints. If his father wasn't holding him, his mother was, or he was sleeping.

It was a time of great content.

A FORTNIGHT LATER, shortly after Mireille gave birth, Rafe, Nicole and Leo traveled to Paris to meet the new baby. The visit was tearful and happy, joyful and poignant; Henny's son had entered the world. The baby bore a startling resemblance to his late father. He had Henny's ginger hair, his fine-bridged nose and sturdiness; the baby's faintly tilted eyes achingly familiar. The fates had been kind.

"Have you decided on a name?" Rafe asked. Mireille hadn't when she'd first called.

"You know Henny didn't like his name, or more aptly the long list of aristocratic names he'd been given. But, Wolfgang, was one he didn't mind. For personal reasons, I think. While he rarely talked about his family, he told me about his grandmother."

"Sophie."

"You know her?"

"I only know of her. She died when Henny was still young, but he remembered her fondly. She called him Woffer."

Mireille smiled. "He told you."

"Yes." There was nothing he didn't know about Henny. Two little nine-year-old boys alone in the world and forced to grow up too fast had had much in common; their bond had been deep and strong.

"Woffer suits him," Mireille said, touching her son's soft, fuzzy hair. "When he's older he can choose whether to acknowledge his title. Henny never did."

Rafe smiled. "Sometimes he did—on those occasions when some pissant in boarding school tried to flaunt his title. Henny would cut through the swagger by mentioning his family put Charlemagne on the throne in 768." Rafe paused for a moment as though in recall, and his voice when he spoke, was softly sardonic. "No one could shut down bullshit better than Henny."

"He had a pretty clear notion of what was important in life," Mireille noted.

"You had a calming effect on him. When we were young, his ideas of what was important were damned irresponsible. Like our expedition to the Eiger." Rafe smiled. "I see he never mentioned that to you. Fortunately, he moved on to Provencal cooking and that sudden shift saved our lives."

Mireille chuckled. "His volatility was one of his many charms."

"Yeah." Rafe's voice was soft. "He didn't believe in slow and steady or caution."

"Or doubt," Mireille said.

"No. Doubt was anathema to him."

As the lengthening silence testified to the enormity of their loss and Mireille's smile wavered, Nicole deliberately interceded. "Rafe, didn't you want to take some photos of the boys?"

After looking at her blankly for a second, he blinked. "Thanks for the reminder." Turning to Mireille seated on a chaise with Woffer in her arms, he smiled. "Could we put the boys side by side somewhere? Either the sofa or maybe that hassock has better light."

Taking Woffer from Mireille, Rafe waited while Nicole placed Leo on the canary yellow hassock before setting Henny's son next to him. The bright fabric was a colorful foil for the two babies attired for summer in blue short outfits; the similar nautical theme pure accident.

Rafe experienced a little jolt seeing the babies dressed almost identically; it reminded him of all the school uniforms he and Henny had worn, of all the years of friendship they'd shared. More than anything, he wanted the boys to be best friends like their fathers had been, but in a world of grace this time, without the ill-treatment he and Henny had suffered. He would see to it. He let out a little breath then, the thought filling him with satisfaction.

Moving to address the best light, Rafe began snapping shots while Nicole made soft cooing sounds to gain the babies' attention.

Until outside—

A police siren ripped through the quiet of the room, the sharp knife blade of sound quickly fading.

But the piercing siren had startled Woffer, and rigid with shock, he began to wail.

In an instinctive gesture of comfort, Leo reached out and touched Woffer's arm.

The wild cry abruptly stopped. Woffer's little chest lifted on a breath and he quietly exhaled.

Tears sprang to the women's eyes.

Rafe's heart went still.

Since Henny's death Rafe wondered, no, *hoped* there was a world beyond the stars where every question didn't need a rational answer, where rigid rules didn't apply, where the archaic *outre mer* was a road home for old friends. He smiled. *Hey, Henny, see that? Our boys are gonna be like us. Best mates."*

As if in confirmation, the babies' eyes locked, Leo gurgled, Woffer cooed in reply, and linked by unspoken thoughts of better days, the adults smiled.

THE CONTINI FAMILY stayed in Paris for several more days, becoming acquainted with the newest member of what would become their extended family. When it came time for them to leave, Mireille made plans to visit Monte Carlo the following month.

Rafe entertained Leo on the short flight home, discussing plans for Woffer's visit, telling him of the playground currently under construction, smiling at Nicole when she teased him for talking to their son with such seriousness. "When he gets tired of listening we'll do something else. So far he's enjoying the plans for his playground."

"We're all going to love that playground."

Rafe grinned. "That's the idea. I told Ramon to design a park for family fun."

Leo's tiny fist closed on a handful of Rafe's hair and gave it a tug, as if to say don't forget me.

"You hear that Leo?" Rafe said, turning back, his voice soft, the prospect of a future together sending an undercurrent of happiness through him. "We're a family. Can you say- -the best of all possible worlds for daddy?"

Responding to the query in his father's voice, Leo delivered a stream of conversational bubbles, along with a winning smile.

His parents, charmed by their son's cleverness, exchanged tender glances and experienced the rare glow of knowing they were in perfect harmony with the people they loved most in the world.

52

Since Leo was cared for solely by his parents, Nicole went to her six weeks checkup alone. They'd agreed, taking Leo to the appointment would have been distracting for the doctor as well as possibly disruptive.

It was early afternoon when Nicole entered the playground and found Rafe and Leo in one of the pavilions. The green and white striped canvas awning shaded them from the sun, a necessity in August in the Mediterranean.

"Those are darling," she said, pointing at Leo, lying in an infant swing Rafe was gently pushing. "Where in the world did you get baby sunglasses?" Leo had sunglasses with soft, rubber frames secured to his head with a narrow rubber filament.

"Louis sent a bunch." Rafe smiled. "Notice the color coordinated ensemble." The red frames matched Leo's sunsuit. "How'd your appointment go?"

"Need you ask. I'm ridiculously healthy."

Rafe raised one brow. "Is that a confirmed medical opinion?"

She raised *two* brows and threw in a sniff. "You don't

believe me?"

"I believe you." Reticence in every syllable; he'd not forgotten the perilous trauma of her delivery.

"No, you don't. But I'm one step ahead of you. Ta-da!" She pulled out a folded envelope from her cornflower blue linen slacks pocket and held it aloft. "Signed, sealed and delivered, oh ye of little faith."

He smiled. "For real?"

"Damn right. I've been listening to all your polite reservations about having sex: it's too soon after my delivery; Leo might wake up; you might hurt me; what's the rush when we have all our lives. That one scared the shit out of me. It sounded like you were thinking years. So, I figured I'd better have a rock solid, seal of approval from Moncur." She tossed the envelope to him.

Catching it, he took his hand off the swing, slipped his finger under the flap, took out a notecard and looked up with a grin. "Seriously, she has a seal?"

"As you see. Apparently, she's a notary on occasion for those couples who need their birth certificates on the fly. You're not the only billionaire globe trotter she ministers to. And she was sympathetic to my plight having watched you in action."

He smiled faintly, thinking Dr. Moncur could hold her own with the best of them. "She said that?"

"Not in so many words. She didn't call you an arrogant ass. She was polite."

Rafe laughed. Reading the single line designating Nicole completely healed and in robust health, he pocketed the note and said very gently, "So then, tonight's the night?"

"Oh, yes," Nicole murmured, feeling a little shiver race up her spine. "It's been way too long..."

Leo took exception to the swing stopping with a squeal,

instantly displacing his parents' amorous thoughts with more mundane realities.

Giving the swing a push, Rafe held Nicole's gaze and said, "I wish I could offer you guarantees, unfortunately..."

Nicole smiled. "We're resourceful. *And* our darling boy has slept through the night twice in the last few days."

"Certainly encouraging."

Nicole's smile widened. "I have a good feeling."

IT WAS after ten when Rafe shut the door to the baby's room, leaned back, slid his long hair behind his ears with a flick of his fingers and softly exhaled. "He's sleeping." His brows rose. "What?" Nicole had pushed herself upright in bed and was staring at him.

"The way you slip your hair behind your ears with smooth, long-fingered grace. It's super sexy."

"Habit, that's all." He smiled. "And everything's sexy to you, lately."

"Jeez, I wonder why?"

"Wonder no more, pussycat," he said with a grin, pulling his grey t-shirt over his head. "But with our son's erratic sleep schedule"—Rafe pointed over his shoulder—"I'm thinking the first time should be under five minutes. Any objections?"

Nicole grinned. "Why so long?"

"Gotcha." He dropped the t-shirt on the carpet. "By the way, I'm using a condom. Don't argue."

"I told you I'm on the mini-pill birth control."

"Still, just to be safe I'm using a condom."

"Why? The mini-pill is effective. It's made for situations like this when I'm still nursing"—

"We manufacture it. I know what it's for."

"Oh." She paused a fraction of a second. "Well then, we're good."

He looked up from unzipping his black linen shorts. "No. We're not taking chances."

"I told Moncur we might not agree on this subject."

A flash of astonishment in his eyes. "You told her what?" He pulled the zipper back up with a neat snap.

"I said you might be suspicious."

"Jesus, what the hell else did you tell her?"

But his frown wasn't threatening, just grumpy, so she took a chance and smiled. "Nothing earth-shaking. I just knew how you'd feel about this, that's all."

"Fuck if you do."

"Well, about me and birth control anyway," she said, undeterred by his dismissive tone. "Come on, pretty please," she coaxed. "Call Moncur. I explained some of what had happened in the past and made a point of taking the pill in her office so I'd have a witness. Seriously, I don't want you to use a condom." Nicole smiled. "You know...it could be a long, maybe even a wild night."

Rafe snorted. "Dreamer. Leo will probably be up in a couple minutes."

"Maybe not. We had a little talk while I was nursing him. I explained, mommy and daddy needed some private time."

His mouth twitched. "Oh, hell then, not a problem."

"Exactly," she said, ignoring his sarcasm. "Call Moncur."

"It's after ten. She's probably sleeping."

"I told her it might be late."

"Sounds like you had quite a conversation." His smile was conditional; he took exception to a public airing of his private life.

"Women talk, that's all. Don't take it personally. Just ask her if I took the pill. Simple."

What was simple for his wife was almost incomprehensible for a man who until recently had been emotionally uncommunicative. And now he was expected to discuss his goddamn sex life with a doctor he barely knew? *Jesus Christ.*

"I heard that. You don't have to call. It's okay."

"We'll just use condoms for a while."

"No, we won't."

He went still. "I'm not having this discussion ad nauseum."

"Then don't. I took a pill today. Everything's fine."

"Pardon me." A sardonic edge to his voice. "Suddenly your word is unimpeachable?"

She gave him an unblinking stare. "Am I ever going to live that down?"

"I don't know about *ever*," he said, his voice pitched low, "but with a new baby sleeping next door, it might take me a while. And seriously, pussycat, your delivery put the fucking fear of God in me. Let's not play Russian roulette."

"If you don't want to take my word for it, and I understand completely if you don't, then *call* the doctor," she persisted, watching him, wishing she had his bloody self-control. "Moncur will put your doubts to rest."

"I'm done with this conversation." His voice was ultra-soft.

How could he go utterly motionless like that; even his breathing was invisible. "Look, I don't want to fight. I've been looking forward to this"—

"This?" he growled. "You mean, doing what you want—like last time?" He stood taut and exasperated, his nude, muscular torso sleek with tension, his bare feet planted in manifest resistance.

"I'm sorry I didn't tell you when I went off birth control last summer. I shouldn't have done that," she said, as impatient with the argument as he, but circumspect in her velvet smooth enunciation; she had plans. "Please don't be mad," she murmured, sliding off the bed, walking across the room, taking his hands and ignoring their slackness, pulling them around her waist. She waited a moment in the event he'd relinquish his hold and when he didn't, continued her apology. "Everything turned out fine in the end, perfect in fact and I'm healthy as can be." Trailing her fingers up his ridged abs and toned pecs, she slid her palms gently over his shoulders, melted into his hard, unyielding body and lifted her blue, heated gaze to his. "And I'm *telling* you what I did this time. Full disclosure. So please, it's been a really, *really* long time," she whispered, sultry and low. "I need to feel you *deep* inside me..."

Every man had his breaking point. That he'd never gone without sex for more than a few days in the decade past meant the last two/plus monastic months had left him acutely susceptible to his wife's heated plea. Not to mention, her soft, warm, voluptuousness under his hands and against his body was firing up every randy nerve in his psyche. *Fuuuck.*

He could have disengaged himself; he thought about it. But his erection was hard against her stomach, his dick swelling higher with each beat of his heart, and, suddenly, issues of responsibility and personal autonomy mattered less. Still, it took another restive moment before he said, "I'll call."

"Thank you," Nicole whispered with a flare of relief, and pulling his head down, she kissed him hard and fast. "I love you madly, deliriously, even complacently," she added with a grin, "if that puts you in a better mood. And"--leaning back enough to see the rising humor in his gaze, she winked--"Leo's going to sleep all night. Just wait and see."

Dropping her hands, she reached for the zipper on his shorts, and squealed as his hand closed on hers in a crushing grip. But a second later, his fingers loosened slightly and gracious to his misgivings even while personally discounting them, she gave him a sweeter than sweet smile. "Forgive me, I presumed."

Rafe grinned. "Goddamn. Sounds like I'm in charge."

"Aren't you always?"

"Actually no, nor am I delusional. You're playing nice because you want sex."

"Specifically, sex with you. Now, if you're done being troublesome"—a slight frown marred her perfect brow—"call Moncur. Or give me your phone, I'll punch in the number."

He released her hand. "I have the number." Along with every other doctor, here and in Paris, that might possibly be needed should Nicole or Leo require care.

Nicole's smile this time was a high wattage, super-sized beam of sugary sweetness. "You're always so efficient. I'm in awe."

Pulling his phone out of his pocket, he gave her a sardonic glance. "Give it up, Tiger. You don't know how to kiss ass."

"Yes, sir," she purred. "Whatever you say, sir, although I *am* your ever loving, adoring sweetie pie, and that's a fact."

"Adoring?" he drawled, tapping Moncur's number, his gaze amused when it lifted. "That'll be the day."

"I could be." A rosy blush crept up her cheeks. "Maybe. Oh, hell, you wouldn't know what to do if I was adoring. And FYI, I'm so damned sex deprived, I'm not sure I actually need you."

"Course you do. I have those G-spot skills you like."

Her breath caught in her throat. "Oh, God, hurry," she

said, in a suffocated voice. Taking a quick breath, her next words were more familiarly assertive. "Consider that an order."

He was still smiling when the doctor picked up. "Rafe Contini here. I apologize for calling so late, but I'm in a trust-but-verify mood, and Nicole said she already warned you I might call."

"She's on the mini-pill. She took one before she left the office. If you're concerned, you can monitor her future pill intake. She's statistically impregnable. But you know those percentages better than I. Will that do?"

"Yes, thank you."

The line went dead before he could say goodbye. "Talk about efficient," he said with a quirked brow. "No hello, no goodbye. She was, however, convincing."

With her horniness approaching redline status, and Rafe's mood still in the dicey range, Nicole attuned her voice to a polite, well-mannered civility. "Good. Happy now?"

His gaze held hers for a moment. "Satisfied at least."

"Perfect." She didn't say *unlike you, rose-colored glasses largely illuminate my world and once I climax, life will indeed be perfect.* "Thank you for calling."

Rafe shrugged, weary of the argument. "I like your skirt," he said, changing the subject. "You look like a beautiful, fey nymph."

She ran her hands over the floaty layers of colorful, floral print muslin grazing her bare feet and smiled. "Perhaps Alessandra was aware of your interest in nymphs."

"Take it off." A quick breath, a softer tone. "Please."

"Short conversation?"

He smiled. "You interested in talking?"

Damn, that sexy smile, and the lurid undertone to his query that was offering her something ten times, a thousand times, better than talk. "Maybe later," she said, trying not to openly pant.

"Sure."

Really, the difference between men and women--that Mars and Venus divide--was on full display, his off-hand reply casual to the point of indifference. And if he wasn't currently stripping off his shorts and boxers, she might have focused more substantively on the vast gulf between male and female sensibilities. But the image of his huge, inked dick, waist high and turgid, struck her retinas with dramatic impact, instantly ratcheted up every sexual receptor in her body and effectively vaporized gender issues.

He saw her suck in a breath, took note of her flushed cheeks, viewed her nipples stiffening under her short, green sweater with a connoisseur's appreciation. "Any time you're ready," he murmured, curling his fingers around his rampant erection, sliding his fist up then down, his engorged cock spiking higher, the flaring head swelling. Arching his back against the flagrant pleasure, he transiently zoned out, until Nicole's small, smothered moan registered at some elemental level, and he caught her just as her knees buckled under the lustful jolt slamming through her pussy.

Fully alert now, he took note of her sudden shiver. "You're trembling. This can wait. I'm putting you to bed."

"No!" Her gaze flashed up, wide-eyed. "Don't you dare!" she panted, frenzied, needy, nearly unstrung. "Can't wait—I won't!"

With her sharp commands echoing in his ears, issues of her health and vigor disappeared. "Take a breath, pussycat, relax. Those five second orgasms are rubbish and you know it. Did I tell you I promised Leo a motorcycle ride tomorrow if he sleeps a couple hours?"

A startle reflex, a tiny, grudging smile. "Well played, Machiavelli. Leo on your motorcycle? That stopped me cold. Although," she added, glancing down at his rigid dick flat against his stomach—"your cockblock is temporary from the look of things."

"He'll wait." Unhesitating, confident. "I'd just like our first time in a long time to play out in slightly more than five seconds."

"Personally, I prefer all night, but..."

"Understood. Let's see what our lion cub allows. In the meantime, humor me." His smile lingered in his eyes. "I'm feeling the romance." He wasn't entirely teasing; it felt as though tonight was shiny and new, all the doors slammed shut on his fucked-up past, the future bright.

"Consider me available for anything romantic," she purred, "so long as S-E-X is involved."

He laughed. "I'm aware."

Her brows rose. "A problem?"

"Hell no." Scooping her up into his arms, he carried her to the bed, gently placed her on her back, followed her down with the superb grace faultlessly honed muscles allowed and brushing her skirt aside, settled between her legs, his sudden smile matching the warmth in his eyes. "No panties. We're going to get along."

She smiled. "As always."

Perfectly aware of what was unwise and safe at times like this he smiled back, said, "Yes, always," and slid into her hot, silky sweetness.

"Oh God..." Pleasure flooded her mind. "Oh God, oh God, oh"--

The sudden snuffling on the baby monitor detonated like a bomb.

Rafe froze mid-stroke, shut his eyes, drew in a deep

breath of restraint and taut with nerves, listened to the waking-up baby noises.

Nicole giggled.

He opened his eyes, gave her a jaundiced look. "Tell me this isn't our future."

She shook her head, held up a finger. "Trust me."

Dubious, his expectations shit to nil, he politely smiled.

"I feel you," she whispered, shifting her hips ever so slightly, the tactile flesh to flesh pressure, silken, delectable, rising in splendor. "Nice..."

"Take it easy, pussycat." The tick over his cheekbone seconded the warning. "Seriously, don't move. My dick is in a non-compliant mood." His erection was swelling in breadth and width and length; in general, being a dick.

"I'll try," she whispered.

Either she wasn't trying very hard or his dick was being more troublesome than usual. Probably both, which meant he better shut this down before it was too late.

He sighed. *Maybe next time.* And flexing his quads, he was about to withdraw, when by an act of God, the hand of fate, or because one of Natalie's gypsy charms had haphazardly arrived, the baby snuffles began to diminish.

Rafe's head came up, his attention fixed on the tiny little hiccups and snorts, the soft pitch and softer volume, the slowing cadence, until, with a last, little sigh, Leo's breathing lapsed into the rhythm of sleep.

Nicole grinned. "You're welcome."

"I'm buying you the sun, moon and stars in about five minutes," Rafe said, his voice a husky rasp, his fingers closing hard on her hips.

"I'll settle for an orgasm in two minutes."

"Done."

Dragging her into his rock-hard erection, he dropped his

head to stifle her sudden cry of pleasure. "Don't wake him," he whispered, his breath warm on her lips, spreading his fingers to grip her ass more firmly, forcing himself deeper by slow degrees. Waiting each time for her strained flesh to softly yield, like that...and that—*Fuuuck*...he shut his eyes against the freaking unchecked pleasure, inhaled Nicole's throaty moan, then pushed that nervy distance more where wild, spiking delirium burned away reason.

"More," Nicole panted, a moment later when she came up for air. "More, more, more..."

A muscle along his jaw twitched. "I don't need fucking encouragement."

"You worry too much. I'm fine." She shifted her hips in a seductive heads up, added a sunny smile. "You know how long it's been, right?"

"I do." *To the minute.*

But he hadn't moved. "You want me to beg?"

"Fuck no."

It felt like coaxing a toddler to eat his spinach. If not for his scowl, she might have said so. "Come on, I won't break."

A pause. "I'm not so sure."

She better than anyone knew how well she felt. Grabbing his firm butt, she hauled him as close as his stiff cock allowed and said with exaggerated sweetness, "Are we gonna discuss useless shit until Leo wakes up?"

A deep breath. "Sounds like you'd rather not."

She smiled faintly. "Sounds like you got the message."

"Hard to miss." His voice was whisper soft, his entire nervous system narrowly focused, his dick on full alert.

She moved slightly in teasing enticement.

Instantly swelling inside her, he groaned at the raw pleasure, and abruptly dismissing caution, said, "Forgive me," and plunged into her creamy pussy with dizzying speed, penetrating to an almost indefensible depth, exhaling a perverse grunt of satisfaction at the fierce, unbridled delirium. *Damn, he'd forgotten how bloody fine that felt.* "Ready for more?" It wasn't really a question; he was already flexing his legs, his libido in overdrive, his muscle memory unleashed. Withdrawing marginally, he paused briefly to quash a final reprimand from his conscience then buried his dick hilt deep in a single hard thrust.

Nicole's stifled scream jerked him out of his frenzy. *Oh shit.* He froze. "I'm so fucking sorry"—

Her hand covered his mouth. "Do it again," she said in a low, heated purr. "*Exactly* the same way..."

The tension drained from his muscles. The error light in his brain stopped flashing. She was dewy wet, slick and welcoming. *Focus, dude. Seriously*--added warning to his headbanger nerves--*do no harm*.

"Hey," she whispered, "you still there?"

Dipping his head, he kissed her, so she knew he was, in fact, there. *And here.* A nicely placed, super polite downstroke. *And right the hell, here.* Much deeper, as in light-up-the-universe deep. Inhaling her soft, gratified moan, he went on to execute her requested, *do it again,* with flawless recollection, making an indelible impact on her shimmering G-spot and swollen clit with his chivalrous, well-trained dick. And once all her libidinous nerve endings were figuratively purring in satisfaction, he moved on with a tailor-made, power-stroke targeting, per request, the *exactly-the-same-way* portion of her anatomy.

The result was exactly-the-same too: a stunning surge of ecstasy rocketed through her pussy, raced up her spine, strummed through her brain, spiraled hot and fevered through every overwrought sexual receptor in her body with razzle dazzle splendor. And if not for her brain synapses short-circuiting from carnal overload, she would have complimented Rafe on his fiendishly precise expertise.

She didn't have to; he already knew.

Because that expertise thing.

Settling into a smooth, take-it-home rhythm, he concentrated on the silken flex and flow, the tight, sublime friction, the restrained/unrestrained equilibrium learned long ago that touched all the female flashpoints and supercharged feverish hysteria, until at the peaking last, when Nicole was shuddering on the brink, he held himself at the very extremity of acceptable behavior and went still.

"Count down," he whispered.

"You don't--know—everything," she panted.

He hoped like hell he did because waiting much longer might be a fucking problem for him. But she liked to be boss, so he said, politely, "Let me know when you're ready," rather than *I'll take care of this,* and quickly kissing her, he shoved his tongue down her throat with the naked authority that more or less, okay, always, turned her on.

Her climax exploded.

Check. And instantly, every politely-waiting-to-come nerve in his body fully engaged, an electrifying blaze of heart-pounding rapture coursed through him, raw-edged, strangely tender, the sensation so rare and pure and fine, the world went white and silent.

For only a nanosecond.

His orgasm was coming at him a million miles-an-hour.

It hit him with untrammeled force, streaked through his adrenaline-powered senses, and erupted in an ejaculatory spasm so violent it took his breath away.

Nicole's climax was starkly different: spun sugar soft, shiny and bright, little skid marks of spring-loaded pleasure spinning through her senses. The flickering glimpses of paradise etched on her retinas were part starry-eyed bliss, but more largely the result of Rafe's huge cock straining every shimmering, sexed-up surface of her pussy; his particular genius for that risky balance between delicacy and force world class.

In this schizoid wonderland, with Nicole drifting in a hazy, roseate euphoria, Rafe, wired to the max, and only nominally aware, pumped, poured, flooded his wife's succulent pussy with wave after wave of cum.

Until at last, replete and drained, neither moved.

Coming down from a less violent orbit, Nicole reached a state of relative consciousness first. "If I wasn't still half-dazed"--she looked up through her lashes, her voice wispy--"I'd high five you. That was freaking beautiful. Wanna try for two?"

"Give me a--minute." Eyes shut, breathing hard, Rafe smiled. "It's been...awhile."

"I'm all warm and tingly and walking on air, so"—a flirtatious note in her voice—" I'm thinking, with luck, this could be a fuck-till-you-drop night."

Dream on with a baby next door. "Wouldn't that--be nice." Rolling off Nicole, Rafe lay sprawled on his back, softly panting.

"I need a yes." Scrambling up on her knees, Nicole dropped onto his broad chest with a mutual, "Oof!"

Shocked into full consciousness, he wrapped his arms around her, and kissed the top of her head. "Yes."

Lying heart to heart, they shared a quiet moment of sweet triumph.

Minutes later, because Nicole was getting twitchy and fucking was his special talent, Rafe said, "So then..."

His soft drawl was teasing, and when she raised her

head enough to see his face, his slow, lazy smile could have melted the mythical ice maiden.

As remote from an ice maiden as the current state of intergalactic travel, Nicole's reaction was predictable. Her pulse rate accelerated, her pussy turned greedy stat and her voice trembled when she said, "I should undress."

"Or I could undress you," Rafe murmured. "How's that sound?"

Like heaven on earth, like her favorite chocolate cake with chocolate pecan frosting, like she was being offered sexual pleasure strung with fairy lights and poetry. "Hafiz," she whispered, warmed by his smile.

"Absolutely," he said, understanding. Lifting her aside, he slid off the bed, came to his feet, grabbed two towels from the bedside table, dropped one between her legs, and after wiping her up, did the same for himself. With the lack of time germane, he quickly undressed her. "Now, let me see how our little alarm clock is doing." He held up one hand, fingers crossed. "If ever there was a time for prayer, right?" Then swinging around, he walked toward the nursery.

Seriously, where did Rafe get his energy? Wrapped in her cozy post-coital afterglow, she was content to just lie there in a state of bliss.

Rafe returned shortly. "Sleeping like the proverbial baby."

She smiled. "Told you."

"You deserve a prize for clairvoyance."

She ticked off an air check. "One of my many talents."

A smile rippled across his face. "Damn, that could be a problem."

"As if," she said, lightly. "You know that enigma wrapped in an enigma phrase? That's you."

"I'm better--thanks to you and Leo." Then he nodded

and his voice softened. "Would you like to rest for a minute?" On entering the room, he'd watched her for a moment as she lay, eyes closed.

She shook her head.

"I could entertain you. You wouldn't have to do anything."

"I might take you up on that."

"Thought you might."

"You think you know me?"

His head tipped slightly to one side and he gazed at her in mild amusement. "Maybe just a little…"

"So well-mannered and tactful," she murmured.

"Maybe I have plans, correction, I do have plans. Starting now. Be back in a sec." And turning he walked away.

Coming out of the bathroom a few minutes later, he paused for a moment then said, quietly, "Feel like playing?"

"As in?" A hint of wariness echoed in her voice at the sudden glittering heat in his gaze.

"It's a surprise. Yes or no."

"What are you carrying?" Full-out suspicion now with her question unanswered.

"Jesus, Tiger, I'm not asking you to strip before the Pope. It's a game. You'll like it. Yes or no."

"Show me what you're carrying."

He held his hands out. "Wet, heated washcloths. If I'm going to go down on you, I'd prefer not tasting my cum."

Her smile was dazzling. "Why didn't you just say that?"

"Because I was asking you something else. And you still haven't answered."

"Okay, okay, I suppose."

He laughed. "Such reluctance."

"There was something different in your eyes when you

said, play, that's all. And I thought of--well..." Her voice trailed off.

"Forget it. I'll just hold you."

She sat up like a shot. "No, that's not what I want."

He came to an abrupt stop, kept his voice bland. "I have no fucking agenda other than making you happy, but I'm bad at mind reading. Tell me what you want."

"Sex, orgasms, you, over me, under me, inside me."

He smiled, sat on the bed beside her. "Gotcha. Spread your legs then and we'll get started on your pretty goddamn simple plan."

She sniffed. "We're not all into complicated sex."

"I never said, complicated. Games can be plain vanilla and still intense."

Her chin went up a notch. "Don't tell me how you know that."

"Come on, there's at least a gazillion porn sites on the web."

A lowering look. "Plu-ese."

"Look," he said, softly. "Leo might be up soon. Could we talk about this later?"

"After sex you mean."

"I mean after you come a couple times."

She sighed. "God, I'm sorry. You're always so reasonable, and I'm always troublesome and"—

"Perfect. In every way." His restraint had been honed by bitter experience; it was neither enviable nor virtuous. "Now, lie down, pussycat, relax. Think of me as your personal house boy with benefits."

She leaned back on her elbows and smiled. "When you put it that way, how can I refuse?"

"You can even give me orders if you like." A white lie, a politesse, a means of fast forwarding this discussion.

"In that case," she murmured, lying back on the pillows, "consider me in full autocratic mode."

Good luck with that. But he smiled and said, "Super," because he planned on making her feel so hot and bothered her thoughts would be on something other than giving him orders.

He was right, or maybe she was predictable, or perhaps his expertise wasn't open to debate because after he'd gently washed every tender fold of her pouty, pink pussy, particularly those areas most likely to please her, she was flushed and panting.

"Feeling good?" he unnecessarily asked.

"Just a little," she purred, her gaze heavy lidded, her hips moving faintly in response to the delicious pulsing deep inside, her slowly unfurling smile sumptuously sensual. "Is there more?"

"As much as you want..."

His low, husky whisper vibrated through her body with unnerving impact out of all proportion to its hushed resonance, his blanket assurance both tantalizing and, dammit-- annoying. "Why don't I let you know," she said, a sudden bitchiness in her tone.

"Or maybe I'll decide."

The casual chastisement in his voice sent an unwanted frisson shimmering through her senses, swirling downward and settling wet and feverish between her legs. After taking a moment to find her breath, she spoke with equal casualness. "Is that supposed to intimidate me?"

"Would you like it to?" His gaze was steady.

"No," she said, less firmly than she intended with his hooded, watchful eyes trained on her. "And don't look at me like that."

He shuttered the wildness in his eyes, smiled. "Better?"

Then, his smile still in place, he slid two fingers into her glossy cleft so deeply she gasped at the shocking invasion. "Or is this better?" he murmured, his fingers gentle now, caressing the hot, slick tissue.

"As if you don't know, damn you." A peevish, moody retort entirely separate from her greedy libido laying out the welcome mat without so much as a thought for righteous indignation or independence.

"I wouldn't want to presume," he said, ignoring her petulance, his voice soft as silk, his fingers gliding over her slippery, pulsing warmth equally gentle. "Feel this?" Positioning the pad of his thumb on the crest of her engorged clit, he lightly pressed.

Tiny fireworks left a trail of sparks on the superhighway to bliss. But he was way too smug, so she answered, "Scale of one to ten, a three."

"No shit, a three." His voice was dry. "I better up my game." And he deftly circled her clit with delicacy and finesse, lightly traced the swollen length, took the throbbing little nub between his thumb and forefinger and squeezed with the precise intensity calculated to please; that skill acquired with a blur of women in his decade-long pursuit of pleasure.

And, as usual, appreciated.

Nicole's moan rose from deep in her throat, a fresh surge of lubricant drenched his fingers and he smiled. "You're always a little unmanageable at first. I like that."

"While you're always a control freak—oh, God..." Her voice trailed off in a muted sigh, as he slid his fingers in, then out again, the rhythm measured, sure, the friction, intense.

"Sometimes you don't mind." His fingertips drifted over the cushiony swell of her G-spot with a subtle skimming stroke. "Particularly when I control your *precious* little sweet spot like"—he pushed—"*this*."

She whimpered at the wild rapture coursing through her body, unable for a moment to find sufficient air to speak, then, panting, she looked up and saw his impudent smile. "Damn. I don't know--if I should be--pissed off by your swagger--or thank you."

He laughed. "That's easy." He slid his fingers deeper. "Pleasure first. Rule one. There isn't a rule two."

"These rules of yours." Her gaze narrowed. "They're purely in reference to me."

"Of course." His fingers slid over her slippery flesh whisper soft, then without warning, sank palm deep.

A brief startle morphed into a breathy purr as the tantalizing splendor lit up her erogenous zones with a molten glow and wanting what she wanted, she languidly stretched and met his gaze. "Anytime now." A flash of a smile. "I'm asking."

She reminded him of a sumptuous odalisque from centuries past, beautiful, provocative, tempting as hell, and it took a moment to beat back his deviant impulses. "In that case," he said, his voice deceptively soft, "you know the game. I push you a little, you push back in your inimitable fashion, then I push just a little bit harder, until"--

"No Japanese rope."

Had her voice been less tremulous, it might have been an order. It was instead capitulation and submission, the prospect so limitless his predatory instincts instantly revived. "No, nothing else. Just me," he finally said, having dragooned his demons into a semblance of civility. Then slipping his fingers free, he kissed her gently. "I apologize for that incident. It made you uncomfortable."

Shocked by so bland a reference to hardcore bondage,

she stared at him. "*Uncomfortable*?"

"Perhaps *frustrated* would be more appropriate," he said. "That was entirely my fault."

"Damn *right* it was."

He heard the anger in her voice, briefly considered the resentment and duplicity that had fueled the situation and politely chose not to mention them. "I'm sorry for doing what I did to you. I was out of line." He'd apologized then as well. "And if you prefer wham, bam orgasms from here to eternity, I'm perfectly fine with that."

"Jesus, as if," she muttered. "Just no rope when you're in a crazy mood."

If she hadn't said she was leaving to go fuck other guys that time, he wouldn't have been in a crazy mood. Not an excuse, but a reference point. "I understand. You set the rules. I'm entirely at your disposal, tonight."

Her brows went up. "Wow. So, I'm the boss?"

He smiled. "You are." Only the faintest ambiguity lay beneath the well-bred concession.

Not faint enough; she caught the nuance. "Hey, no second thoughts." She raised her chin, met his gaze. "You owe me. Now, how much time do I have?"

He shot a glance at the nursery door. "Limited, I'd guess."

"Okay, then." A small breath, an uncertain flicker in her eyes, a debating moment to exhale. "How limited?"

He shrugged. "Your guess is as good as mine."

"Jeez, you're annoyingly calm."

"Fuck if I am. I'm horny and edgy and wondering if I can adjust to a six- week-old baby controlling when and if we fuck."

She smiled. "How edgy?"

He smiled back. "I'm trying not to scare you."

"Okay, look, you decide." She did a little wave of her hand. "I'm too lazy to actually set an agenda, or—I don't know...what—make a list, one to ten on how to fuck?"

This was no time to point out that sex was resolutely venturesome and without plan; her sudden volte-face, however, required confirmation. "Wanna change your mind? Just asking."

She hesitated, then said, "No, I'm good."

He was alarmed at his powerful response; he hadn't realized surrender was so freaking arousing. "You sure? Last chance."

She sighed, wrinkled her nose, then held up a finger.

He braced for a second volte face in this super-charged, seriously limited window of opportunity.

"This is off topic, but I'm dead serious."

Not an encouraging comment, but he hadn't had high expectations for the night anyway. Chill.

"I want all those women you tied up in the past erased from your memory, and don't say there weren't any because I don't want to hear a lie, okay? I need a hand to God or a hand on your heart or whatever, cause my jealousy is so far off the charts it's sailing into the next galaxy."

If not for Nicole's semi-dicey mood, he might have answered, "What women?" because in those days his memories of women were fleeting. Instead, he said, "It's only been you and you alone since you walked into my stateroom last August."

She gave him a squinty-eyed look.

Which prompted him to raise his hand. "Swear to God. You're my girl, the sunshine of my life."

"Okay." She let out a small breath. "Thanks, although I can't guarantee that sunshiny thing. I can be a moody bitch."

"Just so long as you're *my* moody bitch, I have zero complaints. But if life sucks, let me know. Or if you disagree or object to something I say or do, make sure and tell me."

"I don't need your permission."

He smiled. "I know."

"Look," she said with tiny shrug. "All you hear is yeses from everyone, everywhere, and you have for years, so I figure I'm here to occasionally tell you no." An eyeroll, a grin. "You know, add a little surprise to your life."

"Sometimes even big surprises like a baby."

She wrinkled her nose. "I'm not going to keep apologizing for that. You adore Leo. I did you a favor."

"Us. You did *us* a favor." His smile was slow and broad, filled with love, and brushing her bottom lip with his finger, he added, "For which I'm deeply grateful. I love you and Leo more than anything." He let out a small breath, each word careful. "Don't ever forget that."

She swallowed to hold back her tears. "I won't," she whispered.

His kiss was sweet, tender, an unspoken measure of his love. And a moment later when he raised his head and held her gaze, they both smiled.

"We were so lucky"—

"To meet, yeah. But from now on," he said in a low rasp, "I'll take charge of our future. I prefer certainty to random luck."

"You think you can control the world." She sighed. "You can't."

"I can control *my* part of the world," he said with soft finality. "See that you and Leo are happy." He smiled. "Which reminds me…"

"We're on borrowed time."

"Fortunately," he drawled, "you're always Miss Impatient, and I happen to know a thing or two or three you like, so…if you'll lie back and think of England or shoe shopping, you don't do that, maybe think of"—

"Your huge cock?"

"Yes, ma'am, that'll work for both of us." He was already lifting her under her arms, sliding her higher on the bed, and a moment later, spreading her legs with an upward sweep of his palms, he smoothly swung between her thighs in a ripple of uber-toned muscles. "Now, let me see if you're wet enough for sex," he teased, slipping downward between her legs, and glancing up from under his long lashes. "Feel free to give me directions." He tongued her clit, felt it immediately swell, nipped it lightly, then smiled faintly as her fingers slid through his hair, gripped his head and dragged him closer. "Or not," he said, licking a cool path up one side of her gleaming pussy, down the other side, the resonance of her soft moan appreciation and approval, impetus to move on to her susceptible little G-spot that was the fluttering lodestar, her all time favorite pleasure point, the quicksilver means of bringing her to orgasm without so much as breaking a sweat. Raising his head slightly, his breath a warm hum on the surface of her pussy, he said, "You have a couple more minutes before my focus narrows. After that, punch me hard to get my attention. Okay?"

Then his tongue plunged inside her and her whimper was audible, heated, graphic with need, her fingers tangling in his hair, pulling him so close he winced at the drag on his hair. Another wince as he raised his head enough to speak. "If I can't breathe, Tiger, you're not getting off."

It took her a second to come back to earth, a second more to release her death grip on his head and a mere millisecond to smile. "Carry on, soldier."

He laughed and she felt his breath on the sensitive,

ready-to-rock surface of her sex. As she did when, he murmured, "My pleasure."

"Au contraire, *my* pleasure. Thanks to you I'm super close to one of the best, most wonderful feelings in the world."

She was so fucking adorable, Pollyanna to the core. Leaning in, he touched her clit with featherlight brush of his tongue, with perfect know-how in terms of nerve locations, and adding his fingers to the heated game, turned his attention to the timely concept of super close.

She sucked in a breath as flame hot rapture flooded her senses, every primal nerve suddenly focused on high pressure bliss and when she finally exhaled in low throaty purr, the sound was one of guileless pleasure.

He half smiled and got back to work; his tongue meticulously accommodating, his fingers delicately opening her wider, giving him better access to her G-spot, her sleek passage, her scented flesh. And very quickly, she was frantic, melting, her pearly fluid coating his tongue and fingers.

"Now," she hissed.

He raised his head. "Soon."

She slapped him. "No, now!"

"Not a good time to piss me off," he said, gently sarcastic, his fingers stroking her G-spot with targeted concentration.

A volatile, spiking ecstasy suddenly coursed through every seething nerve in her body, and a second later, trembling, feverish, aching with need, her hot gaze met his. "Damn you..."

"Yeah, I know. If only you didn't need me."

Her lashes lifted, and her eyes flashed blue flame. "Maybe I don't."

"And maybe I don't believe you. Now, be a sweetheart. I know what I'm doing."

"Don't say that," she muttered.

"Why not?" Although, he knew. And if not for his own jealousy, he wouldn't have goaded her. "Come on, you like what I do to you."

"Shut up."

"Do you want me to stop?" His voice was suddenly cool.

The ensuing silence was fraught with resentment.

"Answer," he softly commanded, "or I'll"—

"Don't stop." Nearly orgasmic, all her senses were centered on avaricious need.

The phrase, *Don't stop,* granted infinite possibilities. Too long a creature of impulse, never in his adult life celibate, it took effort to quell the violence of his thoughts. His whole body stiffened for a second, as though an unseen hand had constrained him, and a second later, he understood that games were out of the question tonight.

His demons were too restless.

Reaching up, he touched her cheek, his voice soft and conciliatory. "Forgive me and my bloody temper. Ready for a happy ending?"

If Nicole wasn't so close to that aforementioned happy ending, she might have replied.

As it was, Rafe's question was largely rhetorical, her feverish desires unmistakable. Intent on not only making amends but pleasing her, he centered his attentions on her dewy clit and pulsing G-spot, his fingers and tongue solicitous, adept, no longer languid, her impatience a palpable drumbeat under his touch. Swiftly pushing her over the edge, he smothered her wild, explosive cry with his hand, waited briefly for her tremors to quiet and while she was still softly panting, brought her to a second even more glorious climax, so intense, her scream erupted before he could muffle it. Moments later, with Nicole already beginning to quiver, Rafe was adjusting his position to more quickly smother her next orgasmic cry, when the baby monitor suddenly came alive.

Two softly uttered expletives resonated in the room.

And a high-strung moment of indecision ensued.

Then Nicole tugged on Rafe's hair.

He looked up, his gaze questioning.

She smiled. "I'm fine. Leo slept way longer than I thought he would. Seriously, I'm counting my blessings."

"Wait a minute."

"Yes, sir." A low, docile purr.

He grinned. "You can be compliant after all."

"Depends on the circumstances," she sweetly said.

His head swiveled toward the nursery. "At the moment those depend on our little boy."

They both fell silent, listening to the restless baby gurgles. Propped on his elbows, Rafe watched the clock. Nicole silently counted while Leo's intermittent gurgles rose, quieted, rose again and on reaching fifty, she spoke the number aloud.

"Want to give it a try?" At the heat in her gaze, he smiled. "Silly question."

"I doubt there's time."

"Watch and learn, pussycat." Drawing on his years of sex as entertainment, he lowered his head, mobilized his sensitivity training, and using his deft tongue and artful fingers with expeditious grace, sweet-talked his darling wife's creamy pussy to a fast and furious, transcendent, star-studded orgasm.

Whether it was the brief setback, the hindered time frame, or more likely Rafe's competence, her climax was karmic in wonder. And when, at last, her nerve endings stopped vibrating convulsively and her panting diminished to a less raucous level, she softly exhaled and blew Rafe a kiss. "You're way, way too good to me. Thanks, a thousand, trillion thanks."

"No problem. You okay for a couple minutes now?"

"Way longer than that. A couple weeks if necessary."

An almost infinitesimal double take, then a polite smile, and rolling away, he lay on his back.

"I don't *want* it to be necessary," she said, propping herself up on one elbow and contemplating his motionless form.

"I know. Me either."

"This—us, the baby's schedule--is going to take a little adjustment, isn't it?"

A sideways flick of his eyes in his otherwise inert body. "Yes."

"Are you mad?"

"No." He smiled a better smile. "I'm adjusting."

She snorted. "Wiseass. Maybe I'll punch you from here to Tuesday, and wipe that smirk off your face."

He laughed. "You could try."

She fell on him, pounding his hard muscled chest and arms, his ripped abs and taut belly; her pummeling quickly shifting into a playful wrestling match in which Rafe allowed her wide latitude until she finally ran out of steam and gasping for air, stopped.

"You're—impervious...dammit."

He grinned. "That's cause you punch like a girl."

Which served to redouble her efforts until he suddenly grabbed her hands and held her still. "Listen."

After long, hushed moments without a sound from the baby monitor, Nicole smiled. "Wonder of wonders."

"He fell back to sleep."

"Your turn," Nicole said, with the sweetest smile.

"*Our* turn," Rafe said, smiling back. "But you're not allowed to scream."

"Oh, damn, then just forget it."

But he saw that she didn't scream…or at least not much. He also kept his reckless libido strictly under control and miraculously, they had time for several deep-in-love, fly-me-to-the-moon orgasms, even a semi-wild one.

Much later, resting in the shambles of the bed, Rafe held Nicole lightly in his arms. "I could get used to that kind of adjustment," he murmured, dropping a kiss on her forehead.

Looking up from under her lashes, she smiled. "I'm not saying I want to wait this long again, but there's something to be said for sexual deprivation in terms of mind-blowing orgasms."

"No doubt."

Her lips pursed. "Is that agreement or disagreement?"

There was only one answer to that recognizable female inflection. "It's complete agreement."

"What the hell kind of tone is that?"

He was silent for a moment, then his eyes fully opened. "It's a tone that means, no, I don't want to wait that long again, and yes, the orgasms were seriously mind-blowing."

A huge smile. "Good. Same here."

His wife's emotional warmth was an unparalleled gift. "It looks as though your little talk with Leo worked out." A twitch of a grin. "Thanks."

"I owe you more thanks than you do me. A bunch of times more."

"My pleasure, pussycat, but keep doing what you're doing and we'll both have reason to be thankful."

She was gently stroking his dick, running her fingers over

the warm, velvety skin, watching the Hokusai *Great Wave* tattoo slowly expand: the huge, blue, white-caped wave dark against the pale pink sky, the manned boats dwarfed by the ocean's power, the inked image broadening in scope as his cock rose. "I knew about this before I met you, you know. Your dick, your gorgeousness, the Hokusai tat were all the stuff of legend."

There was no upside to this topic. He didn't reply.

"No comment?"

"I'd rather not."

She looked up, watching him as if to measure his response. "Why?"

He knew what she was asking, knew all the gossip and scandal; he'd been notorious for a decade. "Look," he said, very softly, "I didn't know you then."

"What if you had?"

"I didn't." Her frown prompted him to add with a sigh, "What do you want me to say?"

"That if you'd met me sooner, you'd never have fucked all those other women."

"I wouldn't have. I never even looked after we met. I swear. And conversely," he said, a sudden coolness in his voice, "you wouldn't have hooked up with anyone either if you'd met me sooner."

"I wouldn't have."

He stared at her for a moment, sensibly discarded several inflammatory comments, and finally nodded. "Good. That's settled then."

"Is everyone in love as irrational as we?"

Exhaling softly, he said, "Probably not."

"How about we consign the past to the past. End of. Case closed. You tell me how much you adore me, I'll do the same for you"—Nicole's mouth twitched into a smile—"and we'll be madly in love, figuratively and otherwise, forever and ever."

He adored her capacity to pivot on a dime, overlook discord, find a silver lining in every cloud. His life had required constant vigilance to forestall hazards and threats; advantageous skills when operating a global business, but less applicable when it came to understanding his wife's benevolent view of the universe.

But he was learning.

"You were my salvation." His smile ticked up. "When I didn't know I needed saving."

"Who does."

"Yeah, hindsight is clear-eyed."

"Do you ever regret your rash and reckless playboy ways?"

"Some, sure. Not all. I wouldn't have met you if I hadn't invited all the wild, young glitterati to my summer party."

She tapped his chest and smiled. "You lucked out big time."

His amber gaze, warm and cloudless, held hers for a moment. "Fucking right I did."

"Speaking of lucking out. Do you think we have time?"

He answered her mischievous gaze in a voice of velvety indulgence. "Sounds like you're all done resting."

"If you don't mind."

"I believe the saying is not while I have breath in my body."

She grinned. "I adore your generosity."

He laughed, a delicious, husky sound. "Pure selfishness. You're going to have to tell me when you've had enough."

"Because you love me."

"Yes, heart and soul, now and always."

EPILOGUE

Eighteen months later...

Halfway down the garden path, Nicole could hear the loud, discordant piano sounds coming from the indoor pool/conservatory where Rafe did his morning laps.

An early riser like his son, Rafe often took on the dawn shift with Leo, and early on, had introduced his son—events permitting—to a morning swim. Initially, Rafe had held the baby on his stomach while he swam, but by the time Leo was ten months old, he could swim alone. Not that he often did, preferring to wrap his arms around his father's neck, and ride on his back while Rafe burned through fifty laps.

The tender, loving father/son relationship they'd forged since Leo's birth was brand-new and precious to Rafe, perfectly ordinary for Leo and a delight to them both.

Nicole opened the outside door, and entering quietly, stood for a moment inhaling the sweet fragrance of flowers, admiring the splendid array of tropical greenery brought in from distant shores in the nineteenth century when the villa had been built. Then her gaze traveled across the pool to where father and son were seated side by side at the Bosendorfer piano.

Rafe was fingering something complicated on his half of the keyboard, unruffled by Leo's sledgehammer thumping. Their hair was still damp from swimming, Rafe's falling in dark tendrils to his shoulders, Leo's shorter, disheveled hair bouncing as he pounded the keys with wild abandon. Their swimsuits had left wet stains on the bench cushion—not an issue for a man with a large household staff; she hoped to teach her son less nonchalance. But, parental aspirations aside, the two figures were charming to behold; their bare backs a contrast in form and tone; one, long, lean, deeply bronzed and sleek with muscle, the other small, sturdy, straight-backed, dimpled at elbow and shoulder, only lightly touched by the sun.

Rafe's hands moved with a fluid grace, his long, slender fingers easily covering two octaves, while Leo made up in noise and enthusiasm what he lacked in grace.

Turning at Nicole's approach, Rafe blew her a kiss, then leaned down and spoke to Leo.

A quick head swivel, a big, wide smile. "Hi Mommie. Me and Daddy no sweep." And he returned to his high-decibel piano playing.

Rafe looked up, his gaze amused. "We saw the sunrise."

"I owe you."

He shook his head, then lightly touched Leo's fingers, and spoke to him in French.

The little boy's hands suddenly went still on the keys and wide-eyed he turned his amber gaze on his father. "*Vraiment?*"

After several more quiet words in French, Leo swung around on the piano bench and offered his mother a beaming smile. "Want me play Twinkie Star?"

"I'd love it."

"Daddy help." He looked at his father. "Me first."

Rafe nodded.

Turning back to the keyboard, Leo concentrated on the keys for a moment, the tip of his tongue visible. Then carefully positioning his small hands, he took a breath, and began slowly playing, "Twinkle, Twinkle Little Star."

After the first few notes, Rafe accompanied him in quiet harmony, keeping time with the toddler execution, readily complying when Leo said, "Sing wit me."

The duet brought tears to Nicole's eyes.

She'd first heard Rafe sing with Leo. When she'd asked him why she'd never heard him sing before, his answer had been so vague she'd dropped the subject.

Once the song was over, Leo turned to face his mother, his little legs dangling over the piano bench, his dimples showing. "Me good?"

Quickly blinking away her tears, Nicole smiled. "Yes, you were wonderful."

"Why you crying?" He turned to Rafe who was sliding around to face Nicole. "Daddy, Mommie crying."

"Something went in my eye, that's all." She pointed up to a flowering jacaranda tree. "Pollen from the flowers."

Rafe's looked at her with mild concern.

"Your song was lovely," Nicole said, meeting Rafe's gaze. "You boys sing well together."

Rafe's expression cleared. "Leo showed me how," he said, understanding the reason for her tears. "He's a good teacher."

Before Nicole could reply, a tiny meow issued from under the piano. Her eyes widened. "Do we have a cat?"

"We do now." Leaning over, Rafe scooped up a little bit of black and white fluff from under the piano and held the tiny kitten out on his palm. "Ramon brought her to us this morning. He found her in the rose garden. Leo's ecstatic." Cupping the kitten in his hand, he held it against his warm chest, and leaned down to catch his son's eyes. "Do you have a name for kitty?"

"*Chatte*," Leo said.

"What?" Nicole asked.

"Cat, Mommie," Leo said, switching to English. "Cat, cat, cat."

"Why not Muffin because she's so sweet?" Nicole suggested. "Or Patches with her spotted fur?"

Leo's jaw firmed. "Cat," he repeated doggedly, then suddenly smiled. "Kitty tell me she want name."

Rafe held Nicole's gaze, a teasing note in his voice when he said in an undertone, "Your son is extraordinarily spoiled."

She laughed. "I wonder why?"

"Mommie happy now?" Another bright smile, reading his mother's laughter as approval.

"Yes, darling, Mommie's happy."

Understanding harmony was restored, Leo said, with artless innocence, "Daddy say me be nice, me get me pony."

Nicole's surprise showed. "Really, Daddy, a pony?"

"Really. And if you're nice to me," Rafe added, very softly, "there's no end of what I might do for you." Smiling, he watched her face turn pink, knew what it meant; her impressionable libido was stirring.

"Hush," she whispered, then turned to Leo. "My goodness, how exciting. You'll have to learn how to ride."

"Daddy show me."

Nicole swiveled to Rafe, her eyebrows raised. "You ride?"

"I used to play a little polo."

"How do you play a *little* polo?"

"I followed the circuit one season." His voice was mild. "Just one. That's a little."

"You continue to amaze me."

He grinned. "One can but hope." Then his expression sobered and his voice when he spoke was softly earnest. "You amaze me every minute of the day, Tiger. Swear to God, I'm so lucky to have you."

"We're both lucky." Leaning down, she kissed him lightly.

"Me like Mommie happy," Leo said, understanding what kisses meant.

She smiled at her son. "It's easy to be happy with you and Daddy."

The toddler turned to Rafe. "Daddy happy?"

"Yes, very happy."

"Me too!" Leo yelled, jubilant and gleeful.

From the mouth of babes, Rafe thought.

Someone once said: Happy families are all alike; every unhappy family is unhappy in its own way.

Rafe wasn't sure whether it was true or not but having survived a schizoid childhood, he was going to make damn sure his own small family was in that happy category. Motivated by his ruinous past, he was determined to nourish and sustain his family's content: with hard work and watchfulness, love and affection and coming from his background, a bone deep vigilance against unknown threats.

"You look serious. Was it something I said?" Nicole murmured.

Rafe glanced down at Leo, saw he was busy petting the kitten. "Have you read Anna Karenina?"

"Yeah, great story, terrible ending." She grimaced. "Women as victims. Ugh. Clearly, it was written by man who didn't have a clue."

"Aren't you overlooking nineteenth century cultural mores?"

"As a matter of fact, I'm not," she replied, crisply, keeping her voice down as he had. "I'll have you know strong, independent women, rich or poor, young or old, have played significant roles in every society since the dawn of time." She held up her fist. "Screw cultural norms."

His expression was amused. "Struck a nerve, did I?"

"More than one. I prefer the concept of female exceptionalism. So, sue me."

"No need. You're exceptional in every way," he murmured. "No question."

"God, you're sweet. That must be why I love you"—she fluttered her lashes in flirtatious play--"well, one of the reasons."

He laughed. "Since that's a totally useless concept right now, would you care to see a pony?"

"Pony!" Leo screamed, the magic word diverting his attention from the kitten. Jumping off the piano bench, he ran toward the outside door.

Nicole's brows rose into her hairline. "Does he know where to go?"

"No." Coming to his feet, Rafe quickly set the kitten in the box it had come in and shouted, "Wait, Leo!"

"It's fine. He can't open the door. Oops," Nicole added, as her son pushed the door open. "When did that happen?"

Rafe grabbed her hand and started to run. "He figured it out yesterday." Exiting the conservatory a few seconds later, Rafe shouted, "Leo, you're going the wrong way!"

Leo stopped, turned, his toddler balance unsteady and after wobbling sideways, once, twice, he fell, landing on his butt, wide-eyed.

Rafe scooped him up a moment later and smiled. "You're really fast. We almost didn't catch you."

Wiggling and squirming, Leo tried to escape his father's hold. "Let go, Daddy! Me see pony!"

Setting Leo down, Rafe pointed. "The pony is at the playground. Ramon has him in the pavilion until we can build a sta"—his voice trailed off; Leo was already out of earshot. Rafe turned to Nicole and grinned. "He listens as well as you do."

She ran her finger lightly over his bare chest. "Leo's father also tends to be hard of hearing at times. Although, with us as parents, our darling baby doesn't stand a chance of being obliging or reasonable."

"But then reasonableness is much overrated." Rafe smiled a heart-melting smile she remembered from long ago. "If either of us had been reasonable, you would have walked out of my stateroom last August, and I would have let you."

"But you didn't."

"Nope. It was written in the stars, pussycat. You and me."

"And Leo."

"Yes, our wild child. Tell me I can spoil him."

She gave him a smartass grin. "Would it do any good if I said you couldn't."

"Probably not." He kissed her lightly. "Thank you."

"Speaking of wildness, I hope someone's at the playground because Leo's disappeared from sight."

"There's quite a few people there unless Ramon fired his entire crew."

She wrinkled her nose in a little irascible twitch. "Sometimes you rich boys can be annoying. You have no sense of proportion. I worry about Leo growing up with too much."

"Hey." He pulled her into his arms, held her gaze and

said, very softly, "I could live in a tent in any outback of the world as long as you and Leo were with me. I mean it. You and Leo are my life. Nothing else matters. If you want to move, we'll move." He grinned. "I know how to build a fire; I can hunt and fish. We'll roast marshmallows with Leo, how about that?"

What almost brought her to tears, was that he meant every word. "Marshmallows sound good." Her smile was a little shaky. "I just want to keep Leo grounded, make sure he knows what's important in life."

"You tell me when I go overboard. Seriously, I know what you mean about annoying rich boys. I grew up with a ton of them; superficial, graceless idiots the lot. And while we're on this topic, I want you to know, I'm opposed to boarding school for Leo."

She kissed his cheek. "That works out then, because he was never going anyway."

He nodded. "Good--definitely soul mates on that subject. And I mean it about a different house. Pick out something smaller if you like."

She put her finger on his lips. "You can't talk that way, like money's incidental."

He smiled. "Sorry. Call me on my lapses."

"And I'll try to be more understanding about the lifestyles of the rich and famous."

"There you go. How can we go wrong? Not to mention I love you more than anything, so the incentive is huge."

"Yeah, love makes everything possible--and nothing impossible." She smiled. "Like Cinderella's fairy godmother."

"Absolutely," he graciously agreed, although in the authoritarian recesses of his mind where old habits die hard, he rather thought there might be times—in the absence of magic--when he might wield that fairy wand himself.

Still, he was willing to concede on most every point, save that of his family's safety. In all else, he was malleable.

"So," he murmured. "Are you ready to meet our new pony?"

"Did you really compete on the polo circuit?"

"I did. Would you like to learn to play?"

A friendly smile. "Would you love me less if I said, no?"

"I'd love you more. In the end, I found it boring--in contrast to Contini Pharma." He shrugged. "Workaholic. What can I say?"

"Don't tell me even the polo groupies were boring. That I doubt."

"Particularly the polo groupies. You're a gazillion times more beautiful and fascinating--not to mention intelligent. I won the lottery with you, pussycat."

"Back at you, handsome," she purred, her hips brushing his in a slow, languid rhythm.

No matter the slight pressure, it tripped every highly charged libidinous wire in his psyche. "Goddamn." He uttered a long groan. "I suppose we can't miss the pony viewing even though Ramon, his crew, the groom and stablemaster are there with Leo."

"Groom and stablemaster?" she said, semi-coolly.

"Oh, shit. Should I send them home?"

And so their world advanced, in fits and starts, hesitantly at times, most often with compromise, but always with unfailing affection.

Marriage and family turned out to be a sweet revelation for two people who hadn't had a serious relationship before they met, had viewed the concept of love as the wildest of fantasies, had had no intention of entering the state of matrimony in the foreseeable future and certainly hadn't considered becoming parents.

It just went to show, no matter how you plan, life can surprise you in the most unsuspecting and totally awesome ways.

ALSO BY CC GIBBS

If You Want To See How It All Started...

US Reckless Series

Book 1: Power & Possession

Book 2: Seduction & Surrender

UK Reckless Series

Book 1: Pushing the Limits

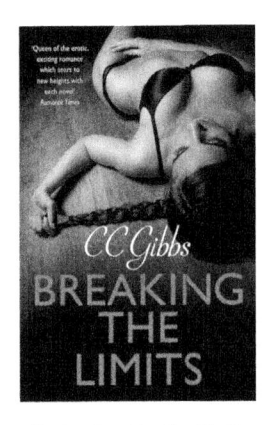

Book 2: Breaking the Limits

You Might Also Like...
US/UK Dominic Knight Trilogy

Knight's Mistress
CC Gibbs
Knight's Game
CC Gibbs
Knight takes Queen
CC Gibbs

ABOUT THE AUTHOR

Stay in Touch with CC Gibbs/Susan Johnson
  Website:
  http://www.susanjohnsonauthor.com
  Facebook:
  https://www.facebook.com/CCGibbsAuthor/
  Twitter:
  https://twitter.com/ccgibbs
  Instagram:
  https://www.instagram.com/cc.gibbs/

Printed in Great Britain
by Amazon